THE EYES OF VICTIMS

-- A WATCHTOWER THRILLER--

MIKAEL CARLSON

WARRINGTON
PUBLISHING

DANBURY, CONNECTICUT

The Eyes of Victims
Copyright © 2023 by Mikael Carlson

Warrington Publishing
Danbury, CT
www.mikaelcarlson.com

Printed in the United States of America
First Edition
ISBN: 978-1-944972-26-4 (paperback)
         978-1-944972-27-1 (hardcover)
         978-1-944972-28-8 (ebook)

Cover designed by JD&J
Editing by Michael Waitz of Sticks and Stones

Novels by Mikael Carlson:

– The Michael Bennit Series –
The iCandidate
The iCongressman
The iSpeaker
The iAmerican

– Tierra Campos Thrillers –
Justifiable Deceit
Devious Measures
Vital Targets
Revealed Secrets
Decisive Endgame

– Watchtower Thrillers –
The Eyes of Others
The Eyes of Innocents
The Eyes of Victims

– The America, Inc. Saga –
The Black Swan Event
Bounded Rationality
Boiling the Ocean

For all those who find the strength to overcome their trauma.

CHAPTER ONE
"BOSTON" HOLLINGER

BANK OF HOGAN
HOGAN'S ALLEY, VIRGINIA

I pull up the car and slam the shifter in park. The street isn't busy, but it isn't vacant either. This could be any small town in America. The more I travel, the more I realize that, despite some dissimilarities, most small towns are alike. This one is no different.

Nadiya opens her door and climbs out of our Crown Vic. I follow suit, slamming the door and surveying the surrounding buildings. Nothing is remarkable about any of them, including the Bank of Hogan. It's a plain brown brick structure with a sign, double glass doors, and a trio of oversized windows peering onto the street. It's strikingly similar to the retail bank that held my accounts before I was legally declared dead.

We walk through the doors and over to one of the tellers. I flash my FBI badge and politely inform her that we're on official business and need to speak to the branch manager. Nadiya studies the patrons as the young woman disappears into an area behind the counter. I make the mistake of closing my eyes, allowing my brain to focus on the signals emanating from the people in the room.

That's a mistake, and I try desperately to change my focus. I'm not here to experience memories. This is routine Bureau stuff. We have a subpoena to serve for records and nothing more.

"Is FBI work always this boring?"

"I suppose so. I'm a CIA instructor, remember? It's not like what you see on television, Boston. Emma says that the little action most agents see is usually followed by a mountain of paperwork. It's not worth it."

"Great," I say as the teller emerges.

"The manager is running an errand. She should be back in about ten minutes. You can wait if you'd like," she says, gesturing to a lounge area behind us. "The coffee is pretty good. Please, help yourselves."

We thank her and adjourn to the waiting area in the corner. Banking has come a long way. Or regressed, depending on one's perspective. Nobody comes to a bank to hang out. The existence of a lounge means there isn't enough staff to handle the number of potential customers needing mortgages, home equity loans, or new checking accounts.

I pull out my phone and open a game to occupy the time. I don't want to probe people's memories, and the apps I have loaded on this thing are useful distractions. It also means that I'm not paying attention to my surroundings, which proves to be a mistake when a man in line begins yelling.

"On the ground! On the ground, now!"

I look up to see a masked man waving a handgun at people. The customers dive to the ground, eager to obey his commands. I'm about to stand and confront him when Nadiya pulls me to the ground.

"Don't do anything stupid, Boston."

I don't acknowledge the warning. The man is barking at people to cover their heads, but we are out of his line of sight. He tosses a bag to the teller and orders her to fill it with the cash in the trays.

Contrary to popular opinion, bank branches don't have millions of dollars on-hand for the taking. While they may have a healthy supply of bills stuffed in a safe, bank tellers typically don't have more than a few thousand dollars in their cash trays. This haul will not be worth a decade in a federal penitentiary.

I watch the man intently, playing it cool because that's what I'm supposed to do. Or so my instructors have always said. Observe and report. Get a good description. That's all an agent needs to ensure the robber is caught. It's crap, but they'd rather let the man walk free and have insurance pay the bank than ensure a criminal is brought to justice.

The teller completes her task, and the man begins backing out of the bank. Then he makes a mistake and turns his back to me. I'm done lying on the floor. This guy needs to go down.

I climb to my feet as Nadiya quietly protests. I pull my weapon out of its holster when I hear a noise behind me. The manager walks onto the floor and freezes. When the door slams behind her, the man with the gun spins. I'm the first person he sees.

"FBI! Freeze!"

I've never seen that work, and this is no exception. The man swings his arm toward me and fires, forcing me to roll to my right. The first shot goes wide, but the next round hits the manager squarely in the chest. She collapses to the ground.

I check the backdrop and return fire, but my three shots miss as he zigzags to the door. I frown. Emma will have something to say to me about that.

"I got this! Call 9-1-1!"

"Boston!" Nadiya screams as I cross the bank's floor.

I rush out the door after the bank robber and am ready for the ambush he prepared. He has already demonstrated once that he's willing to fire a weapon. He's going to do it again.

Bolting across the sidewalk only takes a couple of seconds. I duck behind my vehicle an instant before a pair of bullets strikes the fender. I wait to see if he fires again. Half of his magazine load is gone. I make a mental note and poke my head up to see the man fleeing down the sidewalk. Pedestrians scatter in every direction, trying to stay clear of him.

Fairly certain I have a better chance of getting struck by lightning than him shooting me at this distance, I give chase as he sprints north. My target breaks right at the drugstore and down a side street. I pull up at the corner, fighting to control my breathing. I crouch and glance around the corner. The man was expecting that tactic, but not at this height.

Bullets ricochet off the bricks above my head, right where my face would have been. A couple of shots snap in my ears as they sail past my head when he adjusts fire. I pull back around the corner and hear the telltale sound of his slide locking to the rear. He's out of ammunition.

"Now you're mine, asshole," I mumble.

I move around the corner with my weapon up. The assailant sees me and is frozen in indecision. A car waits for him thirty yards away, but that is a long distance to cover when you're racing bullets.

"I'm a federal agent, so don't even think about it. You'll never make it."

The man grins and bolts toward his car. I chase him down the alley, intending to drop him when he reaches the driver's side door. I stop and take up a combat stance, raising my weapon and lining up the sights on his back.

Another figure steps out from behind the dumpster fifteen feet in front of me. My brain registers the danger too late to do anything about it. His weapon is already out and aimed, and the accomplice fires three rounds in succession.

My chest registers the pressure as all three find it. The pain causes my knees to buckle, and I collapse backward on the sidewalk. I lose grip on my weapon, causing it to spill out of my hand. Blackness closes in on the periphery of my vision. I feel like I'm in a tunnel.

My breathing shallows. I try to reach for the gun, but it's a foot away from my fingertips. It's over. I rest my head on the asphalt and close my eyes, consigning myself to a fate I never expected. This went wrong so fast. Sometimes, life is like that. It's not the first time I have found myself in this situation. That one ended just as badly.

CHAPTER TWO
SSA ZACH FORTE

HOGAN'S ALLEY FBI TRAINING CENTER
QUANTICO, VIRGINIA

Forte storms around the corner to where Boston is lying on the cold asphalt. He left the monitoring room moments after the chase from the bank began. He knew how it would end.

Boston is staring at the sky as he takes short, sharp breaths. Forte leans over him and shakes his head with a disapproving look a grandmother would use to scold a misbehaving toddler. Emma and Nadiya join him as the two "criminals" high-five each other after clearing their weapons.

"You're a special kind of stupid, Boston. That was the dumbest thing I've seen in my entire career. How the hell did you ever survive in Mexico?"

"I didn't expect the bank to get robbed," Boston whines.

"News flash, moron! This is the crime capital of America. That bank is robbed at least twice a week. You haven't even met the drug dealers, mobsters, and terrorists yet."

Hogan's Alley, located at Quantico, is where the FBI trains its new agents. Trainees are immersed in realistic scenarios where basic tactics, investigative techniques, and firearms skills are tested in stressful situations. There is no better test of decision-making skills in all of law enforcement. Boston has a long way to go to refine his.

Named after an 1890s comic strip set in a bad area, the fictional town was built with the help of Hollywood set designers. It has its own ZIP code and features a bank, a post office, a hotel, a laundromat, a barber shop, a pool hall, shops, and homes. Local actors play the town's citizens, making training at Hogan's Alley very realistic. Which is the point.

Boston starts to move before stopping and grimacing. "Can this wait until I can breathe properly again?"

"Oh, hell no. I want you to remember this moment forever. If you think simunitions hurt, wait until you see how far I'm gonna shove my boot up your ass. Stand Captain America here up."

Emma and Nadiya reach down and grab Boston's arms before he can protest. They haul him to his feet, and he immediately checks the three impact areas on the center of his chest. They were lethal unless he had been wearing body armor, which he wasn't.

Simunition, short for simulated ammunition, is accurate, non-lethal, and is fired from slightly modified weapons. It's comparable to paintball, except it hurts like hell. These scenarios are the closest a trainee will ever get to engaging in gunfights without real bullets flying. Face protection is supposed to be used, but Forte opted not to for this training. They can always rebuild Boston's face again if they need to.

"Ow! You know that hurts, right?" Boston screeches after Emma pokes him in the chest.

"Tell that to the civilian that got gunned down in the bank. She's dead because of you. You had no reason to engage the robber in a building full of civilians."

"Observe and report. I know," Boston says, frustrated.

"Yeah. Then why didn't you?" Zach asks.

"I saw an opportunity."

"To what? Miss every shot you fired?" Emma asks, piling on.

"Maybe I should have had you here to punch me in the ribs while I was firing."

She doesn't appreciate the comment. Emma Farris is one of the FBI's best firearms instructors and was assigned to Watchtower for the sole purpose of beating some shooting skills into their newest weapon. Boston has improved significantly, at least on the range at their own training center. He still has a long way to go to apply those skills in the real world, as this demonstrated.

"Life isn't paper targets hung downrange with binder clips, Boston," Emma says. "People don't stand there and wait for you to shoot them. That's not how the world works."

"Say it, Boston," Forte says, causing his protégé to glare at him. "Say it, or I swear to God, I will reserve Hogan's Alley for a month and run you through every scenario the Bureau has ever devised. Your choice."

"Fine. I screwed up."

Zach nods. Boston is not the most coachable man he has ever trained. The hardest part is getting him to admit mistakes and learn from them. Part of that is being a victim of his own success and surviving killing Alejandro Salcido during a solo mission south of the border.

"Everyone meet in the classroom in fifteen minutes. We need to do a post-mortem on this disaster."

Forte stays back as Nadiya, Emma, and a pair of FBI instructors leave, presumably to instruct the actors who were milling around Hogan's Alley or making a withdrawal at the bank before it was robbed.

"Are you staying behind to keep yelling at me?"

"That was nothing. You should have seen the dressing-downs I got when I went through Quantico."

"Did you get someone killed in the bank?" Boston asks.

"Nope. I got five people killed, not including myself. There isn't an agent alive that hasn't died or gotten someone gunned down in that infernal bank."

"That's encouraging."

Forte shakes his head. "That's how we learn, Boston. There is no substitute for experience, and pain is a great motivator."

"You're a masochist. Where did you get shot?"

"We used blue practice guns, not simunitions," Forte says with a smile.

"Oh, so I'm special?"

"You can see people's memories, Boston. You know their secrets. That makes you special, but it also makes you a target. Your gift won't help you when bullets start flying. You need other skills to defend yourself that you haven't fully developed yet."

Boston stares at the buildings lining the alley. Zach brought him here because he was getting too used to the training areas at Watchtower. They are getting a redesign, but that takes time they don't have. He won't be any good to Watchtower if he gets himself killed by being stupid.

"Come on," Forte says. "Let's get this over with so you can get yourself killed in the next simulation."

CHAPTER THREE
ASHLEE TRILLO

SALISBURY LAW SCHOOL RESIDENTIAL HOUSING
SALISBURY, CONNECTICUT

Ashlee leans back in her chair and rubs her eyes. She sighs deeply and closes the law book before retreating from her study. It's Friday afternoon. That's enough for one day. It's not like she wants to graduate at the top of her class. Her peers are smart, driven, and ruthless, and she doesn't care enough to compete with them.

Student housing at the Salisbury Law School is like everything else here: expensive. The on-campus apartment she shares with her roommate is spacious and comes with furniture usually found in upper-middle-class homes. Two studies are built off the main living area with a gourmet kitchen off to one side. A short hallway connects the space to equal-sized bedrooms with separate spacious baths and large walk-in closets.

She grabs a bottle of wine out of the rack in the corner, retrieves a glass from the cabinet, and plops onto the overstuffed white sofa. She's about to turn on the television when she hears keys jingle outside and the door's lock turn. Ashlee's roommate, clad in workout clothes and sucking water from a reusable bottle, drops her keys in the dish on the credenza near the door.

"How was the gym?"

"Great!" Chloe exclaims. "You should try visiting it sometime. Workouts are a great stress reliever."

"So is this," Ashlee says, holding up the glass of Merlot she just poured.

"I don't know how you do it, Ash. You never work out, yet you're toned and impossibly fit. I could run marathons and still gain ten pounds just looking at food."

Ashlee eyes her roommate. Chloe isn't fat by any stretch of the imagination. Her frame is bigger, but she's got curves in all the right places. She would turn heads at this school if not for her complete refusal to wear makeup or style her hair. Instead, Chloe ardently sticks with the "plain Jane" look that rarely attracts male attention. Not that the lack of suitors seems to bother her.

"What can I say?" Ashlee asks with a shrug. "I have good Mediterranean genes."

Her father was born in Italy and came to the United States when he was ten. He's as Italian as he can get. Ashlee's friends all referred to him as the capo when she was out with them. Her mother was born an American to Italian immigrants. She was a strong woman right up to the accident that took her life nearly ten years ago. Ashlee misses talking to her. She always had the best perspective on things.

"Are you heading out tonight?" Chloe asks, plopping down in the matching chair before sipping from her water bottle.

"I'm not sure. Who's hosting tonight's soiree?"

Salisbury, Connecticut, is in the northwestern part of the state. It's basically in the middle of nowhere. On a good day, it's a two-and-a-half-hour drive south to New York City and an additional fifteen minutes beyond that east to get to Boston. The town itself is small and very rural. There isn't much to do here.

That makes the Friday evening parties off the hook. Students take turns hosting parties open to the entire student body at their overpriced apartments. Half the students show up, many with friends or other guests. The campus police keep an eye on things but are rarely called upon to break things up. Everyone here is over the drinking age, so as long as there isn't any depraved activity, authorities and school administrators are hands-off.

"Lucas and Brody are holding it."

Ashlee growls and sets her wine glass down on the modern glass coffee table for a refill. Lucas and Brody were first-year roommates and have become inseparable friends. They do everything together, including going on double dates. Both guys are from wealthy families, so their parties are among the best on campus.

"Still holding onto that grudge?"

"We went on one incredible date, and then he ghosted me. Yeah, I'm still a little salty over it."

"Maybe he wasn't into you. It happens. He isn't worth the time or energy you've spent ranting about it."

"You've met my father, right? Getting over things is not what my family does. Ever. We get even."

"Hon, you need to let it go."

"Chloe, he's been out with almost every girl in this school multiple times except me."

She holds her hand up in the air at shoulder level. "And me. I've never been out with Brody once. Look, he's a player. He has a different girl on his arm every week. It doesn't matter if they study here or if they're imports from New York. I think it's because he has a small penis."

Ashlee nearly snarfs her wine. "What?"

"You heard me. If Brody Prock was a god in bed, every girl on this campus would be talking about it. Hell, there would be a bronze bust of him on a marble pedestal in the student center between John Marshall and Ruth Bader Ginsburg. But that's not the case. I've never heard any girl he's hung out with say what an amazing night she had with him between the sheets. That's a red flag, counselor."

"Objection. Cause for speculation."

"Overruled," Chloe says with a smile. "Ashlee, you're beautiful. And smart. You can get any guy you want."

She cocks her head. "And yet I have no discernible love life. I haven't even been on a date since before Halloween."

"I haven't since Labor Day. So what? If you want some action, then go to the party, find a guy, and show him a good time. Let Brody Prock stew about what he's missing."

Ashlee smirks. "That's not a half-bad idea. Will you go with me? You rarely go to these bashes, but it's almost Christmas break. You can spend one night out with me this semester."

"I could, but I won't. It's almost finals. My parents will disown me if I don't ace my exams."

Ashlee starts to sip her wine and stops at the objection. "They own their own firm, Chloe. I think your future is secure."

"Tell that to them," she grumbles.

Chloe's parents married right after finishing law school and joined different law firms. After the long hours, they both left and hung a shingle on the outskirts of Minneapolis. Her parents made a name for themselves by representing rioters arrested over the summer of 2020. In the years since, their firm has only grown in size and reputation. Chloe likes to think about what her job interview will be like, but Ashlee finds the notion of that ridiculous.

"I'm going to shower and head to the library for a while. Have fun tonight."

Ashlee smiles and sips her wine. Lucas is Brody's best friend, and his hosting the party is an opportunity. The only question that needs to be answered is whether she has the guts to seize it.

CHAPTER FOUR

JAMIESON BOHMER

PRUDENTIAL CENTER
NEWARK, NEW JERSEY

Jamieson stands because everyone around him does. He has no idea what's happening, nor does he care as he subconsciously smooths the front of his jersey. The act of donning it feels like…betrayal. The Brit doesn't specifically hate the New Jersey Devils, but he despises hockey as a sport. It's not a proper athletic endeavor like football is, or as most idiotic Americans call it, soccer.

He would give anything to change into a Manchester City jersey right now, but can't afford to not blend in with the sea of black and red coloring the Prudential Center. Jamieson checks his watch, counting the minutes until he can make this agony end. When it reads the prescribed time, he rises from his uncomfortable seat and heads for the concession stand to find Art Burill already waiting in line.

"Fancy meeting you here," the big man says. "You look good wearing the red and black."

"I'm glad you're enjoying yourself at my expense."

"Just because you stuffy Brits don't have a sense of humor doesn't mean I don't. I can't exactly invite you to my office to talk, now can I?"

He's right about that. Art Burill is a fixture in Newark city politics. He'd win in a landslide if he ever decided to run for mayor. But he won't. Art is content being the chairman of the city's Department of Economic and Housing Development and is too accustomed to the financial "perks" that come with it.

"No, I don't suppose a visit to Room 112 at City Hall would be an appropriate venue for us to conduct business."

Art scoffs. "Ya think?"

Jamieson edges up in the line behind the chairman. "I shouldn't have to meet you at all. The terms of our arrangement were decided years ago."

"Times change. And when they do, the terms need to change with them."

"That's not how I see it."

"You? Or Tomasso? Because you're an arrogant Brit who still thinks his country rules the world, and he's a ruthless developer who knows better."

"Tomasso is an Italian businessman, so *you* should know better. We've paid you handsomely for your cooperation in these matters."

Art nods. The central planning board prepares the city's master development plan, reviews site applications, and recommends zoning ordinance changes to the municipal council. While his official responsibilities have weight, his real value comes from his relationships. That's what makes his services worth "purchasing."

"I have steered tens of millions of dollars' worth of contracts to Brick City Development," Art says, his voice turning graver. "You are the number one developer in Northern New Jersey because of me and my close relationships with the mayor and city council. So, when I say a change in our arrangement is needed, it is."

"Why?"

"Federal dollars and the politics that come with them."

"What do you mean?"

Art glances over his shoulder at the Brit. "Don't play dumb, Jamieson. Washington is about to fork over billions in aid to cities, and we're gonna get a big check for our urban renewal efforts. Pay up if you want a seat at the table."

The two men make it to the counter and place their orders at different registers. Art gets enough food to feed a small army, while Jamieson settles for a single hot dog. He looks around as he pays. They are talking openly, but nobody here is listening. The Devils just went up two to nil, and the place is going bonkers. Not that anyone eavesdrops on conversations in a line like this, which was the point of meeting here.

"You don't think we can earn the business on our own?" Jamieson asks when he joins Art at the condiment station.

"You can roll the dice if you choose. This contract will go to the lowest bidder, and the bids will be sealed. Go ahead…take your chances."

"Nah. I don't think it will come to that. You won't risk losing your chance to fatten that off-shore account."

The big man smiles at the warning. "You think Tomasso is the only player that has offered me a bribe? I get monthly solicitations."

"Then why us?" Jamieson asks, slathering his hot dog with mustard.

"Because you pay the best. I'm offering you the chance to keep your spot as the top dog. You can seize it, or you can take a pass."

"Yes, it would be a shame for you to get hemmed up for corruption."

Art stops what he's doing and looks at Jamieson for the first time in the entire conversation. The corner of his mouth curls up.

"I go down, and so does your boss. It's simple math."

"How much?" Jamieson asks as Art goes back to preparing his food.

The chairman looks around to ensure nobody standing behind them is paying attention. "A twenty percent increase, payable to the same Cayman account."

"Ten percent, with a kicker depending on the size of the contracts."

Art collects his food in his arms and turns away from the condiment station to allow another patron access to the ketchup.

"Done. It was good seeing you again, Jamieson. Enjoy the game."

As if enjoying the game was even a possibility. Jamieson got the answer he wanted. He turns and walks down the concourse, listening to the shouts from the crowd as two men on the ice toss off their gloves to start hitting each other in the face. What a ridiculous sport.

He tosses his uneaten hot dog in the trash as he heads for the nearest exit. Tomasso isn't going to like this one bit. Ten percent and a bonus is a steep increase. Jamieson hopes his boss orders him to put a bullet in Art's head instead. That's an assignment he can get behind. Maybe he'll even wear this infernal hockey jersey for it.

CHAPTER FIVE

JOHN PROCK

ESTATE OF JOHN PROCK
SCARSDALE, NEW YORK

John checks his watch when he hears the doorbell ring. Nine p.m. This man's punctuality is borderline annoying. He rises from the sofa and heads to the foyer to open the door.

For as much as this place costs, his house should be the size of Versailles. The picturesque Westchester County village of Scarsdale is one of New York City's most affluent suburbs and ranks among the wealthiest towns in America. John's five-bedroom, three-thousand-square-foot house on a quarter acre is by no means a mansion but would easily sell for a cool two million if he were to list it.

The shipping magnate opens the door and steps aside. "Good evening, Lothar. Come in."

"Thank you for agreeing to meet me."

John leads him through the house to the door leading to the basement. The study on the first floor is just for show. The real work happens on the lower level. The rest of the house may have a colonial, traditional Northeastern feel, but he wanted an ultra-modern look to his workspace. The surfaces are glass, and there is LED accent lighting, stainless steel, and futuristic furniture that looks straight out of a science fiction novel.

"Drink?"

"Oh, you know it."

"This must be important if you're here on a Friday night," John says as he moves to the bar cart along the wall and pours bourbon from a crystal decanter.

"I'm afraid it is."

John hands him a half-full crystal tumbler. Lothar is an American success story. He immigrated to live with a relative as a teenager after his parents were killed on the Autobahn. The man he lived with was a drunk, and Lothar was left to fend for himself. At eighteen, he began work in the industry, and John hired him for the new startup when he was twenty. Over the next two decades, Lothar worked his way through the ranks to become a valuable employee. He has a knack for business operations and a certain street savvy. The mix made John eager to put him to work on his newest endeavor five years ago.

"This can't be good news, so out with it. And please tell me this isn't about that large shipment from Mexico."

"It isn't. A worker in one of our Bronx stations has been arrested."

John shakes his head and then takes a sip of his drink. "Drugs?"

"Domestic violence."

"Is he talking?"

"Not yet, but the NYPD knows how to apply pressure effectively to squeeze out a confession. He beat the crap out of his girlfriend, so the physical evidence is damning enough. The urge to trade information about our activities for a lighter sentence will be irresistible."

"Which puts the operation in jeopardy and increases the risk of authorities identifying our buyers and suppliers. That won't sit well with our partners."

"Which is why I'm here on a Friday night," Lothar says, nodding.

The German is more than an operations manager – he's a COO, even if he doesn't officially hold the title. His contributions are invaluable. Since John can't acknowledge them through positions and corporate titles, he compensates the man well. Very well.

"Shut down the station immediately."

"Plans are already in motion. They will expend their production supplies tomorrow. The scheduled shipment of their product inventory has been moved up. Then it will be easy to dump the lease and move to a new location."

"Good."

"That only solves half our problem. He could name names."

John doesn't like losing competent employees. He handsomely rewards the men and women who meet his demands of loyalty and silence. They may not know who he is, but they all know at least a subset of their coworkers. Given enough names, even an incompetent investigator could put enough pieces together to lead them to AMLOG's doorstep.

Every business has risks that need to be mitigated. AMLOG is no different, except the risks associated with failure are far more cataclysmic than bankruptcy. His clients are very demanding.

"Fire them," John orders, staring at Lothar to convey the true intent of the words.

The German nods, understanding the message. "It will be taken care of."

Lothar shows himself out. He knows the way, having spent more time in this house than John's son has.

The president and CEO of AMLOG turns to stare at the large silver and glass world map bolted to the wall. Thin blue LED lights mark the main shipping routes his company has established. They've come a long way since their days being simple truckers. Now, they are a logistical powerhouse and growing fast. The money to fuel that growth has to come from somewhere.

John sets his glass down and turns the lights down in the study. That's not the right name for this room. It's an operations center, not a place to lounge in leather upholstered furniture and read old first editions of the classics. He has no time for that with a successful business to run.

CHAPTER SIX

ASHLEE TRILLO

SALISBURY LAW RESIDENTIAL HOUSING
SALISBURY, CONNECTICUT

College parties look a lot alike. Even the ones at a swanky, prestigious law school tucked into the Northwestern Connecticut hills look much like the drunken bashes at America's biggest party schools. People are everywhere, spilling outside in the near-freezing temperatures without coats. There is a lot of screaming and laughing. The music is blaring. Everyone is having a good time.

Ashlee walks into the apartment and is familiar with the layout. Most of the housing on campus is the same two-person apartment design. The only difference is the furniture, much of which has been moved to make room for the hundreds of guests, most holding red Solo cups.

She imagines that about half the student body is here. The living room is jammed, and the breakfast counter above the sink has been turned into a wet bar stocked with bottles of hard alcohol. The kegs are tapped on the patio, which may be why the apartment isn't more crowded.

Ashlee maneuvers her way to the makeshift bar and evaluates the selection. She hates cheap booze. It's a byproduct of raiding her father's liquor cabinet as a teenager. He always had expensive tastes and wouldn't think twice about dropping thousands of dollars on a single bottle of scotch whisky.

"I had the same thought," Lucas says, shouting over the din. "Most of this stuff tastes like engine degreaser."

Lucas is a catch by most women's standards. He is the triple threat: tall, dark, and handsome, not that his attractive qualities end there. Lucas is also well-groomed, cultured, intelligent, can dance, and comes from a wealthy family. In many ways, he and Brody are the perfect roommates.

Ashlee cocks her head. "How exactly do you know what engine degreaser tastes like? Is this something you drink frequently or tried by accident? Did you—?"

"Whoa! Easy on the cross-examination, counselor," Lucas says, holding his hands at shoulder level. "It was a metaphor."

She shrugs. "Just checking."

"I haven't seen you at one of our parties in a while, Ash."

"Yeah, well, I've been busy. I need to keep my grades up. We all don't have…a family job lined up like my roommate."

That's not what she was going to say. She was going to make a snarky comment about having a trust fund. Lucas has one rumored to be seven figures that he can fall back on. Not wanting to offend her host, Ashlee changed her mind last second, hoping he's too lit to notice.

Lucas smiles before picking up a bottle. "I'm glad you came tonight. Let's celebrate with some of the good stuff. Come on."

He sets the bottle of cheap silver tequila on the counter, and they weave through their peers clustered in the living area. The hallway that leads to the bedrooms is short, and he turns into the one on the right. Typically, bedrooms are off-limits at these soirees. She imagines that Lucas and Brody will use them for whichever women get caught in their webs tonight.

"There's the man of the hour!" Brody says, sitting in a chair and holding court with a couple of friends.

"And you're being rude. There are two hundred people here, and you're hunkered down in here drinking my stash."

"Sorry, Bro. I'll head out in a bit. Who did you…? Ashlee?"

Ashlee stuffs her hands in her pockets and leans gently against the jamb. "Hi, Brody."

"Ok…I think this is going to require a shot," Lucas says, feeling the tension that has gripped the room in its icy grasp.

He pours Patron Platinum Gran Tequila into a sextet of shot glasses. They all slug them down. Ashlee isn't a fan of tequila, but this is smooth. At two hundred fifty dollars a bottle, it ought to be.

"I haven't seen you in a while, Ashlee."

She wipes her mouth. "That's by design."

"I thought we had a fun date back in October."

"It was September, and we did. It was so good that you couldn't wait to ask me out on a second one."

Brody averts his eyes. "It wasn't—"

"Or walk me to the door…or kiss me goodnight…."

Brody's friends make a range of surprised and horrified faces at the slight. Lucas noisily sets his shot glass on the small table against the wall.

"Okay…that's our cue to leave. C'mon, guys, let's give them some space."

"I'm sorry, Ashlee," Brody says after they clear out and the door is closed behind them. "I know it isn't an excuse, but I was dealing with some…stuff."

"Stuff. Sure. You must have dealt with it fast because I saw you out with Charlene Mazzaron a week later."

"I—"

Ashlee holds up a hand. "Don't bother explaining."

She moves to the table and pours two more shots. Brody doesn't follow her. He heads to the nightstand and picks up a baseball signed by Aaron Judge. She wonders if it's a home run ball. Probably.

"My life is complicated, Ashlee. I didn't mean to blow you off."

Ashlee swirls the liquor in the glasses and hands him one of the shots. She salutes him with hers, and they both fire their drinks into the back of their throats.

"It's fine. I'm used to men hurting me. It's been that way for a while now."

"I'm not like those men."

Ashlee frowns. "All evidence to the contrary. I liked you, Brock. I really did. I thought we had a connection."

He nods. "Look, I'd like to make it up to you."

"A little late for that now, isn't it? How could you—"

The door swings open, and four of her peers barge in with Lucas on their heels. Brody sets the baseball down on the lacquered pedestal he picked it up from.

"Sorry, man, I tried to stop them, but they found out about my bottle of Ciroc Ten vodka. The Smirnoff out in the kitchen isn't cutting it."

"It's okay. Come on in, guys. We were just leaving."

Brody nods, and Ashlee follows him into the hallway. Instead of turning left and heading back into the party, he pulls out a key and unlocks his bedroom door.

"An exterior door lock?"

"I installed it myself," he says with a smile. "We keep all our valuable stuff in my room during these parties. You know as well as I do that lawyers are crooks."

The pair enters the room. Ashlee sits on the bed while Brody closes the door and locks it behind him. He rests his head against it.

"You okay?"

"Yeah. Too much tequila too quickly. You?"

"I'm a…I'm a little woozy, actually. How do you think you'll make up for the fact that you ghosted me?"

Brody grins and sits down next to her on the bed.

* * *

Ashlee is going to get bloody-knuckled from banging on the door. Their doorbell hasn't worked since they moved in, and the calls to maintenance haven't resulted in any action. She raps the door even harder until she hears someone stirring.

"I'm coming. I'm coming. Geez…."

Chloe opens the door to find her disheveled roomie standing on the stoop in last night's clothes. Instead of pushing into the apartment, Ashlee is like a statue. She doesn't move an inch.

"Wow. You must have had one hell of a night. Did you forget your keys?"

It was meant to be a playful inquiry. Instead, Chloe gets no reaction. When Ashlee lifts her head, she sees the look on her face, and the mascara-tainted tear tracks down her cheeks.

"Ashlee, what's wrong?"

Her roommate looks around, her jaw quivering. She holds her arms against her chest and begins sobbing uncontrollably.

"Ash? Tell me."

"I was…I need you to take me to the campus police," Ashlee says between sobs.

"Why? What happened?"

Ashlee only begins crying harder. She holds herself tightly. It doesn't take a genius to recognize the trauma and put the clues together.

"Oh, my God! Yes, I'll take you. I'll get my coat."

CHAPTER SEVEN

JOHN PROCK

In many respects, John knows he's leading the perfect life. His wife may be tragically gone, but she left him a son who will graduate with a law degree and go on to do great things. Being a widower in his early fifties means he gets to live a bachelor's life in an amazing house in one of the country's wealthiest areas. Best of all, he makes a fortune from the business he started and runs and still has enough vigor to bed whichever woman happens to pique his interest.

Those are the obvious benefits. One of his favorites is nobody telling him what to do. He doesn't need to plan or coordinate with anyone. No spouse, mistress, or girlfriend is standing over his shoulder and nagging him about his health. If he wants three scrambled eggs, six strips of bacon, and a toasted bagel for breakfast, then that's what he has. It's also exactly what he just made.

John slept in this morning. He's a workaholic and is known to take much of it home to the massive, modern workspace he constructed in the basement. Not today. John didn't feel like waking up early this morning, so he didn't. The coffee is made, the clock is approaching ten, and it's a perfect day of peace and quiet.

And then the phone rings.

The shipping tycoon puts down the forkful of eggs and walks over to the handset sitting on the charger in the kitchen corner. He's the tail end of the last generation that still sees the need to keep a personal landline. He isn't sure why. He never uses it, and only telemarketers, spammers, and political pollsters ever call the number. That's why he's surprised to see the name when he checks the caller ID.

"Brody? To what do I owe this unexpected pleasure of you calling your old man?"

"Hi, Dad," he says, in a tone best characterized as morose.

"I pay a small fortune to that school for you to study and learn, not to party. It sounds like you had a tough night."

"You could say that."

John listens to the silence on the other end of the call. He even pulls the handset away from his ear to see if the line is still connected. It is.

"All right, Brody, you called me, remember? What's wrong?"

"I'm…I'm at the state police barracks in Canaan."

It takes a moment for John to process that news. A thousand questions run through his mind like it's the Boston Marathon. His first emotional reaction is disbelief, but that quickly begins to change to anger. His son is reckless. Now he's gone too far.

"What? Why are you at a police station? What did you do?"

"Nothing!"

"Don't tell me that. You didn't call me because it's 'nothing.' It must be something if you're under arrest."

"I'm not under arrest. I'm being questioned."

"For what?" There's another long pause, and John stares at his breakfast impatiently. "For what, Brody?"

"Sexual assault."

John closes his eyes. "You raped a girl?"

"I didn't! I swear to God!"

His son is a player. He wasn't shy in bragging about his conquests when he was an undergrad at NYU. That carried over to his studies up at Salisbury. John doesn't mind enduring the "sowing his wild oats" phase. It beats the alternative.

But now it looks like he may have taken things too far. It could be a misunderstanding. The girl could have cheated on a boyfriend and lied to protect herself from the repercussions. It could be something else. He's not sure what to believe, but regardless, steps must be taken.

"Okay, okay."

"Dad, you need to believe me. I didn't rape her!"

"Brody, are they still questioning you?" John asks with a sense of urgency in his voice.

"Yeah."

"Don't answer any more questions. I'll contact our attorney and get him to meet me up there. Do *not* say anything more. Nothing. Do you understand?"

"Y-yes."

"I need you to say that you understand. No answers. Even if they ask if you want some water, you don't respond. Say it."

"I…understand. Don't answer anything," Brody says, his voice quivering. "I'm so scared, Dad."

"It'll be okay. I'm on my way."

John disconnects the call and squeezes the handset tightly. He doesn't have time to deal with this. Unfortunately, it needs to be his highest priority. He stares at his untouched breakfast. A meal can wait. There's work that needs to be done.

CHAPTER EIGHT
"BOSTON" HOLLINGER

WATCHTOWER TRAINING FACILITY
SOMEWHERE IN VIRGINIA

There are two distinct kinds of silence in this world: quiet and awkward. The former is often a relaxing, zen-like state where nothing in the world exists around you. The latter is the frustrating, uncomfortable absence of conversation between two people who should be talking. I should be used to this. Most of my appointments with Dr. Kurota are like this at one point or another.

Asami puts down her pen and pulls a pair of reading glasses off her face, folding its arms as she stares at me intently. "What's wrong, Boston?"

"What makes you think something's wrong?"

"I have three medical degrees and am a trained psychiatrist, but mostly, I'm not stupid."

I lean back into the overstuffed chair. "I'm pretty sure one medical degree is evidence enough."

"You've sat in this office every week for over a year. In all that time, you've never gone this long without complaining about why you're here. What's wrong?"

"Nothing."

Asami shakes her head. "That's a woman's answer when a man asks that question, and it always means something is. Tell me, or I can summon Nadiya and have her beat it out of you."

I force a smile. "That would go against your motherly instinct."

"Call it tough love."

"Okay. You practically have an aneurysm every time I go on a mission. When I get back, you grill me for hours. Why do you do it?"

Asami cocks her head. "That's my job, Boston."

"I know that. I want to know why you chose to do this. You're intelligent, educated, and respected in your fields. You could do anything you want, so why are you here? Why the interest in me?"

"Because of what you can do…and how you do it. We still need to learn much about your gift, but it's more than that. There's a psychological component. I like you, Boston. You're one of the best men I know, and I've seen the mental toll this takes on you. Nobody could possibly understand the impact. I've made it my job to explain it to them."

I clasp my hands and wring them. "You're right. It does take a toll. A big one."

The doctor sits up a little straighter. "I didn't think you would ever admit that."

"If it makes you feel better, I'm a touch scared about what happens now that I have. I'm afraid you'll try a Vulcan mind meld on me."

"Do my ears look pointy to you?" she asks, brushing her long, black hair back for effect. "Why are you bringing this up now, Boston? Did something happen?"

I shake my head. "Are we off the record?"

"Uh…not really," Dr. Kurota says, pointing at her yellow legal pad.

"Can we be? I need a friend, not a doctor who recaps every session with Matt and Zach."

Asami rubs her chin and fidgets in her chair. It's a bigger ask than most people would think. She gets grilled for every detail about my well-being, and keeping me sane is her job. This would mean that the next part of the conversation could never be relayed to anyone at Watchtower and could be a career-ending move for her.

"Okay."

"How are you coming along with your inhibition drugs?"

Whatever she thought I was about to say, that wasn't it. The blood drains out of her face.

"I don't know what you're talking about."

"Nice try. Don't lie to me, Asami. Watchtower thinks I'm a weapon that they only have tenuous control over. They need to install a safety switch. Brass must have instructed you to find a way to negate my gift if he ever needed to give the order."

"That's not how—"

"Asami. Please. I would have ordered the same thing in his position. Do you have one or not?"

She presses her lips together. "No. Not yet. Are you asking because you're afraid we'll use it or because you want to take it?"

The awkward silence returns with a vengeance after I break eye contact. She doesn't press me for a response. The lack of an immediate denial answered the question, but I know I won't get off the hook that easily.

"I'm not very good at being an agent. If my experiences in Hogan's Alley taught me anything, it's that. My gift is the only reason I'm here. I don't have the instincts for the rest of it."

"Your exploits in Arizona and Mexico lead to a different conclusion."

I shake my head. "I was lucky. And angry. And Sol rode in on her lime-green steed to save the day."

"And Forte showed up in a pair of helicopters with special forces. You had support, yes. You also had the wits to make it that far."

I relive a memory of my own. I was pinned down at the coast by Alejandro Salcido's thugs when Sol, the sister of one of the trafficking kingpin's henchmen, defied my instructions and saved the day. We escaped north, but Salcido was well-connected. A small army was waiting for us as we reached the border. They were pissed I had eliminated him and surrounded us before Forte, Emma, and Nadiya showed up in two military gunships to extract us from Mexico.

"I will never be the asset they expect me to be."

"You did fine at Quantico. You didn't do any worse than most trainees."

"I know, but there's a difference: Trainees want the job. I don't."

She squints, and I suddenly feel pressed between two pieces of glass under a microscope. "Nice try."

"It's true."

"Partly true. You don't want to be an agent, but you *do* want to make a difference. That's what propelled you in Arizona. That's why your missions are successful, while your training performance—"

"Sucks?"

"I was going to say 'is lacking.' Why are you really asking about the inhibitor? Is this about Tara?"

I understand the question, even if I don't like it. I only knew Tara for a matter of days. That short amount of time with her was enough. I felt more connected to a woman I barely knew than I did my traitorous late fiancée. I still do.

"For once, no," I say, standing and walking over to the window that overlooks the parking lot. "It's about seeing things I don't want to. The missions are bad enough, but now that Forte and Matt let me out once in a while…I see things…horrible things."

Asami doesn't say anything. That's a skill most people don't have. She is easy to talk to because she listens, even if it's only to diagnose me and report her findings. She doesn't bother asking a probing question or prompting me to continue. She already knows that I will.

"I was on the Metro a couple of weeks ago. A man got on at Foggy Bottom and sat next to me. He wasn't a politician or CEO…just another lawyer in a city full of them. Then I saw his memories…I saw him beating his wife and children."

Asami closes her eyes. She can't possibly know what emotional traumas I see other than what she writes down on that pad. But she's a woman who has a past. In that history is trauma. I've seen it and know that's what drives her.

"That had to be hard," she croaks.

"The imagery was bad, but…I could feel the guy's rage. He hates his wife and kids and despises everything about his life. I wish I could say that was the worst part of the experience. Then I opened my eyes and realized something."

Asami leans forward. "That you couldn't do anything about it."

I nod. "Watchtower needs its weapon, and that requires me to be anonymous. I'm forbidden to act and am forced to ignore all the evil in this world…repress all the things I feel."

She leans back. "Superman had to be Clark Kent. Batman had to be Bruce Wayne."

"I'm not a superhero," I argue.

"Aren't you? You have a special power. You have enemies. You have a history and even a bat cave," Asami says, spreading her hands at the training facility. "You even have sidekicks."

"I'll give you a hundred dollars if you tell Forte he's Robin."

Asami smiles and then stifles it. "Our time is up, Boston."

"Really? I figured you would try to milk me for every bit of information you could now that I've opened up."

"You've said enough," Asami admits. "I do have one question for you. What would you do if you didn't have to abide by Watchtower's rules?"

I stare hard at her. "Easy. I'd start administering some justice in this world."

CHAPTER NINE
JAMIESON BOHMER

Jamieson raps on the sturdy oak study door and opens it to find Tomasso toiling at his desk. Work doesn't stop, even on a Saturday. The Italian developer may be many things, but lazy isn't one of them.

"Is she back?"

"Safe and sound up in her room," Jamieson says, not bothering to sit in one of the matching chairs in front of the ornate lacquered desk.

Tomasso nods. Jamieson can't understand why a father wouldn't rush to be by his only daughter's side after such a tragic incident. He was perplexed why the man didn't accompany him to Connecticut to pick her up. It is very un-parental, if not unexpected.

The Trillo family patriarch's life has little room for sentimentality, affection, or love, even for his only daughter. He isn't sure if it has always been that way or has something to do with the loss of his wife, Viviana. Either way, it's irrelevant. Jamieson isn't paid to understand this dysfunctional family dynamic, so he quit trying years ago.

"How is she?" Jamieson's boss asks with all the concern of a parent asking if a child took out the trash.

"Eager to not be here."

He sighs. "I bet. Did Ashlee say anything on the ride back from Connecticut?"

"No."

"Did you ask her what happened?"

"I did. Your daughter ignored any attempts at conversation and just stared out the window for the entire two hours."

"Has she been interviewed?"

"Campus police took her initial report, and state police detectives followed up. Sharon Hospital conducted the medical examination. Outside of that, no."

"I heard that the state police are involved."

"And they handed it off to the feds." Tomasso looks up. "Given who you and the boy's father are, a special request was made to the FBI. Apparently, a team is being sent up from Washington. They're going to want to speak to Ashlee."

Tomasso frowns and shakes his head. "We don't need this right now."

"Your daughter didn't ask to get raped, sir."

Jamieson knows he crossed a line but is incapable of feeling regret. If his boss is angered by the observation, he can stand here and take the retribution. Some things need to be said, and Tomasso must guard against presenting himself as indifferent or uncaring when the FBI comes knocking.

"Ashlee went to that party for a guy," Tomasso says evenly after leaning back in his chair. "I'm sure she was dressed provocatively and had too much to drink. She may not have asked to be assaulted, but she might as well have. She put herself in a situation to be taken advantage of."

"She's young."

"And I taught her better than that. The world is cruel, and nobody knows that better than she does. You have to be ruthless to survive in it. Instead, she made herself into a victim. She's still playing one."

Jamieson imagines most people would be repulsed hearing those words. He isn't. Nothing rattles him. He avoids getting emotional about situations and applies logic and reason to solve problems. That's why he's the star employee of a man who views empathy as a weakness.

"Inform the house staff and guards that Ashlee is not to leave this house under any circumstances. Take whatever precautions are necessary to ensure she remains restricted to her room. Confiscate her phone and computer. I don't want her communicating with the outside world."

"I'll see to it."

"Ashlee will think she's a prisoner and complain about it to everyone," Tomasso continues. "I don't care, and neither should anyone else. This is for her own good and the good of the family. Explain that to her. Be blunt, if needed."

"As you wish."

The lawyer understands his boss's reaction. This incident is starting to gain media attention. It has all the ingredients for the perfect story: powerful, politically connected families, a prestigious law school, allegations of sexual assault, conflicting accounts, and lots of opinions from people who weren't there. There is no doubt that media outlets will climb over each other to get the next scoop.

As stories get pumped out, the public will begin expressing their outrage. That will result in more salacious reporting as the cycle reinforces itself. Jamieson doesn't think hiding Ashlee in Rapunzel's tower will help control the narrative. It will likely make matters worse for them.

"Jamieson, there's one more thing. I'm going to need you to do some things. We cannot have the feds snooping around. We're too exposed. Find a way to slow down any investigation while I take some precautions."

"Are there any limitations I should adhere to?"

Tomasso leans forward in his chair and begins shuffling papers around his desk.

"Use your judgment," he says, refusing to make eye contact.

The loud and clear message is to make this go away as fast as possible. Ashlee isn't going to get the justice she thinks she deserves. Tomasso will never let things get that far. It will be a further opening of the rift between father and daughter, but that's his problem. Jamieson has another assignment, and he will see it through.

CHAPTER TEN
SSA ZACH FORTE

Training is important in any endeavor. The American military is a lethal fighting force because they constantly hone their skills in realistic scenarios. Soldiers maintain physical fitness and technical proficiency during training cycles established at the battalion, brigade, or division levels. This is no different.

Boston needs to sharpen his skills. He may have a gift that provides insights into his targets, but he needs to know how to react to situations and survive if it comes to that. He got lucky in Mexico. That is undeniable.

When the request to report to Matt's office came, Forte assumed it was some bureaucratic exercise. On the way into the administrative building, he had another, more disturbing thought. Something is up.

Zach raps twice on the door jamb. "You wanted to see me?"

Matt leans back and waves him in as Asami turns to watch him from her seat across his desk. Zach parks himself in the other chair and leans forward. Whatever this is can't be good.

"We have a new assignment."

Zach looks at the pair, confused. "We're in an operational standdown."

"We *were* in one. Then we got handed a mission."

"Handed?" Zach asks.

"This one comes directly from Brass. Lord knows who turned him onto it."

David Brass isn't an FBI agent. Zach has long suspected that he's CIA, but they won't have a record of him either. As a cover, Brass is responsible for bringing American farm goods to international markets for the Department of Agriculture. Before Boston's assignment in Arizona, he had only met the normally hands-off program director a few times. His presence has been more of a constant as Boston racks up wins. Watchtower went from almost being dissolved to one of the country's most effective teams.

"You're okay with this?" Zach asks, turning to Asami.

"It's not my job to determine what assignments Watchtower takes."

"I never said it was. Are you *okay* with it?"

"Dr. Kurota," Matt interjects, "what Zach is trying to ask is whether Boston is in a mental place where he can take on another assignment after being promised a break."

Asami takes a deep breath. She looks like she has something to say but stifles the urge. "Yes."

"That's good enough for me," Matt concludes.

Zach shakes his head. "What's so important that we need to get involved? Political corruption? Drug ring? Espionage?"

"A woman accused a man of rape at a law school in Connecticut last night."

Zach waits to see if Matt has anything more to offer than that. He doesn't.

"At the risk of sounding crass and uncaring, doesn't that happen at schools all over the country?"

"Regrettably, yes. The act itself isn't what warrants Watchtower's involvement. It's who the accuser and accused are. Ashlee Trillo and Brody Prock."

Forte waits for more information and, once again, doesn't get any. Matt must expect him to know the names, or at a minimum, who the families are. He doesn't and holds his hands out to prompt some elaboration.

"Ashlee is the daughter of renowned Newark developer Tomasso Trillo. He's the founder and president of Brick City Development, one of the most notable urban-renewal companies in the country. Brody Prock's father is John Prock. He owns the fastest-growing international shipping company in the country."

"Okay…so are we talking political connections?"

"Lots of them. Both men donated enough money to local and national campaigns to start political action committees. They're on a first-name basis with everyone from mayors to congressmen to New York and New Jersey governors."

"Have any of these politicians begun leaning on the FBI?"

"Not yet, but they will. Considering the sensitivity of the allegations and the kids involved, the Connecticut State Police called the Bureau. Salisbury is only served by a resident state trooper, and the CSP wants to ensure the proper resources are dedicated to it. This investigation needs to be by the book and the conclusion airtight."

Forte rubs his chin. Agreeing to an assignment like this is out of character for Matt. There are too many eyes on this, and the whole point of Watchtower is to remain secretive. This order may have even come from above their overlord.

"Did you try to dissuade Brass?"

Matt fidgets as he stares at some papers on his desk. "This isn't a hill I'm willing to die on. We're going to handle this assignment quickly and quietly."

"What do you want Boston to do?"

"Accompany the team to New Jersey and interview the alleged victim. It involves a recent trauma, so any memory of what happened will be clear. We need to know beyond a shadow of a doubt."

Zach looks at Asami. She doesn't like the idea of Boston reliving that experience, but she isn't being vocal in protesting it either. He understands that the FBI is terrified about being wrong. In a high-profile case like this, the possible emotional damage to Boston cannot be understated.

"Doctor, we watched what happened when Boston saw through the eyes of innocent children. You aren't concerned about what happens when he sees through the eyes of a victim?"

Asami's jaw tightens. "I'm concerned about everything he sees, Special Agent Forte. But this is going to get national media exposure. Activists will use it to advance agendas, and lives could get destroyed. We need to know the truth unequivocally."

"And Boston?"

"I will keep an eye on him as always, as I'm sure you will."

Matt has heard enough. "Ashlee Trillo is with her father at their house in Northern New Jersey. You'll leave first thing in the morning. She clammed up during the state police's interview, so see what you and the team can get out of her. You can set up shop in Manhattan."

"The FBI field office?"

Matt rubs his chin. "Near them. Brody Prock has lawyered up. His father has already brought in a high-powered defense team. I'll see what I can do to get through them, but it may take a couple of days. You can work from there without attracting unwanted attention."

"Okay," Forte says, rising from his chair. Asami remains seated. Whatever conversation she is having with Matt isn't finished.

"Good luck, Zach. Keep me posted."

CHAPTER ELEVEN
ASHLEE TRILLO

TOMASSO TRILLO FAMILY ESTATE
ENGLEWOOD CLIFFS, NEW JERSEY

Ashlee lays three outfits on the bed and stands back. She's partial to the black spaghetti strap top, but the red has a certain wow factor when she wears matching lipstick. It might be too chilly outside to wear the blue dress, so it's eliminated from consideration. She picks up the black shirt and jeans, then changes her mind.

"Definitely the red," she says, holding it in front of her long floor mirror.

Her favorite clothes are still up at school, but Ashlee has a closet full of designer outfits to choose from here. She doesn't like to pack when she comes home. Her father left for the office an hour ago without even checking on her. He may be a douche, but at least he's generous with loaning her his credit card.

There is no way she's staying here tonight. She may hate school, but being back in Englewood Cliffs is worse. This house has a crypt's warmth and a dead battery's energy.

Ashlee pulls off her t-shirt and stops to admire her black lacy bra. It's new, and it looks fabulous on her. She needs to get a few more of these in different colors.

The bedroom door flies open, and Jamieson stomps in. Ashlee grabs her shirt to cover her chest. Jamieson is a creep, and this isn't a peep show.

"Don't you knock? What the hell are you doing?"

"When it suits me," he says, noticing the outfits on the bed. "I should ask you the same thing."

"I'm going out."

"No, you aren't."

Ashlee's brow crinkles as she cocks her head. "Excuse me?"

Jamieson closes the door and turns to face her. "You aren't leaving the house. In fact, you're not leaving your room. Meals will be brought to you, but you are restricted to your bedroom until further notice."

"Oh, I don't think so."

Ashlee grabs the red outfit off the bed and tries to walk past him. He grabs her upper arm and spins her around. She yanks it away and glares at him defiantly.

"You don't get a say in where I go and what I do!"

"That's true. I don't. But your father does."

"He doesn't get to, either."

Ashlee tries to walk past him again. He grabs her arm, and she struggles against his grip. When he doesn't let go, she draws her right arm back and lets her fist fly. It hits nothing but air.

Jamieson gnashes his teeth. That was the last straw. He crosses his right arm in front of his chest and swings it hard in an arcing motion. The back of his hand contacts Ashlee's cheek, and the momentum turns her face hard to the left.

He releases her, and time seems to stand still. She touches her cheek tenderly with her fingers and looks at him with fury. Slapping your boss's daughter across the face would normally be a career-ending move. In this case, Tomasso will understand.

Ashlee charges at him in a rage. Jamieson doesn't need to react. He was expecting her to do something rash because that's how petulant, spoiled brats behave. He arrests her momentum and grabs her throat with his hand. She grabs at his wrists as he forces her backward onto the bed.

She strikes his wrist to break his grip, but he only clenches her throat harder. He climbs on top of her, pinning her down. Jamieson releases her throat and grabs her wrists, pinning her arms over her head. Ashlee gasps for air now that she is free to breathe. He waits until she catches her breath and leans close to her face.

"Does this feel familiar?" Jamieson asks, pressing himself harder on her. "I bet it does."

Ashlee stops fighting against his grip. He expects her to burst into tears when memories of what happened at Salisbury come flooding back. She doesn't. She just stares at him with hatred and disgust.

"I frankly don't care where you go or what you do, Ashlee, but your father does. Since you have a glaring incapacity to honor him or this family, he must make decisions that are in everyone's best interests."

"Yeah, I'm sure he has my best interests in mind."

Jamieson doesn't react. "Your time up at school has caused you to forget the rules. Let me spell them out. You will not leave this house. I'm taking your phone because you won't need it. I am also taking your laptop and have changed the wi-fi password. The Internet is off-limits. You will follow these rules, or else."

"Or else what? What are you going to do to me?"

Jamieson's lip curls. "Hurting you doesn't give me joy, Miss Trillo. I will not regret it, either. It will just be something that…happens. Like taking out the trash. It must be done."

"My father would never agree…." Ashlee's voice trails off.

Tomasso has never protected her. At least, not like a father would be expected to protect a daughter. Why would he start now?

"Are you certain?"

Jamieson releases her and climbs off. Ashlee doesn't move. She remains lying on the bed, staring at her bedroom ceiling. He stops when he reaches the door.

"The FBI will be coming to interview you tomorrow. Dress modestly…if you can. We don't want them to think you're a slut. They will have lots of questions. Tell them what happened at Salisbury and nothing more."

"Aye, aye, sir!" she says with a sarcastic salute, still not looking at him.

"Heed my words, Ashlee. This will be the only warning I give you. You're home now. Remember that."

Jamieson leaves her bedroom and closes the door. He pauses and leans his ear close to the door. Unlike the sturdy oak that shields Tomasso's study, these hollow core doors let all kinds of sounds through. The sobbing he hears almost causes him to smile. Almost.

CHAPTER TWELVE

JOHN PROCK

AMERICAN LOGISTICS OFFICES
HUNTS POINT, BRONX, NEW YORK

A hub was needed to base their operations when American Logistics was established. Hunts Point, already home to one of the world's largest food distribution facilities, was the perfect location. Once a vacation spot for the city's elite, apartment buildings replaced mansions, and convenient access to the Tri-State region via rail lines led to increased industrial and commercial activity.

As the business grew, John Prock contemplated moving the company's headquarters functions to a swanky office building in Manhattan. He decided against it. He hired loyal people to work for AMLOG, and they wanted to be close to the corporation's beating heart. None of them live on that expensive, overpopulated island. This company started in this facility, and there is no good reason to move it.

John wasn't going to let them work in spartan conditions. The outside of the building is decrepit, and the dingy distribution part of the facility doesn't reek of corporate success. So, he invested in the office space. It's not as nice as something constructed in luxury skyscrapers, but it's at least comfortable.

The executives have already gathered in the conference room. The men and women who run this company have been with John for years. Despite the familiarity from working together every day, they avoid eye contact as he finds his seat at the end of the long conference table.

"There's no reason to be cagey. I know this is bad. You're all here to tell me how bad, not blow sunshine up my ass."

"I'll go. I'm not scared of your ass," Brianna Brown, the company's public relations officer, says.

Brianna is one of the newer executives. She worked in customer service for a public utility when John called one day to report an outage. She was polite, straightforward, and had street smarts most college-educated PR reps could never match. He liked her skills, so he hired her on the spot at a fifty percent increase in salary. It was money well spent.

"I expected nothing less."

"None of what happened at Salisbury should reflect on the company, but all of it does."

"That's stupid," one of his managers says from the other end of the table.

"Welcome to the Modern Age. It's a character thing. John is AMLOG's founder, and people will think his son's behavior reflects his values. It doesn't matter whether the accusations are true or not. The damage is done."

"Who's feeding this to the press?" Johns asks. "Is it the girl's family?"

"No, I don't think so," Malcolm Gumm, the vice president of corporate communications, says. "At least there's no evidence of that. Tomasso Trillo is a bigshot developer in New Jersey. He's the patron saint of the city's redevelopment efforts. He won't want the publicity that comes with this."

"Because he's shady as shit," Brianna moans. "I have a cousin who lives there. It's the city's worst-kept secret."

"Then who?" John presses.

Malcolm leans forward and places his hands on the table. "Not who. What. The media is driving it. It's the perfect clickbait story. The entitled son of a wealthy shipping tycoon rapes a fellow student at a snobby law school. I'm surprised this incident doesn't have its own hashtag yet."

"Is there any chance they'll lose interest in the story?"

"Sure," Brianna says. "All stories fade in time. How much time depends on their ability to keep viewers, subscribers, and readers addicted."

"That's why we need to get ahead of this, John," Malcolm warns.

"You mean by issuing a statement."

"Not commenting will create an information vacuum that the media will find ways to fill, likely with unfavorable opinions and viewpoints."

"Or worse, they'll start making BS up."

"Why would they do that?" another manager asks.

"Ask the committee investigating Russiagate," Malcolm says. "When you don't have the goods, you run with whatever sounds good."

There's a moan at the table. John isn't sure what the political leanings are of the people at the table, but he also doesn't care. This isn't the time or place for that discussion.

"So, we release a statement from AMLOG. Malcolm will draft one and get it out for the people in this room to review. What else?"

"Business impact," Emily Perkins says.

John leans back. Of all his hires, she may be the best one. Not only is Emily a fantastic VP of Account Management, but she's easy on the eyes and has a set of legs that belong in a magazine. John has always preferred brunettes, but when her long hair curls gracefully down her neck and shoulders, he becomes a devotee of blondes.

In her mid-thirties and unmarried, John has been warned that she has more than a passing crush on him. He has avoided mixing business and pleasure, even though there is no corporate policy against it, and his wife is long gone. Maybe someday she'll wear him down, and he looks forward to that journey.

"Are we losing clients?"

Emily checks the paper in front of her. "We've lost a couple, but that number is likely to increase in correlation with the story's viral velocity."

John shakes his head. "All over a stupid allegation."

"Companies have to be careful," Brianna adds. "Activist groups may be small, but they make a lot of noise, especially on social media. They will come under immense pressure to cut ties with you and AMLOG. Some are doing it preemptively."

"Emily, I need you to plug the leaks in the dam the best you can. What's the best way to prevent more clients from leaving?"

She looks around the table before settling her eyes on John. "Make this go away as fast as possible."

CHAPTER THIRTEEN
SSA ZACH FORTE

TOMASSO TRILLO FAMILY ESTATE
ENGLEWOOD CLIFFS, NEW JERSEY

The driver pulls the Suburban into the estate's semi-circular driveway and stops in front of the house. Not that "house" is an accurate description. It looks more like a stately European manor than something you'd find in Northern New Jersey.

This place is ridiculous. Eight large windows dominate the white brick two-story façade, and a massive arched window open to the foyer dominates the space above the double front door. The driveway is painstakingly constructed from gray paving stones, and the landscaping alone must have cost more than Zach's annual salary.

Boston, Nadiya, and Emma climb out of the vehicle and join their boss in staring at the structure. There is no obvious security, but this is a newer construction, and Zach is certain the grounds are covered with cameras. He takes the lead up to the covered entryway and presses the doorbell. Zach can hear the faint chimes inside and expects to see Lurch open the door. Or Geoffrey, the butler from *The Fresh Prince of Bel-Air*. Instead, Tomasso Trillo appears when the rightmost door swings open.

"Mister Trillo? My name is Special Agent Zach Forte with the FBI."

"Yes, your office called, and I was told to expect you. Come in."

Zach exchanges a look with Boston. Tomasso Trillo's greeting had all the warmth of a bag of ice. He could understand that the stress of his daughter's ordeal would take a toll, but the FBI will be instrumental in putting her attacker behind bars. It wouldn't be erroneous for most people to think he would welcome their involvement.

The quartet enters the white marble foyer behind Tomasso, who stops and turns to face them. "I didn't expect four agents."

The developer eyes the two women. Both have their hair up and are dressed professionally in blouses, tailored suit jackets, and pants. The clothing is not form-fitting, but Nadiya and Emma would look good in garbage bags or potato sacks. Tomasso does a not-so-subtle once-over on both of them. Nadiya's eyes narrow at the overt leering.

"Your case is getting a lot of special attention," Zach says, code for politicians and senior Bureau administrators taking an active interest.

"I see."

The admission didn't have the effect Zach thought it would. The man is politically connected and should have been leveraging those contacts to ensure the proper authorities are involved in his daughter's case. That doesn't seem to have happened. Instead, Tomasso appears more annoyed at their presence than grateful for it.

"I'm Special Agent Emma Farris," the firearms instructor says, extending her hand, which he takes.

"Special Agent Nadiya Jesperssen."

"Special Agent Andrew Dufresne."

The introductions are completed, and Tomasso gestures to his left. "Why don't we chat in the study?"

"We would rather see your daughter, sir," Zach says, recognizing the offer as a stall tactic.

"Please, I insist. Follow me."

The heels of our shoes echo in the cavernous foyer as they click on the marble. The two women fall in behind Tomasso, likely wanting to plant a knife in his back as they walk. Zach uses the din to lean over and whisper to Boston.

"Andy Dufresne?"

Boston grins. "It's better than Will Smith."

Eugene Hollinger no longer exists, at least legally. So far as the world is concerned, he was killed by Gina Attison on his living room floor. As a result, each mission he embarks on requires an alias. The first one Zach chose when they were in Arizona was Will Smith. Since then, Boston has picked his own, based mostly on movie characters.

"Someone will get wise to your fictional characters sooner or later."

Boston shrugs. "Probably."

They enter Tomasso's study and stop near the heavy oak desk. The study is situated in front of the mansion and has long and narrow dimensions. It's not the dark space Zach envisioned. Two of the oversized windows allow plenty of light. The interior wall and the far side contain ornate bookshelves stocked with cloth-bound novels and literary works. He wonders if one is a lever that activates a secret door to a fortress of solitude.

"Will one of you tell me what this is about? My daughter was the victim of a sexual assault. She wasn't kidnapped and taken across state lines. Why is there federal involvement? And don't say it's because this case is somehow 'special.'"

"Once the report was made, campus police involved the Connecticut State Police, and they contacted the Bridgeport field office. We were dispatched from Washington to ensure that the investigation is thorough."

"As opposed to all the other ones?" Tomasso says, causing Zach's jaw to tense at the slight. He bites his tongue. "My daughter has already been interviewed by campus and state authorities. That should suffice."

"I'm afraid it doesn't," Nadiya chimes in. "Sexual assault cases are difficult to prove in a court of law. There is some physical evidence but no eyewitness testimony. It becomes an exercise of 'he said, she said,' and juries often base their decision on which story is more believable."

"The best way to overcome that is ensuring her account of the assault is well-documented," Emma says, picking up the argument. "A follow-up to her initial report will provide the clarity for prosecutors to move forward with a case."

"So, you want her to relive her trauma?"

Zach thinks they made a good argument, but Tomasso is rolling out a good tactic. Nobody wants the young woman to needlessly suffer, and by arguing that point, the Watchtower team will seem cold and uncaring.

"Sir, I can't begin to imagine what Ashlee is going through. No man can. This isn't about forcing her to relive her pain."

"Less than one percent of rapes in this country lead to felony convictions, Mr. Trillo," Nadiya interjects. "Too many women fail to report assaults because of their fear of not being believed. Ashlee did because she wants justice, and so do we. I'm sure she understands this interview is necessary to deliver it."

Zach suppresses a grin. Nadiya flipped the script on the developer. What father wouldn't want justice in his daughter's attack? This one, apparently, but he would never risk his reputation by looking indifferent to his daughter's plight.

"Very well," Tomasso concedes. "But I want to be present."

"I'm sorry, sir, but that's not possible," Zach declares.

"Why not?"

"Because rape is a personal crime, Mr. Trillo," Nadiya continues. "It's a violation of human dignity. And it's sexual. Your daughter won't feel comfortable discussing those details in front of you, and you won't want to listen to them."

"Okay. Then my attorney should be present."

"Your daughter is a victim and has no need for an attorney. Ashlee isn't suspected of any crime, and we're not here to determine if she committed one."

"Unless there's another reason you don't want your daughter talking to us," Boston says after he opens his eyes.

Everyone focuses their attention on him. Tomasso doesn't shy away from the insinuation nor look keen to directly challenge it.

"Of course not. I will get Ashlee. You're free to use this study for your interview."

"Thank you," Zach says as Tomasso disappears and turns for the foyer and the grand staircase that leads upstairs. "Agent Dufresne, any thoughts?"

Boston shakes his head slightly and rolls his eyes around the room. It's his signal for "not now because this place is bugged." With little else to do while they wait, the women begin arranging the chairs in the study. There is just enough for the four of them, plus Ashlee. Boston sits alongside the dusty tomes filling the bookshelves. He likes to be a passive observer in these situations but is more reticent than usual. He didn't like whatever he saw in the memories of Tomasso Trillo.

CHAPTER FOURTEEN
"BOSTON" HOLLINGER

TOMASSO TRILLO FAMILY ESTATE
ENGLEWOOD CLIFFS, NEW JERSEY

Ashlee stops walking when she reaches the study's threshold. Seeing four federal agents in your house can be intimidating, but this reminds me of those YouTube videos of owners dragging their pets to the veterinarian. She finally summons the courage to slowly enter, staring at the floor as if expecting it to open up and send her plunging into the depths of hell.

I close my eyes as Forte encourages her and starts with the introductions.

The memory is clear and absent the haze and fog that accompany most memories. It's either new or traumatic enough to remember every detail. The study looks different, yet the same. Tomasso is sitting at his desk with an open bottle of alcohol. His eyes are puffy, and he wipes them as I enter.

"The hospital just called. Your mother died."

A surge of raw emotion flows through me. I want to cry. I want to scream. I feel...pain...and anguish.

"I don't know why you're upset. You're responsible. Your mother never should have been out last night. It's your fault."

"I didn't...It's not my..." I can't get the words out.

"It is!" Tomasso shouts, circling the desk.

He stands in front of me, looking wounded...and angry.

"You killed your mother, Ashlee. Your irresponsibility is why...you're not my daughter. I could never have raised such a despicable person. Your mother is dead because of you. You'll have to live with that."

"Father, I—

"I can't stomach looking at you right now. Go to your room. Go anywhere. I don't care where. Just get out of my sight."

"Is Agent Sleepyhead over there okay?"

I hear the question and open my eyes to find everyone staring at me.

"I apologize, Miss Trillo. Special Agent Andrew Dufresne typically works nights," Zach says with a frown.

"I'm sorry," I say, desperately trying to shake off the emotional shock of the memory.

"Shall we begin?" Zach asks, moving things along. "We know you met Brody Prock when you first started at Salisbury. You went on your first date with him almost three months ago, not long after the semester began. Is that correct?"

"Yes. Brody asked me out. I agreed."

"Tell us what happened on that date."

Ashlee begins walking everyone through it. Emma and Nadiya interrupt for a couple of details, but they mostly let her tell the story. Everyone is taking notes except me. I close my eyes again as she tells the story. The memories I see with them open are a little like watching television in the bright sunlight. I want clarity, and that means looking like I'm napping. Zach will have to get over it.

I see the memory of the date and her being dropped off. She wanted Brody to kiss her. She really wanted him to accompany her inside her apartment. He was having none of either of those. The story she tells matches the memory almost perfectly. There is no deception or purposeful omissions due to embarrassment.

"He didn't try to kiss you?"

"No. Brody didn't even walk me to the door. I got out of his car, and he drove off."

"And was there any contact after the date? Calls or text messages?"

"No. Brody basically ghosted me."

Emma leans over to Zach. "Ghosting is when—"

"I know what it is, Agent Farris."

"Just checking. You're kinda old."

The interaction was meant to get Ashlee to loosen up. Maybe even crack a smile. She doesn't. There is no reaction from her at all.

"How did that make you feel, Ashlee?" Nadiya asks.

"I...I was disappointed. We had a great time that night. I liked Brody. I guess he didn't feel the same about me."

Ashlee zones out, and I close my eyes. There is a quick succession of memories, I think mostly from her teenage years. Most of them involve some kind of rejection. This young woman may be in a prestigious law school but suffers from egregiously low self-esteem.

Zach moves them along to the night of the assault. Ashlee begins by talking about how her roommate told her about the party after returning from the gym. She explains that she decided to go and try to avoid Brody, but he was very talkative when they bumped into each other. He had already been drinking for a couple of hours and made one for her.

I close my eyes when she gets to the part I was waiting for.

The party is crowded, with everyone hanging around on the back patio or in the main living area. There are about sixty people there, all with cups in their hands and having a good time. The music is blasting. Some of the kids are doing lines of cocaine on the coffee table.

I see Brody in the bedroom. We exchange words, and I have a shot. The other guys leave, and I pour a drink. My hand is shaking. I don't know why until...wait

The memory continues. I can feel the effect of the tequila. We walk across the hall into another bedroom. Brody sits beside me on the bed, and one thing leads to another. What happens next isn't what I expected.

"You made the report as soon as you woke up that morning?" Emma asks softly as I open my eyes.

"I didn't know what else to do."

"Where was Brody?" Zach asks.

"He was…sleeping in the bed next to me. He was still naked."

"That had to have been hard…waking up next to the man who raped you," Nadiya says.

Ashlee closes her eyes and gives a few quick nods as she hugs her chest harder with her arms. Zach is about to speak when Nadiya touches his arm. She remains silent as she stares off into the distance.

"Who picked you up from Salisbury?" I ask, earning an immediate glare from my combatives instructor.

"Why does that matter?" she asks in a defensive tone.

"It doesn't. I'm just curious."

"Jamieson Bohmer," Ashlee says in a near whisper after swallowing hard. "My father's attorney."

The memory of the slap is fresh. It may have only happened yesterday or this morning. I study Ashlee's face and see the heavy coat of cover-up foundation makeup on her neck and cheek. Lawyer, my ass.

"Why didn't your father pick you up?" I ask, continuing to press her for details.

Ashlee offers a slight shrug. "He was busy."

"Too busy to rush to the side of his daughter, who just experienced a traumatic sexual assault?" Nadiya asks.

"What does he do for a living?" I ask.

"He's a developer."

"I assume you don't mean film," Emma asks, prodding her to be more specific.

"No. Buildings. My father owns Brick City Development and does work for the City of Newark."

Zach looks at me. We were briefed on the family and their backgrounds. He knows that I fully understand what her father does for a living. I need her to focus on him, and Forte is wondering why. The scope of this investigation is what happened to Ashlee up in Salisbury, but I don't think it's that simple.

"Are you close to your father?" I ask. The question gets the desired result.

"You will do as I say!" Tomasso shouts as he swings his arm and slaps me with an open hand across the face. I feel my cheek burn from the hit, and my vision blurs from tears forming. Anger turns to profound sadness…and fear.

"As close as any college kid is to her dad, I suppose."

"Has he ever committed a crime?" The question commands the attention of Zach and the three women.

"What?"

"Answer the question, please, Ashlee," I insist before Nadiya can scold me. "Has your father ever committed other crimes besides repeatedly abusing you?"

Ashlee's mouth hangs open, and then she averts her eyes. I'm about to press for an answer when the study doors burst open.

CHAPTER FIFTEEN

JAMIESON BOHMER

TOMASSO TRILLO FAMILY ESTATE
ENGLEWOOD CLIFFS, NEW JERSEY

The entrance was more dramatic than Jamieson intended, but it had the benefit of stopping the interview cold. The four FBI agents stand at the sudden interruption, three forming a phalanx in front of Ashlee with the fourth remaining along the wall.

"This interview is over," Jamieson says, striding across the study.

"This interview is over when we say it is," the older agent argues. "Who the hell are you?"

"Jamieson Bohmer. I'm the Trillo family attorney. Miss Trillo is a cooperating witness, and I would expect your questions to be directed at what happened leading up to and on the night of the assault. Your line of questioning leads me to believe that you are after something else."

"And how would you know that?" one of the female agents asks.

"Legal instinct."

The agent farthest away from the group catches Jamieson's attention. He's so focused on him that it's distracting. Then he closes his eyes and scrunches his brow. The lawyer is about to say something when the lead agent enters his vision.

"Mr. Bohmer, this is about confirming the statement to bring justice—"

"Yes," Jamieson says, holding a hand up to stop him. "Tomasso told me how you appealed to his duty as a father to bring justice for his daughter. You also know that Miss Trillo is entitled to legal representation during an interview with the FBI or any other law enforcement agency."

The lead agent shrugs. "She didn't indicate that she wanted or needed any."

"Did you ask her?"

"We did as the interview commenced," the dark-haired agent says.

Jamieson grins. "Miss Trillo, would you have been more comfortable with legal representation in the room during this interview?"

Ashlee lowers her eyes. "Yes."

"There you go."

The agents look at each other. He knows what they're probably thinking, but there isn't much they can do about it. Ashlee has rights, and Jamieson has every reason to insist on his presence. Not that his plan is to sit here and listen to anything.

"Fine," the lead agent says. "Then we can continue with you here as an observer."

Jamieson presses his lips together as if he's thinking it over. He slowly shakes his head.

"No, you won't."

"Excuse me?" one of the women asks.

"You were deceptive and are flouting procedure while violating my client's legal rights."

"We did no such thing!"

"And I disagree," Jamieson says, staring at the beautiful blonde. "I don't think you're acting in my client's best interests despite your previous assurances to my employer. You cannot be trusted."

"We are investigating a reported crime, not serving as advocates. Our duty is to uncover the truth."

"Yes, as recent events have shown, I'm sure."

The older agent's hands ball into fists. Jamieson is certain he has no intention of using them, but the reaction lets him know the comment hit a tender spot. FBI agents can't be held responsible for the political actions of their leaders, but that doesn't mean the Bureau's misdeeds can't be used as leverage against them.

"Are you implying that—"

Jamieson holds a hand up. "You're only involved because of Tomasso Trillo's and John Prock's political connections. Let's not pretend otherwise. The Connecticut State Police are more than capable of investigating this independently."

"I resent your characterization of our motives," the lead agent seethes.

"I don't care. This interview is over. If you come back, it will need to be with a subpoena that I wish you good luck obtaining. Leave now, or I will draft a statement describing this interaction and release it to the press. It's your choice."

The lead agent stares at Jamieson for a long moment. He returns the stare, completely unfazed. Gold badges don't intimidate him, and the men and women America puts through Quantico don't impress him. This one has a chip on his shoulder, but underneath their cheap suits or FBI-emblazoned windbreakers, they're all the same.

"Let's go," he finally commands.

"Agent Forte...."

"Let's go, Nadiya."

The other male agent in the study stops in front of Bohmer and takes in his appearance.

"What kind of law do you practice, sir?"

Jamieson takes his measure of the man. The agent is confident, self-assured, and can handle himself. All good things to know.

"Does it matter?"

"No, not at all. I'm just curious."

"I practice family and corporate law."

The agent nods. "You have mud on your shoes. You should get them shined."

Jamieson looks down to see his Oxfords caked in mud. He stifles a scowl about forgetting to clean them after today's adventures.

"Thanks for the tip. Good day, Agent...?

"Dufresne. Special Agent Dufresne."

He grins and follows his team out. Jamieson moves to the window and watches them load up in their vehicle. The younger agent stops and looks at him. The two men lock their eyes and hold their stares until he finally climbs in and closes the door.

"I didn't tell them anything," Ashlee says from behind the desk.

He knows exactly what was said in this room, but there's no reason to explain that. It's better for everyone if Tomasso's petulant daughter is kept off-balance and defensive.

"Return to your room. Remember the rules and the consequences for failing to abide by them."

CHAPTER SIXTEEN

ASHLEE TRILLO

TOMASSO TRILLO FAMILY ESTATE
ENGLEWOOD CLIFFS, NEW JERSEY

Ashlee doesn't waste time returning to her room after Jamieson's interruption. She may despise the man, but she wasn't fond of answering the FBI's questions either. The intervention was a welcome one. He already knows what's being said in that room. Her father has most of this house surveilled by video and wired for sound. The study is no exception. Jamieson also won't want to confront her, so Ashlee is reasonably sure she won't be bothered in her cell.

It's an appropriate metaphor since her home feels like a prison. Living here is akin to being incarcerated. This isn't the first time she has been banished to her room for a long period. There were long stints of house arrest while she was in high school. That's when she worked out a prison economy with the house staff.

Inmates have plenty of time on their hands. It should surprise nobody that markets developed for everything from contraband goods to the first shot at the cute new guy on the cell block. Those goods have to be purchased, and in the absence of currency, things like cigarettes, fish, and ramen served as adequate substitutes because they're nonperishable, come in standard units, and have intrinsic value.

In Ashlee's prison, she traded things with the staff for phone time. It worked up through graduation. Once she went to college, she took measures in case of another stint in solitary confinement. Most people only own one cell phone. A subset of the population also has a work phone, but since Ashlee is in law school and not actively employed, that was never a concern. Her father should have known better and installed a jammer just in case. Mercifully, he isn't the most tech-savvy man.

Ashlee opens the top drawer of her nightstand and retrieves her Bible. She has never been overly religious, but a gift is a gift, and there is a use for this one. She opens the cover and the first few pages to the hollowed-out portion and retrieves her disposable cell phone.

The battery is fully charged, and she opens up the contacts. There are only a few loaded in it. She selects the one she needs and types a short text to her roommate.

Ashlee >>> Hey.
Chloe >>> Hey. You're done already?

Ashlee smiles and replaces the Bible in the nightstand drawer before settling onto the bed, lying on her stomach and propping her chin up with a pillow. If she's wrong and

Jamieson decides to pay her a visit, she can quickly hide the silenced phone before he sees it.

Ashlee >>> Yeah, Jamieson interrupted it. The feds started asking questions about my father.
Chloe >>> Why?
Ashlee >>> No idea. Sorry that it took so long to get in contact. Dad took my cell.
Chloe >>> I figured. Can't believe you put up with that.
Ashlee >>> You don't know my father.
Chloe >>> So? Leave the house. What can he do?
Ashlee >>> I have too much to lose.

Her roommate will never understand. Chloe's childhood was under the watchful eyes of caring, supportive parents. Ashlee's father is anything but caring or supportive. Since her mom's death, she feels more like a liability than a beloved daughter. She tried to explain that to Chloe over a pizza and a bottle of wine one weekend, but it needs to be experienced to be understood.

Chloe >>> All right. What did the FBI say?
Ashlee >>> IDK, not much. They asked questions and made me recite what I told the police.
Chloe >>> Unbelievable. Do they have the results of the rape kit?
Ashlee >>> Not sure. They didn't say.
Chloe >>> What the hell? Brody should be in jail by now. What are you gonna do?
Ashlee >>> I don't know.
Chloe >>> Is there any way I can help?

Help. It's not an offer that Ashlee gets very often and something she has spent her late teens and early twenties not expecting. She appreciates the offer, but this is her problem. She can't bring her roommate into it.

Ashlee >>> Other than busting me out of here? Not sure how.
Chloe >>> I have an idea that may help get the cops and feds to get off their fat asses.

"That would be a nice change of pace," Ashlee mutters quietly.

Ashlee >>> I don't think you should get involved. You were there for me at Salisbury. That was enough.
Chloe >>> I don't mind. What happened to you was horrible. They aren't making it any better. Trust me. I got this.
Ashlee >>>Okay. Thanks, Chloe.
Chloe >>> No prob!

The urge to ask for details is almost irresistible. As much as Ashlee wants to ask, it's better that she doesn't know. If Chloe does something that her father doesn't like, it's easier to plead ignorance and mean it than lie during the subsequent inquisition.

Ashlee >>>I have to go. I can't get caught with this phone. I'll text you later.
Chloe >>> Stay safe. Keep your head up.

Ashlee closes the chat and powers down the device. There isn't a need to charge it, so she replaces it in its hiding spot and closes the drawer. She rolls over onto her back and stares at the ceiling. At least one person in this world is on her side. It isn't the police, FBI, school administrators, or even her father. It's a roommate that she has almost nothing in common with. Now, Ashlee's afraid that her one ally is about to stick her head in the lion's mouth.

CHAPTER SEVENTEEN

JOHN PROCK

The reporters and cameramen huddle in their vans across the street. The ones who have dared to mill around the street look uncomfortable. This isn't the nicest neighborhood in the city. John watches as a cameraman exits the back of a satellite truck and sparks a cigarette. His head is on a swivel. Knowing this is the last place the man wants to be posted causes Prock to smile.

As reports of the alleged rape at Salisbury capture more of the country's attention, the appetite for new angles to the story is becoming insatiable. That's what has led the media to his doorstep and workplace. It was everything he feared would happen. He's under a microscope.

A knock at the door precedes Emily walking into the office. The vice president of account management has had a dour look on her otherwise pretty face for days. He can't blame her for being in a foul mood. The more AMLOG is mentioned in the reports about Brody, the more customers get pressured to find someone else to handle their logistics. Since it's her job to keep them happy, there has been nothing enjoyable about coming to work.

"Look at these vultures. What news do they think is possibly going to happen here?"

"This story is starting to get teeth. They want footage of you covering your head in shame or charging out to them and making a fool of yourself. They need a video to lead their evening broadcasts."

"Why does anyone even care?"

Emily shrugs. "Because someone in an office decided that people should. Why did the media cover JonBenet Ramsey or Caylee Anthony? Kids disappear all the time. What was so special about Amanda Knox? Trayvon Martin? George Floyd? None of those were unique stories, yet most Americans recognize those names. Why? It's because the media created sensationalized narratives, and then they cashed in."

"And you think my son deserves this?"

"Nobody deserves this," Brianna says, striding into the office without knocking. "I hope I'm not interrupting anything."

"Not at all. What can I do for you?"

"Do for me?" she asks with a raised eyebrow. "Go outside and answer all the questions those reporters shout at you so they'll leave."

"Yeah, that's not going to happen."

Brianna sighs. "I didn't think so, but you need to do something. Your son's silence makes sense. The accused are instructed by lawyers not to speak to the press. Parents of the accused don't get that luxury. It lets the press create the narrative that your silence means you have something to hide, and people believe what they're told."

John goes back to staring out the window. Being the face of his son's defense is the last thing he wants. He has spent a lifetime in the shadows. He has quietly built his business and avoided the flashy trappings of power in doing so. Wandering into the searing hot spotlight wielded by the national media will subject him to unwanted scrutiny.

He turns away from the window and moves behind his desk. John's eyes settle on his PR rep. She's a tough woman with an edge, but her demeanor is different. So is her body language.

"Brianna, do you think my son is guilty?"

"I wasn't there, John."

"That wasn't my question."

Brianna presses her lips together and looks around the room like it's the last time she'll ever see it. "Your son has a reputation as a playboy. He's a womanizer."

"So, you do. What about you, Emily? Is Brody capable of rape?"

She cocks her head. "Considering the men I've had relationships with, I think anyone is capable of anything. That isn't the question you should be asking. Did he do it?"

John stares at his desk. "He says no. I don't think he'd lie to me about that."

"Then that should be enough for you."

"Yeah, but what about them?"

"The media won't be on your side, but they are your conduit to the masses. You need to convince them that the truth is on your side."

"That's where I come in," Brianna chimes in. "Everyone is going to think he's guilty. He's a rich white kid studying to become a lawyer at an elite school. They want him to be the villain."

"What do I do?"

"Create a new villain."

"How?"

Brianna shakes her head. "That's not my job. I run PR for AMLOG, not for the Prock family. All I know is that this will hurt the company if you don't do something. I'm sure Emily agrees. Malcolm and I will do our parts, but you need to give us some direction. You need to do it fast, too, because the barbarians are at the gate…literally."

She glances out the window at the assembly of satellite trucks and media vans and shakes her head before leaving. John watches her go. Brianna is right — it isn't her job to represent the family. She's a valued employee of AMLOG who knows what she's doing.

"Change the narrative. Brianna makes it sound easy," John moans as he sits at his desk."

"Maybe it is," Emily says, taking a seat in one of the visitor chairs. "Everyone assumes that your son is lying. Nobody is even asking whether Ashlee Trillo is. We need to get them to ask that question."

"How?"

"I'm not sure. I don't know much about communicating with the media, but I know a thing or two about people. They're more likely to believe something when they see a plausible alternative. It's how conspiracy theories are built. Show them a soundstage, and they'll assume that's where the moon landing footage was shot."

"I see where you're going with this. Take Brianna's advice and create another villain."

"Exactly. We start casting suspicion on the Trillo family. Her father is a developer, right? Make this some sort of family rivalry. Like the Montagues and Capulets."

"I don't even know the man."

She reaches out and takes his hand into hers, and squeezes.

"Since when does the truth matter to reporters? I'll help you for as long as it takes. Let's take an hour and work through some options on how to make the Trillos public enemy number one."

He forces a smile. It's the first one he's tried to wear since Brody's phone call on Saturday.

"Okay."

CHAPTER EIGHTEEN
SSA ZACH FORTE

JACOB K. JAVITS FEDERAL BUILDING
NEW YORK, NEW YORK

The forty-one-story Jacob K. Javits Federal Office Building is located in the Civic Center neighborhood of Manhattan. The skyscraper is one of over forty Manhattan buildings in the city with its own ZIP Code. The building falls under the jurisdiction of the United States Federal Protective Service and is home to a number of agencies, including the Department of Homeland Security, the Social Security Administration, and the General Services Administration.

The Federal Bureau of Investigation's New York field office is on the 23rd floor. Composed of over two thousand agents and task force members, it has the largest field office staff in the FBI and serves a population of over thirteen million people.

That means they should have complete anonymity, but that wasn't good enough for Matt Remsen. He procured them space on another floor where people wouldn't ask too many questions. Watchtower doesn't officially exist. He's determined to keep things that way, even from the Bureau.

The conference room is spacious enough to host a team twenty times the size of the one that accompanied Zach to New York. A videoconferencing unit was set up at the far end of the table, and Matt connected as everyone gathered an appropriate distance away in the middle.

Boston has a lot of explaining to do. Unfortunately, he remained silent following the Trillo interview and subsequent interruption. That's uncharacteristic for a man with a big mouth and a propensity to use it. He must have gotten strong memories from Ashlee, which is why Zach didn't press him. The lawyer is another situation entirely. Boston should be able to read him like a book but won't speak about it.

"What do we have?" the director asks, his eyes welded to papers scattered on his desk instead of the camera.

Forte gives him the rundown on the bookends of the Trillo mansion visit, beginning with his impressions of Tomasso Trillo and ending with Jamieson Bohmer's abrupt entrance to end the interview. Matt listens patiently before waving a dismissive hand.

"I get Trillo is an ass, but one with significant political connections. Get to the meat of the interview. What about the daughter?"

"Sir, she had all the classic signs of a rape victim," Nadiya concludes. "Shame, guilt, insecurity, trust issues…she will need significant therapy to help her deal with the trauma."

"So, you think she's telling the truth?"

"Yes, sir," Nadiya states confidently. "No doubt about it."

"Emma?"

"I'm a firearms instructor, not a profiler. But, if she's lying, she thought her story through. The memory gaps were explainable, and the details that changed were small enough to conclude that her statement was based on truth, not deceit."

"I concur, Matt," Zach agrees. "She relayed the key events of the evening substantially as she did in her initial reports to campus and state police."

"Boston?"

"You want my opinion?" the dream machine asks, causing Zach to cock his head at the obvious stall tactic.

Matt raises his eyes and stares at the camera above his screen. "We don't keep you here for your charming smile and good looks. I've heard the investigative angle. Now I'm looking for you to confirm it. Did you see anything about that night?"

Boston clenches his teeth before speaking. "Memories don't come with timestamps, sir. It's hard to glean when the events I see transpired within the framework of someone's life."

"But you saw one."

"I saw a lot of them."

"And?"

There is a long pause. Boston steals a glance at Nadiya and then at Emma. Zach is about to prompt him to answer when he loudly sighs.

"Did Ashlee have a relationship with Brody at any time in the past?"

Zach riffles through the papers in the folder until he finds the one he is looking for. "They went on one date in September."

"Ashlee said it ended abruptly. Is there any evidence that she's lying? I need to know if they slept together."

"There was no sexual contact. Apparently, Brody didn't even kiss her goodnight. She confirmed that."

"Has anything indicated whether there was a second date or any romantic involvement that she didn't tell us about?"

"No."

"You're certain?" Boston presses.

"According to statements," Forte surmises, "Brody is a playboy who uses women as arm accessories. None of the interviewed students mentioned them being an item outside of that one date."

"What about a hookup or late-night tryst?"

"Where are you going with this, Boston?" Matt asks, growing impatient. "What did you see?"

Boston looks at each of them. "I saw everything that happened that night through her eyes."

"That had to be hard," Nadiya mumbles.

Boston frowns at the unintentional pun and shakes his head. "It wasn't at first. It took a while."

"What do you mean? State it plainly," Forte commands.

"Ashlee Trillo wasn't raped. Brody Prock was."

All eyes turn to Boston as mouths hang open. Even the usually stoic Matt Remsen wears a look of shock on his face. The silence that grips the room is suffocating. Boston isn't interjecting detail or defending his conclusion. He is just sitting there, patiently waiting for the inevitable responses.

"What?" Nadiya asks in a sharp tone piercing the quiet room like a klaxon. "Have you lost your mind?"

"No. That's what happened."

Nadiya slams her hand down on the table. "How could you—"

"She had his semen in her vagina," Zach interrupts, trying to regain control of the conversation before Nadiya rips Boston's arms off and beats him with them.

"I never said they didn't have sex."

"How was it not rape, Boston?" Nadiya asks, making the question sound more like an accusation as it escapes her lips. "She had flunitrazepam in her system! Rohypnol is the world's leading date rape drug."

Boston nods. "Did he have any in his?"

If the word "incredulous" had pictures next to it in the dictionary, the looks on the women's faces would fill the space. Worse, each of their reactions has a hint of betrayal behind it. Boston is a friend, a fellow agent, and someone they figured would subscribe to the notion that all women should be believed.

"Why do you ask, Boston?"

"Because he was unconscious in the memory, and *she* was on top of *him*."

Nadiya throws her arms up in the air. She stands so abruptly that her chair flies backward and violently crashes against the conference room wall.

"I'm not going to stay here and listen to this!" she shouts, her face contorted from fighting strong emotions.

She storms out, and Zach notices Boston close his eyes. Within a few seconds, he opens them and violently tries to shake the image out of his head. Whatever he saw was something he didn't want to experience.

"Nadiya?" Emma asks as her friend reaches the door, starting to get up from her chair to follow her out.

"Leave her be. Trust me." The words were more a warning than instructions, and Emma takes that seriously when they come from Boston.

"How sure of this are you?" Matt asks as Emma tenuously sits back down.

"If everything you told me about their history is true, one hundred percent."

Matt nods. This assignment just got far more complicated. There is nothing Watchtower's director hates more than unexpected developments. He clearly didn't think the case would take this turn.

"Okay. You're all dismissed. Zach, stay behind, so we can talk about next steps."

"Give me a minute, Matt," Zach says, muting the mic and stepping out of the camera's view. He motions Boston over to the wall.

"Is Nadiya okay?"

"I'm not sure. I'll go check on her."

"Do you know what's wrong?"

Boston grimaces. "It's nothing to worry about. Yet. I'll let you know if that changes."

Forte nods. "What exactly did you see through Ashlee's eyes? The women are gone, so be blunt."

"Brody was buck-naked and unconscious on the bed. Ashlee was riding him like he was Secretariat. I'm not going to pretend I'm an expert in any of this, but tell me if that sounds like *he* raped *her*."

Zach feels the pit in his stomach grow larger. He almost wishes that Boston had lied. This assignment is about to take a turn for the worse. If the media gets a hold of that narrative, the resulting public inferno will consume everyone, including Watchtower.

CHAPTER NINETEEN
"BOSTON" HOLLINGER

FOLEY SQUARE
NEW YORK, NEW YORK

I don't know if Nadiya's here, but I know she didn't stay in the building. She would want to be alone yet still around people. This is as good a place as any.

Foley Square is a stone's throw away from the federal building and contains a small triangular patch of grass and trees named Thomas Paine Park. It sits on the former site of Little Collect Pond, one of the city's original freshwater sources. The small reservoir was drained and filled decades ago after becoming polluted and blamed as the source of typhus and cholera outbreaks.

Nadiya is a vision on her worst day. Even dressed professionally without much makeup and her hair tied in a bun, she turns heads. When she puts any effort into her appearance, she stops traffic. That makes her easy to spot. I walk over and park myself next to her on the small set of stairs that ring the Triumph of the Human Spirit sculpture.

"I'm sorry I lashed out at you," she mumbles.

"You don't need to apologize. You want to talk about it?"

Nadiya turns her head to look at me. "Do I need to? I'm sure you already know."

I face the sculpture, not wanting her to think this is an interrogation. "I don't. I saw part of the memory, which was enough to know it wasn't something I wanted to experience. So, I forced myself to focus on something else."

She smiles weakly. "Thank you for that. Do you really want to know?"

"Only if you want to tell me. It's none of my business."

Nadiya stares at her hands for a long moment. "I was fifteen. That summer, I went to a pool party because a boy I liked was going to be there. Phillip. I remember going shopping for the perfect swimsuit to impress him."

I feel Nadiya glance over at me, looking for a reaction. The thought of Nadiya in a bikini would make any heterosexual man drool like a Saint Bernard. I don't. She is beautiful, but she's a colleague in pain right now. That thought is furthest from my mind.

"It turns out I impressed him, all right. As the sun was going down, things got a little crazy there. Phillip grabbed me by my arms and dragged me into this shed that served as a pool house. I don't know if anyone saw us. Or maybe they thought I was going willingly.

"He pushed me inside, and I screamed. The music was loud, so nobody responded. It was the only chance I had. He clamped his hand over my mouth and pulled down his swimsuit. I froze. My whole body went numb. I couldn't move. I knew what was going to happen and was powerless to stop it."

Nadiya brushes tears from her eyes as she struggles to keep from breaking down. I have my own struggle. I remember Tara's explanation of how my visions worked when I discovered how I could see memories. She explained that people's brains broadcast like a wi-fi signal. The power of the emotions or underlying trauma is directly correlated with the strength of that signal.

Nadiya's signal is overwhelming. I don't need to close my eyes to focus on the memories. It's staring at a screen in a dark room, not the white-hot sunlight. They are trying to play out in my mind no matter how hard I fight to stop them. I can feel my body begin to react to the panic and fear. I don't want to feel this pain.

"He ripped off my bikini top, and…. After he was done, he tossed it at me and walked out of the shed like nothing had happened. I curled into a ball on that dingy floor and cried harder than I ever had. It's amazing how fast your life can change. I went to that party as a typical teenager. Lying on that shed floor, I had lost my pride, my security…my innocence."

Nadiya wipes the tears from her eyes. I feel myself fill with rage. That's my emotion, not the memory. I want to plant Phillip deep in the ground for hurting her.

"Rape isn't about sex. Had Phillip dated me, there's a good chance he would have gotten that eventually. It's about power. He wanted to dominate me…use me. That's why he tossed my bikini back at me when he finished. I was trash to him. Something to be discarded.

"I stayed in that shed until it was time to go. My older sister picked me up. I started crying as soon as I got in her car. I had so many thoughts racing through my mind. I remember wondering if it was my fault or what I would do if nobody believed me. Waves of emotion washed over me: shame…guilt…anger…fear. But most of all, disbelief. How could this happen to me?"

"Did you tell her what happened?" I ask in a near whisper.

She closes her eyes and nods. "She insisted that I tell my parents, and I reluctantly agreed. My whole family was crying…even my father. Mom called the police, and we filed a report. An officer took me to the hospital to have a rape kit done. They went to Phillip's house that night, and he told them it was consensual. Nobody saw anything. It was his word against mine, so the charges were dropped.

"I saw him in school every day after the summer. I heard whispers in the hallway. The emotional damage of rape is far greater than any physical injury. Fear and helplessness during the assault get replaced by guilt and self-blame. It's how most victims cope, but it hampers the healing process. I had flashbacks, fell into a depression, and even had an eating disorder for a while."

Nadiya wipes a fresh set of tears from her eyes. I'd offer her a tissue if I had a purse to carry them in. She inhales deeply and straightens a little, finding new strength to face this dark chapter in her life.

"What changed?"

"I did. I was tired of being a victim. I knew I couldn't erase what happened…couldn't undo it or force myself to forget. So, I swore it would never happen again. I wanted my power back. One day, after school, I went to a karate dojo. I dedicated myself to learning everything I could to defend myself, and my sensei was eager to teach me.

"Then I studied judo, krav maga, jiu-jitsu…you get the point. I had become an expert in all of them by the time I finished college."

"And then the CIA came knocking."

Nadiya forces a smile. "Yeah. I dismissed the idea at first. I didn't think girls would make good spies."

"They probably make the best ones," I say, trying to lighten the conversation so that I don't have to fight the visions so hard.

"I know that now. The Farm needed an instructor to teach agents, and I thought I could leverage their resources to track Phillip down for some payback. Stupid, I know."

"The Farm" is a colloquial term for Camp Peary, an ultra-secret nine-thousand-acre, densely wooded training facility run by the Central Intelligence Agency. It's used for training its clandestine officers and is located near Williamsburg, Virginia. That's all I know about it.

I shake my head. "It's not stupid at all. Did you find him?"

"Yes, but I never did anything about it. I had to let my hatred go. Phillip's out in the Midwest. Still single, so far as I know."

"I asked Forte how you ended up at Watchtower. He said Matt had told him that the last guy who groped you landed in the hospital."

Nadiya smiles and shakes her head slowly. "That's the politically correct version the CIA tells to avoid embarrassment. I play along to avoid the memories it conjures up. It wasn't groping. A senior guy at Langley tried to force himself on me one night. I'll spare you the details, but let's just say that I put my martial arts training to good use. Seeing him in the hospital in multiple casts and his jaw wired shut was cathartic, but my superiors were displeased. I took this assignment to get away from them."

"I don't blame you."

We watch people pass by for a couple of minutes. The intensity of her brain signals has diminished enough that I don't need to constantly fight it. If it's this brutal for me, I can only imagine what it's like for her. Regardless of the clarity of the memory or the strength of the emotion I feel, it can never compare to actually living it. I'm amazed by the baggage that people carry with them.

"Boston, nobody knows about what happened to me. Are you going to tell Zach?"

"Nope. It's none of his business."

She grabs my hand and looks at me through wounded eyes. "You should. I'm compromised on this assignment."

"Nadiya, I see the worst of the worst. I'm compromised on all of them. I need your perspective on this."

She stares down at the ground. "I'm not sure I can be impartial. I *want* to believe Ashlee. Are you sure that she's lying?"

"Yes, I'm sure. The truth is going to come out, one way or another. When it does, it'll be another high-profile false accusation that prevents women from getting the justice they deserve. You didn't lie, and it's still haunting you. She did. I need you to help me uncover why before the truth comes out and does unspeakable damage."

Nadiya doesn't say anything. Instead, she slides her hand under my arm and rests her head on my shoulder. Zach and Emma can wait for a while. I'm in no rush to go anywhere.

CHAPTER TWENTY

JAMIESON BOHMER

This is a movie that Jamieson has seen before. It plays more often than Seinfeld reruns. He understands the anger because Tomasso is such a passionate man. At least, that's what his friends would say. His enemies would call him "unhinged."

This study is wired for both video and audio. The lawyer may need to add this rant to his collection of classics. Tomasso seething at all the media coverage. He could be looking at this issue with Ashlee as a net positive. His daughter was violated, and the country is on her side. Sympathy is powerful, and the media have ensured that most people believe her accusation.

That's not how the owner of Brick City Development sees it, as he has made crystal clear in this latest irate monologue. After his wife's death, he viewed his daughter as a liability. Nothing has happened in the subsequent years to change that perception. Instead of supporting her through this difficult time, as any decent parent would, his resentment has only grown exponentially.

"Why couldn't she just keep her mouth shut?" he almost shouts as he looks out the window of his study into the front yard.

"She was raped, Tomasso."

"There are other ways to get justice, Jamieson. You know that about as well as anyone. She should have kept it in the family."

Jamieson turns in his chair and stares at his back. "What would you have done? Rushed to her aid?"

"I don't know, but now I have the FBI probing my business and a horde of media outside my house. That's bad enough, but now our competitors are trying to steal our contracts."

"They won't."

Tomasso turns to meet Jamieson's gaze. "We need to make sure of it."

"How?"

"By whatever means necessary. Burn their offices to the ground if that's what it takes."

The emotional response isn't for Jamieson's benefit. There would be no point in the exercise. This isn't hyperbole or posturing from an Italian with a knack for dramatic expression. Tomasso is dead serious.

"I wouldn't advise that."

Jamieson can feel his boss's eyes burning into the back of his neck. He's not intimidated and doesn't bother turning to face him. Instead, Tomasso leaves his post at the window and moves back around his desk. He sits in his chair and plants his elbows on the sturdy oak desk, wringing his hands as he stares at his lawyer.

"Really? Mister 'he who dares wins' doesn't think we should act?" he asks, quoting the SAS motto.

Jamieson smirks. "The SAS drew on their wartime experience to identify seven characteristics of the ideal recruit: initiative, self-discipline, stamina, independence of mind, an ability to work without supervision, and a sense of humor. Their seventh ideal is patience. You should see this as an opportunity to practice some."

"You're saying that I should sit back and do nothing?"

"Tomasso, you built your business by being discreet. Brick City flies under the radar, and it has earned you vast riches and a never-ending supply of new work. People view you as a savior, not a scoundrel who cheats and breaks whatever law he feels is inconvenient. Why jeopardize that?"

"Because, as you are fond of saying, it has to be done."

"I think NASA and Hitler would agree with you."

Tomasso offers a quizzical look. "What?"

"The biggest contributor to most failures is impatience," Jamieson says after a sigh. "In 1986, NASA *needed* the PR of sending a teacher to space and wouldn't stomach another delay. They rushed the launch of Challenger in frigid temperatures, and seventy-three seconds into its flight, it disintegrated in front of millions of viewers.

"By the end of 1940, Hitler had issued Führer Directive 21, codenamed Operation Barbarossa. It didn't matter that an attack on the Soviet Union would face challenging logistics and overstretched supply lines. The invasion *needed* to happen. We know how that ended."

"I get your point. We're not launching rockets or fighting wars."

"No, of course not, but that doesn't mean we aren't fighting those who want what we have."

"You want me to let the feds do whatever they want?"

"A couple of agents poking around isn't a threat. A task force that gets created because we do something stupid is one. Tomasso, your success is a result of making smart decisions. Be smart, and let fools rush in."

It's easier said than done. Men of action don't like waiting for others to make the first move. They fix their enemies and defeat them before they know what's coming. Patience is a virtue that few possess. Those with it in their arsenal can wield it as an effective weapon.

"Then what?"

"I believe Napoleon Bonaparte said it best: 'Never interrupt your enemy when he is making a mistake.'"

CHAPTER TWENTY-ONE

JOHN PROCK

John enters the outer office and expects to see some old, decaying woman serving as secretary. Nope. The girl manning the desk outside the president's office could be a model. She smiles and bats her long lashes as he answers. Either this woman can type, or the old codger behind the door is an absolute dog.

"Mr. Prock? The president is waiting for you in his office. You can go right in."

"Thank you so much," John says, returning her smile.

Donald Malfatto is seated at his desk. He stands to greet John, and the two men shake.

"I'm glad you could meet with me."

"Of course. Why don't we sit down," Donald says, gesturing to his right.

The school's president walks him to a sitting area in his office with four high-back leather chairs and an antique coffee table. Nothing about the school is old, but its buildings, furniture, and appointments look like they came out of Victorian England.

"I'm happy you reached out to me, John. We all found the allegations made against your son surprising. Rest assured, we are doing everything we can to get to the bottom of it."

John offers a brief smile. "I'm sure you are. That's what brought me here. It feels like Salisbury Law may be taking sides."

"Oh? How so?"

The inquiry annoys John. So does Malfatto's innocent tone. He's a lawyer and is used to putting on a show as he lies to a jury. He's also a school administrator, making him skilled in deflection and a user of ridiculous banalities. That's how most elites treat people. Donald believes everyone he meets is dumber than he is.

"I watch the news and read articles online. All of them contain statements that your campus police made to the media. Your staff loves offering their opinions to any journalist willing to print their name. Why are you allowing anyone to discuss this?"

Donald immediately shifts into a defensive posture. "I don't like to restrict free speech on my campus."

"Of course. America's colleges and universities are bastions of free speech these days," John says, not masking his sarcastic tone. "Your employees are causing harm to my son. You and this school are indirectly taking sides."

"I understand why you might think that. I'm sure if Mr. Trillo was here, he would say the same thing. I can't imagine how you feel as concerned parents."

The corner of John's mouth curls. "I'm more than just a concerned parent, Donald. Do you need to be reminded of that?"

Very few things in life amuse John. Watching the Mets win or celebrating holidays does little to excite him. What he really enjoys is making smug, pompous, arrogant elites like Donald Malfatto uncomfortable. It's better than drugs.

"That's a separate issue," Donald says with a dismissive wave of his hand.

"No, they're very much linked."

"Your son was accused of sexual assault. Based on that allegation alone, he would have been expelled from any other university."

John presses his hands together and stares at them for a long moment. "This is a law school. Considering the amount of tuition I pay, I hope you understand and instruct the concept of innocent until proven guilty. I'm certain your legal department advised you what the lawsuit against you would have looked like if you had done that."

Malfatto shifts his position in his chair again. John knows that he just went up two-nothing on the scoreboard.

"Brody is a valued member of our student body, as is his accuser."

"No, you can't afford to be wrong, get sued, and lose. Let's stop playing games."

"I don't think I like where this is going," Donald says, his tone becoming harsher and more agitated.

"I don't care. Since you clearly have a lapse in memory, let me refresh it. You approached me with a problem last year. Despite having an astronomical tuition, this university was somehow in the red. I can't imagine how that would happen unless you factor in fraud or incompetence, but I didn't press you about the reasons. I wrote you a check."

Donald thrusts his chin out. "There was no quid pro quo stipulated with that donation."

"No, there wasn't. I did it as a courtesy. I also did it anonymously. Most people would want a building named after them for a million dollars. It's not unreasonable to believe that a courtesy or two would be reciprocated."

Donald exhales and presses back into his chair. "You're asking me to interfere with a federal investigation."

"I'm asking no such thing."

"Then what are you asking?"

John leans forward aggressively. "That you understand I have value. That my son does. And that nothing is gained for this school from a random, uncorroborated investigation into something that never happened."

"We don't know that!"

"I do, Donald, and I can't be expected to support an institution that doesn't share my beliefs and values. It will force me to publicly state where I stand." John spreads his hands theatrically. "Who knows what I could say?"

"You wouldn't." It was an accusation more than a statement.

"I wouldn't *want* to. But things get said in the heat of battle. I mean…what would your administrators and professors say? What would your board say? I can only imagine."

"I refuse to be extorted," Donald says, crossing his arms.

Make that three-zip.

"I'm not extorting you, although I can see where you might believe this meets the legal definition. I'm simply reminding you how much I appreciate our relationship and why you shouldn't forget its value."

Donald looks like he's about to be sick. To him, John Prock is a trucker who pees in a milk jug on long trips across the country. A nobody who eats his meals in roadside diners and sleeps on a small bed in the cab. He doesn't understand what it took to build a massive logistics company that major Fortune 500 corporations rely on daily. He could never know where his other revenue streams come from.

John rises and buttons his suit jacket. "This is a difficult time for Salisbury, President Malfatto. I wish you the best of luck in navigating these waters. I can't imagine the board could have picked a more worthy captain for this ship."

The haymaker finds its mark. Malfatto is lying prone on the mat as the referee counts down. John leaves, winking at the attractive assistant on the way out of the office. That's why you never take an underdog for granted. The smug president of one of the country's most esteemed law schools just learned that lesson the hard way. There is no better education than graduating from the school of life.

CHAPTER TWENTY-TWO

ASHLEE TRILLO

TOMASSO TRILLO FAMILY ESTATE
ENGLEWOOD CLIFFS, NEW JERSEY

It's almost time. Ashlee collapses on her bed facing the television and bites the end of the sleeve on her sweatshirt. The texts came fast and furious as Chloe set this up. It turned out to not be that hard. Nearly every media outlet in the country has reporters on campus. All she had to do was walk up to them and say, "Hi, I'm Ashlee Trillo's roommate. Wanna talk?" This morning show interview is the first of about a half dozen she has lined up today.

"Welcome back," the anchor says after returning from the commercial break. "We are now joined by Chloe McCarthy from our Hartford affiliate. Chloe is the roommate of Ashlee Trillo, the young woman who accused one of her peers of rape at the elite Salisbury Law School. She's here with us today to share her story. Thank you for joining us, Chloe."

"Thank you for having me."

Ashlee takes her sleeve out of her mouth and rubs her chin, wondering how Chloe could look that calm and collected. She would be a basket case. Her roommate always came across to her as insecure. Now, she's a confident young woman who is being interviewed live on national television.

She deftly answers the first couple of the anchor's questions before transitioning to what happened. Chloe's voice begins to rise, and her face reddens as she talks about the campus police's reaction to the report and how the state police conducted themselves.

"I know this is a difficult subject for you to publicly discuss. You sound angry about how this case is being handled."

"I am angry," Chloe says. "At what point in this country will we start believing women? One in five women in the United States experienced rape or attempted rape during their lifetime. Twenty-five percent of sexual assaults were reported to police in 2018, down from forty percent a year earlier. Do you think that's because women are more comfortable disclosing such a personal crime? No, it's because they're less confident that the report will lead to prosecution for reasons like this."

"You're very well-informed on the subject."

"I'm studying to be a lawyer. I know how to conduct research and present facts. Here are a few for your audience about what happened to my roommate. No fewer than a hundred people saw Ashlee at the party that night. At least three of our peers saw her enter Brody Prock's bedroom. She had his semen inside her, as confirmed by doctors at Sharon Hospital and via a DNA test administered by the Connecticut State Police with the assistance of the Federal Bureau of Investigation."

"Brody's supporters say that the intercourse could have been consensual."

"Yes. It's the easiest defense against bad behavior. I would argue that consenting adults don't routinely need Rohypnol. It's a date rape drug, and Ashlee had it in her system. When the preponderance of the evidence is considered, the only conclusion is rape. So, why hasn't Brody Prock been arrested?"

"That's a question for the police," the anchor says as a way to transition to her next question. Chloe doesn't let her.

"Have you asked it? Has anyone in the media demanded it? The FBI, campus, and state police have stopped doing press conferences. Maybe you should be beating down their doors to ask what their justification is for not arresting Brody."

"I understand your passion, Chloe, but you must admit you're close to this. People could argue that your emotion is clouding your judgment."

Chloe's face wears a melancholic look. "I was the first to see her the morning after it happened. Her emotional trauma can't be faked. I took Ashlee to the campus police and went with her to the hospital. I don't think men understand what rape is. It's the ultimate violation. It destroys trust, impairs relationships, and leaves scars that will linger for the rest of her life.

"So, yeah, I am emotional. I'm outraged, and I'm betting a lot of other Americans are, too. Men should be equally enraged. What if this was your wife or girlfriend? Mother or daughter? Would you want to see their claims ignored? Wouldn't you want the guilty punished?"

"Guilt is established at a trial," the anchor argues.

"Yes. A jury of Brody's peers gets to make that determination. It's the end of a process that requires him to be *charged* first. How much more evidence do they need to bring those charges? Or is there a reason they don't want to?"

Ashlee mouths "wow" at her television. Chloe is going to make one hell of a lawyer. The last question wasn't an innocent one – it was loaded. It's the last line that everyone watching will remember. The longer it lives in people's minds, the more it will turn into a call for action. Social media has its purposes. Mobilizing people to get a specific result is one of them.

"We'll have to leave it there. Thank you for joining us this morning, Chloe."

Ashlee smiles. Chloe did an amazing job. If this doesn't get the FBI's attention, then nothing will.

CHAPTER TWENTY-THREE
SPECIAL AGENT ZACH FORTE

SALISBURY LAW SCHOOL OFFICE OF THE PRESIDENT
SALISBURY, CONNECTICUT

Zach gives their names to the attractive admin, and the school's president is summoned to come out and greet him and Boston. They are shown into the office, and the senior agent is already feeling uneasy. He has never liked lawyers and finds their stuffy, book-strewn offices ostentatious. They are filled with mahogany, leather, and the smell of elitism.

The dean of students is there, and more introductions are made. Lincoln Drewitt is the kind of elderly attorney you would expect to be an administrator at a law school. He's also not a man of many words, which is rare in Zach's experience. Most lawyers love to hear themselves talk.

The men start with perfunctory chatter about how this ordeal is a tragedy and how valued their students are. The conversation is tense, and the demeanor of the administrators is ice-cold. The dean says nothing, standing like a statue behind his boss seated at his beefy desk.

Zach begins pressing for more cooperation from school officials and campus police and gets canned responses. The men are deflecting. The senior agent finally loses his patience.

"I'm told that the campus police were forthcoming with information until yesterday," Zach says. "What changed?"

The two administrators briefly look at each other quizzically. "Nothing, to my knowledge," President Malfatto says. "We are doing what is asked of us."

"I understand that you are in a difficult position. You are being forced by the media to take sides in this."

"We love and appreciate all our students. No sides are being taken."

Zach clenches his jaw. "From the interviews I have seen with the faculty, I would disagree."

"No restrictions are placed on free speech in this institution, Special Agent Forte. Our faculty are free to say what they please so long as they make it clear that they aren't speaking for the university or other staff members. The same applies to our students."

"I see. Thank you for the clarification," Zach says, nodding. "Then…why did it suddenly stop?"

"I'm sorry?"

Zach leans back in his chair and steeples his hands. "Not a single interview has been given today by your facility. There have been no comments on social media either. Who gave the order that instructed them to avoid speaking to the press?"

The senior agent enjoys watching the mental gymnastics meet in the president's head play out on his face. The one thing about snobs like Donald Malfatto and Lincoln Drewitt is they think they are better than everyone – better informed, better educated, and better thinkers.

Except that isn't always true. While these men may have more education than Forte, they don't have the information he does. That places them at a disadvantage that has made them uncomfortable since this meeting began. They don't know what he knows.

"To my knowledge, nobody," Malfatto says, clearing his throat slightly. "I'm not sure what you're fishing for, but I agreed to this meeting out of respect for your investigation. Unfortunately, I'm a busy man. So, unless you have anything important to discuss, I will ask you to excuse me."

Zach glances at Boston, who offers a little grin before closing his eyes and shaking his head in disbelief. They want this meeting over before either of the men tells a lie they can't escape from. It's not a requirement to get one. Zach wanted to make them uncomfortable, and that mission has been accomplished. He already knows the truth and has Boston with him to fill in any missing pieces.

"Of course. Thank you for your time, President Malfatto."

The two men exit the administrative building and walk across the quad. They don't speak on the way out. Zach is content to put some distance between them and that office before they do. Boston has different ideas. He checks behind them before turning to Forte.

"He was lying."

"No kidding," Zach grumbles. "He gave that order to the faculty. Someone got to him. What did you get?"

"Malfatto has a lot of skeletons in his closet, but nothing specific to Prock, Trillo, or the rape allegation. This school is rotten to its core, though. They have big financial problems that he's covering up."

"No doubt, but that isn't our concern. We'll have to do this the hard way. Did you pack a bag for the trip up here?"

"Yeah, but I thought we were heading back to the city," Boston says, watching his breath condense in the cold Northern Connecticut air.

"Change of plans. I'll book us rooms at an inn down in Lakeville. We'll head back to the city tomorrow. I want to snoop around for a while to get a feel for the school."

Boston gives him a dose of side-eye. "The school isn't suspected of rape. Brody Prock is."

"And since he's lawyered up and inaccessible, I want to meet the people who know him. Faculty, staff, students…everyone. I'll work with Nadiya on it."

"What about Ashlee Trillo?"

"If you're right about Ashlee making this up, maybe we can uncover the why. Talk to the roommate tomorrow, and take Nadiya with you. She was pissed off in that morning show interview and might not be comfortable talking to a male agent after her roommate's accusations."

"All right. One more order of business – did you ever get Watchtower to get you a dossier on Jamieson Bohmer, attorney-at-law?"

"I've been waiting for you to ask. First, why does our friendly lawyer in New Jersey matter?"

"Humor me."

Zach nods. "There wasn't much on Bohmer before he emigrated from London. He grew up middle-class in West Yorkshire before coming to the U.S. in his late twenties. He worked odd jobs for a few years before attending Cornell Law. After graduating, he was immediately hired as the head legal counsel for Brick City Development and the Trillo family."

"I don't think he's just their lawyer, Zach."

"What did you see?"

"Nothing. That's the problem. I'll explain another time."

"Suit yourself. Let's drop in on the campus police and rattle their cages."

Boston spots someone and stops walking. Zach scans the far sidewalk to see Dean Drewitt leaving the admin building and heading in the direction of his office near the student center.

"I'll meet you there. I need to find something out first."

Zach doesn't know why Boston thinks a conversation with the dean would be valuable but has learned not to question it. He can handle the police on his own. Dean Drewitt barely uttered a word in that meeting. Maybe there are some memories Boston can exploit to make this trip to Connecticut worthwhile.

CHAPTER TWENTY-FOUR
"BOSTON" HOLLINGER

SALISBURY LAW SCHOOL CAMPUS
SALISBURY, CONNECTICUT

The Salisbury campus isn't that big. They don't have much in the way of athletic fields or a huge student population that requires housing. The administrative and classroom buildings are clustered close to each other and make up the heart of the campus. Residential areas are sprinkled around the periphery, with stands of trees breaking up sightlines. This whole campus must have been engineered by an architect who knew what he or she was doing. While pretty with the Christmas décor being hung by maintenance workers, it must be absolutely gorgeous when the leaves change color in autumn.

I do some quick calculations and turn left down a different sidewalk. This is a guess but an educated one. There won't be much time to rectify the mistake if I'm wrong. I turn the corner of the building and spot the man under a covered area, taking a long drag from his Marlboro.

"How did you find me here?" Dean Drewitt asks as I approach. "You followed me?"

"I didn't need to. I could smell the cigarette smoke on your suit and knew you would burn one before returning to work. Since this campus has designated smoking areas in its public spaces, I chose the secluded one close to your office."

Lincoln nods. "Well done. You're a good agent."

I frown. "The jury's still out on that."

The dean takes another drag. "I'm sorry that you wasted your time tracking me down. I have nothing to say."

"I know. I'll just keep you company until you're done giving yourself cancer."

Dean Drewitt grins as I close my eyes. I want to see if the memory returns. I'm still unsure if what I saw was from his perspective or President Malfatto's.

I can feel the concern. It isn't panic, or at least, not yet. But I can feel it building with every step I take. There is a leash coiled up in my hand. My head is on a swivel. It makes me feel like I'm back in the Army in Syria.

"Glaston! Come on, boy! Glaston!"

The announcements are met with silence. There is no barking or signs of a dog charging out of a neighbor's yard. I turn and walk back to the house.

"Glaston is right here," a man says, sitting next to a little girl in a flower dress pouring imaginary tea from a kettle. "I'm having a little tea party with your lovely granddaughter. Why don't you join us, Dean Drewitt."

"Who are you?"

"A man who gets things done. Thank you, sweetie," he says to the girl, who beams as he takes a sip. "This is excellent tea."

"Get out of my house," I say, trying to tamp down my panic.

"That would be rude. Excuse me, love, while I talk to your grandfather."

The man stands and walks over. He pats the dog on his head.

"There is an investigation happening at Salisbury Law. State and federal authorities are getting involved. You will ensure that the campus police and the administration don't cooperate. Do as I say, or this won't be my last visit. Mention this to anyone, and I'll kill your dog. Fail me, and your granddaughter will have a tragic accident."

I open my eyes and turn to him. "Your dog's name is Glaston?"

The dean's head spins around as he crushes his cigarette under his heel. "What?"

"Your dog's name? It's Glaston?"

It takes a moment for him to form the words. "I named him after the town of Glastonbury, where I rescued him. How did you know?"

"The FBI is thorough. Jamieson Bohmer came to your house and threatened you, didn't he? He said he would kill Glaston and arrange a tragic accident for your granddaughter to cow you into silence."

"He did no such thing," Drewitt says in an automatic denial.

"Yes, he did. What did Mr. Bohmer want?"

Drewitt lowers his eyes. "I can't tell you. He was very clear."

"I understand. He made you promise not to talk to the FBI, which is why you aren't talking to me. I don't blame you. He doesn't seem like a man that should be trifled with."

"My granddaughter is my world. Glaston…I can't imagine living without him."

"I wouldn't ask you to jeopardize my family. Let me guess: He wants you to tell campus police not to cooperate with the investigation."

The dean doesn't say anything. He also doesn't have to. His silence speaks volumes and would convince me even if I didn't know the truth. Drewitt pulls out his cigarettes and pulls another from the pack. He lights it with a Zippo and slaps the cover shut. It's a smooth move that he's practiced a dozen times a day for probably forty years. It's also a signal that he wants to talk. Otherwise, he would have retreated to his office.

"Enough of that business. As dean of students, you know Ashlee Trillo and Brody Prock."

He nods. "Only by name. Nothing that can help you with your investigation."

"Jamieson Bohmer is under a different impression."

The dean takes another long drag, looking around at the empty campus behind me. "Not really."

"Tell me about Brody and Ashlee."

He shrugs. "They were second-year students. Prock gets decent marks and has a reputation for being a ladies' man. Ashlee is a 'C' student who doesn't seem like she wants to be here."

"What do you mean?"

"I mean, the young men and women who come here are serious about their studies. Most have grand notions about serving on the Supreme Court or becoming a senior partner in one of the country's largest or most prestigious law firms. She doesn't. Her attitude toward her education is…indifferent."

"Have the campus police found anything at the scene that they didn't share with the state police or FBI?"

The dean eyes me and takes another long drag from his smoke. He remains silent, so I take a stab in the dark.

"That's why Jamieson wanted to dissuade the school from cooperating with investigators. That's why he threatened Glaston and your granddaughter. He thinks you can force them to stop cooperating."

"I wouldn't know anything about that. All I can say is that you're a good agent."

I take that as the intended confirmation. "Okay. Thanks for taking the time to speak with me, Dean Drewitt. I promise that this discussion stays between us."

"Agent Dufresne? Will I get another visit from Jamieson Bohmer?"

The man is dangerous. If he is willing to threaten the life of a little girl and a dog over something so trivial, then he's a special kind of evil. He may go after the dean if he even thinks he was betrayed. There's no point in telling him that, though.

"It won't be because of anything I report. Lock your doors, and don't have your granddaughter over for a while. Be diligent about keeping Glaston on a leash. Stay alert, take precautions, and everything will be fine."

The dean nods and heads into the student center building through the back door. I walk back toward the campus police station, where Forte is likely shaking some trees. The quad is quiet and peaceful while the remaining students study for the remainder of their exams. It gives me time to think.

The bond people have with children and pets is special. Threatening them is often more effective than threatening friends, parents, property, or even someone's own life. Using them as leverage against a man who has nothing else is a no-brainer. It also makes Jamieson Bohmer a complete scumbag.

The mud on Jamieson's shoes wasn't from skulking beneath the window in Trillo's study to listen in on her interview like I thought. The psychopath went through the woods to access Drewitt's back door. It's rural Connecticut. Nobody locks their doors. The ground is soft, the frost hasn't set in, and he never cleaned the mud off before returning to New Jersey. If Jamieson kills a little girl or a dog, it will be among the last things he ever does. I'll make sure of that.

CHAPTER TWENTY-FIVE

JAMIESON BOHMER

AMERICAN DREAM MALL
EAST RUTHERFORD, NEW JERSEY

The traffic is light, and the drive from Newark only takes a shade over twenty minutes. Not that Jamieson is behind the wheel. He ordered a rideshare for this trip and watches from the back seat as the driver steers his sedan up Route 21 and then East on Route 3. This isn't a meeting that he wanted to bring his personal vehicle to.

In the shadow of MetLife Stadium, home to the Giants and Jets of the National Football League, is a retail and entertainment megaplex that took seventeen years to design and complete. It was first envisioned in 1996 and had several owners, multiple starts and stops, and a litany of bad press surrounding the multicolored eyesore that the then-governor called one of the ugliest buildings in the country.

The American Dream Mall is the second-largest shopping center in the nation and one of the largest in the world. It's a fusion of entertainment and retail meant to redefine the shopping experience in the age of point-and-click selling from online retailers. It features a Nickelodeon theme park, an NHL-regulation-size ice skating rink, an indoor ski slope, and more than thirty other rides and attractions.

Jamieson makes his way into the megamall, which is busy but not crowded this time of day. The directions of where to meet are vague, and the timing is fluid. He sits on the fountain wall in the Garden Plaza and waits for the man to arrive. He hates shopping in general and malls specifically. As a military man, Jamieson doesn't like large crowds. People are too panicky and unpredictable when something happens. If he were to shoot his gun in the air right now, ten people would die, not from the bullets, but from the resulting stampede to the exits.

"I didn't expect to have to meet up here," Jamieson says as the big man nonchalantly takes a seat next to him.

"I needed to finish some Christmas shopping," Art Burill says, not looking at him. They are just two ships passing in a busy shipping lane. Just like last time.

"There are malls in the state that aren't complete tourist traps."

"There is anonymity in numbers, Jamieson."

The lawyer smirks. "I'm aware. I had to endure a Devils game, remember?"

"I doubt you stayed," Art says, amused.

As pleasant as this chat is, it's among the last places Jamieson wants to be. The Newark bureaucrat knows that, at least on some level. Sporting events, malls…if this relationship continues, he's expecting an invitation to Disney on Ice or the Macy's Thanksgiving Day Parade next.

"Are you here to extort me for more money?"

"You want to get right down to business," Art says with a chuckle. "Okay. No, you can keep your money. I'm here to terminate our business relationship."

"That's not going to happen," Jamieson says, shaking his head.

"Yeah, it is."

"Why?"

Art glances over at the lawyer. "You know why."

Maybe there was some merit to Tomasso's recent rant. He said that competitors were circling like vultures. It's entirely plausible that Art Burill found himself a more lucrative deal. He doubts that this has anything to do with what happened in Salisbury.

"Tomasso's daughter was raped. That has nothing to do with Brick City Development."

"Except the feds are crawling all over you. Police handle rapes. The FBI is using that tragedy as an excuse to dig because they know something. I don't want holes in my backyard."

"And the contracts?"

Art shrugs. "You can still earn them…legitimately. Brick City is the biggest developer in Northern New Jersey. I'm sure you can win contracts on your own."

"Don't do this, Art," Jamieson warns in a tone that would make a mobster take pause.

"I *am* doing this. It's over, and before you decide to threaten me, know that I will go public. It will end me, but Tomasso Trillo will have an adjoining cell. We've had a good relationship, but it needs to end. Honor the business we've done by respecting my decision."

Jamieson hangs his head. "Okay. Tomasso is going to be disappointed."

"He's a very rich man because of me. I'm sure that counts for something." Art stands, stretches, and looks around. "I think the food court is calling my name. See you around, Jamieson."

The bureaucrat heads back into the bowels of the mall, leaving Jamieson alone at the fountain. A minute goes by before two parents park themselves next to him as they watch their kids run around. He hangs his head again.

The lawyer knew this was the likely reason for the meeting. Art can pretend that a relationship like this can be terminated, but deals with the devil don't have an expiration. Business is a "what have you done for me lately" endeavor, and now the bureaucrat is a loose end that must be tied. That's something Jamieson fears Art will have to learn the hard way.

CHAPTER TWENTY-SIX

JOHN PROCK

ESTATE OF JOHN PROCK
SCARSDALE, NEW YORK

There is no sense of time here. Outside of the digital blue LED clock on the wall, it could be midday or the dead of night, and John wouldn't know the difference. In this case, he knows the approximate hour because he left the AMLOG office early to finish some other work. Instead, he's found himself pacing in his subterranean operations center.

The quiet stillness of the room allows him to think and strategize with minimal disruption. Today isn't one of those times. He can't focus. There are too many variables to account for in this equation. He's being forced to be reactive rather than proactive, and that's not a feeling he enjoys.

A door opens above him, and John hears the telltale footfalls of someone descending the stairs. If it were the feds, the intrusion would have been preceded by a loud bellow of "FBI." At least, it would if they played by the rules. It could be a reporter, but he doesn't think any of the lemmings outside would be that brazen. That means it must be Lothar. Hopefully, he comes bearing good news.

His operations manager reaches the bottom of the stairs and turns to notice his boss's nervous gait. John watches as he moves to the map of the world on the wall and smirks.

"Relax, John. Our operations are secure."

"For now."

"Do you expect that to change?"

John shakes his head and returns to his desk. "You know as well as I do that people talk. All it takes to unravel this whole thing is for the feds to find the right string to pull and give it a tug."

"Our people are more loyal than you give them credit for," Lothar says in an annoyed tone.

"Loyalty is a commodity. People are quick to trade it for things like money or freedom."

Lothar frowns. "Let me worry about keeping our people in line. I'm going to go out on a limb and say that I don't think that's what's bothering you."

He's right. It isn't. John rubs his chin before pointing at the television, which happens to be turned off.

"Did you see that bitch's interview this morning?"

"I heard about it," Lothar says with a nod.

"Chloe McCarthy made my son sound like a monster and her roommate a candidate for sainthood."

"It wasn't flattering, but people see through that."

John squints. No, people don't see through that at all. They unquestioningly believe anything the media tells them. At least, most people do. Precious few challenge the narrative that is laid out for them daily. That's how false narratives morph into sacred truths.

"She hadn't said anything to the media since the story broke. Now, she's making the rounds like she's promoting the next great summer blockbuster. Why the sudden change? Do you think the Trillos put her up to it?"

"I don't know. It's possible."

"I think they did. We need to send a message."

Lothar shifts his weight. "John, we're already under a microscope. This is becoming a media phenomenon. If things start getting violent, the magnification and number of people studying us will only increase."

"If we don't, our business will be negatively impacted, and I'm not only talking about AMLOG," John says, crashing into his chair and leaning back while interlacing his fingers. "If people want to talk, fine. They should come to understand that words have consequences."

The operations manager clearly doesn't agree. John understands why. He's tasked to keep a lucrative operation in the shadows and fears anyone shining lights in his direction. Lothar has also been asked to do some unsavory things to that end. This is no different, other than the stakes are higher.

Despite his obvious reservations, John knows the man will do what he asks. AMLOG is his creation, as is their side business. Bosses are entitled to do what they want, even if their employees believe it's reckless and unnecessary.

"What would you like me to do, sir?"

"Do we have some expendable men with a taste for violence and untrammeled loyalty working for us?"

"No, but you wouldn't want to use them anyway. I have contacts I could leverage. They'd be useful for the right price, depending on what you want them to do."

"We need to send a message. A loud one."

"What do you have in mind?" Lothar asks, sitting in a chair and checking the length of his fingernails.

After hours of wasted time pacing, a brilliant plan pops into his head. John offers him a smile that the Joker would be proud of. He may be playing with fire, but that's one of the things that fire is good for.

CHAPTER TWENTY-SEVEN
SSA ZACH FORTE

There isn't much to do in this area. Zach is under the impression that people up here prefer it that way. So, when it came time to track Boston down after discovering he wasn't in his room, his first stop was the Lakeville Brewing Company. The brewpub means they have a restaurant operating alongside an onsite brewery. It's Zach's kind of place.

The parking lot isn't full but still has a healthy number of cars. Zach finds a spot and makes his way to the entrance. The brewpub has the rustic feel of an old colonial tavern and is trying to recreate its historical importance. "Public houses" were once prominent in conducting government, community, and personal business. The news was read aloud from pamphlets and newspapers, meetings were held in them, and people posted signs to offer items for sale. It was a simpler time.

Zach checks the menu to find hand-crafted beer and classic homemade cuisine influenced by flavors from around the world. The beer they brew is available to take home in thirty-two-ounce crowlers. They also have a full bar and wine list and three seating areas, including their dining room, patio, and bar.

An attractive young hostess wearing a tight t-shirt featuring the LBC logo returns to the podium. "Welcome to the Lakeville Brewing Company. Would you like a table, or do you just want to sit at the bar?"

"I'm actually looking for a friend of mine. He's about my height and looks a little like Matthew McConaughey. I'm pretty sure he's here, but I don't see him."

"Oh. He's out on the patio," the hostess says matter-of-factly, cocking a thumb over her shoulder.

"A little chilly for the patio to be open, isn't it?"

"It's not open. Your friend insisted on sitting outside. Since I already bent the rules, you can join him."

"Thanks."

Zach walks to the bar and orders a stout that he adds to Boston's tab. He swings open the patio door and heads outside. It's cold, although not frigid out here. He would prefer the warmth of the heated bar area, but Boston has other ideas. He doesn't flinch when Zach sits beside him at the lone table.

"Are you sitting in nature's freezer for a reason?"

"Yeah, I wanted to enjoy a pint without seeing the highlights of everyone's trauma like they're movie trailers."

Zach looks back through the large windows into the busy tavern. "Sometimes I forget how annoying that must be. How did you talk the hostess into letting you sit out here?"

"She thinks her boyfriend is cheating on her."

"Is he?" Zach asks, wondering how that's relevant.

Boston shrugs. "I haven't met him, so I don't know for sure. I just said that women can sense those things. If it feels like he is, then she's probably right."

"That's harsh."

"Not really. She needed to hear it and was thankful enough to let me sit out here. What's so important that you needed to track me down?"

"I got off the phone with Remsen a half hour ago. He's pulling us off this mission."

"What? Why?"

Zach sips his stout before answering. "Mission accomplished, or so he says."

"The hell it is," Boston grumbles.

"It is for our purposes. Matt will warn the field office that there is more to the story than Ashlee Trillo has divulged. The point was to steer the Bureau away from potential embarrassment. He doesn't think there's more to be gained from our involvement."

Boston turns to look at Zach for the first time. "How about getting some facts and uncovering the truth?"

Truth and fact. The two words are closely related and used by the masses as synonyms. However, truth is grander in scale because it considers feelings and beliefs, whereas a fact is true everywhere and for everyone.

It's a fact that this brewpub is in Lakeville. It's a truth and not a fact that Boston and Zach are there. Why? They will leave in an hour or two, making the statement untrue. But this place will always be located here. Not that Boston would care about any of these musings, even if Zach felt like explaining them.

"The FBI doesn't care about the truth. They're looking for a way to kick the case back to the state police."

"Of course they are. You know what that means, right?"

"Yup. Since there's no hard evidence, it becomes the dreaded 'he said, she said' argument. It's unlikely that the case will ever get prosecuted."

Boston nods. "And since the allegation is out there, the media will lament that Ashlee never got the justice she deserved. For the rest of his life, Brody Prock will live with everyone believing he's a rapist."

"It's not fair," Zach says in agreement.

"It's also not the truth."

"Unfortunately, the only people who know that are him, her, and because of the wi-fi antenna installed in your brain, you."

What Boston sees cannot be faked. This isn't *Total Recall*. Memories cannot be planted into someone's mind. Therefore, he is a walking, talking, living, breathing polygraph machine. Video can be manipulated and deep faked, and audio can be manipulated. Boston can take his visions out of context, but they are facts. It has to be frustrating to know what he knows and not divulge it outside Watchtower.

"When's the mission officially over?"

"In a day or two, most likely. Matt needs to brief Brass, and getting on our overlord's calendar is sometimes tough. Why?"

"Because I'm not content to end this without the truth getting out there. What good is this gift if I can't use it when needed most?"

Zach can't argue with that. Not that he wants to. While he can't understand how Boston's gift affects him, he can understand the frustration that comes with it. Criminal justice is a messy business. Too often, there are no winners. In this case, they know the truth and can't do anything about it. Officially. It doesn't mean that they can't do things unofficially. The two men silently enjoy their beers as they contemplate what that means.

CHAPTER TWENTY-EIGHT

ASHLEE TRILLO

TOMASSO TRILLO FAMILY ESTATE
ENGLEWOOD CLIFFS, NEW JERSEY

There's no reasonable hope for people to understand Ashlee's predicament, not that she expects them to. They don't walk in her shoes or have her life experiences. Chloe didn't get it, nor did any of her friends in college. It's why she chooses to isolate herself on an emotional island.

The advantage of her paternally imposed prison sentence is that it gives her plenty of time to think. Ashlee wonders how she would rationalize her choices to the police if they ever asked. Not that they would. She's legally an adult working toward a law degree at one of the most prestigious schools in the country. There's no reason she should allow her father to banish her to the bedroom like she's a misbehaving toddler in time out…except there is one.

Her father is not a good man. Evil would be too strong a word, although his detractors wouldn't be bashful about using characterizing him as the Antichrist. He comes from a different era and believes it's his house and his rules, with no exceptions. That isn't a model of modern parenting, but it could be at least understood. He's hardly the first to take that approach to child-rearing.

Unfortunately, his anger and domineering bring it to a new level. He changed after Ashlee's mother died. He became cruel, and his behavior toward her was more akin to torture than love. She was no longer a cherished daughter. She was a hated liability.

A knock on the door summons Ashlee from her thoughts. The big oaf of a security guard opens it and orders her down to the study. At least he has the courtesy of not walking her down there himself.

The door is open, and Ashlee strolls in. She hates this room and what it symbolizes. She hates her history in it and, most of all, the man who spends most of his time here.

"You summoned, Master?"

Tomasso glances up from his desk and sneers. "Lose the attitude."

"What attitude?" Ashlee asks innocently. "I thought that's how you would want me to address you. Or do you prefer Your Majesty? Perhaps something more Italian, like Il Duce."

"Enough!" her father barks. "What is your relationship with Chloe McCarthy?"

Ashlee clenches her jaw. She knows what this is about.

"She's my roommate at school. I told you that."

"Are you friends with her?"

"I live with her."

Tomasso leans back in his chair. "Are the two of you communicating?"

A shiver runs down Ashlee's spine. The tone was less than an accusation but still more than a question. It's like he is searching for confirmation of a suspicion. That disposable cellphone is her only lifeline. She can't afford to lose it.

"You took my computer and cell phone, remember?"

Tomasso bites his lower lip. He rises from his chair and moves around the desk to stand before her. Ashlee stands a little straighter. She doesn't want to appear intimidated.

"You're in law school. You know what deflection is. Answer the question. Are…you…communicating?"

"No."

"I see. Then why is she suddenly talking to every media outlet that gives her an audience?"

Ashlee shrugs. "Because she's a big girl and has something called freedom."

The slap comes fast and hard. It catches Ashlee square on the left cheek, and the force knocks her head violently to the right. She leaves it there as she fights back her tears. Her father grabs a fistful of her hair and twists her head until she's forced to stare at him. Her hands instinctively reach for his, but she's powerless against his grip. He looks at her with pure contempt.

"You are a leech that squanders everything you're given. You're an unthankful degenerate, and I own you until you can provide for yourself. If you don't like it, you can run away and whore yourself on the streets for money. Is that the life you want? You have no skills for anything else. No friends. No boyfriend to care for you. You're nothing, and without me, you always will be."

Ashlee stares at him in horror. It's not the slap or even the threats. It's the realization of a truth: He has made it so she can't leave. That's the real reason she's still here. She depends on him for her survival and wouldn't know where to start without his financial resources. Maybe that will change when she graduates. It's her only salvation…if she can last that long.

"You want to leave. I see it in your eyes," her father says, releasing the fistful of hair. "Then leave. Here is your only window of opportunity. There's the door. I will instruct the guard to let you pass. You will have your freedom…and nothing else. Ever."

Ashlee glances at the door before lowering her head. She wants to accept the offer. It isn't an exaggeration when he says it will be the only one she gets. Life on the street would be hard, but anything is better than this. Except that isn't true. Everything she has worked for will be gone, and she knows it.

Still, it's worth the risk. Ashlee wills her legs to move, but they don't. Her anxiety surges, locking her knees and cementing her legs to the floor. She tries to fight it, but fear overwhelms her. It's another byproduct of growing up in this house.

"I thought so," he says, reading her eyes as they give her thoughts away. "You are weak and useless. Maybe you can do one thing that redeems your miserable existence."

Tomasso steps back toward the desk and snatches up his phone. "You will call Chloe McCarthy and tell her to stop giving media interviews. Say that it's damaging you emotionally. Convince her, or I will send Jamieson to do it for you."

Her father hands her his cell. She has no defiance left. Reluctantly, she briefly closes her eyes before pressing the numbers on the screen. It begins ringing, and she can only hope and pray that her only friend has the sense not to answer.

CHAPTER TWENTY-NINE

JAMIESON BOHMER

AMERICAN DREAM MALL
EAST RUTHERFORD, NEW JERSEY

The meeting went as anticipated, if not as desired. So be it. People make choices that determine the direction of their lives and must live with the consequences. Jamieson would love to leave this tourist trap mall, but work needs to be done. He chooses his first target carefully, although he doesn't need to. Teenagers are eager to make easy money for a simple task, especially in the sums he's offering.

With that part of his plan set, the challenge begins. Jamieson needs to pick the moment, brief his new "employees," and then get them to execute the plan at the precise time. Kids may be eager, but they're also unreliable. This is going to be tricky.

The food court is crowded with holiday shoppers, which works to his advantage. It will make his approach difficult to spot. One hint of recognition at an inopportune time, and the whole plan goes in the crapper. Then he will have to explain the failure to Tomasso. That's untenable.

He gestures the kids into position. One of them nods, and they chat among themselves. Their responsibility is simple enough and shouldn't take this much coordination. Jamieson waits patiently until they signal him in return. The man is eating away without a care in the world. It's go time.

Jamieson begins walking deeper into the food court. He tries to look like every other holiday shopper and knows he's failing miserably. He's a fish out of water in a place like this. His dress is appropriate, but his body language is…off. He's hoping that a mall security guard doesn't become too suspicious. Mall shootings are a thing in this part of the country, and the security here is trained to notice anything that looks weird.

When he gets within ten feet of his target, he gives the kids the "go" signal. One of the teens stops short and turns before shoving the kids behind him. The boy takes immediate offense and pushes him back, causing an immediate fracas within the group and the tables around them. His target leaps into action, standing and inserting himself between the feuding boys. There is plenty of shouting but no other physical violence.

The distraction has the desired effect. Jamieson swiftly covers the remaining distance to the table and spots the drink with the lid off. Removing that protective cover was a bad move. He uncaps a small vial and dumps the fluid quickly in as he breezes by the table. To avoid being spotted, Jamieson immediately turns to the right and walks away, his back to his target.

The commotion behind him quiets down. The lawyer joins the tail end of a restaurant line before hazarding a look back. The kids did their job. Peace has been restored, and the group moves off. Content that the drama is over, his target sits back down and takes a long swig of his cola. That's more than enough to cause Jamieson to smile. Now it's a waiting game.

The man finishes his food and picks up his tray. He stops and places his hand over his chest but keeps moving. He exits the food court toting several large shopping bags and heads back into the bowels of the mall. Jamieson follows him, stopping only when the kids show up to collect the other half of their bounty. It's money well spent.

He ambles far behind his target. There's no reason to get close, even if he would have preferred a dozen other methods for dispatching the traitor. A garotte in the parking garage would have been far more satisfying, but it would have been messy enough to make the evening news. That would have upset Tomasso, especially considering Jamieson's lecture about being patient. This is a more elegant yet still risky solution.

The man stops abruptly before staggering to his right and collapsing on the tile floor. A woman screams, and several other people urgently shout the alarm. A couple of Good Samaritans rush over to the man but are helpless to do anything to aid him. A half dozen bystanders immediately pull their phones out to report to 911 dispatchers that a man suddenly collapsed in the American Dream Mall.

Jamieson squeezes the small glass container in his pocket. He hoped that he was wrong and didn't need this. Aconitine is a highly toxic poison with a rich literary history. As little as two milligrams may cause death from paralysis of the respiratory center or cardiac muscle. It appears in Oscar Wilde's *Lord Arthur Savile's Crime*, a short, macabre story about a man desperate to fulfill his destiny to become a murderer as a precondition for getting married. James Joyce also used it in *Ulysses* as the poison Leopold Bloom's dad used to commit suicide.

It's time to go. Jamieson wanders away from the scene, his curiosity satiated. He doesn't rush or make a show of his exit. There is no real reason to beat feet out of the mall. The lawyer even stops at a few stores on the way out. He opens the app and orders a rideshare as he reaches the exit and sees it's only three minutes away.

The man's death will be labeled a tragic heart attack before the holidays. Aconitine is untraceable in an autopsy unless someone specifically looks for it, which they won't. There is no reason to. The overweight man was a civil servant with a history of heart disease, not a gangster or politician.

Dead men tell no tales. Art Burill will no longer be a problem for them. Replacing him and getting the lucrative contracts for the city steered back in their direction is another issue.

CHAPTER THIRTY

JOHN PROCK

BRODY PROCK'S RENTAL APARTMENT
EAST VILLAGE, NEW YORK, NEW YORK

John parks along the far curb and crosses the street. This is a quiet section of Manhattan. At least his son got that right. He hops up the short set of stairs and rings the bell, tapping the butt of his holstered weapon as he looks up and down the street. He's naturally paranoid, but his business endeavors have made him even more so when visiting the city.

New York only issues concealed carry permits to residents, part-time residents, and those who work in the state. He applied for and received his after completing a firearm training class and demonstrating a need, which he manufactured. That was then. The Supreme Court overturned the Sullivan Act in 2022, eliminating the limitations on individuals seeking concealed carry permits in the state. Since then, all law-abiding citizens need for approval is a proper gun safe and a smile.

"Who is it?" his son asks over the intercom after John rings another three times in quick succession.

"Open up, Brody."

The buzzer sounds, the lock disengages, and John pushes the door open. He is about to knock on Brody's ground-floor rental when the door swings into the apartment.

"Dad. What are you doing here?"

"Visiting," he says, brushing past his son and surveying the apartment's interior. "This is nice. How much is it costing me?"

"More than it would if you had let me stay in my house."

"You mean *my* house."

"Why are you here?" Brody asks, moving into the kitchen.

John stops in the middle of the living area. He reaches down, snatches the remote off the coffee table, and mutes the television.

"Did you see the interviews this morning?"

"Watching television is about all I have to do here. Yeah, I saw it."

"Do you know Chloe McCarthy?"

"Salisbury is a small school. Everybody knows everybody. She's nice…well-liked."

"Is she lying?"

"Not on purpose. Chloe is probably regurgitating whatever story her roommate spun for her."

"The one you raped."

John studies his son's face for a reaction. He gets one. At first, it's a flash of surprise and then anger. He knows that his son resents him. It's been that way since before he went to college. There is nothing about this incident that will bring them closer together.

"I didn't rape anybody."

"Don't lie to me, Brody! I can't help you if you do."

Brody folds his arms across his chest. "I'm not lying."

John shakes his head. "So, you're claiming that this Ashlee girl is making this all up? You're a womanizer, son. I've seen your social media profiles. It's all pictures with different women."

"I date a lot."

"And I think one of those dates going too far is more believable than a woman who has your semen inside her lying about rape."

"I guess I shouldn't have expected you to believe me. Did you know, according to the FBI, between one-and-a-half and eight percent of rape accusations are determined to be false? Even if it's only two percent like the Department of Justice claims—"

"I don't care about statistics!" John snaps, cutting his son off. "I care about what you did. She has no reason to lie."

Jackie Coakley told *Rolling Stone* that she had been gang-raped by fraternity members at UVA. In reality, she invented a rapist and used a fake text messaging service to convince her friends he did to make one of them jealous. 'The Mean Girls' from Seneca High School claimed a male classmate sexually assaulted them. Three girls admitted they lied, but the boy was still labeled a 'predator' and had to leave school. Do you know why they did it? One of the accusers plain didn't like him."

"Brody—"

"Tawana Brawley claimed she was raped by four white men in a 1987 hate crime. Reverend Al Sharpton used the media to make her a household name. It took a jury to conclude that Brawley faked the crime so she wouldn't get in trouble at home."

"Okay, I get your point," John says, rubbing his forehead. "None of that explains why Ashlee Trillo is lying."

"Maybe she wants attention or sympathy. Maybe she's mentally ill…there are a dozen reasons she could be lying. Why don't the police do something novel and ask her?"

"The FBI tried. The interview ended abruptly."

Now it's Brody's turn to shake his head. "I wonder why."

John shifts his holster and sits on the sofa. He stares at his hands as he rubs them together. This conversation is making him uncomfortable. He half expected his son to admit what he did, not launch into a passionate defense.

"I know it happens, but I still find it hard to believe. You went on a date with Ashlee, right?"

"Back in September."

"And then you ignored her."

"It's called 'ghosting,' and I didn't mean it to be malicious. I wasn't interested in pursuing what Ashlee wanted," Brody says honestly. "And if you're looking for a motive, there it is. A woman at the University of Colorado accused a man of sexual assault and later admitted to investigators that she 'stretched the truth' because she was angry at him for not wanting to date her after their encounter. She made the report to scare him."

Brody moves into the living area and crashes into the chair. He lets out a loud sigh before straightening. He looks at his father with serious eyes…and a wounded expression.

"I know that my dating history is causing me problems. But let's not pretend that my case is unique. Countless men have had their lives ruined by nebulous allegations. 'Believe all women' is a great notion if all women could be believed. Unfortunately, they can't. Some of them lie, just like men do."

"Oh, so you're an expert?"

"I'm in law school, Dad. I'm studying to become one. So yeah, I may have some insights into what's happening to me."

"Then you also know to keep your mouth shut. You must be thinking about rebutting what Chloe McCarthy had to say. Don't. Not to the police and definitely not to the media. You have a lot to lose. So do I."

The attorney gave a play-by-play of the damage control runbook while John was driving to Salisbury to pick up his son. The accused has a right to remain silent and should use it to avoid being tricked into making an incriminating statement. Even if the person knows they are innocent, they should let an attorney do the talking. The last thing the accused should do is talk to a reporter. Brody must understand that.

His son folds his hands and nods. "It wouldn't do any good anyway. I've been convicted in the court of public opinion. Even when I'm found not guilty in a courtroom, my name will always be attached to this. My life is ruined."

CHAPTER THIRTY-ONE
"BOSTON" HOLLINGER

SALISBURY LAW SCHOOL RESIDENTIAL HOUSING
SALISBURY, CONNECTICUT

The campus is nearly empty. Christmas is coming, finals are ending, and students are heading home for their winter break. Even so, nobody here would mistake Nadiya and me for FBI agents. Dressed in jeans, boots, and a puffy coat and having her hair down, she looks like a student herself. I'm a little too old for that, even with my casual look and government-funded facelift, but I could easily be the T.A. she's sleeping with.

We walk across campus to the residential housing area. There are precious few cars parked in front of their units. Even the media has largely begun abandoning their posts to move on to chase juicier parts of this story elsewhere. There's no reason to be reporting from an empty campus. That's what B-roll footage is for.

"Let me take the lead in talking to Chloe," Nadiya says, breaking the silence as we stride down the sidewalk.

"Naturally."

"I mean it," she says, turning to me as we walk.

"So do I."

I'm not sure why she expected an argument from me, but I don't bother asking. We turn down the small street and spot her car parked in the drive. That was expected. The shouting and pleas for help that come from her apartment aren't.

"Was that a scream?" I ask, confirming I'm not mistaking a vision for reality.

"Yeah, it was," Nadiya says, drawing her weapon and breaking into a sprint that I easily match.

We reach the door and stop. There is another shout from a woman who is in clear distress. We have no eyes or ears in there. It's a blind entry with an unknown number of assailants who are likely armed. Unfortunately, there's no time for backup.

"Help! Help me! No!"

Nadiya nods and holds three fingers up. I reach for the door handle. It's unlocked. She counts down on her fingers. Three, two, one…. I swing the door open, and Nadiya rushes in.

"FBI! Drop the knife!"

I enter behind Nadiya and tack to her right, my weapon outstretched in front of me. "Knife" is a charitable word. The tatted-up man is wielding an eighteen-inch machete over his head. One downward chop will lop Chloe McCarthy's head clear off her shoulders. The man stops at the sight of unwanted visitors and glances to our left.

I catch the blur in my peripheral vision a split second before Nadiya does. She doesn't have a chance to react before a kitchen stool crashes down on her arms. The combatives instructor yelps as her gun breaks free from her grip and drops to the floor. I keep machete man covered as I hear the telltale clack of a switchblade locking into position. He's going to need a lot more help than that.

"Take care of Chloe," Nadiya commands, shaking out her arms. "This asshole is mine."

I take several steps to my right to give them space and get a better angle on his machete-wielding partner. He still hasn't flinched, more interested in the badass blonde who's channeling Chuck Norris as she ties her hair back into a ponytail. The guy with the cute little switchblade has no clue what kind of medical attention he will need in the next few minutes.

My vision blurs. It's dark in here. A man is on a table. He has flesh hanging off him as he yelps in agony. Men, many without shirts on, whoop and holler. I feel...joy. Contentment. I feel the heft of the knife in my hand. It's my turn. I slice the blade through his pectoral muscle's upper layers of skin. He screams, and I notice something else: I'm smiling.

I shake the image. That's a new wrinkle for Asami. I usually feel the pain of trauma in these memories, not emotions bordering on ecstasy. There's no time right now to contemplate how that happened. I have work to do.

The scumbag locks eyes with me. I don't know if it's his memory or his friend's, but it doesn't matter. You are the company you keep. I creep forward, and Chloe sees her chance to scamper away. The man spots the escape attempt and stomps on her leg, causing her to yelp in pain. He grins as his arm twitches.

"Move, and I'll drop you," I say evenly.

I hear the scuffle behind me, followed by a clank on the hardwood floor. The man wouldn't have much of a shot against Nadiya armed with a lightsaber, much less a knife. Now unarmed, he has none. A couple of pops come next, likely his nose being broken and his jaw fractured. Ouch.

"Drop the machete."

The command was a simple one. The man with more ink than skin doesn't reply.

"*¡Suelta el machete!*"

I have no idea if I barked that order correctly. I could have ordered the thug to hit me with the machete, for all I know. I'm not that deep into the Spanish classes I insisted on taking after meeting Sol during my escapades in Mexico. It's time to get back to my studies.

He doesn't respond. Instead, he turns to Chloe and jerks his arm higher before bringing the machete down. I double tap, aiming for center mass. The two bullets hit him square in the chest, and the knife falls from his hand onto Chloe.

The woman screams as the man drops beside her. I turn to see Nadiya break her attacker's arm. She slides around to his back. I know what's coming next. I've seen three versions of that move, and none ended well. With Nadiya's man under control, I move to Chloe, who is sobbing uncontrollably on the floor.

"It's okay. It's okay. You're safe now."

She throws her arms around me and squeezes hard. I stare at the man I just shot. His lifeless eyes stare back at me. There's no need to check for a pulse. He's gone.

I check back with Nadiya, who has the other assailant face-down on the floor. He's gushing blood from his nose and mouth and is writhing in pain. He has already been cuffed, and Nadiya has her knee planted in his back. She offers me a shrug and a smile as she pulls out her cell phone. I listen as I turn my attention back to Chloe, who has a death grip on me as she weeps into my chest.

"Zach, we have a problem," Nadiya says, pausing briefly. "Get to Chloe and Ashlee's place. Bring the campus police and paramedics."

I nod over at the corpse three feet away from me. Nadiya smirks when she gets the hint.

"And a coroner."

CHAPTER THIRTY-TWO
ASHLEE TRILLO

TOMASSO TRILLO FAMILY ESTATE
ENGLEWOOD CLIFFS, NEW JERSEY

Timing is everything. It's true of every situation and human endeavor. First, Ashlee had to come to terms with the consequences of leaving. Now, it's about making it out the door without being seen by the dumbest slab of beef in Northern New Jersey.

The house has been still for a while now. Her father is in his Newark office, no doubt fleecing the taxpayers by charging massive cost overruns for substandard housing. She doesn't know where Jamieson is, only that he isn't lurking around the grounds. He's likely terrorizing the population by pushing old ladies and kicking puppies.

That leaves her babysitter. The security guards Ashlee's father employs work in shifts. When the moronic night guy comes on, a brief changeover is conducted in the driveway. Their foremost concern is for her father's safety. When he isn't here, they relax and take their sweet time about things. Those valuable extra few minutes provide her with an opportunity.

Ashlee stuffs a backpack with clothing and a few toiletries while mentally reviewing the plan. Her immediate need is to overcome her anxiety, which has already made an appearance. Assuming she beats that, she needs to get out undetected. Once out of the house, she can head south to Palisade Avenue to pick up bus route 156. The New Jersey Transit line runs from there to the Port Authority Bus Terminal in Midtown. She has several transit options and time to plan her next move from there, despite having no idea what that might be.

The housekeepers are gone. She checks the clock next to her bed. The night guy should be coming on soon. This is her chance. She takes a deep breath and slowly eases the door open. No sounds are coming from the house.

She eases out of her bedroom and skulks down the hall to the foyer staircase. She glides down the stairs, carefully avoiding the ones she knows squeak. The rubber soles of her sneakers make little noise against the marble in the otherwise cacophonous foyer.

Ashlee is tempted to peek out the windows alongside the double doors leading to the driveway. The shift change happens out front, meaning the back should be clear. The house alarm won't be on. This is going to work.

Another surge of anxiety grips her. She looks back up the stairs at her bedroom. She shouldn't do this. If she gets caught, there will be hell to pay. If she succeeds, her fate could be worse. She'll be alone with nobody in the world to help her. Ashlee takes a deep breath and forces her legs to move.

A quick peep confirms that the gourmet kitchen is completely empty. Ashlee smiles as she resists the urge to rush to the door. She can almost taste the freedom on the other side of it. She opens it, slides through, and turns to ease it closed as quietly as possible. Her escape was nearly silent. She takes a series of sharp breaths. She can do this.

"Are you trying to get me fired?"

She nearly jumps out of her skin at the deep baritone sound of the walking tree trunk who works the night shift. Chaz Sabia is a brainless meathead. She knows the type well. Most of the guys she hung out with during her undergrad years were just like him: all muscles and very little common sense. Unfortunately, his timing couldn't have been worse.

He takes a final drag on his cigarette and crushes it in the can near the door. "Where ya goin'?"

"For a walk. I've been cooped up in that room for a while now."

"With an overnight bag?"

Ashlee grasps the strap of the backpack slung over her shoulder. She doesn't have an answer to that.

"I'm not stupid," Chaz decrees.

Reasonable people would disagree with that, but she isn't in a position to argue the point. "I never thought you were."

"Then why are you lyin'?"

Ashlee decides to change her tactics. "Because you'll get in trouble if I tell you the truth."

"I need to tell your father about this," Chaz says, completely expressionless.

"I wouldn't do that if I were you."

"Why not?"

Ashlee hangs her head in mock reluctance. "Because he'll wonder how I managed to get out of the house. Or my room, for that matter. He'll accuse you of not doing your job and wonder why he's paying you when you can't control a twenty-three-year-old woman."

"That's not—"

"Reasonable? You've met my father. He's not a reasonable man. How do you think he'd react?"

Chaz takes a moment to think about it. "He'll be angry and yell at me."

"Exactly."

Ashlee waits for him to agree with her line of thinking. She would have been a fantastic lawyer. Not that a mental exercise with Chaz requires much exertion.

"I'm not letting you go," he declares, folding his massive arms in front of him.

"I know. You see how it is here, though. Can you blame me for trying?"

Chaz looks around the backyard. He thinks they are at an impasse. Ashlee considers pressing her luck with her escape attempt but doesn't think he'll agree to it in the end. It's better to retreat and reevaluate what she's doing. Her central nervous system is already shot because of this.

"What do we do now?"

"Well, it's best for both of us if we don't discuss this with anyone. I got some fresh air, and nobody needs to know about this. No harm, no foul."

That's only partially true. The entire property is covered in cameras. Jamieson reviews the tapes like he's concocting a game plan for a Sunday football game against a division rival. She can only pray that he has no reason to check them tonight when he returns.

"I'm supposed to report stuff like this."

"Yelling…lots of yelling," Ashlee reminds him.

Chaz nods. "Stay in your room. Don't try to leave again."

"Okay. You're a good guy, Chaz," she says, popping him on the shoulder. "Far better than how they treat you."

Ashlee steps back inside as the moose sparks another cigarette. She closes the door and leans against it. She was so close, but maybe this is for the best. Her hippie friends would call it a sign. Perhaps she isn't supposed to leave here. She has plenty of time to contemplate that as she retreats to the prison cell she calls a bedroom.

CHAPTER THIRTY-THREE
SSA ZACH FORTE

SALISBURY LAW SCHOOL STUDENT CENTER
SALISBURY, CONNECTICUT

The conversations with the Connecticut State Police captain and the tiny campus security department chief went about as well as they could. Neither disputed that it was a good shooting and that Zach's agents likely saved Chloe McCarthy's life. On the other hand, they don't like the FBI. It's a turf thing. Policing this campus is their job, and they're militant about reminding Zach that FBI assistance isn't really needed or wanted for a simple rape case.

They got the required statements and information from Boston and Nadiya and exiled the pair to the student center to wait. Emma met them there, and seeing the two women with Boston will likely give every straight male still on campus a reason to loiter there with their tongues out.

The student center is nice in a snobby elitist intellectual kind of way. There is lots of mahogany furniture, dark leather seating, big windows, and warm lighting. The three team members are parked in a lounge area with steaming cups of java served by the barista at the coffee bar a couple dozen yards away.

"How's Chloe?" Boston asks when Zach sits in one of the oversized leather chairs.

"Shaken up but alive," he says, surprised it was Boston who asked and not one of the women. "She's very grateful to the two of you, and so are her parents. They were getting ready to leave Minnesota to pick her up when they got news of the attack."

"Where is she?"

"At the hospital getting checked out. She was slapped around a little before you two rode in on your white horses. Some butterfly sutures and a couple of aspirin are all that's stopping her from getting released in an hour or two. You guys are cleared, in case you're interested."

"Was there a doubt?" Boston asks.

"Not in my mind. Unfortunately, the state and campus police needed a little persuasion. They don't much like us."

"Jerks," Nadiya mumbles.

"Cut them some slack. They're in a tough spot. The media just left, and now they're doing U-turns in White Plains to haul ass back here. The locals aren't used to dealing with a press horde, let alone investigating an accused rape and a vicious assault in the same week."

"Any word on the two assailants?" Emma asks.

"Yeah," Zach says, digging into his jacket to pull out his phone. He brings up an email and scans it. "The one Boston shot was Luis Cabezas. The guy in custody is Julio Tadeo. Both are illegals from El Salvador and likely members of MS-13."

"There's no doubt about it," Boston mutters.

Mara Salvatrucha is also known as MS or just Mara, but they are most commonly referred to in the United States as the dreaded MS-13. They started in the 1980s in Los Angeles before growing into a seventy-thousand-member international organization. The level of brutality they employ makes ISIS look gentle. They earn truckloads of money through human trafficking, sexual slavery, street-level rackets, and helping the Sinaloa cartel's United States drug market.

"Is he talking?" Nadiya asks with a smirk.

"Not yet. Tadeo is still receiving medical treatment. That will take care of his physical issues. He'll need therapy for the psychological ones once his boys hear about the whooping you put on him. Thank you for not breaking his jaw completely off, at least."

Nadiya grins enthusiastically. "You're welcome!"

"Where are they from?" Boston asks.

Zach glances at his phone. "Newark, New Jersey."

"The home of Brick City Development," Emma says, leaning back.

"Owned and operated by one Tomasso Trillo," Zach adds, understanding her point.

The team all stares at their hands as they contemplate that. It was the first leap Zach made when he read the email. He's content to wait to see what conclusion they reach.

"That makes no sense," Emma finally says. "Chloe McCarthy was backing Ashlee's accusation. Why would her father send men to attack her?"

All eyes turn back to Zach. "I don't know. It's a question someone should ask."

"Why not us?" Nadiya asks, picking up the intended message in his choice of words.

"Because we're off this case. We'll caravan down to Virginia tomorrow, per Remsen's orders."

"Not yet," Boston decrees before giving Zach a hard look. "Find a way to keep us in New York."

"Boston…."

"I'm with him, Zach," Emma says. "We're not done yet. This mission isn't over until we say it is. Screw what Remsen orders."

Zach looks at Nadiya. "There are too many unanswered questions. I won't sleep well until they are."

The senior agent stares at each member of his team. They're serious about this. Three months ago, he would have said, "orders are orders," and dragged them back to Watchtower if he had to. That was then, and this is now. He's tired of that game. This team is the best he has ever seen. If they want more time, he will find a way to get it for them.

"You guys are impossible. All right. Boston, did you get anything useful from the guys in the apartment?"

"Nothing you want to hear about. They were violent. That's it. I had no time to focus for long on what I was seeing. I didn't want to accidentally shoot Chloe and end up facing Emma's wrath."

"Good call," she says with a wink. "You're learning."

"I have a good teacher."

"If I agree to run interference with Matt, I need a reason. Mister MS-13 isn't going to talk, so what's your play, Boston?"

Boston tightens his jaw and wrings his hands. "What does the referee do before he flips the coin at a football game?"

"Shows the teams the two sides," Emma says, causing Zach to cock his head at her. He didn't peg her as a football fan.

"Exactly. We have only seen one and need to eye the other. I need to confirm something with Brody Prock."

"What?"

"I'll let you know. You'll have to trust me on this."

"This isn't the time to play coy, Boston. Brody lawyered up. His blood-sucking attorneys won't agree to any meeting with the FBI."

"Ask anyway. The worst they can say is no. Ladies, would you mind taking a walk with me?"

"Where are we going?" Nadiya asks.

"The hospital. I still want to chat with Chloe McCarthy. I need to know what she experienced with Ashlee after she arrived at the front door of their apartment."

CHAPTER THIRTY-FOUR

JOHN PROCK

It's become increasingly hard for John to focus. His work is demanding, and he typically pours his heart and soul into growing AMLOG into a logistics powerhouse. This is not one of those days. The strain of his side business and his son's legal troubles have distracted him.

Hard decisions come with the territory. Every business leader makes choices and must live with their consequences. It's as true for the owner of a small suburban nail salon as it is for the CEO of a Fortune 500 company. John has never shied away from making the hard call. He has made a living evaluating information, weighing options, selecting a course of action, and managing the result. Today is no different, except in the ways that it is.

Business is war. It's a tenet John learned early on, and he has ruthlessly treated it that way. His interests must be protected at all costs. Colleagues are not friends, and partners are only valuable if they contribute to a goal. Rivals must be defeated, and new ventures need to be quashed before they can become competitors. Those all get added to the balance sheet of running a successful business. Assets must be protected, and liabilities erased. And that's his problem.

His son has become one of those liabilities. He can't do much about that. He warned Brody that his philandering was going to cause problems one day. It turns out that the talk was prophetic, even if his obstinate son failed to heed the advice.

Since he can't eliminate the liability, he must protect the assets. John can tamp down the noise by sending a message to the people doing the chirping. That's the point of today's mission. The stakes are high, and the blowback could be severe. He trusts Lothar to make the necessary arrangements to insulate him, but not all risks can be eliminated.

Lothar knocks on the door jamb and enters the room. He doesn't look happy. Part of that is his not spending much time in the office. Likely, most people working for AMLOG wouldn't even recognize him, despite his lofty title.

He closes the door and stares down at the handle. "Chloe McCarthy was attacked in her residence at Salisbury a couple of hours ago."

"That's horrible!" John screeches, a little too excited. "Is she okay?"

"She's traumatized but otherwise fine, outside of some cuts and bruises."

John's exuberance deflates. That's not what he expected to hear, not that he dares utter that. The office is not a safe space to discuss details of a crime they should know nothing about. The shipping industry is cutthroat. It wouldn't shock him to learn that a competitor bugged his office, even if he isn't big enough for corporate espionage.

He also doesn't trust the FBI. They've been known to illegally eavesdrop on the unsuspecting to build their cases. Gone are the days they worry about pesky things like Constitutional rights and warrants. It's a brave new age in America.

"Thank God for that," John says, grinding his teeth. "Do the police have any suspects?"

"The attackers were confronted by federal agents during the assault. One was killed when he tried to lop her head off with a machete. The other is in custody."

John shakes his head. He would have thought that MS-13 would have been more effective at this. Brutal violence is their modus operandi.

"I assume he's being interrogated. The police and FBI will want a motive."

"No doubt, but the man is hospitalized, and it doesn't sound like he's talking. His friend certainly isn't."

"Do you think he'll talk?"

Lothar glances around the room. "If they are correct that it's MS-13, talking would be out of character for such a ruthless gang. Silence is a badge of honor for them."

"Well," Johns says, clasping his hands together. "I'm glad to hear that she's okay. At least physically. I hope the police get to the bottom of it. That school has seen enough drama over the past week. Thanks for the information."

"I thought you would want to know. The feds may think you had something to do with it."

John nods. "Yes, along with other insane accusations like my son raping a girl. I will inform our legal team to expect a call. Anything else?"

"Yes, one more thing. We have an opportunity to expand one of our hubs in the Midwest. I can swing by your house later tonight to discuss some interesting possibilities if you're available."

It's code. Whenever Lothar wants to discuss their other operation, it's always a line about expansion. The region is the key to the topic. The East is a product problem, the South is personnel, the West is suppliers, and the Rockies is law enforcement. When the issue isn't covered by one of those broad categories, he gives the name of a state or city. Midwest is the code for the need to discuss a development in more detail.

"Come over at eight. I'm not keen on expanding in this market climate, but we'll talk over some options."

"See you then," Lothar says before leaving.

John looks out the window at the remaining satellite trucks. Most of the journalists have moved on, but several holdouts are still chasing this part of the story. John can't afford to throw them a bone. That's what will happen if this failure is linked to him. Lothar is thorough and careful, but mistakes happen. People can be compelled to talk. He needs to know what went wrong and why.

CHAPTER THIRTY-FIVE
JAMIESON BOHMER

BOSTON POST ROAD
DARIEN, CONNECTICUT

Darien is an idyllic New England town. Situated just east of Stamford, it boasts an estimated median household income of over $200,000. The schools are good, the cost of living is ridiculous, and the crime rate is nearly non-existent. It's also the smallest town on Connecticut's Gold Coast and features countless parks, two beaches, and two train stations serving Manhattan's Grand Central Terminal.

The center of the town's business activity is along U.S. Route 1, known as the Boston Post Road, which runs roughly parallel to Interstate 95. The number of traffic lights and crush of vehicular traffic make tailing his target difficult, but not impossible. At least he doesn't need to worry about getting spotted. He is following several cars back, and there is no reason for the kid to think he's being followed.

The gray Audi pulls into a fitness center and slides into a spot along the sparse tree line separating a trio of businesses from their neighbors. He hustles into the building without even looking in Jamieson's direction. He planned on doing this at the house when the kid was alone, but this could work to his advantage.

Jamieson checks his watch. The kid is already dressed in stylish workout clothes. He could be there for anywhere from a half hour to two hours. The timing is important, and the lawyer needs to guess. He doesn't want to be exposed for too long to the foot traffic entering and leaving the fitness center.

The strip mall with a nail salon and liquor store across the road has line-of-sight to the parking lot in case Jamieson's forty-five-minute estimate proves incorrect. He does a U-turn and steers his car over there to wait. When the requisite amount of time elapses, he pulls back into the fitness center parking lot that is shared with a small restaurant and dry cleaner.

Instead of finding a random spot in the small lot that wraps around the rear of the structure, he spots a fortuitous empty spot beside the gray Audi. He pulls in, leaving only six inches between his car and Lucas's driver's side door. He once saw this in a movie and won't take credit for the tactic when Tomasso presses him for details.

Jamieson climbs out of his vehicle and passes through the line of trees separating the two parking lots. He ducks behind an SUV and monitors the fitness center door. He timed it almost perfectly. The kid comes out five minutes later, mercifully before the owner of the dark Mercedes GLA he's ducking behind comes to retrieve his or her vehicle. That would have been awkward.

Lucas Noland throws his arms in the air when he notices Jamieson's parking job. Resigned that he'll have to do this the hard way, he climbs into the passenger side and shimmies over the center console. He eases into the driver's seat and reaches across to close the door. Jamieson is already sliding into the Audi's passenger seat and closes it for him.

"What the hell are you doing?" Lucas Noland shouts in shock. "Get out of my car!"

Jamieson retrieves his weapon from the shoulder holster and slams the butt of it into the young man's chest. Lucas gasps, and his eyes lock on the H&K VP9 Jamieson chose for this task. It was a good selection. This weapon just looks scary.

"Wh-what is this?"

"A conversation, Lucas," Jamieson says evenly.

"At gunpoint?"

Jamieson jams the pistol into his holster and retrieves his Fairbairn-Sykes British commando dagger. The long, slender black blade may be more intimidating than the gun.

"Knifepoint, actually," he says with a smirk.

"What do you want to talk about?" Lucas asks, edging closer to the driver's side door. The extra distance will do him no good, and there is no escape that way.

Jamieson leans closer to him. "Brody Prock."

"What about him? He's my roommate at school."

"Oh, he's much more than that," the lawyer says, gauging this kid's reaction. "He's a rapist."

Lucas shakes his head vigorously. "That's a lie! He isn't. That chick is lying, and I won't say otherwise. I don't care if you start carving me up with that thing."

"I didn't think you'd find a physical threat against you credible. It is, by the way, but I also don't expect you to believe that. The truth is, I don't want you saying anything about what happened at Salisbury. To anyone. Ever."

A range of emotions flashes across Lucas's face. Surprise at Jamieson's admission is quickly replaced with anger and then defiance. This generation is so entitled. This kid legitimately doesn't understand how close his life is to being ruined…or ended.

"I support Brody and always will. You can't coerce my silence."

Jamieson smiles, amused. Lucas has spirit. It may be misplaced and ultimately irrelevant, and it'd be admirable if he were willing to back it up. Which he won't.

"Challenge accepted," the lawyer says, with some theatricality. "You will agree to my terms, or I will provide the media a name: Angel de la Rosa."

Lucas goes pale. "How…how could you…?"

"Your generation still has no concept of how social media works. You spent years documenting your entire lives and leaving digital fingerprints everywhere. The more time someone spends online, the more information can be found. I employ a small army of private investigators who can find…well, pretty much everything."

"You'll destroy him…me," Lucas stutters, his lower lip quivering after hearing a name he never thought he would again.

"Yes. It's called 'scorched earth.' You will do one simple thing for me, or I will burn your life to the ground. And Angel de la Rosa's. So, what do you think, Lucas?"

"What are you asking?"

"Very simple. Keep your mouth shut. You don't speak to the media and will stop cooperating with law enforcement. You don't say anything about Brody Prock or Ashlee Trillo, bad or good, to anyone from this point forward. If you agree to those terms, your secret remains just that. You understand what will happen if you don't."

This is the problem with modern society. Everybody crumbles like a cookie at the first hint of adversity. This is truly a generation of keyboard warriors. Comfortable men living comfortable lives are among the softest. Lucas doesn't want to lose the life of secrecy he's built. It will cost him his schooling, career, and the seven-figure salary he's likely to make plying his trade. It will result in personal embarrassment and likely some familial strife. Instead of facing that to support his "friend," he'll fold faster than a poker player unwilling to go all in with one pair.

"That won't be necessary."

"Good man," Jamieson says, opening the car door.

"Who are you? Who do you work for?" Lucas asks, defeated.

"Neither of those questions should concern you. Remember our arrangement, Lucas. Trust me when I say that I'll be watching."

Lucas wastes no time firing up his Audi and tearing out of the parking lot. Jamieson watches him go. He rattled the kid, and it was with the name more than the gun or knife. Brody's roommate may have spirit but lacks grit. He wouldn't have lasted two days in the SAS. The spineless ones are always the first to wash out.

CHAPTER THIRTY-SIX

"BOSTON" HOLLINGER

SHARON HOSPITAL
SHARON, CONNECTICUT

I'm not sure what is causing me the most angst. It could be the smell, the sight of lab coats and scrubs, or even the color of the walls. Whatever it is, I hate hospitals. I mean, I really hate them, and emergency rooms are the worst.

Chloe is sitting on a bed in a patient examination area bisected by a curtain. Introductions are made, and her eyes lock on me. She is genuinely gracious that we arrived at her apartment in the nick of time. If I had taken a shot of tequila for every thank-you she utters, I'd need to have my stomach pumped. At least I'd be in the right place for it.

I melt into the wall as Nadiya and Emma lead her interview. The first question Chloe asks the ladies is the obvious one: why she was attacked. Emma provides the information Forte acquired on the two MS-13 gangbangers, and Nadiya adds a few details along the way. Their answer hits Chloe like an anvil and sparks a degree of disbelief.

"So, this was random? Because it didn't feel like it."

I don't think it was random at all. Someone unleashed those men on her, probably because of what she said in the interview. It could have been John Prock's intention to silence her, but that would invite media and law enforcement attention that he seems keen on avoiding. I'm not ruling out Tomasso Trillo, even though the roommate supports his daughter. He wants this to go away almost as badly.

I shake my head at Nadiya, who turns to Ashlee. "We'll know more once we interrogate your surviving attacker. Right now, that's our conclusion."

"Okay," she says, lowering her head as she comes to grips with the terror that her life almost ended in a random home invasion. "What did you want to talk to me about?"

"The morning Ashlee came home. Do you remember it?"

"I remember everything about it. At first, I was annoyed that Ashlee woke me up. Then I opened the door and saw her. She was a mess."

"A mess? As in, emotional?"

I close my eyes after Nadiya asks the all-important question that should trigger the memory I'm looking for.

I open the door, feeling groggy and annoyed at being woken up. Ashlee is standing on the stoop, completely frozen and motionless. That makes me even angrier, but I feel myself trying to tamp it down.

"Wow. You must have had one hell of a night. Did you forget your keys?"

Ashlee doesn't move. When she finally lifts her head, I see the wounded look on her face. Her eyes are puffy, and her tears carry what's left of her mascara down her cheeks. My attitude immediately changes.

"Ashlee, what's wrong?"

She looks around before sobbing. Not gentle sobs, but brutal, uncontrollable ones.

"Ash? Tell me."

"I was…I need you to take me to the campus police."

"Why? What happened?"

My answer was reflexive. My stomach turns because I already know what happened. Ashlee begins crying harder. Now I feel horrible about being annoyed with her banging on the door.

"Oh, my God! Yes, I'll take you. I'll get my coat."

"Her eyes were bloodshot and swollen from crying," Chloe continues as I open my eyes. "She didn't have her purse with her. She was so distraught that she left it and her phone at Brody's."

"That's why she knocked," Emma confirms. "Her keys were in the purse."

Chloe nods.

"Have you ever been on a date with Brody?" Nadiya asks.

"No. I mean…I would have because he's…I never thought I had a shot with him."

Chloe is pretty in a very girl-next-door kind of way. She will never turn heads on the street or be the first approached at a bar. She's what most men would consider "wife material." She's smart, attractive but not beautiful, caring, and loyal. I've only known her for a few minutes and conclude she's the type you bring home to meet the parents, not to your place for a one-night stand.

"You know him, though. Is Brody the aggressive type?"

She looks warily at the two women, who look back at her with sympathetic eyes. That's why I wanted them to talk to her. Coming from a man, the question would somehow be construed as a defense of Brody, regardless of its intent.

"No, not that I've ever seen."

"We know he goes on many dates with other women. There's never been any stories or rumors…anything you've heard about other possible assaults?"

"No, none. That's why I was so shocked initially. The girls he goes out with don't talk much about their dates with him. He's broken a lot of hearts."

"Nothing about him being sexually aggressive or kinky?"

She shakes her head. "Never. That doesn't mean he didn't do it."

"We know," Nadiya says, reassuringly touching Chloe's knee to ease her defensiveness. "We're just trying to establish if there is any behavioral pattern."

The interview lasts another half an hour. Chloe walks us through meeting Ashlee and their relationship as roommates. I just sit and listen. There's nothing I can contribute to the conversation.

"I think we're done here," Emma says, stealing a glance at me and getting a nearly imperceptible nod in return. "Thank you for meeting with us, Chloe."

"I have a quick question," I say, pushing off the wall. "How do students communicate on campus?"

"You mean, like, when not in person?"

"Yeah. School stuff…group projects, whatever. How is that coordinated?"

"We use a chat program called mIRC. There is a whole bunch of campus groups, and we also create our own."

"Thank you."

"Anything I can do to help."

Emma gives her a card with instructions to call us if she needs anything or remembers any details we didn't discuss. Nadiya reaches the door first, and I track behind Emma before stopping.

"Chloe, has Ashlee ever talked about her relationship with her father?"

"Uh, sometimes. She said he was demanding."

"Has he ever been violent with her?"

Chloe shifts her weight and begins to fidget. "Why does that matter?"

I offer her a knowing smile and pull out my own card. "It doesn't. If Ashlee ever comes to you for help and you learn she's in over her head, have her call this number."

"Why isn't your name on the card?" Chloe asks, holding it up between her index and middle fingers.

"Because the only people I give it to already know who I am."

"What makes you think she'll need you?"

"It's just a precaution," I say, knowing it isn't the first lie we've told Chloe in our time here. "Have a safe trip back to Minnesota, Miss McCarthy. I'm glad you're okay."

Emma and Nadiya don't say anything as we head out of the hospital toward the parking lot. They may have been busy ignoring the leering of male doctors, orderlies, and nurses. Some female ones, too.

"What do you think?" Emma asks.

"If I ever see another hospital again, it will be too soon. I hate these places."

"About Chloe, Boston," Nadiya says impatiently. "What do you think about Chloe?"

I got the answer I was looking for from Chloe. I think I know the whole truth about what happened in Salisbury, why it happened, and why Brody isn't defending himself. I just need one more piece of the puzzle to prove it.

"That she's going to be the rarest member of the human species: an honest lawyer."

CHAPTER THIRTY-SEVEN

ASHLEE TRILLO

TOMASSO TRILLO FAMILY ESTATE
ENGLEWOOD CLIFFS, NEW JERSEY

Nervous energy is incredibly hard to burn off. Ashlee would never characterize herself as a fitness maven but could use some quality time on a treadmill or elliptical machine. She's been cooped up in here for far too long.

Her secret burner phone is a lifeline to the world outside these stone walls. It's also her last crumb of sanity. She opens her drawer and retrieves the device from the hollowed-out Bible. A press of a button powers on the cell, and she expects to see a bunch of unread text messages. Or maybe she just hopes to, but the result is the same: still nothing from Chloe.

She chatted with her roommate only briefly after her interviews. It's unlike her to go radio silent for this long. Ashlee's fingers type out another text message:

Hey Chloe. Haven't heard from you and am getting worried. Text back.

Ashlee performs the ritual in reverse in case her father's manservant stops in for an unannounced visit. She turns on the television, which is already tuned into cable news. That's how pathetic her life has become. The remote slips from her hand when she sees the chyron at the bottom of the screen.

"Details are scarce as law enforcement continues their investigation," a journalist reports from a spot between Salisbury's housing area and the quad. "Sources have confirmed that two men entered a campus residence during the attack and that there was a police response. Unconfirmed reports have indicated that the student was Chloe McCarthy of Minneapolis, Minnesota. She is the roommate of Ashlee Trillo, the woman who filed a rape report here last week. There is no word if this physical assault has anything to do with that report."

Ashlee hears the front door open downstairs and doesn't wait for the reporter to finish speaking. She jumps off the bed and yanks open her bedroom door. It slams hard against the door stop screwed into the baseboard trim and feels like it shakes the house.

"You bastard!" she shouts from the railing. "What the hell did you do?"

Jamieson stops in the middle of the foyer and stares up at her. He doesn't say anything, prompting Ashlee to charge down the staircase.

"Answer me!" she demands, violently shoving him with both hands. "What did you do to Chloe?"

"What are you talking about?"

Ashlee shoves him in the chest again. "Liar!"

She brings her right hand back and opens her hand. She arcs it forward, aiming it at the lawyer's face. As fast as the movement is, it's not fast enough. Jamieson catches her hand mid-flight. Before she can retaliate, he digs his middle two fingers into her wrist, causing her hand to go limp.

"Control yourself, Miss Trillo."

Ashlee struggles against his grip. "You asshole!"

Jamieson changes his grip on her in an effortless, well-practiced move. With his hand positioned on top of her wrist, he sharply bends her hand forward. The torque on her joint causes a jolt of pain to rush up her arm and down her spine. Her knees buckle at the sensation.

"I said control yourself," Jamieson says, his voice steady and tone easy.

Ashlee stops resisting. Sensing that she has regained some control of her emotions, Jamieson releases her. Her first action is to back away from the menace and rub her wrist.

"Now, let's have a civil discussion. Instead of accusations, use your words and tell me what you're talking about."

"Chloe McCarthy."

"What about her?"

"She was attacked on campus!" Ashlee says, again growing agitated.

"Okay…."

"Where were you, Jamieson?"

It wasn't a question. It was an accusation. Ashlee knows that the lawyer was somehow involved in this. He may not have been among the attackers, but she's willing to bet he was watching from nearby. That's how he operates.

"Manhattan. I had nothing…how did you know she was attacked?"

"Are you kidding? It's all over the news."

"No," Jamieson says, staring up at her bedroom door. "You've been talking to her."

"What? How? You took my cell phone! I can't talk to anyone!"

The lawyer's lips crease into a smile. "Thou doth protest too much."

He covers the ground between them quickly and grabs her by the hair. Ashlee screams but is powerless not to follow him if she wants to have a scalp. The security guard comes rushing into the foyer, his gun drawn.

"Mind your post!" Jamieson shouts as he ascends the stairs, towing Ashlee by her hair.

"Let me go, you psycho!"

"You're in no position to be calling me names," the lawyer says, pushing her through her bedroom door. "Where is your other phone?"

"I don't have one!"

"I don't believe you. Where is it?"

She points at the television. The daytime anchor is still talking about the attack with a guest. What he's an expert in, she doesn't know. The split screen transitions into a shot of her apartment at Salisbury, complete with the red and blue flashing strobes of law enforcement vehicles and obligatory yellow police line tape.

Jamieson sees the coverage and turns to stare at her. His eyes are locked on her for several intense seconds. It makes her skin crawl.

"I don't answer to you, Miss Trillo. I do as your father sees fit. In this case, I had nothing to do with any attack against your roommate. If I had wanted Miss McCarthy attacked, she'd be dead."

"You're sick."

"So I've been told," Jamieson says with a grin before looking around her room. "Don't let me catch you outside this room until your father says so. And don't ever assault me again. The next time you place a hand on me, I promise you'll end up with more than a sore wrist."

Ashlee watches the man leave, pulling her bedroom door closed behind him. She closes her eyes and exhales as she rubs her scalp. It hurts more than her wrist does. She knows Jamieson's threat wasn't an idle one. Every moment she stays here, it gets more dangerous for her. It's a scary world outside. It's become even scarier here. Something needs to be done, her anxiety be damned.

CHAPTER THIRTY-EIGHT
SSA ZACH FORTE

LAKEVILLE COUNTRY INN
LAKEVILLE, CONNECTICUT

The team offered Zach the opportunity to join them on a morning ten-kilometer run. Despite the beauty of this area, he took a hard pass. The last time he ran that far, the Boston Red Sox were still trying to win their first World Series since World War I. Even if he did want to abuse his knees trying to keep up with the younger agents, he couldn't. He needs to wait for the call that he knows is coming.

The conversation will be short and have two main focuses. The first will be a pointed question about why they aren't on the road back to Virginia. The second is the result of the request to Brody Prock's legal team.

The call comes in and plays out just as Forte thought it would. After hanging up with Matt, Zach makes his way down to the lobby area and to the small eating space adjoining it. Boston, Emma, and Nadiya have showered and are enjoying a New England breakfast for the ages. On each of their plates are healthy portions of corned beef hash, eggs, bacon, sausage, home-fried potatoes, and pancakes. The team is washing the meal down with fresh black coffee whose aroma is to die for.

"What's the verdict?"

"Exactly what you think it is. Brody's lawyers said a manned mission will be launched to Pluto before we talk to his client. He'll tell his story if he gets subpoenaed for a deposition and not a moment before."

"Wonderful," Nadiya moans.

"Anything else?" Boston asks before jamming a forkful of eggs into his mouth.

"Yeah. We're to report to Virginia immediately."

The team keeps eating. Zach expected a chorus of protests and denials. Instead, he's greeted with an unnerving silence. He plays along with the waiting game until they finally look at him.

"We must report back to Virginia…or else what?"

"What do you mean?"

Boston puts his fork down. "What will Remsen do if we don't walk in the doors at Watchtower? Is he going to send the black helicopters after us? Black bag us in the middle of the night and haul us off?"

"You've seen too many movies, Boston."

Zach's answer is tongue-in-cheek, but he raises a fair point. Matt can issue orders, but the team doesn't have to follow them. The chain of command at Watchtower is unambiguous, but there are no actionable consequences to disobeying directives.

Boston proved that in Mexico. Alejandro Salcido was a horrible human being, but what Boston did to end his reign of terror smacks of vigilantism. If an actual FBI agent had been that brazen, it would be the end of a career. It only embellished his, at least in the eyes of Remsen and Brass.

Boston is a man of their own creation. Without consequences, there is no control. Zach has already learned that. It appears that his bosses are about to. Part of him is okay with that.

"I'm serious. What can Matt do?" Boston presses.

Zach shrugs. "Nothing."

They exchange looks before Nadiya takes up the questioning. "Is this the point where you plead with us to do as instructed?"

"Nope. You're not going to listen anyway."

"And you agree with us," Emma concludes.

"To a point, yes," he says as the gracious innkeeper who cooked this magnificent meal brings him coffee. "I don't want to know what your next move is. Prock's lawyers said no, and you knew they would, so I assume you made other arrangements."

"Yeah. Stop in Scarsdale on our way to Manhattan and knock on his door," Boston says.

"And kick it down if necessary," Nadiya adds.

"He's not there."

"What?"

Zach leans back and takes a long sip of the strong coffee. They know how to brew beans up here.

"Apparently, Brody Prock is secreted away at an undisclosed location. He isn't at his house. His legal team professes that he's in hiding to avoid unwanted media attention."

"That's convenient," Emma muses.

"Anyone who knows where Brody is isn't telling us, so you'll need to find him first if you want to talk. Fortunately, we have people who are good at that sort of thing. You just need them to do it on the down low. If Remsen finds out, he'll quickly shut any inquiry down and then take you behind the woodshed for a whuppin'.'"

Zach is likely to find himself working a desk in Alaska if Remsen learns that he's advising the team on how to circumvent his authority. He shrugs off the thought. He owns a warm jacket or two.

"Is that a challenge?" Boston asks.

Forte grins. "I don't know, is it?"

The senior agent drains the rest of his coffee and leaves the table. He should have breakfast but isn't really hungry. He knows he'll catch hell for his team not following instructions, but he's tired of being the go-between. These are his people, and he trusts them. Even Boston. He might not know why the dream machine insists on talking to the accused but is betting that there's a damn good reason.

CHAPTER THIRTY-NINE
"BOSTON" HOLLINGER

JACOB K. JAVITS FEDERAL BUILDING
NEW YORK, NEW YORK

Talking to yourself used to be a sign of insanity. Now it's a sign of status. I don't know where the expression came from, but it beautifully explains the streets of Manhattan. Bluetooth earpieces were all the rage a decade ago. People would be on the phone doing everything from strolling in the mall to mowing the lawn. The devices have fallen out of fashion in this era but are still useful. Sometimes you don't want to be seen with a phone to your ear.

I announced my need to go for a walk to stretch my legs and left the federal building. That's usually a sign Forte interprets as my being up to no good. There is little doubt that either he or one of the women is keeping tabs on me. They can always pull my phone records to confirm whether I'm making a call, but it'd only make sense if I gave them a reason to think I did. Thus, my trusty Bluetooth earpiece.

I had already set the phone on the elevator to dial the number. When I reach the lobby, I press "send." Five seconds later, Wesley answers from the Watchtower operations center.

"You owe me big for this, Hollinger," he whispers into the phone.

I smile as I cross the street and stroll past Thomas Paine Park on my right.

"Do I? How's your kid sister doing? No more problems with her verbally abusive boyfriend, I hope."

Wesley sighs after getting the point. "Fine, this makes us even then."

"Does it? That'll depend on if you found what I'm looking for."

"What the hell, man? Do you think I work at the Geek Squad or something?"

I stifle a laugh. "I think you're insulting everyone who does work there."

"Whatever," Wesley screeches. "You were right. Brody's still checking his social media. Based on the IP address, he's in Manhattan. You'd think he'd know how to use a VPN."

A virtual private network is a cheap means to guarantee online privacy and anonymity by using software to create a private network from a public internet connection. VPNs mask internet protocol addresses, making online actions virtually untraceable. As nefarious as that sounds, it's a useful privacy tool for users who connect to the internet from public places such as coffee shops and hotels.

"Just because the kid is smart enough to get into law school doesn't mean he's tech savvy. Can you get him a message?"

"I'm assuming you don't mean DM."

"Yes, by all means, let's send him a direct message so that a disgruntled tech company activist can release to TMZ that Public Enemy Number One is having a chummy conversation with the FBI."

"Yeah, yeah, I get your point, Boston. Getting him a message any other way will be a challenge. I'd have to create a back door if there isn't one on his computer. He won't click on links in an email to release spyware, so I have no way to remote into his system."

"He has mIRC chat. Can you use that?"

Internet relay chat is used by individuals and organizations to communicate and collaborate with each other on IRC networks. The mIRC client has served the Internet community for more than two decades and is a reliable piece of technology.

"Sure, if he has it open."

"He will. It's how he's keeping in touch with his roommate."

"How do you know that he is?"

I smile again as I stare at the federal building from the park's east side. "Gut feeling."

"All right. Assuming I can reach Brody, what do you want me to say?"

I think about that for a few seconds, not having fully fleshed that out in my head. I thought it would be more of an argument to get Wesley to help me. I didn't plan out the message.

"Give him my Dufresne alias. Explain that I'm with the FBI and think he's innocent. Tell him I want to meet. He can pick the time and place."

"That's it?" Wesley asks.

"Yeah, that should be enough."

I can almost hear Wesley thinking of ways to punch holes in this plan. I understand it's a long shot, but it's worth a try. There's no way I'm getting through the phalanx of lawyers his father assembled, so I might as well try to flank them.

"What if he presses me for more information?"

"Tell him 'take it or leave it.'"

"All right. You realize I'll be working an outpost in Mongolia if I get caught doing this for you. Remsen's ruthless."

"A fifth grader could do this without getting caught. You're at least that good, aren't you?"

"Duh."

I'm tempted to continue goading Wesley by using his nickname, but I let it go. So far as handles go, there are a ton worse than "Crusher." He hates it, though, and I don't want to antagonize him more than I have.

"I'll let you know when I reach Brody," he says, and ends the call.

I continue my walk around the park. It feels good to stretch my legs as I nonchalantly brush the Bluetooth earpiece out of my ear and into my pocket. What Zach doesn't know won't hurt me.

CHAPTER FORTY

JOHN PROCK

AMLOG CORPORATE OFFICE
HUNTS POINT, BRONX, NEW YORK

It's amazing how quickly life can change. Fortunes can be made and lost in the blink of an eye, and a serene life well-lived can turn into an unimaginable hellscape in the length of a sentence. John has two thriving businesses, one legal and aboveboard and the other operating in the shadows. Money is pouring in from both of them. He sits on the throne of an empire in the making.

Then an accusation is made. It has nothing to do with him or AMLOG except in the minds of those poisoned by the insinuation. There is no presumption of innocence with the American public. Judgment is immediate, fostered by narratives conjured by pundits who relish telling others how to think. John is guilty by association at best or the father of a monster at worst. He will be made to suffer for the alleged sins of his son.

John's employees are loyal, but they're also frustrated. People whose opinions he values vehemently disagree with him not making a public statement. Brianna and Malcolm are among the most vocal. It's understandable. They're on the front lines of this media war and resent the company being dragged into it.

Emily is more forgiving but is under considerable pressure to plug leaks in the dam. Clients, customers, and vendors are voicing their discontent and threatening to pull their business. Corporations used to have a backbone but have succumbed to the modern tactic of activists applying social media pressure to humiliate them into compliance. Sometimes the ploy fails. Other times, it doesn't. Either way, John is learning that cancel culture is a real thing.

"Who wants to go first?" John says, sitting at the head of the conference table.

"I thought we were rounding the corner," Brianna opens. "The media was moving on. Then Chloe McCarthy gave her interviews and renewed the outrage. The timing sucked, but we could have survived that onslaught except…."

"Except she was attacked up at school," John finishes. "Are the media blaming us for that, too?"

"Indirectly," Malcolm says. "Most people know you weren't there."

"Most?"

"You would be shocked to learn how many people believe in conspiracies. A lack of information combined with an illogical event causes people to fill those voids with whatever their imagination can create."

"So, now I'm the shooter on the grassy knoll? The attack was a couple of thugs from some gang!"

"It was MS-13, according to media reports," Brianna adds with all the enthusiasm of someone explaining a computer issue to tech support for the twentieth time.

"What more information do people need? Do they think I routinely hang out with violent thugs?"

"It's not that simple, John," Malcolm interjects. "They think the extensive media coverage inspired the attack—"

"And the coverage wouldn't be necessary had your son not raped one of his peers," Brianna interrupts.

"My son didn't *rape* anybody," John says through clenched teeth.

"Only the public doesn't believe that. They haven't heard Brody's side of the story. You haven't made a statement that—"

"What difference would it make?" John asks, slapping his hand down on the table.

He's tired of playing defense with his own people. As chief executive, he made the call to remain silent in the face of enormous media pressure. They need to get on board with that decision, even if they don't agree with it.

"Other than giving the media machine their sought-after sound bite, what difference would a statement make? Whose mind are my words going to change? You and Malcolm are the experts, Brianna. So, tell me, if the crazies believe I was present for an attack without any proof, what can I say to convince them otherwise?"

The room is bathed in a silence reserved for monasteries and outer space. Executives gathered around the table shift their eyes away from John, unwilling to argue that point. Everyone except Brianna, that is. She is always willing to argue her point until he sees things her way.

"You aren't trying to convince those people," Brianna says. "You can't fix stupid, but you can appeal to those expecting you to defend your son. Your silence is only confirming reasonable suspicions that you're hiding something."

"Except my protests would be construed as defending evil. I am in a no-win situation. Emily, what are the clients saying?"

She sighs and scans a paper in front of her. "We've lost a couple of companies who took a wait-and-see approach. This second round of negative publicity compelled them to sever ties."

"And the others who are on the fence?"

"I'm not optimistic. We may retain a few of them, but we should also expect reduced business contracts. They will siphon off work to our competitors wherever possible, even if it isn't the entirety of their logistics need."

"What does that do to our portfolio?"

Emily refers to another report. "The current losses, plus the new and likely ones, will be a thirty-one percent loss in our client base. That translates into an approximate forty-one percent reduction in AMLOG's revenue."

"Can we get them back?" John asks quietly. Those numbers are sobering.

"If they sign contracts with our competitors, they're gone. Considering the negative press, no new clients are in the funnel to replace them."

"What if we cut our rates? We'll take a hit on the margin, but we can keep them in the fold."

"You're missing the point, John," Brianna says. "This isn't a cost issue for them — it's a perception issue. Sure, cutting rates will save them money, but then they'll need to publicly justify profit over moral responsibility to the legion of activists out there."

"That's what companies exist for. Morality in the business world is relative."

"Tell that to their customer base. People want to believe the nameless, faceless companies they do business with share their values. Corporations enjoy the benefits when they do."

John leans back and rubs his chin. The world is insane. He isn't hearing anything he doesn't already know, but it doesn't help his present situation. Anybody looking for any corporation to be the exemplar of moral behavior is setting themselves up for disappointment. It's only a matter of time before the veil of carefully curated lies gets lifted, and a company is exposed for what it really is: A money-grubbing whore obsessed with profits at any cost.

"Is there anything that makes this go away?"

Brianna looks over at Malcolm and hangs her head. When she looks at John, it's with a modicum of regret.

"Throw your son to the wolves. Tell the world he's guilty and disavow him."

The surge of anger overcomes John and is about to set him off. Instead, he grabs the end of the table and takes a deep breath. He asked their opinion. There's no point in crucifying them for offering it, regardless of how insane it is.

"My son is innocent. You know that I won't do that."

"Then, no, nothing will make this go away."

"Thank you, everyone."

There is no small talk or additional encouragement before the leadership team leaves him alone in the conference room. Even the playful Emily doesn't look at him before she departs.

John has a choice to make. For most people, he imagines it would be an easy one. Not for him. AMLOG is as much his child as Brody is. Now he needs to decide which is more important.

CHAPTER FORTY-ONE
JAMIESON BOHMER

Jamieson pulls into the semicircular drive and parks his car near the front door. He doesn't plan on staying long. The house is quiet, and the light in the study is on, per usual. That's where he will find Tomasso, who is undoubtedly sulking over something.

Chaz Sabia greets the lawyer when he enters the foyer and closes the door behind him. The beefy guard is well-dressed, appearing closer to a roided-up butler than hired security. He's capable but not overly impressive. Jamieson would consider him too young and inexperienced to be counted on. That's why he's working as a guard for a New Jersey developer instead of training to become a Ranger or Navy SEAL.

"Sitrep," Jamieson commands.

He may no longer be in the SAS, but the experience of being a soldier hasn't left him. The word has little meaning in the civilian world, but "sitrep" in military parlance is short for "situation report." It would be just as easy to ask the young stud what's happening.

"Everything's quiet."

"And Ashlee?"

"In her room watching television."

Jamieson takes a deep breath as his eyes track up the grand staircase to the bedrooms above. She is being uncharacteristically compliant. He wonders what she's up to.

"Tomasso wants to see you in the study."

Jamieson nods. That almost goes without needing to be said. His footsteps echo as he crosses the foyer and knocks twice on the door before entering. Tomasso is glued to the television on the wall. The lawyer recognizes where the local reporter is standing before he hears him discussing Art Burill's tragic death.

"You've been busy."

Tomasso mutes the television, prompting Jamieson to launch into a detailed explanation of his trip to the American Dream Mall. Tomasso's face softens when he reaches the part of the explanation that includes the late Art Burrill's thinly veiled threat. When Jamieson gets to the part where the man's drink is laced with aconitine, the developer looks impressed. He can't be sure whether it's because of the methods or the forward-thinking he exhibited.

"Why didn't you tell me?" Tomasso demands when Jamieson finishes the tale.

"It's not something to discuss over an unsecured cell phone connection."

He nods. "Where have you been since?"

"I had a pleasant conversation with Lucas Noland."

"Maybe a pleasant one for you, but I doubt he would say the same."

"True," Jamieson agrees before describing that encounter and the resulting confirmation of the information he discovered about the young man.

"That's interesting. Very interesting."

"I don't understand what the big deal is."

Tomasso eyes the man. "A son is a reflection of his father. Every man who raises a boy understands that. You aren't a father, so you couldn't possibly understand. I assume Lucas is on board, given our discovery?"

"Enthusiastically. He won't be a problem for us."

"Good. What about your other assignment?"

Jamieson slides his hand into his suit jacket and pulls out a slip of paper. He hands it to Tomasso, who eyes it before returning his gaze to Jamieson.

"You're nothing if not efficient. How certain are you that this is his whereabouts?"

"I trust my source."

Jamieson may not know jack about parenthood, but he knows how to run an operation. The investigators he works with may not be elite, but they know how to do the job. From what he's seen, Dusty is the best of them. When he hands over information, you can take its accuracy to the bank.

"Do the police or FBI know where he is?" Tomasso asks.

"I don't know, but I doubt they care. If Brody is indicted, he'll be expected to turn himself in. John Prock won't risk himself or his business by abetting his son's attempt to evade justice."

The developer returns the slip of paper to Jamieson, who tucks it into his pocket. "Can you use that leverage on Brody Prock?"

"You're the father. You tell me."

Tomasso offers a look of disapproval before turning to gaze out the window. Brody likely shares a secret with Lucas. It's equally likely his father has no idea about his son's activities. If his learning would cause upheaval in their relationship, he could be convinced to do anything to prevent it. That's how sons interact with their rich parents.

"Convince Brody Prock to admit to the rape. You have a penchant for being very persuasive. Do it quickly because we need to replace Art Burill and can't do that with this investigation hanging over our heads. This needs to end now. I'm counting on you to end it."

Jamieson nods and leaves his boss alone in the study. He has work to do. This has to be handled just right. There is a fair chance that Lucas didn't heed his warning about alerting his roommate. That would be a shame. He's a good kid. He'll learn if Brody knows he's coming when he gets to him.

CHAPTER FORTY-TWO
"BOSTON" HOLLINGER

CHURCH OF SAINT MARY THE VIRGIN
NEW YORK, NEW YORK

It was unnecessary to park the Suburban four blocks away. It's a federal vehicle, and even if an officer in the NYPD was bold enough to issue it a parking ticket, neither Emma nor I am responsible for paying it. The truth is, I wanted to walk and clear my head. Exercise is the only real relief from the constant barrage of memories.

"Are you afraid of driving in Times Square or something?" Emma asks, keeping stride with me west down 46th Street after we turn off 6th Avenue.

"A little. I didn't want to pull up to the church with it."

"Speaking of which, do you know why he picked this place?"

"No."

"You think it's close to his hotel?"

It would make sense. There are countless hotels in the Midtown area within walking distance. Of course, it would be logical that he wouldn't want to meet anywhere near where he was staying. That would allow him to hit the subway and make several transfers to ensure he isn't being followed. That might be more tradecraft than something a young law student would do. Then again, everyone watches movies.

"Since we don't plan on following him, does it matter?"

"Just making conversation to keep warm."

Emma and I stop in front of the towering gray edifice. The Church of Saint Mary the Virgin was founded in 1868 to serve the residential neighborhood in Midtown, once known as Longacre Square. It's much smaller than St. Patrick's Cathedral but still features a rose window and heavy oak double doors.

"I thought the church would be closed to visitors by now."

I point to the sign that changes their hours in December and smile.

"Showoff. I know you don't want to hear this, but we could be walking into a trap."

"Why do you think I brought you along?"

"My rocking body and awesome personality?"

I smile. "Nah, those are just bonuses. I don't think Brody Prock plans to ambush a pair of federal agents. He's a scared kid running from something more than a rape allegation."

"Like what?"

"That's what I'm here to find out," I say, swinging the door open.

This church is beautiful. Lines of white candles flicker, and the light bounces off columns and gothic arches. There are breathtaking wood carvings, murals, and artwork everywhere. A huge white altar sits at the far end, adorned with flowers and poinsettias as Christians begin to celebrate the coming birth of their Savior.

Emma peels off and stays toward the exterior wall as I walk up the center aisle after spotting a single figure in the pews. I stop at the one Brody is seated in and slide in. He doesn't even look at me. Not so much as a glance.

"Your partner isn't going to join us?" he says, still staring at the altar.

"She thinks you're here to try to kill us."

He snickers. "I thought you were here to arrest me."

"I wouldn't have needed to send you a note to do that. I would have gotten a warrant and shown up with thirty agents armed with assault weapons."

"That's a little unnecessary, don't you think?"

"Very unnecessary. Go big or go home. I'm Special Agent Dufresne."

"You work out of New York?"

"D.C."

Brody doesn't respond. He's a smart guy, so he's probably working through why an agent from the nation's capital is working a case originating in rural Connecticut when there are five field offices capable of handling it. I'd be curious, too.

"Your note said that you know I'm innocent. How?"

I shake my head. "It doesn't matter."

"It matters to me."

The memory sweeps in with the force of a tsunami. It's more graphic and emotional than I was expecting. It's also something I didn't want to experience sitting in a church. I know everything about Brody Prock I need to. As much as experiencing memories is a curse, it does simplify things.

"I know it does. Your secret is safe with me."

The comment rattles him. He shifts his gaze down to his trembling hands before clasping them and looking at me for the first time.

"How did you find out?"

"Nobody ratted you out if that's what you're worried about. There were inconsistencies in Ashlee's story. I was able to piece some things together."

"There's no way you uncovered that by chance."

"You'd be surprised, and I didn't know for sure until you confirmed it just now."

"So, you have the truth. Does that mean I'm in the clear?"

"It's not that simple, unfortunately. The investigation needs to run its course. If you want this over faster, you need to—"

"I'm not doing that...I can't."

I decide not to press him. That's his choice. "Okay."

"If you're not ending the investigation and already know the truth, why did you want to meet me?"

"Confirmation. And to let you know that not everyone is against you. That the truth about the allegation will come out."

"I need that to be the only truth."

Now it's my turn to face straight ahead and admire the beauty of the altar. I don't like making guarantees. In this line of work, they often end up empty and unfulfilled. Someone is likely to uncover Brody's secret. The end result is the same whether it's an agent or a journalist.

"I can't promise that."

He gives a couple of knowing nods. "Then I've already lost everything."

The kid stands and starts to make his way out of the pew to the side aisle.

"Brody?" I pull a card out of my jacket and hand it to him. "Just in case you need me or want to talk."

He studies the card, and his face betrays his confusion. I would be confused, too. All that's on it is a phone number and the FBI seal.

"No name?"

"Everyone I hand that card to already knows who I am," I say, repeating the same line I used with Chloe. It seems to be acceptable.

He nods and shuffles out of the pew and up the side aisle. I hear the door and then spot Emma coming down the center aisle. She slides in next to me.

"That was a quick conversation."

"It didn't need to be long," I admit, staring at the altar to uncover what Brody found so interesting.

"What did you learn?"

"Let's go back to the office. I'll tell you all at the same time."

We slide out of the pew, and I say a quick prayer before turning and walking up the aisle. I don't consider myself religious, but I could use some divine guidance for this case. Having the Big Guy in my corner wouldn't hurt.

"You know that Remsen is going to be pissed if Zach tells him about this meeting," Emma concludes.

"Yeah. Why break tradition?" I say with a smile, knowing I won't have one a couple of hours from now.

CHAPTER FORTY-THREE

ASHLEE TRILLO

TOMASSO TRILLO FAMILY ESTATE
ENGLEWOOD CLIFFS, NEW JERSEY

There isn't much to see in the inky darkness. Ambient lighting from nearby houses does little to penetrate the black shroud covering the backyard. Ashlee can't see the patio at this angle but doesn't need to. The exterior lighting her father installed is activated by motion sensors. She can tell where his security guard is just by watching the lights activate around the house.

She has sat and watched the patio light click on and off three times in the past two hours without convincing her body to move. Anxiety is the natural stress response and affects everyone in different ways. Her fear and apprehension about what's to come never subside and often intensify during stressful situations. Everyone feels this to a degree, but Ashlee was diagnosed with an anxiety disorder because of the strength of those emotions.

Her fears are debilitating and omnipresent. She has worked hard to overcome her anxiety since high school, but it still stops her from enjoying life. Doctors indicated it was post-traumatic stress disorder from losing her mother at an early age. She knows better. That was a traumatic event, but her father's treatment since that fateful day is responsible for the PTSD.

Ashlee glances at her coat lying on the bed. She didn't bother packing a bag this time. A clunky backpack or duffle will only slow her down her escape and require her to lug it wherever she goes. Instead, she filled her jacket pockets and purse with the essentials, including the burner phone.

The patio light is activated, and she can see a shadow moving. That's her cue. Chaz is out for another cigarette. They'll kill him if his father doesn't do it first when he finds her missing.

"Okay. Now or never, Ash," she whispers for the third time.

Instead of remaining motionless and watching from the window, Ashlee slips into her coat and opens the bedroom door. The house is still. Her father is at a late dinner meeting, and Jamieson is nowhere to be found. She can do this. She just needs to slip past Chaz successfully this time.

Ashlee glides down the stairs and opens the front door. She peeks out, crosses the threshold, and closes it behind her. The entry light is on, so she hurries onto the driveway and breaks into a jog. The motion-activated spotlights illuminate her. They often get triggered by small animals, passing cars, and blowing leaves. It won't raise any immediate red flags.

So far, so good.

Ashlee speeds up a little as she turns onto the road. There are no oncoming headlights. She glances behind her…once, twice, and a third time. The doubt begins creeping back in. It's not too late to change her mind. She could go back. If she gets caught….

The anxiety begins to overwhelm her, forcing her to run faster. Her arms pump as her sneakers hit the worn, cracked asphalt. She makes a left turn down a side street and then a right. She stays off the roads her father will drive to return home.

She kicks her heels up and pushes harder, now in a dead sprint. Her lungs are burning as she tries to provide oxygen to her muscles. She should have gone to the gym with Chloe more often.

She turns south and crosses Palisade Avenue before she knows it. She can't use this street because her father often takes it. He might not notice her coat in the darkness, but why take the risk? Instead, she goes a block south and heads east on Dillingham Place. Exhausted and with legs that are screaming, Ashlee slows to a walk and catches her breath.

The suburban road is lined with nice two-story homes and has no sidewalk. A flashlight bobs up and down ahead, almost causing Ashlee to stop in her tracks.

"Act natural. You're not escaping prison. Not a *real* prison," she whispers to herself.

She waves at a woman walking her dog, and the lady politely returns the gesture as they pass. Two ships in the night. She sees Route 9W and cuts through a gas station on the corner. It's open but has no customers and an inattentive clerk working the counter.

The bus station is just across the street. Ashlee needs to time this just right. She talked the housekeeper into giving her a bus schedule. It should be coming any minute now.

Ninety seconds later, the distinctive silhouette of the bus appears under the streetlights to the south. Ashlee bursts ahead, breaking into another sprint before crossing the street. She catches the bus just as it's beginning to stop. The door opens, and she swings onto it.

She pays the fare and finds a seat on the otherwise empty bus. Self-doubt begins to creep into her thoughts again. Ashlee can't believe she went through with it. The thought of being on her own in the world is terrifying, but it's happening. She can do this. She has to.

Ashlee rests her head back, knowing she's safe from her father and Jamieson. It's a feeling that will be short-lived come morning. All hell will break loose when her father realizes that his daughter broke his first cardinal rule: She disobeyed him.

CHAPTER FORTY-FOUR
SSA ZACH FORTE

JACOB K. JAVITS FEDERAL BUILDING
NEW YORK, NEW YORK

The building isn't completely empty, but it is desolate enough that Zach doubts Emma and Boston will run into a single person on the way up to the floor they're squatting on. After Emma called and told them they were inbound following the unsanctioned meeting with Brody Prock, he made coffee and joined Nadiya waiting in the conference room.

"You're going to drive me to drink, Boston," Zach complains as the pair enters and sits on the opposite side of the table.

"Isn't that how you ended up at Watchtower?" Boston asks, cocking his head.

Zach frowns, wishing he hadn't told him that story. Matt enlisted Zach's help while the senior counterintelligence agent was drowning his sorrows in a run-down D.C. bar. He was as good as out of the FBI, so there was no reason not to take Matt up on his offer to investigate a congressional staffer. He never could have known that it would lead to this.

"How did you get the guys at Watchtower to send Brody Prock a message without Matt finding out?" Zach asks, ignoring the question.

"You'd be surprised how many favors I do for people."

"You monetized your gift?"

"No, that would be ridiculous. I trade my talents for the occasional favor."

Zach leans back. He wouldn't be so annoyed if Boston weren't so smug. He kicks himself for not realizing that anyone with that gift would create a black market information clearinghouse. At least he isn't engaged in insider trading…yet.

"Is that how you got roped into this?" Forte asks Emma.

"Nope. I volunteered."

He looks at Nadiya, who shrugs. "I would have gone if she didn't."

"At least you brought support with you this time. I assume you talked to Brody. What did he have to say?"

"Not much. The Procks have a familial distrust of the FBI."

"I work for the Bureau and don't trust them. What else?"

"Brody was surprised that we know as much as we do."

"Yeah, I wouldn't expect him to think we have someone who can replay memories like he's at the movies. How much did you tell him?"

"Very little."

Forte waits for more and doesn't get any additional information. He sips his coffee and leans forward, planting his elbows on the table.

"Did his memories confirm the memories you got from Ashlee Trillo?"

"Not directly. Brody has no memory of what happened after the pair went into the bedroom."

"Which means he was unconscious," Emma concludes.

"Or felt no guilt over it," Nadiya argues.

"Who wouldn't feel at least some guilt over raping a woman?" Zach mumbles.

"A psychopath, as I'm starting to learn."

Zach stops sipping his coffee and stares at Boston. "All right. So, Brody's a psychopath?"

"No," Boston says, shaking his head. "In fact, he's very sensitive."

Nadiya scoffs. "Even if he didn't rape Ashlee, he's still a playboy who's been breaking hearts since high school and leaving a long train of emotional baggage in the process. He can't be that sensitive."

"Yeah, I thought the same until I sat next to him in that church."

A full fifteen seconds of silence pass before Forte loses his patience. "And?"

"Did you know that 'macho' is derived from the Spanish term for 'male animal?' We use it to mean someone who is hyper-masculine or virile."

"I didn't realize you were moonlighting as an anthropologist," Forte moans.

"We also use it derisively to describe someone trying to act that way," Boston continues, ignoring his boss's interruption. "When a guy buys an expensive sportscar, he's compensating for other inadequacies. Men with round or young faces are more likely to have assertive and hostile personalities than their more chiseled peers. Males are pressured by societal norms to be a certain way, and they manipulate or manufacture their image when their masculinity is under threat."

"I need to start monitoring your sessions with Asami," Forte moans.

"While I don't disagree with any of that," Nadiya interjects, "how does it apply here?"

Boston takes turns looking at the three people sharing the room. Forte braces himself against the back of his chair. He knows that look. The last time he saw it, the bombshell sent Nadiya fleeing from the building. This is going to be another one.

"Brody *wanted* to be seen with women. He *wanted* rumors about his conquests circulating because it's the easiest way to keep up the charade."

"What charade?" Emma asks.

"Brock's philandering is misdirection. When you don't want to come out of the closet, the easiest way to avoid suspicion is by convincing everyone that you aren't in it in the first place."

"Wait…closet…what?" Nadiya asks, perplexed.

"Are you saying…?" Emma asks, her voice trailing off.

"Yeah, that's what I'm saying. He isn't the womanizing man whore the world thinks he is. Brody Prock is gay."

CHAPTER FORTY-FIVE

JAMIESON BOHMER

ASTOR PLACE SUBWAY STATION
NEW YORK, NEW YORK

The Astor Place station became part of the city's first subway line when it was constructed in 1904 for the Interborough Rapid Transit Company. The station's platforms were lengthened in the late 1950s, and the station underwent a renovation in the mid-1980s. Jamieson steps off the six train onto the southbound platform. He took the Lexington Avenue Line downtown from Grand Central after arriving with the early Metro-North commuters from the Scarsdale station.

Jamieson has a love-hate relationship with mass transit. On the one hand, he likes the anonymity it provides. Whether riding a train or bus or strolling through a terminal or station, he's just another face in the crowd. That leads to the hate part.

He has never liked people. One-on-one and small group interactions are tolerable, but crowds give him agita. People are dangerous because they're unpredictable in an emergency. They panic at the first indication of danger, and panicked people in large numbers lead to chaos that feeds the fear. Jamieson habitually avoids crowds, which is likely why Art Burrill forced him into an arena full of fans at a Devils game.

At least the subway platform at rush hour is more bearable than Grand Central. Only a handful of people exit the train with him after it screeches to a stop and the doors open. The rest, many dressed professionally, remain seated on their way to the financial district to spend the day ripping hard-working people off.

The lawyer emerges from the covered access in the triangular sliver of land between Lafayette Street and Fourth Avenue. He looks around to get his bearings. The grid layout for most of Manhattan makes this borough of New York City easy to navigate. Jamieson turns and faces east and is mentally calculating the most efficient route when his phone vibrates.

"Yeah?"

"Where are you?" Tomasso asks in a tone best described as urgent.

"Manhattan."

"Why are you there?" he demands.

Jamieson pulls the phone away from his ear and stares at the screen to ensure he's talking to his boss and not a complete imbecile.

"I'm paying our friend a visit like we discussed."

"Never mind that. We have a problem. Do you know where Ashlee is?"

Alarm klaxons sound in his head. Now he understands the urgency.

"She should be in her bedroom."

"She isn't. She's not in the house at all. She must have left during the night."

Jamieson curses under his breath. Chaz is a moron incapable of even the simplest tasks. The house has an alarm and enough high-definition and infrared cameras to act as the set of CBS's *Big Brother*. There is no way she should have been able to make it to the grass, let alone slip off the property.

"Why didn't the alarm sound?"

"The guard disarmed it when he stepped outside for a smoke."

"Unbelievable. What time was that?"

"We're not sure. Apparently, he had a night full of cigarette breaks."

"Did you fire him?"

"I was too angry to even look at him. I will let you take care of that when you return."

Leaving the comfort of her father's estate is a bold move for Ashlee. She might hate her life there, but it's all she has. Without resources or close friends to lean on, she'll discover how unforgiving the streets can be.

"She won't make it far. I'll get my people on it. We'll find her."

"See that you do."

The line goes dead. Jamieson checks to confirm that it's disconnected and pockets his phone.

"You're welcome," he mutters.

Brody Prock will have to wait. He has good people who can help him find Tomasso's wayward daughter, but they need notice and time for planning. Time is the one thing he doesn't have. Ashlee won't have much cash, but buses out of the city aren't ridiculously expensive. He doesn't want to waste time tracking her across the country.

He is counting on her being too frightened to leave her comfort zone. New York City may be a big, scary place, but it's familiar. The rest of the world isn't. She won't rush to leave what she knows, and that gives him time to find her before she musters the courage.

CHAPTER FORTY-SIX

JOHN PROCK

AMLOG CORPORATE OFFICE
HUNTS POINT, BRONX, NEW YORK

Hunts Point doesn't come to mind when people think of New York City. This section of the Bronx is far removed from the perception of the city in every possible way. Instead of gleaming skyscrapers, the area is filled with dilapidated commercial buildings. There is nothing romantic or sexy about this area, but it's his second home.

John pulls his Mercedes into the parking area beyond the gate. He doesn't bother locking it. It is safe enough in this lot, and his employees wouldn't breathe on the car, much less steal it.

The facility is still winding down from the overnight shipping work, and the day shift has yet to arrive. The corporate office is still dark and still, except for the one area near his office. The motion-sensing lighting has been activated there, and John finds Lothar sitting on his assistant's desk outside his door.

"Lothar, you're one of the hardest-working men I know. In all that time, you've only beaten me to the office a handful of times, and it was never with good news."

"That streak isn't going to be broken today."

"Yeah, I was afraid you'd say that. Come on in."

The two men enter the office, and Lothar closes the door behind him. The CEO obviously has the largest space in the building, but it feels exceedingly small compared to his workspace in Scarsdale. It also has a different feel. Instead of the ultra-modern décor, this office has a more utilitarian, industrial vibe.

"What's the word? Do we have an operational problem?"

"No, this is more of a personal nature. It's about your son."

John grimaces as he stands behind his desk, checks the handwritten notes his admin left, and starts to log in to his computer. "What has Hugh Hefner done this time?"

"He met a woman and a man in the city last night."

"A threesome. That's kinky."

"The man and woman in question have gold-plated resumes."

John freezes in place. For a moment, he isn't sure he heard that correctly. He shifts his gaze and settles on Lothar's impassive face. The time for worrying about his office being bugged is over.

"What? Why is my son talking to the feds?"

"I don't know."

"Did he set up the meeting, or did they?"

"I'm afraid I don't know that, either. I only know the meeting happened. It was a short one, if that makes a difference."

"It doesn't."

After Brody was bailed out, it was clear that the media circus would follow him. That's reason enough to stash him in an Internet rental in Manhattan, but it also means the authorities won't need to visit. John has an army of lawyers that can run interference and protect their interests. It's their job to keep his son out of jail. It's John's responsibility to keep the feds out of his business.

"Lothar, how much does Brody know about our operations?"

"You raised him, sir. I'm sure he knows a lot about AMLOG."

"You know that's not what I'm talking about," John says, using a grave tone.

"Brody is a smart young man. I'm sure that he's figured out that one plus one does not equal three. Your lifestyle is not completely aligned with your income. He could know about Jackpot, at least conceptually, but I doubt he knows any specifics."

"Jackpot" is not an official business name. His side business doesn't have one. It's what Lothar uses to describe the operation, and John is warming to the moniker.

"But the feds could turn him into a source. That's why you're here."

Lothar clasps his hands behind his back. "The thought crossed my mind, yes."

"Brody wouldn't do that."

"John, you entrusted me to safeguard the operation. If it meant staying out of prison for rape, can you be sure he wouldn't talk? What I'm about to say comes with the utmost respect: You and your son don't have the best relationship."

The CEO slides papers around his desk. It's something to do with his hands as he thinks about how to reply. Lothar's conclusion is objectively true, but there is much more to it. He used to be close to his son. That ended a long time ago.

"I've been tough on him, but I'm still his father."

"Most sons have demanding fathers."

"And I love him."

Lothar lowers his head. "As most fathers love their sons. Yet, you've never trusted him enough to share all aspects of the family business. 'Father' is more than a biological title – it's a role someone fills when raising a child. One that you have abdicated since your wife's…accident."

John's glare could burn a hole through his long-time confidant. He's about to lash out when he stops to study the man's face. There is regret in his eyes…and even some fear. There is no ill intent behind the words. Lothar was relaying something that needed to be said.

"Will you know if Brody meets with the feds again?" John asks, turning to look out the window.

"Of course."

John doesn't want to know how Lothar could find out. He's uncomfortable having his son followed and watched, even for his benefit.

"Let me know if he does. This time I want to know what he tells them."

CHAPTER FORTY-SEVEN
"BOSTON" HOLLINGER

GRAND CENTRAL TERMINAL
NEW YORK, NEW YORK

Brody's instructions were to meet at the clock, but I can't be that cliché. It is the perfect meeting spot in a busy train station for tourists, which I'm not. I decide to wait on the north side of the main concourse at one of the portals leading to the platforms. With a clock in front of me, I don't need to check to see that he's ten minutes late.

"I miss the days of the old flip boards," I say when I sense a presence slide up next to me. "They had a certain Old World charm that these new LED screens can't replicate."

"I'm too young to remember them," Brody says, joining me in staring at the three massive displays over the ticketing area.

"Technically, so am I. Why do you want to see me?"

"You alone?"

"Yeah. My colleague has siderodromophobia. It's a fear of trains," I say, anticipating his next question.

Brody rewards the comment with a quizzical look but doesn't probe further. "Good. Follow me."

We move through the concourse to the S train. The Shuttle is the shortest line in New York City, dedicated to ferrying tourists and commuters to and from Times Square. When we arrive at the other end, Brody gets his bearings and walks west toward the river before turning north on 8th Avenue.

"Was there a point meeting me at Grand Central just to come here?"

"I wanted to make sure we weren't followed."

I don't have the heart to tell him we are being followed. Emma has been shadowing us since we left the terminal and was in the same subway car. He still hasn't spotted her. That rules out a future career in countersurveillance.

Brody steers us into a small restaurant that caters to tourists and the Broadway show crowd. It's chock full of old European artifacts and vintage decor. It's also mostly empty. He gives the hostess his name, and she checks her system for a reservation before seating us in the far corner.

"Is there anything you need to tell me?" Brody asks.

"You called me, remember?"

"I did. I need to know when this investigation is going to end. For real."

"I already told you in the church. It will be measured in months, not hours."

He leans back in his chair. "That's not going to be good enough. It needs to end now."

"Why?"

"A lot of reasons."

I'm staring at Lucas sitting on the sofa across from me. I'm upset but not angry. From the look on his face, so is Lucas.

"Are you ever going to?"

"The moment I tell my family, my relationship ends with them," he says in a near-whisper. "They won't have a son. I won't have a family."

"Is it worth it? Sacrificing yourself to keep a secret from others?"

"Nobody said life was fair, Brody. I live a privileged life because of my parents. Maybe someday I'll be willing to sacrifice that, but it can't be right now. It doesn't matter how much I care for you."

"One big one. Lucas hasn't said anything to the FBI about your relationship if that's what you're worried about."

"How…what? How do you know it's him?" Brody asks, wide-eyed.

"It was a safe bet. Just because people think FBI agents are idiots doesn't mean we are. You know, Brody, I'm no lawyer, but you can take a big step in making this whole thing go away by—"

"Coming out?" He shakes his head. "Being a homosexual isn't a defense for rape. People can conjure up a thousand reasons why a gay guy would rape a woman. It's not worth…I can't."

"You're right. People will do anything to validate their opinions. That doesn't explain why you're hiding who you are."

"Are you gay, Agent Dufresne?"

"No, I'm as hetero as you get," I answer honestly.

"Then you won't understand," Brody says, lowering his eyes.

"No, I won't. Not completely, anyway."

"I've known I was gay since middle school. I didn't find girls pretty or have any attraction to them. I thought something was wrong with me until I realized why. Then I accepted it, knowing my father and friends wouldn't. I didn't want to deal with the stigma behind it.

"Then I went to college. I saw the mistreatment of the LGBTQ community, even at a progressive school like NYU. The distasteful jokes, verbal insults, unequal treatment…sometimes I even saw physical violence. I didn't want to be a part of that."

Our meals come, and we put the conversation on hold. The timing is perfect. Brody could use an emotional break. We talk about school, sports teams, and life in general. He's a smart kid, and he knows something about everything. It makes conversations with him easy.

"Brody, ridicule isn't why you're afraid of coming out, is it?" I ask, transitioning back to the subject as our Reubens disappear off our plates. "It's because of your father.

Before you answer, remember it's not the 1950s anymore. It's not even the 2010s. Society has changed. He might be more understanding than you think."

"He won't be. Trust me. My father is paying for Salisbury. If I come out, it ends like that," Brody says, snapping his fingers. "I've read the pamphlets that LGBT groups put out. They say 'acceptance is a process' and 'it takes time.' Whoever wrote that doesn't know my father. I may accept my sexuality, but he never will. Never."

"That's why you've gone to such lengths to hide it. All the dates with women…."

Brody nods. "Everything with my father is about perception. His business, our house, his friends…he cultivates the image he wants people to see. He needs to, so I do the same."

"Because your father is a major drug dealer."

I'm playing with fire. There is no way the FBI could know that. The problem with invading people's memories without their knowledge is I need plausible cover stories to explain how I know. Fortunately, I'm quick on my feet, and my Watchtower instructors have trained me on how investigations work.

"How do you know that? No…wait. It must be another guess."

"Your father's lifestyle doesn't match his salary as CEO and founder of American Logistics. The difference could be passed off as shrewd investing, but his tax returns don't indicate that. He has a side hustle, and given he works in the transportation industry, drugs made sense."

"So, you *are* investigating him. That's why you saw his tax records."

I shake my head. "I requested them after you called because I think you came here to horse trade. I wanted to know what you had to offer. You said in the church that you had already lost everything, so I figured you wouldn't come out and take Lucas down with you. But if your father goes down for selling…meth?"

"Fentanyl."

I nod. "Then you are free from him…you can finish your studies or do what you want and be with who you want."

"It's not *that* easy, but yeah."

"Because Lucas isn't ready to come out, either. You're protecting him as much as yourself. Maybe even more."

"His parents are religious. They have no clue about his lifestyle or belief system. They sit around the table at holidays and talk about how gays need therapy to 'cure' them. They think homosexuality is a mental illness, and not providing treatment is unethical. I can't betray his secret."

"And you're ready to betray your father to keep it?"

He pulls out a baggie and slides it across the small table. It's filled with different colored pills and a vial with clear liquid in it.

"He has an office in our basement. It's where he and Lothar Schwarz run the operation from. He has manufacturing facilities, logistics records, supplier information, transportation schedules…everything."

It sounds too good to be true. Even if the information is encrypted, the act of finding it in Prock's home would be good enough for a jury to send him up the river for the remainder of his days. Then again, cloud storage and other off-site storage locations can be compromised. He will have a backup plan to protect that data, but having it close isn't the worst idea for anyone capable of staying off the radar.

"It's risky to keep it there," I say, checking to see how much Brody knows.

"Why do you think he wants this investigation over? It's why I'm in the city and not staying at the house. He doesn't want the police or feds traipsing through."

I finish the last of my fries. "Does your father know that you know?"

Brody shakes his head. "I don't think so. My father said he wanted me to hide out in Manhattan so the media wouldn't harass me. I knew the real reason, but I thought it'd be easier if I played along."

I take the drugs and put them in my pocket. I probably shouldn't have left them out in the open on the table as long as I did. The information about his father is a game-changer. While these drugs aren't concrete proof of his father's involvement in illegal drug manufacture, I know Brody isn't lying. It's time to consider the next steps.

"I'm not authorized to make any deals, Brody. All I can do is run it up the ladder."

"I figured."

"Then why tell me all this? Outside of your needing someone to talk to?"

Brody shrugs. "I don't know you, but I think you're carrying as many secrets as I am. And I trust you."

I drop a hundred down to cover the check and the tip. Brody probably has more money in his trust fund than I make in a decade, but it's the least I can do. He was under no obligation to come here at all.

"Are you staying in the city?" I ask, getting a nod. Give me a couple of days, then I'll be in touch."

I walk out of the restaurant with plenty to think about. It's filling up as customers report to the hostess stand for their lunchtime reservations. I turn left and head east down the sidewalk. Emma will have plenty of questions, and she launches her first after materializing at my side.

"Want to talk about it?" she asks, matching me stride for stride despite her shorter legs as we walk toward Times Square.

"Not really. Let's just say this assignment just got a lot more complicated."

CHAPTER FORTY-EIGHT

ASHLEE TRILLO

THE PLAZA HOTEL
NEW YORK, NEW YORK

She needs to think like an outlaw. That's what Ashlee keeps telling herself. She took a class on this during her undergraduate studies in criminal justice. Attending afternoon tea at one of the most notorious hotels in the county probably isn't something most fugitives would do. There's a method to her madness.

Her father's sadistic manservant will be combing the city for her. He'll assume she doesn't have much in the way of cash on her. That means his minions will monitor her credit and debit cards for transactions. The moment she uses one, they will narrow down her location. That won't do.

What they don't know about is her jailhouse mentality. She has far more cash on her than they'd expect and will use it as necessary, but most hotel reservations need to be secured with a credit card. They will search the seedy spots that don't require them first. That will buy her some time.

The last place they would expect to find her is at the Plaza Hotel. It was once said, "Nothing unimportant ever happens at The Plaza." Ashlee hopes that nothing important happens to her here. This is one of America's most celebrated hotels, hosting kings, presidents, and celebrities for over a century. The notoriety of this place disqualifies it as a spot she would be expected to go. At least, that's what she's counting on.

Ashlee picks up her phone and powers it on. Until now, she has only sent SMS messages from it. It's weird to dial a number on it for the first time.

"Hey, Ashlee!" her roommate squeals after answering. "It's great to finally hear your voice."

"Hi, Chloe. Yours, too. Where are you, still in Connecticut?"

"My parents booked us a room at the TWA Hotel at JFK. This place is awesome! We have a flight back to Minnesota first thing tomorrow morning."

Ashlee closes her eyes. That's not what she was hoping to hear.

"I need your help."

"Sure thing. What's wrong?"

"I left," Ashlee almost whispers.

"Left?"

"I snuck out of my house. I couldn't…be there anymore. I'm sure my father has people looking for me by now."

"Where are you now?" Chloe asks with a higher sense of urgency in her voice.

"Manhattan. I don't have much money, and they'll find me before long."

"There are like a million and a half people on that island. They won't find you. If you're afraid they will, get on a bus and leave."

"You don't know my father or Jamieson. Trust me, they'll find me. The first places he will put people are at the Port Authority Bus Terminal, Penn Station, and Grand Central."

"What is he, CIA?"

Ashlee knows that Jamieson was military but doesn't have the details. He may have been to law school and passed the bar, but he is anything but a lawyer. At this point, the particulars don't matter. He's a predator, and right now, she's his prey.

"Something like that, I think. I need to lie low tonight. He'll know I came into the city and will have people combing the streets. I will pay cash for a room tonight, but I need you to make the reservation. This phone doesn't have the Internet on it."

"Okay. Where am I making it?"

Ashlee closes her eyes. Chloe expects her to say Hilton or Marriott on the high end. Or maybe a boutique hotel downtown. She's a little concerned about how this is going to come across.

"The Plaza."

There is a sharp exhale on the line. "Are you serious?"

"This is as serious as it gets. I need to be somewhere I know my father's henchmen won't look."

"All right. Hold on."

Ashlee hears the clicking of a keyboard as Chloe gets to work on her laptop. There is a possibility that they are monitoring Chloe's transactions, but she isn't that close to her roommate. They don't know that Ashlee put her up to do the interviews that enraged her father.

"Done. I had to provide your name for check-in since it's my information on the reservation. Is that okay?"

Ashlee grimaces. She would rather not leave any semblance of a paper trail but knows that a desk clerk isn't handing her a key card if her name isn't somehow associated with the reservation. Jamieson may be resourceful, but she doubts he can access The Plaza's systems, assuming he would even think to.

"It will have to be. Thank you, Chloe. I promise that there will be no charges on it. Can you meet me tomorrow?"

Chloe lets out a deep sigh. "I don't know, Ash. I want to help, but I'm not sure I can convince them to stay here. They're spooked after what happened to me at Salisbury and want me home."

"I understand," Ashlee says, meaning it. "I'm sorry to ask you. The attack up at school must have been terrifying. I just have no one else to turn to."

"You can always go to the police."

The suggestion was meant to be helpful, but Ashlee isn't interpreting it that way. She's emotional and nervous. Both feelings are difficult to repress.

"And say what? I ran away from my rich father because he wasn't nice to me? They can't help me. I need to talk things out with someone I trust."

There's a long silence on the line.

"Okay. Let me talk to my parents. I'll text you in the morning."

"Thank you," Ashlee says, relief dripping from her voice.

"I need you to stay safe until then, Ashlee."

"I'll do my best. Thank you, Chloe," she says, ending the call and powering down the phone.

Ashlee looks around at the people enjoying their afternoon, seemingly without a care in the world. She looks for signs of trouble and finds none. Even if the odds of Jamieson finding her here are remote, she can't shake the feeling that she's in danger. She has no idea what to do. Hopefully, Chloe can point her in the right direction. It's a lot to ask, but she is out of options.

CHAPTER FORTY-NINE

JOHN PROCK

BRODY PROCK'S RENTAL APARTMENT
EAST VILLAGE, NEW YORK, NEW YORK

The last thing John wanted to do tonight was to drive into the city. Unfortunately, the news about a second meeting set events in motion. There are a dozen reasons Brody is talking to the feds, and none are good. Lothar's fear is that he's making a trade. His operations manager is convinced that he could be using information about Jackpot to strike a deal.

John has his doubts, but there is only one way to find out. He needs to look his son in the eyes and drag the truth out of him. He just needs to be slick about it to get Brody to confess. It would be a betrayal for the ages. Unfortunately, he has already started down that road by talking to the FBI in the first place. It needs to end right now.

Brody opens the apartment door after letting his father into the building and turns back inside without a word. John shakes his head and closes the door behind him. He will never understand this generation. That level of rudeness when he was his son's age would have resulted in his old man beating his ass.

"Is that any way to greet your father?"

"You only visit when you want something. It's late. What is it this time?"

"To save your skin," he says, causing his son to make eye contact with him for the first time. "Your legal team thinks the police have convinced prosecutors in Connecticut to convene a grand jury. We met to align our strategies for your defense when the indictment gets handed down."

"I didn't rape Ashlee."

"It appears that a jury will need to decide that. If this goes to court, you will need character witnesses to testify on your behalf. The lawyers are going to talk to every woman you've ever banged. They'll be convinced to tell the world you're a gentleman and great lover who would never hurt a fly. Studies have shown that rapists exhibit a pattern of behavior. We'll show the world that you don't match it."

"You can't do that," Brody mumbles.

"Why not? Because it isn't true? Are you violent with women in bed? Have you raped anyone before?"

Brody's jaw quivers, but no words come from it. He stares blankly at his father before his face contorts into a twisted mess of shock and emotional pain.

"How can you ask that?"

John throws his hands in the air. "Because all I hear out of your mouth are hollow denials. The burden of proof in a court of law may be on the prosecution, but it's on you in the court of public opinion. I've seen your social media profile. I think you documented every date you've ever been on. There are a hundred women you can call to the stand…unless there are reasons not to."

"No, nothing like that."

"Then what?" John demands, grabbing Brody's arm as he tries to turn away.

"Nothing."

"Tell me, Brody. Your life hangs in the balance."

"Is that why you brought your gun?" his son asks, nodding at the holster clipped to John's belt. "You plan on shooting me if I don't do what you say?"

"This?" John unholsters it and sets it on the breakfast bar. "Tell me. You're a womanizer. You've left a trail of broken hearts a mile long. How many women have you forced to get an abortion?"

"None!" Brody shouts, tears forming in the corner of his eyes. "I've never been with a woman!"

John twitches. He mentally dissects those words several times without gleaning the intended meaning.

"What?"

Brody exhales. He presses his eyes closed and clenches his jaw. Then he physically lets go of his angst.

"I've never been with a woman. Not even once."

"Brody, don't lie. I know you aren't a virgin—"

"Do you really want to know what secret I'm hiding from the world…from you? I'm gay. There, I said it. Now you know the truth. Are you happy?"

"That's…not possible," John says, shaking.

"It's true. I've been in a relationship with my roommate since we started at Salisbury. I had a few lovers before him in high school and college."

"No, no, no," John says, swaying as he pushes his hair back from his forehead with both hands. "My son isn't a faggot."

"I am a gay man, Dad. It's who I am."

John stares down at the floor. His son was lying to him. He never expressly condoned Brody's serial dating but also never dissuaded him from it. John met and married his mother when they were young. A big regret in his life was not taking the time to sow his wild oats. He was proud of Brody for taking that path he never did.

"You've been lying to me all these years?"

"Yeah, as if I couldn't tell you the truth. I knew you'd react like this. You reject anything that doesn't conform to your narrow-minded view of the world. It was better for me that you didn't know."

"When? When did you…?"

Brody softens his stare. "I've known since I was eleven."

John's mind races. He wasn't even a teenager. Not even old enough to understand the decisions he was making.

"Who did this to you? Huh? Did one of your teachers convince you of this?"

Brody scoffs. "I didn't need anyone to tell me. It took a long time for me to understand why all my friends were chasing girls and I had no interest. I thought I was weird. I wasn't. Just different."

"Different. That's one word for it. You're also a liar. A charlatan."

"That's why I didn't tell you. I don't expect you to understand."

John doesn't understand. He can't begin to process how a man can be attracted to another man. Lesbians he gets, at least on some level. But the thought of intercourse between two men nauseates him. He needs to get off this subject.

"Did you talk to the FBI?"

Brody's head snaps at the sudden change of direction.

"What?"

"It's a simple question, Brody. Have you been talking to the FBI? And don't you dare lie to me."

"No. I haven't talked to anyone."

"I see. Thank you. That makes this easier."

"What?"

John narrows his eyes and glares at his son. He can ignore many of the things his boy does that he doesn't agree with. There are some things he won't. Lying is the second red line Brody has crossed since John arrived here.

"I know you met with them. Once at a church and again at a restaurant near Times Square." Brody's face registers shock, which is all the confirmation his father needs. "So, here's what's going to happen. I'm cutting you off. No more legal team. No more Salisbury. No more stipends so you can enjoy romantic evenings with your fag lover. Then I'm going to the police and will tell them you admitted to raping that girl."

"You can't do that!"

"I can, and I will. And let me tell you, I'm a very compelling witness. You'll be found guilty and go to prison. You might like it there. General population is full of other rapists and will do wonders for your sex life."

"You're a monster!" Brody shouts, shaking and crying. "What father would do that?"

"I don't know. Not many, most likely. Then again, a loyal child shouldn't be so willing to lie to his father. You hid things from me. Then you went to the FBI after I explicitly told you not to. No, from this point forward, you aren't my son."

Brody picks the gun up off the counter and points it at John. His hands are shaking. He'd be lucky to hit the wall if he squeezes the trigger.

"What? Are you going to shoot your old man? Are you blaming me because you're queer? Go ahead, fairy, pull the trigger. I'm the evil man. Put me down, but it won't change anything. You will still be a faggot, and a narc, and I'll have neither for a son!"

"It's who I am. I can't change that," Brody says, tears streaming down his face. "I didn't do it because I'm confused, or someone convinced me it's cool. It's who I've always been."

"I don't care. You're the sick faggot, not me."

"It's not an illness. I am who I am!"

"You're a pervert. Go ahead, shoot me. Pull the trigger, coward."

Brody lowers the weapon. John is tempted to yank it from his hands but doesn't bother. Fags aren't capable of violence. They're too feminine. That's why they always play the victim to enhance their power.

"That's what I thought. You don't have the balls. Not that you use them for anything, anyway. What a waste of a promising life."

Brody brings the gun up, anguish on his face. John closes his eyes and waits for the shot. The noise fills his ears when it finally rings out.

CHAPTER FIFTY

SSA ZACH FORTE

THE METROPOLITAN MUSEUM OF ART
NEW YORK, NEW YORK

It could be worse. Asami could have picked Rockefeller Center for this meeting. At least this is inside. It's not frigid in the city, but the brisk wind makes the high-thirties temperatures feel anything other than balmy. The major drawback to meeting here is that the subway station at Lexington Avenue and 86th Street is a ten-minute walk away.

Forte climbs the stairs, grumbling with each step. He didn't bother counting them, but it was too many. He enters the Great Hall to find the doctor waiting for him.

"We have a perfectly good office building downtown. Why did you drag me up here to meet first thing in the morning?"

"Would you rather have this discussion in a stuffy office building where federal employees would wonder why an FBI special agent is talking to a shrink?"

Zach considers that for a moment. "Fair point. But nobody knows me there."

"So you think."

"Okay…but really, a museum?"

"You have something against the arts?"

"Do I look like the kind of guy who appreciates Impressionists or Asian art?"

Asami runs her eyes up and down his rumpled suit. "No, I'd expect to see you guzzling beer while wearing a mustard-stained hockey jersey at a Rangers game."

He left the door open for that dig. "For the record, I prefer football."

"I don't care. I bought you a ticket. Follow me."

He follows Asami through the Medieval Art wing and to the right toward the American Wing. The huge open space is remarkably quiet and peaceful. That's probably why she wanted to come here.

The doctor gets them coffee at the American Wing Café, where patrons can enjoy coffee, wine, beer, or another beverage with a snack. Zach selects a seat at one of the sterile white plastic tables with a view of the courtyard and waits for her to arrive with a desperately needed hit of caffeine.

"This is my favorite part of the museum," she says, setting a cup down in front of him.

"It's nice. Now tell me why you wanted to meet here."

"I don't want Boston to know I spoke to you."

Zach leans back and sips his coffee. "He isn't tracking my cell phone. I think we're here because you know I'm not going to like what you're about to tell me."

Asami's lip curls. "What's happening with Brody Prock?"

He definitely isn't going to like this. Zach gives a synopsis of Boston's meetings with Brody yesterday and the night before. He explains what he saw and what the problem with the truth is. For good measure, he throws in the interview with Ashlee and Boston's caginess about Jamieson Bohmer.

"I read the report about Ashlee. Troubled girl."

"What makes you say that?"

"I know Boston better than I know my own parents. I have spent more time with him than anyone except Nadiya, and she spends her time beating on him. When I read his reports, I don't focus on what he's saying. What's more interesting is what he's omitting."

Zach grunts and takes another swig of his coffee. He never looked at it that way. Then again, he can only imagine the horrible things Boston sees in these memories. Most people spend their lives trying to forget trauma. He lives it every day, and none of it is his.

"Okay, so what do you want?"

"To evaluate his mental state back in Virginia."

"He's in the field, Asami," Zach argues. "I can't remove him from duty because his doctor thinks he needs a checkup."

She nods. "Okay."

"That's it?"

"I did what I was instructed to."

Zach scoffs. Matt is a friend as much as he's a boss, but the man has his own agenda. He has no wife or children, so Watchtower serves as the stand-in for both. If he thinks it's in trouble, there is nothing he won't do to protect it.

"Remsen sent you here."

"He thought it was the best way to extricate all of you from this."

"That's a bold move, considering he sent us here in the first place," Zach moans.

Asami looks around. They shouldn't be talking like this in the open, but the only other people in the café are a small family who looks like they came to the city from Nebraska.

"He didn't. Brass did. He vehemently disagreed with that decision, not that he'd tell you that. This situation is toxic, and it's political. Nothing is going on here that should involve Watchtower."

"I'm not so sure. Both Tomasso Trillo and John Prock are likely involved in illegal activities. And I know that Boston is a little freaked out about Jamieson Bohmer."

"That's because he just met his first psychopath," Asami says with the lack of passion people have when ordering a pizza.

"I would have thought Alejandro Salcido was one."

"No, he was a sociopath."

"There's a difference?" Zach asks.

He knows the mental health field doesn't officially diagnose people by either term. Doctors use "antisocial personality disorder." It's a ridiculous word salad, and simplicity is the key to understanding. Zach calls them potentially dangerous nutjobs.

"An important one. A key difference between a psychopath and a sociopath is the little voice inside our heads warning us that something is morally wrong. A psychopath doesn't have one. He or she would have no moral qualms about beating and robbing you before leaving you to die in the street. If any emotions are displayed, it's a deception to make others believe they aren't different.

"A sociopath has a conscience, but it's weak. They will know that beating, robbing, and leaving you to die is wrong but will do it anyway. That's Alejandro Salcido."

Zach spends a lot of time thinking about all the women and children taking that scumbag out saved. Human trafficking is one of the world's most despicable crimes, and Boston putting a bullet through Salcido's forehead was a gift to humanity. It could have been years or even decades before law enforcement caught up to that piece of crap.

"Going up against a psychopath doesn't sound like something that would bother Boston."

Asami clearly disagrees, and she would know best. "Look at it from his perspective. He can read and interpret memories, even when he doesn't want to. He's gotten used to seeing the worst in everybody. Except now, when he's run into someone who's a black hole. This Jamieson guy is a blind spot for him…he's his Kryptonite."

"Okay, so what do I do about this?"

"The easy answer? Wrap up this case and get back to Virginia."

"That's it?"

"No, but it's the safest way to keep Boston out of harm's way," the doctor admits. "Psychopaths are cold-hearted and calculating. They carefully plot their moves and aggressively take out anything or anybody standing in their way. I don't know who this guy is, but he sounds dangerous. If he's trained, Boston would be matching his skills with Jamieson's on an even playing field."

Asami stands and pushes her chair in. "I'm going to enjoy the museum for a couple of hours before getting back on the Acela. I did what I came to do. The rest is up to you and Boston."

"Will he let this go?"

She stops and turns. "Was the Joker allowed to run roughshod over Gotham?"

CHAPTER FIFTY-ONE

JAMIESON BOHMER

Most of the normally quiet tree-lined street is cordoned off with yellow police line tape. The NYPD activity has naturally drawn quite a crowd. Neighbors and curious passersby stand outside the thin plastic barrier and crane their necks to see what the fuss is about. Jamieson decides to join them.

He shouldn't get this close, but the odds of anyone knowing who he is are remote. He spots Dusty talking to an officer manning the perimeter to keep onlookers and the smattering of media at bay. More will come as the word spreads about whose body was found in that apartment.

Jamieson already got that heads-up from Dusty. It's why he rushed over here. The rest of the world is playing catch-up. All he needs now are whatever details the aging police veteran has managed to extract from his former colleagues.

The grizzled private investigator spots him and casually walks over. He stands next to Jamieson, not making it evident that they know each other. He surveys the scene and shakes his head.

"What a mess."

"What do the police know?"

"Not much. A neighbor called 911 about a single gunshot around ten thirty last night. Officers reported to the scene and didn't initially find anything unusual. They began knocking on doors, gained access to the bottom floor apartment, and found a body on the floor. Their initial report labeled it a probable suicide."

Jamieson nods. That's the official story, but like most, not the whole one.

"What really happened?"

"A man showed up. Fifteen minutes later, there was a gunshot. Then someone exited the apartment about five minutes later."

"Was the shooting accidental?"

Dusty presses his lips together and shakes his head. "Based on what I know, it's unlikely. It looks like murder to me. Most people don't legally own handguns in this city, and nobody flees the scene of a suicide."

Parent-child relationships are complicated. If the former SAS warrior has learned anything from the Trillo family, it's that. But they should share bonds almost as strong as the ones he formed with his brothers-in-arms in combat. They may not have the shared war experience, but they are still each other's flesh and blood. Children are extensions of the parents who brought them into this world. He can't understand why animosity exists between them at the level it does in society.

"Did you tell the police anything?"

"No."

"Were they wondering why you're here? You looked a little chummy with that uniform over there."

"I was on the force for twenty years. The NYPD is a brotherhood. I told him I was checking on a stockbroker cheating on his wife in lower Manhattan and heard the report."

"He bought that?"

Dusty snickers. "Most stockbrokers cheat on their spouses. It's hardly a unique story."

Jamieson doubts that's true but has no data or willingness to refute the conclusion. Infidelity is a global pandemic, so he supposes the percentage could be higher than the general population among the rich and overstressed masses who work on Wall Street.

"Has the body been removed?"

No, they're waiting for a tent and curtain screen. The coroner doesn't want to pull the body out in front of rolling cameras. This is already going to dominate the news cycle for a week. Why give them good footage to accompany it?"

Jamieson nods. That makes sense. Reporters are vultures who make a living uncovering the next big story, and their outlets cover it until the nation becomes addicted. Americans have watched continuous coverage of murders, disappearances, wars, political scandals, and race riots on their televisions and smartphones over the past several decades. Once the media realizes they can turn an event into clicks and advertising dollars, they latch on with the strength of a pit bull.

This will lead to another major problem. The media pressure to interview Ashlee will become unbearable. They will camp outside the estate just like at John Prock's house in Scarsdale. Tomasso isn't going to be happy.

"You find the girl?" Dusty asks, changing the subject.

"Not yet."

Tomasso is going to be even less happy about that. With his daughter out in the wind, who knows what could happen when she hears this news? If she decides to talk to the media…Jamieson doesn't want to think about how her father will react. He needs to get in front of this before Tomasso channels his legendary anger in his direction.

The phone in his pocket vibrates, and he retrieves it to find a text message from another source:

McCarthy family changed their flight. Still in city. Instructions?

He taps out a quick message in reply:

Tail her and report movements.

"Let me know if you hear anything new," Jamieson orders as he turns for the walk back up the street.

"You got it."

Jamieson looks back to ensure nobody is paying him any attention, and then he places a call. He holds the phone up to his ear as he reaches the corner.

"Have you found my daughter?" Tomasso asks without a greeting after the call connects.

"It's only a matter of time. Ashlee can't run forever. I'll find her."

"But you haven't found her, so why are you calling me?"

"Because of what you're about to see on the news."

"What will the news say that I possibly care about?"

Jamieson looks back at the flashing strobes of the police cruisers and emergency services vehicles.

"That Brody Prock is dead."

CHAPTER FIFTY-TWO

ASHLEE TRILLO

THE MET CLOISTERS
FORT TRYON PARK, NEW YORK, NEW YORK

This is one of Ashlee's favorite places. A hidden gem in one of the world's most iconic cities, The Cloisters, a branch of the Metropolitan Museum of Art, is dedicated to medieval Europe's art and architecture. They couldn't have picked a better spot to construct it. The five French cloisters, three chapels, Gothic-style terraces, galleries, gardens, and arcades were built overlooking the Hudson River in Fort Tryon Park. The museum features five thousand art pieces, but Ashlee has always been mesmerized by their renowned Unicorn Tapestries.

She isn't here to appreciate them today. This museum has two qualities she needs right now. It's a public place Jamieson would never think to look for her, and it isn't jammed with patrons and tourists. Crowded places like Times Square make it easy for professionals to spot people who think they're anonymous. Unlike The Met Gallery next to Central Park, few tourists visit the northern tip of Manhattan, making the museum feel desolate outside of a couple of die-hards and a handful of staff.

Ashlee doesn't wander far from the Main Hall while waiting for Chloe to arrive. Learning about Brody's suicide has rocked her to her core. She may not have seen or talked to him since that fateful night, but she feels responsible for his death. The overbearing feeling of guilt has sapped her energy, and regrets about Brody have replaced the fear of being on her own.

Chloe arrives, striding up to her with a sense of urgency. The two women embrace and hold the hug, neither wanting to let go. They've both been through a lot.

"Are you okay?" her roommate finally whispers.

"Define 'okay.' I have no home, little money, one friend, and I'm being hunted by my father, who will ruthlessly punish me for disobeying him."

"How do you know he's looking for you?" Chloe asks.

Ashlee nods to the side, and they wander deeper into the museum. "Because that's what my father does."

"You know that sounds insane, right?"

It is insane. Ashlee knows she's a grown woman. She should have slipped from her father's control the moment she graduated high school. It's not that simple. He has maintained his dominance over her through college and now law school. That control will continue until she is free of his financial support and learns to be self-sufficient.

"My father doesn't like to lose. He likes to be in charge of everything, including me. Disobeying him is a personal affront. Trust me, he's looking for me."

Chloe stares at her roommate out of the corner of her eye. "You heard about Brody?"

Ashlee lowers her head and presses her lips together. "It's my fault he's dead."

"No, it isn't. Brody killed himself out of shame for what he did to you. That's not your responsibility. It's *not* your fault."

"It is."

"Look at me, Ashlee. You're a victim. He's a predator who took advantage of you in one of the worst ways imaginable. I'm glad he's dead."

"Don't say that."

"Why not?"

Ashlee lowers her head again and shakes it. They enter an arcade, and she sits on one of the wooden benches. It's chilly outside but unseasonably warm for late December in New York. Her coat is warm, and the cold air on her face feels good. The women remain silent until Chloe digs through her purse and pulls out a wad of cash.

"I'm sorry I couldn't get more."

"This will help a lot, thank you. I'll find a way to pay you back."

"Don't worry about it."

"Were your parents mad that you wanted to stay?" Ashlee asks as she stuffs the money into her coat pocket.

"Not mad, but they weren't happy either."

"I'm sorry to have dragged you into this."

"Don't be. You didn't do anything wrong. Brody dragged me in when he raped you. You're my roommate and my friend. If the roles were reversed, you would have done the same for me."

Ashlee forces a smile, unsure about the truth of that conclusion. She tolerated Chloe more than she was friendly with her. It's been like that with every friend she's ever had. Nobody is allowed to get close or get admitted into the circle of trust.

"What are you going to do now?"

"I don't know…I think I need to talk to the police."

"Why?"

"I just do."

Chloe reaches into her purse and pulls out a card. She hands it to Ashlee, who studies the front, not that it takes much concentration. Outside of the FBI logo, it only has a phone number printed on it.

"What's this?"

"The agent who saved me from my attackers gave it to me at the hospital. He said to give it to you if you ever need help."

"He said that?" Ashlee asks, surprised. Chloe nods. "There's no name on it."

"It belongs to Agent Dufresne." The twinkle of recognition in Ashlee's eyes is unmistakable. "He's a really good-looking guy. It looks like you know him."

"He interviewed me at the house with three others."

"He's perceptive. He didn't say much when we were in the ER, but it felt like he knew everything. If you need to talk to someone, start with him."

Ashlee turns the card over a few times in her hand. The decision she makes right now may very well change the course of her life. She had a plan to escape the confines of the house but didn't think much past that. Actions have consequences. She knows that better now than ever, but there is no other way. This needs to end.

"Can I borrow your phone?"

CHAPTER FIFTY-THREE
"BOSTON" HOLLINGER

ESTATE OF JOHN PROCK
SCARSDALE, NEW YORK

Forte is a lot of things. A bad driver isn't one of them. I figured that he would handle the SUV like Hoke Colburn in *Driving Miss Daisy*. Instead, my ten-minute head start after leaving the federal building has evaporated to about thirty seconds. And it's not like I'm driving slowly.

The news of Brody Prock's suicide has shaken me. The kid was under immense pressure from the rape allegation and distressed that his father would learn his secrets. But there is no way he was suicidal. I refuse to believe it. That leaves murder, and there is only one prime suspect. All I need to prove it is to be in his presence. Then I will bring his whole world down on top of him.

I check the rearview mirror. I first caught sight of Forte not long after getting on the Bronx River Parkway. He has his lights on, same as I do. There is no way I'm going to lose him. He knows where I'm heading anyway.

My phone rings in the seat next to me. I don't need to see the caller id to know who it is and let it go to voicemail. There's no doubt he'll call back. I expect it to ring all the way to Scarsdale incessantly.

I press the accelerator harder, weaving through traffic until I reach the exit. Once on the side streets, this race will become a matter of who takes the most efficient route and who gets unluckier with the traffic lights. It's time to put that to the test. I run the red, almost causing an accident in the intersection. What good is having strobes and federal plates on the vehicle if you don't use them?

That will let me pull away from Zach. I tear through the side streets and pull hard into Prock's neighborhood. The line of satellite trucks and news vans acts as runway landing lights straight to his front door. His neighbors must be thrilled.

The local police keep the media corralled on the other side of the narrow street. None of the uniforms stop me as I steer into the driveway, but they quickly rush to confront me when I exit the Suburban. I flash my badge, and they let me through their cordon.

It's almost a first for me. I rarely show my credentials and tuck my wallet back into my pocket as I storm up the sidewalk to ring the bell. The clock in my head is ticking. Time isn't on my side. Forte can't be far away.

The door opens, and a tall man in a suit with no tie answers. I was hoping it would be John Prock himself. Instead, I'm greeted by the Bavarian version of Lurch from the Addams family.

"Can I help you?"

"I need to see John Prock. Right now."

"I'm sorry, Mr. Prock is not taking visitors."

I flash my badge again. "I wasn't asking."

The man fills the doorway. "Unless you have a warrant or subpoena tucked in those credentials, I don't care whether you're asking or not."

I offer a slight nod and cock my head. "What's your name?"

"Lothar Schwarz."

"Thank you, Mr. Schwarz. What's your relation to John Prock?"

"No relation. I'm an executive at AMLOG."

"And what do you do for AMLOG besides open the owner's door like a common butler?

The comment sparks an emotional response that has the desired effect.

The place is a pigsty. Sealable plastic containers are everywhere. Pizza boxes and forty-ounce bottles of beer litter the counter. A pill press, drug-making paraphernalia, and bags of red, blue, white, and yellow pills are on the dinette table.

I walk through what is otherwise a common apartment and grab a man by his long hair, pulling him out of the chair. His friends don't react as I make him kneel before me.

"You've been talking to the police."

"No, señor. No he hablado con nadie."

"I don't believe you. My sources said you have, and that's good enough for me."

I feel my finger move to the trigger and pull it back. The firing pin hits the primer, igniting the powder charge in the cartridge. The explosive gases propel the bullet down the barrel, where the rifling spins it until it exits the muzzle. From there, the bullet goes straight through the man's forehead.

"Unless that subpoena you don't seem to have has my name on it, you're not entitled to know."

The comment cuts the vision short. This guy has a wealth of memories, but I don't have time to sort through them right now. I got one thing I am looking for — confirmation of Brody's assertion that his father, president and chief executive officer of American Logistics, is also involved in the illegal manufacture and distribution of fentanyl.

"Mr. Schwarz, obstruction of justice is a tricky thing."

"So is an abuse of power," he snaps.

"Agent Dufresne!" I hear Zach bark from behind me.

I didn't even hear him pull in. I glance over my shoulder to see him standing in the middle of the front yard. Five officers are watching the interaction with more than passing interest.

"Uh, oh. It looks like your boss is angry."

The corner of my mouth curls. "He was born that way. Last chance because hell comes with me the next time we meet."

Lothar's eyes narrow. "I don't respond to threats."

"I don't issue them. Only facts."

"Special Agent Dufresne! I'm not going to ask again. Step…off…the porch."

"Daddy is waiting," Lothar sings out.

I take a few steps and stop when I reach the edge. I watch too many movies and appreciate the flair for the dramatic. Cinema nails it better than real life, but I take a shot at it anyway.

"One more thing, Mr. Schwarz. You should read United States Code, specifically USC eight forty-one through eight sixty."

"Why would I do that?"

"Because the Federal Controlled Substances Act lists all the penalties for the illegal production and distribution of fentanyl. I'll see you around."

That wipes the smug smile off his face. I step off the front stoop and cross the yard, stopping in front of a very pissed-off Forte.

"Get in your SUV and drive away right now," Zach says through clenched teeth.

I sneer. "Your wish is my command, Master."

CHAPTER FIFTY-FOUR

SSA ZACH FORTE

Zach swings into the diner's parking lot and stares intently at the rearview mirror to ensure Boston follows. He does. "Agent Dufresne" has followed him since he took the lead out of John Prock's Scarsdale neighborhood. While the first thought must have been a trip straight back to the Javits Federal Building, Zach isn't quite ready to report to the office.

The two men park the behemoths next to each other, and find a quiet booth in the corner after entering the diner. Boston orders a coffee while Zach opts for a diet soda before they endure a long silence between them. When the beverages arrive, their orders are placed: Breakfast for Boston, who hasn't eaten since last night and prefers bacon and eggs over most dinner options. Zach gets a turkey club with fries and a small dish of cole slaw. Diners in the Northeast have the best club sandwiches.

The waitress leaves to get the cooks busy. Boston looks around the nearly empty eatery, likely waiting for Zach to lay into him for confronting Prock's minion. It'd be hypocritical if he did that. If their roles were reversed, he would have gone to the Prock house to throttle someone, too.

"Are you going to say anything?" Boston finally asks after growing impatient.

"Only that someone needs to take my SUV in for an alignment. It keeps pulling to the right."

"I can't figure you out."

"Good. I despise being predictable. Do you want me to yell at you, Boston? Dress you down for going off the reservation and confronting Prock? I will if it makes you feel better, but my heart's not in it."

"Then why did you stop me?"

Zach scoffs. "Gee, let me think about whether I should have let you commit career suicide."

That's what it would have been. Boston wouldn't have gotten anything except grief from John Prock, who, in turn, would have complained to the FBI that one of its unhinged agents came to his door. The FBI would have started asking inconvenient questions, like 'who the hell is Special Agent Andrew Dufresne?'" Then the fun at Watchtower would really begin.

"What are we doing, Zach?"

"Having an early dinner."

"That's not what I meant, and you know it. Stop playing games and answer me."

Zach unwraps the silverware bundled into a napkin and secured with a paper strip. "We're doing what we're asked to."

"Yeah, but have you ever thought about who's doing the asking and why?"

"It's above my pay grade. I don't play the political game, and I don't know a damn thing about why Brass does what he does."

"He isn't interested in truth or justice."

"Or the American way," Zach adds with a smirk.

Boston shakes his head. "We weren't brought in to bring this case to a conclusion. We're being used to prevent the FBI from making another mistake."

"Yeah, that pretty much sums it up."

"That doesn't bother you?"

It bothers him, but he can't tell Boston that. Five years ago, Zach would have been leading the charge over the cliff his team member was dancing on the lip of. This isn't the time to be a kindred spirit. He needs to walk him back.

"I've learned to accept the things I can't change. You should, too."

"I'm not sure that's ever going to happen."

"Clearly," Zach says, sipping the cola through his straw.

"So, what's our next move?"

"Officially? We load up and report to Belvoir. Unofficially?" Zach shrugs.

The waitress arrives with the food, and the men dig in. The only interruption comes when Boston gets a call. He wags his phone from side to side when he sees the caller id.

"It's Ops," he says to Forte before holding the phone to his ear. "Yeah?"

"What? Are you kidding? Hold on…"

Boston looks around, prompting Zach to do the same. Nobody is sitting near them. At least, not within earshot.

"Put her through."

Zach holds his hands out impatiently as he places the call on speakerphone.

"This is Special Agent Dufresne."

There's a long pause before a female speaks. "It's Ashlee Trillo."

Zach stops before shoving the French fry he's holding into his mouth and sets it back on the plate with its friends. Of all the calls Boston could get, she ranks somewhere between Kim Kardashian and Elton John near the bottom of the list.

"How did you get my number, Miss Trillo?" Boston asks.

"I'm with Chloe McCarthy. You gave her your card, and she gave it to me. I need to talk to you."

"Okay. Where are you?"

"The Met Cloisters. Have you heard of it?"

Zach shakes his head and digs his phone out. He immediately taps on the Maps application.

"No, but we can find it. When do you want to meet?"

"As soon as you can get here."

"Okay. Sit tight. We're on the way. We should be there in…" Zach holds up three fingers and then makes a fist. "Half an hour."

"We'll be waiting."

Forte grabs a fistful of fries and drops a pair of twenties on the table to cover the bill and tip. Boston is already out the door. He understands the urgency. There was something in her voice…fear. Whatever is going on with Ashlee, it isn't good.

CHAPTER FIFTY-FIVE

JOHN PROCK

When John was younger, he had a friend who wanted to become the next great photojournalist. He liked booze and talking more than taking pictures, and his career never got off the ground. Back when his unambitious friend was optimistic, the pair would stay up until the wee hours of the morning throwing back shots and philosophizing about everything from who really killed JFK to alternate endings for the movie *Spaceballs*.

One night, the subject turned to the media. The conversation predated the emergence of social media titans like Facebook, Twitter, and YouTube and was long before "fake news" entered the national vernacular. Smartphones were yet to hit the mainstream outside the legion of BlackBerry users.

His friend asked if he ever wondered how stories became stories. Why were the murders of Nicole Brown Simpson and Ronald Goldman headline news? Why was a slow-speed chase of a white Ford Bronco carried live on network television? Why did one trial captivate the country for eight months? He cited several other examples, but that was the one that stuck in John's mind.

His answer was simple: drama. The media doesn't exist to inform – it exists to survive. In the era when newspapers and nightly news broadcasts dominated, it was about ratings and circulation. The Information Age changed the math to count clicks, likes, and views. The recipe for visibility remains the same, regardless. The more dramatic the story, the more coverage it garners.

The accusations of sexual assault on a college campus would hardly break the Internet. One of the saddest commentaries on modern society is that it happens all too frequently. His son's accusation received attention because it has all the story elements editors and producers drool for. Despite the two patriarchs never meeting, they have made their two families out to be the Montagues and Capulets or Hatfields and McCoys.

Nor is the media bashful about showing the players in this drama. Ashlee could be a model with her tinted Mediterranean skin and gorgeous black hair. His son, with a square jaw, perfect hair, and fashionable clothing, is portrayed as a resplendent predator.

The drama and the mystery the media conjures come from John and Tomasso. Neither has made a statement since the media first reported the incident. There have been a hundred attempts to lure him out of his silence. He's certain that Tomasso has shared a similar experience. Now is the time to fulfill the hopes and dreams of every wary reporter camped across the road. The war is about to escalate, and John wants to ensure it's on his terms.

He exits the house by the front door and steels himself for the realization that every move he makes will be recorded and photographed for the world to see. The reporters breach the police line and pour across the street. Additional officers rush in to control the horde and bark orders for them to return to their vehicles. They are ignored as John comes to a stop.

Questions are shouted in rapid succession. Most overlap as nobody is waiting for an answer. The experience is intimidating, which is one reason he hasn't wanted to do this. The questions begin to die down as John stands there. When there is a brief moment of quasi-silence, he makes his move.

"My son was my life. I built a thriving company from one truck and a single client to fleets of vehicles with hubs and offices worldwide. I would give everything that it has become to have Brody back. He took his own life last night," John says, visibly struggling to fight back the tears. "Why? Because he was depressed? No. He took it because you people left him no option."

There is some nervous shuffling among the journalists, and most of the audible sounds are cameras clicking. The reporters remain silent. He stares many of them in the face before continuing.

"Are you proud of yourselves? Are your families proud of what you do? You aren't reporting the news. You're trying to shape opinion. I always thought that was some obnoxious right-wing talking point. That's what you and your defenders pass it off as. Then you turned my son into a monster before he even had the chance to defend himself because you think he's guilty. You believed Ashlee Trillo's accusations without a shred of proof. Then you went on air and told the world to believe you because you know best. You acted as judge and jury. Last night, you became the executioner."

The cameras stop clicking. The reporters stop breathing. Even the birds who haven't migrated south for the winter have ceased chirping. The world is still and silent, at least in this small part of Westchester County, New York.

"I'm sure your next move will be to absolve yourselves of responsibility. You'll plead to your viewers and readers that you only reported facts. You'll speculate that I somehow must have been involved. The FBI thinks that, so it must be true. You saw them leave here. Perhaps you won't rest until I take my own life, too.

"I find myself grieving again. My wife tragically passed years ago. Now my son is dead. I'm a broken man with nothing left. You got the justice you wanted. The monster you created to sell horror stories to people has been slain. Congratulations. You did your job well."

John turns and walks back through the front door to his house. He expects questions shouted at his back from intrepid reporters but hears none. If it's drama they wanted, that's what they got. That was his opening salvo but not his last. That thought almost causes him to smile as he reaches the front door.

CHAPTER FIFTY-SIX

JAMIESON BOHMER

THE MET CLOISTERS
FORT TRYON PARK, NEW YORK, NEW YORK

This walk feels like it takes Jamieson longer than it did to arrange the transportation and drive to the northern tip of Manhattan. He didn't want to be seen pulling up in front of the museum and decided to leave his vehicle in a lot deep in Fort Tryon Park. From there, it's a ten-minute walk up the dark path that runs roughly parallel to Margaret Corbin Drive. Or so the route on his navigation app says.

It takes him longer because he needs to get the lay of the land. Even in a best-case scenario, he'll need to retrace his steps with an unwilling hostage. Jamieson doesn't want to worry about the route back to the car while he keeps Tomasso's ill-tempered daughter under control.

He stops every hundred feet and turns to check the view from the other direction. The sun is almost down. In another twenty minutes, it will be dusk. Twenty minutes after that, it will be too dark to see much of anything in this park without streetlights. That will only help his effort.

Jamieson walks up the stairs to the cobblestone drive and enters through the double black oak doors that mark the main entrance. He pays his admission at the Main Hall and unfolds the map in the brochure he was handed. During the Middle Ages, cloisters were places of religious seclusion in monasteries and convents for the faithful to reflect and recharge.

Architecturally, it's a covered walk with an open colonnade on one side, running along the buildings' walls facing a quadrangle. There are five cloisters here, and Jamieson doesn't expect his target to be in any of them. There are rooms with art exhibits and chapels, and they're warmer. He starts moving clockwise through the museum, admiring the artwork.

It's what he needs to avoid suspicion. There are only two non-emergency exits; both are back the way he came. Ashlee won't get past him. He meanders through the Late Gothic Hall and checks the Boppard Room. Then he pokes his head into the two tapestry rooms before descending the stairs.

There is nobody at the Trie and Bonnefont Cloisters. The Gothic Chapel and Glass Gallery are equally deserted. Jamieson climbs the stairs back to the first floor, having already cleared half of the museum. It makes sense that she would stay close to the museum staff manning the gift shop located off the Main Hall.

Jamieson checks three more halls before reaching the entrance to the Fuentidueña Chapel. He stares at the massive ornate crucifix suspended above the apse before his eyes wander over to two women huddled on a bench.

"Who is that?" the blonde asks as Ashlee stares at him in disbelief.

"Jamieson."

The look on her face is strangely satisfying. Her whole life since her mother's death has been dominated by fear. He's been a part of instilling it.

She looks across the chapel at the stone portal.

"By all means, go that way, Ashlee, please."

He studied the map. That door leads down to the lower bathrooms. There is no exit except back into the chapel. If Ashlee makes a break for it, this next task will be far simpler.

Chloe says something to her, and both women stand. They begin walking toward him as he reaches into his pocket and wraps his hand around the handle of his commando dagger. They get within ten feet of him.

"Run! Now!"

Ashlee starts to dart past him. Jamieson reaches out with his left arm to snag her when Chloe charges into him. She's not a big woman and doesn't knock him off balance when she crashes into him. Undaunted, the woman begins beating on his chest, but the hits aren't effective other than to distract him long enough for Ashlee to slip past.

He slides his right hand back into his pocket, pulls his Fairbairn-Sykes, and jabs it into Chloe's abdomen. Her eyes grow large as the pain registers. He pulls the dagger out and is tempted to stab her again for good measure, but there's no time. He can't let Ashlee get to the Main Hall.

Jamieson bolts after her in pursuit. He glimpses her fleeing through the Romanesque Hall before turning into the Langon Chapel. He picks up the pace. She's going in the wrong direction, which suits him fine. He slows to a walk as he reaches the chapel and peers around the corner. She isn't in the Cuxa Cloister. That leaves one possible option.

He takes the door leading out to the West Terrace and feels the blast of chilled air on his face. He can hear the soles of her sneakers scraping on the stone. Jamieson walks easily around the chapel's apse and sees his quarry staring over the edge.

"There is nowhere to go, Ashlee. Be smart. It has to be a thirty-foot drop, and that jump will break your legs. Just come with me, and I'll take you home to your father."

She takes a couple of steps back when he holds out his hand. He can see the fear etched on Ashlee's face. She takes another look over the edge, and before he can open his mouth in surprise, she hops over the short wall.

Jamieson rushes over and peers down at the ground below. Ashlee landed on a grassy patch and seems to be okay. Lucky. She stands, looks up at him, and then bolts toward the road.

"I'm getting too old for this," Jamieson mumbles.

He isn't about to jump. The days in the SAS when he wouldn't have thought twice are long in the rearview mirror. He rushes back through the museum and out the main entrance. He descends the short concrete stairs and follows the path to the south before stopping to listen.

There is plenty of ambient noise in any large city. There are always car horns, sirens, and the sound of activity, creating a white noise that only denizens get used to. This area of Manhattan is different. It's quiet, almost rural. He can hear Ashlee's footfalls on the asphalt in the growing darkness. She's heading down to the park. It's almost perfect. He takes off down the path on an intercept course.

CHAPTER FIFTY-SEVEN
"BOSTON" HOLLINGER

THE CLOISTERS LAWN
FORT TRYON PARK, NEW YORK, NEW YORK

It took Emma and Nadiya as much time to make their way up Manhattan as it took us to get here from Westchester County. The three beefy black Suburbans pull into the semicircular access drive off Margaret Corbin drive with me in the lead. I slam the vehicle into park and open the door.

A panicked museum staffer rushes out as the sounds of a girl screaming echo in the trees after we pull up and exit. I look at Forte, who signals Emma and me to investigate.

"Nadiya, you're with me," he says, charging into the museum.

I don't wait for Emma. I accelerate into a dead sprint down a path that leads through groups of trees. The visibility sucks, and I spend more time staring at the ground before me than scanning what's ahead. I hear another scream, and I steer myself across the street onto a grassy area.

Two figures are up ahead. I see the man grab Ashlee as she lets out another scream. "No! Stop! No!"

I stop thirty meters away and pick up a solid firing stance.

"Freeze! FBI!" Emma bellows from another ten meters behind me, having done the same.

The man pulls something from his jacket and hurls it toward us. It looks like a rock but has a smoother and more cylindrical appearance as it nears. I recognize too late what it is and am powerless to do anything about it.

The magnesium-based charge releases a burst of light of around seven million candelas. I was schooled on how bright that is during the early days of my Watchtower training. A twenty-five-watt fluorescent light bulb emits about 135 candelas. The flash overloads the light receptors in the eyes as a thunderous bang destroys my hearing.

I fall to the ground in a heap. It takes a minute to regain my senses. Emma tugs at my arm and helps me to my feet, where I'm unsteady but otherwise mobile. We begin walking over to the figure lying motionless on the grass. Emma is scanning the area for threats, but I doubt she can see any better than I can. Either way, the man is gone. The question is, how far?

"Boston, you okay?"

"This sucks," I moan, unable to see or hear well.

"What was that?" Ashlee says between sobs on the ground.

"It's called a flashbang," Emma says, kneeling beside her as I cover us. "I'm going to check you for injuries. Remain still."

"A flashbang?" she asks, her voice quivering.

"It's a stun grenade designed to temporarily disorient someone without killing them," I explain. "It creates a bright light – the flash – and a very loud noise – the bang. Flashbang."

"Did you get a look at him?" Emma asks me as she runs her hands over Ashlee, who seems to be uninjured.

"No."

"It was…Jamieson Bohmer. He…works for my father. He stabbed Chloe!"

"The lawyer?" Emma asks.

"How many lawyers stab people and carry flashbangs?" I say, shaking my head. "He's much more than the family's attorney."

Emma helps Ashlee up. My vision has mostly returned, and I watch her check herself before looking around in a panic.

"How did he find me?"

"That's a good question. Take off your coat."

"We need to check on Chloe!" she shouts, panicking.

"This first."

Bohmer could be tracking her cell phone, but there are other possibilities. I start searching the pockets as she watches me intently. They're empty except for a few personal items, so I begin feeling around the seams of the puffy winter coat. Nothing is there.

"She's clean. Let's go."

The three of us walk across the grass, cross the road, and follow the path through the trees to the museum's front. It's not hard to find. The entire area is bathed in the light from red strobes atop the dozen police vehicles jamming the drive. Uniformed officers are standing around, most talking into radios or to museum staff.

Nadiya emerges from the building and turns in their direction. She holds up a small square piece of plastic before handing it to me. It's a simple yet elegant solution to track someone without them knowing it.

"Ashlee, this is my colleague, Special Agent Nadiya Jesperssen."

Nadiya offers a cool, forced smile as Ashlee nods at her.

"What is that?" Ashlee asks.

"A GPS tracker. They're small, cheap, effective, available on Amazon, and a great way to locate everything from luggage to the roommate of a rebellious runaway."

Emma frowns. "You could have missed one on her."

"I doubt it. We could tell her to strip and find out, but it's a bit chilly for that. I can check her on the way." I flip the tracker to Emma. "Can you take that back to the office in the Suburban with you?"

"You got it."

"Where are we going?" Ashlee asks.

"A place where your father won't find you."

"Like a hotel? No, no, no."

"Would you rather sleep in a subway car tonight?"

"I'm not spending a night with a strange man after what happened to me."

Nadiya scoffs, and I warn her off with my eyes. "I know exactly what happened that night, Ashlee. The only question is where you got the Rufinol and how you managed to drug Brody."

Her mouth hangs open. "You…know?"

Paramedics wheel a gurney out the main entrance of the hotel. A woman under a blanket is strapped to it. That's a good sign. It's not a body bag. They load her into the back of the waiting ambulance as Ashlee looks on with tears in her eyes.

"Let's talk about it later,' I say, turning to Nadiya. "Is Chloe going to be okay?"

"Yeah, I think so," she says. "She's suffering from a single stab wound to the abdomen and will need immediate surgery. I'll ride in the ambulance with her to the hospital to ensure she gets there okay, and then take the subway back to the office."

"Okay, thanks. Where's Zach?"

"He's coordinating the search with the NYPD. They didn't react well when they found out the assailant used a flashbang. They think he could be armed and want to shut down the parkway."

The Met Cloisters lies just to the east of the Henry Hudson Parkway. The ten-mile thoroughfare connects Manhattan's West Side Highway to the south with the Saw Mill River Parkway to the north. Shutting down the road at the end of rush hour would cause chaos and make the impending media spectacle even worse.

"It won't do any good. If Jamieson is half as good as I think he is, he'll have a backup escape plan. He's long gone."

"Agreed. Forte's trying to keep your name out of this. Emma, you're going to need to make a statement and do some paperwork."

"Wonderful."

I pull Nadiya gently by the arm away from Ashlee. I look around and spot Forte still conversing with an NYPD captain.

"I'm going to stash our Ashlee at the safehouse. I don't want the FBI anywhere near her for the time being. Not yet."

Nadiya purses her lips. "All right. I'm not sure how long we'll be able to keep that from him."

"Do what you can. Every second matters."

"Yeah, okay."

Nadiya walks away, not happy, but not angry either. I'll discuss it with her later, but I need to get Ashlee out of here. It's harder to slip away than I thought it would be. Police scenes are usually chaotic, but everyone was hyper-vigilant at this one, even in the darkness. Ashlee and I cross Margaret Corbin Drive and use the paths through the trees to reach the playground. Beyond that are Riverside Drive, the intersection with Dyckman Street, and its namesake subway station.

"That Nadiya woman wasn't very friendly," Ashlee says as we walk. "That or she doesn't like me."

"She's a little sensitive right now. You're not her favorite person," I explain.

"Why not? She doesn't even know me."

I turn my head to look at her. "Nadiya was raped, Ashlee. For real."

"How long ago?" she asks quietly.

"Does it matter? Come on. We need to walk faster."

CHAPTER FIFTY-EIGHT
ASHLEE TRILLO

FBI SAFEHOUSE
CHINATOWN, NEW YORK, NEW YORK

The ride down the island to Lower Manhattan has mostly been in silence. This agent isn't the talkative type, at least with her. He is zoned out as taxicabs and rideshare drivers blare their horns and weave around him. That's okay with Ashlee. She just watched her friend get stabbed and barely escaped the clutches of her father's mad dog "lawyer." A conversation about any of that doesn't rank high on her to-do list.

The agent pulls the Suburban up to the curb on a Chinatown side street and makes a call. He climbs out of the driver's seat, prompting Ashlee to unfasten her seatbelt and do the same. They walk up the street the way they came and then up to a second-floor apartment in a three-story walkup.

"Make yourself at home," the agent says, locking the door behind them.

"This is cozy, Shawshank. Is this your place?"

He immediately heads for the fridge and retrieves a pair of beers. "No. It's a Bureau safehouse. Shawshank?"

"Really? Andrew…Andy Dufresne? That's either an obvious alias or your parents hated you."

The man smiles as he hands her a bottle and sits in the overstuffed armchair on the other side of the living room. Ashlee plops on the sofa and takes a swig of her beer.

"You looked like you could use that."

"Or something stronger. Do you really think it's a smart career move to be here alone with a rape victim?"

"I'd be more concerned if I were here with one."

"Why don't you believe that I was raped?"

He shakes his head. "Because I know for a fact that you weren't."

"You're wrong."

"I'm not. You drugged Brody. When he passed out in his room, you undressed him and then rode him like you were on a bronco at the Texas Rodeo Championships."

"That's not true!"

"You had two orgasms, Ashlee. The second was stronger than the first."

The shock on her face couldn't be masked. It is pure disbelief. Outside of video evidence, there is not a soul in the world that could know that.

"How…I mean, how…?"

"It's not important. I know everything that happened. Everything. When the deed was done, you gave yourself a half dose of Rufinol so it would show up in your system during an exam. When you woke up, you left, concocted your story, and used Chloe to help it play out. What I want to know is why you did it. Why did you accuse an innocent man of sexual assault?"

"Innocent? That's *not* how I would characterize Brody Prock."

Shawshank cocks his head. "How would you characterize him?"

"He's a playboy. A womanizer. Someone with no respect for women."

Ashlee's voice gets louder as she practically spits the sentences out. She expects him to react with an urgent tone and staunch defense but gets neither. He just nods.

"And that's how you got back at him? Or was this really not about him at all?"

"Are you a shrink, Shawshank?" Ashlee asks, leveling it more as an accusation than a question.

"God, no. I'm a guy trying to understand why a beautiful, intelligent young lady with a promising future accuses a man of rape, knowing it will ruin his life."

"You seem to know everything else about me. Why don't you explain it?"

The agent sips his beer. "I'd rather you did."

"Brody is…was…every girl's dream, and he knew it. The girls at school worshipped the ground he walked on. He was brilliant, gorgeous, athletic, driven—"

"And gay."

"What?"

Shawshank presses his lips together. "Brody was gay, Ashlee. He was in a homosexual relationship with his roommate."

"No…Lucas? That's not possible. He was almost as bad."

"The reputation for womanizing is how Lucas and Brody hid the truth from their religious and homophobic fathers. It's why Brody never spoke publicly about your allegation. He had the ultimate defense and couldn't use it."

The suicide makes more sense now. Brody was cornered. He couldn't tell the police what had happened because he couldn't tell his father who he really was. A pit forms in Ashlee's stomach.

"Is that why I'm here? For you to tell me that?"

"Not exactly, but would you rather have this conversation in front of a room full of FBI agents all judging you?"

Ashlee folds her arms across her chest, clutching the bottle in her right hand. "Isn't that what you're doing?"

"No, I'm not. I don't think you're a bad person, Ashlee. I think you did a bad thing. Those are two very different things. I want to know why you did it."

She cocks her head. "I think you already know."

"And I think your healing won't begin until *you* tell me the whole story. Are you hungry? The smell of Chinese wafting up here is starting to drive me nuts."

The sudden change of subject catches Ashlee off-guard. She offers a weak smile. "I haven't eaten in a while."

"Let's fix that," he says, rising and moving to the kitchen. "Emotional conversations are no fun, especially on an empty stomach."

Ashlee watches the agent read one of the paper menus on the counter as he places a call for takeout. His movements are non-threatening. They aren't aggressive at all. She has never had a man in her life whom she trusts. That might be changing. He isn't what she expected, at least for a federal agent. He seems like a man who has his own pain. That makes him someone she can relate to.

CHAPTER FIFTY-NINE
SSA ZACH FORTE

JACOB K. JAVITS FEDERAL BUILDING
NEW YORK, NEW YORK

It had to be checked. Since Zach's arrival, the team hasn't interacted with their FBI brethren on the floors above them. There was an outside chance that Boston went there with Ashlee, although he thought it was unlikely. Once he confirmed that nobody upstairs had heard of Agent Dufresne or seen Ashlee Trillo, Zach had one option to get answers.

He takes the elevator back down to their desolate floor and strides past the empty cubicles to the conference room. He storms in to see Emma and Nadiya sharing a pizza. They stare at him without moving.

"What the hell?"

"What?" Emma asks. "We saved you a couple of slices."

"That's not what I meant. Where's Boston?"

The two women exchange looks and take bites out of the pepperoni slices folded in their hands. Zach crosses his arms as he waits for one of them to swallow. It's become a contest of who could chew more slowly. He needs to speed up the process.

"Boston left the Cloisters with Ashlee before the two of you did. Yet, you're sitting here stuffing your faces, and he's nowhere to be found. Where is he?"

"He took her to his safehouse," Emma says as if it isn't the most insane thing she could utter.

Zach's jaw hangs open. "He's alone with a *rape* victim?"

"A woman who is alleging rape, yes," Nadiya confirms in a matter-of-fact tone. She must be coming around to Boston's line of thinking.

"Do either of you realize how stupid that is? Why not bring her here?"

Emma shrugs. "Have you talked to Matt yet?"

"No. Why?"

"No reason."

Zach plants his hands down on the desk. "Spill."

"Tomasso Trillo is politically connected," Nadiya says, wiping her mouth with a napkin. "Brass sent us on this assignment for that reason."

"And?"

"The man is a control freak. I don't need a psych profile to tell me that. How do you think he'll respond to us having his daughter?"

Forte only met the Trillo patriarch once, and that was with the team. He came across as cold and calculating. Zach pegged him as a shady man who considers himself the master of all he surveys. If Tomasso wants his daughter back, he'll know which strings to pull to make that happen. Brass will start getting calls, but Remsen calls the shots.

"Matt wouldn't give that order."

"He would if Brass told him to," Emma says, pulling out a hundred and laying it on the conference room table. "Put your money where your mouth is, Forte."

Zach sits and rubs his eyes. Boston is going to be the death of him. That man has a nasty habit of putting everyone in compromising situations.

"Orders are orders."

"What order?" Nadiya asks. "You didn't tell him to come back here. You were busy with the NYPD and assumed he would come back here. Don't be pissed at us because you were wrong."

Forte hangs his head, thinking back to his time at the museum and his discussions with the NYPD…she's right. He never spoke to Boston and is certain that his problem child avoided him by design. He planned this the moment he rescued Ashlee from her assailant's clutches.

"Zach, Boston knows what he's doing," Emma piles on. "I know you want the full story behind why Ashlee made her accusation, and he's going to get it."

"We know the story."

"No. We know *what* happened. We don't know *why*."

"And Matt isn't going to care about the why," Nadiya concludes. "The question is, do you? Slice?"

There is no arguing with these women. They are going to drive their future husbands insane. Zach sits in the chair and takes the pizza Nadiya offers. He refolds it and shoves the first third in his mouth. It's not like the tomato sauce will make his indigestion any worse.

CHAPTER SIXTY

JOHN PROCK

MILITARY PARK
NEWARK, NEW JERSEY

John withdraws a cigarette from the new pack he bought at the nearby convenience mart. He's not a habitual smoker. Unlike most people, he can enjoy the occasional pack of cancer sticks without becoming addicted. It comes in handy at times like this. Alone in a desolate park with no reason to be there on a cold December evening, feeding a nicotine habit is a convenient excuse should anyone become curious.

He leans against the wall of the closed outdoor bar in the middle of the park and sparks the cigarette with a disposable lighter. Military Park is a formerly underutilized six-acre plot that attracts children, local residents, and office workers to an inviting outdoor space. Before its new life as a revitalized town square, the park saw occasional military use as a training ground during the French and Indian War and as a campground during the American Revolution and the War of 1812.

Military Park fell into disrepair until conservation efforts reclaimed the space. It now features the Wars of America monument created by Mount Rushmore sculptor Gutzon Borglum. That monument forms the base of an eighty-yard-long concrete sword built into the ground. There is a certain satisfaction standing here. Tomasso Trillo was instrumental in the rehabilitation effort.

John takes another long drag and stares at Park Plaza. The road parallel to the space's eastern edge is as quiet as the offices and shops that line it. Still nothing. One of the narrow, four-story brick buildings with arched windows stoically stands among its larger neighbors. John checks his watch, hoping nothing is wrong.

He takes a final puff and crushes the cigarette with the sole of his shoe. The flash lights up the area before John hears the deafening boom accompanying it. The explosion rips through the second floor of the brick structure, demolishing all three oversized windows. Flames pour out of the building and lick the facade.

John's lips crease into a smile. The blast wasn't subtle. The message he is sending with it should be just as clear. Within seconds, the building is engulfed in flames. Distant sirens begin shrieking and wailing as a Newark police squad car rips around the corner and stops two doors down from the burning building.

It's time to go. Fires draw curious onlookers like moths to a literal flame. He doesn't want to be spotted here. He shouldn't be here but had to see it for himself.

The shipping tycoon walks around the park's west side, keeping the open space between him and the burning building he's watching over his shoulder. Fire crews arrive and begin their work. Hoses are unfurled, and ladders are extended. Water is poured on the flames in a futile attempt to douse the inferno before it claims the building.

John continues south along the edge of the sword. From the ground, it looks like an empty fountain. He stops and watches the fire department do its work. He's just another observer in a growing crowd. The building will be a complete loss, and the visitor center on the ground floor is collateral damage in this newly declared war.

A car pulls over to the curb and stops. John takes a long look at the burning building and turns toward the waiting vehicle. Lothar looks at him impatiently as he walks around the front, opens the door, and slides into the passenger seat.

"Seen enough?" he asks with a degree of irritation. He didn't like the idea of this course of action at all.

"For now. Any problems?"

"No. The men made a clean getaway."

"Good. Let's get back to Scarsdale and turn on the news."

Lothar pulls back into the lane and steers the car for home. John watches the fire through the window. He smiles. In the morning, Tomasso Trillo will need to think about building Brick City Development a new office.

CHAPTER SIXTY-ONE

JAMIESON BOHMER

Jamieson has changed back into lawyer mode. The failed attempt at snatching Ashlee left him with wounded pride, which will eventually heal after he gets some payback. A physical injury would have been harder to hide. Fortunately, he emerged unscathed.

Fleeing to the north had the desired effect. The NYPD was looking in the wrong direction when he doubled back to his car and slipped away. He found a quiet neighborhood and changed into his suit, ditching the clothing in a dumpster behind a restaurant.

Now he finds himself outside the Jacob Javits Federal Building with half a mind to storm up to the FBI and demand Tomasso's daughter be released into his custody. It's not the best idea considering he lobbed a flashbang at two agents. Most people would claim he's emotional and is making an irrational decision, but he doesn't get emotional. He's just running out of options.

Jamieson's cell phone rings with the call he's been dreading receiving. He stares long and hard at the contact name that pops up on the screen. He takes a deep breath and connects the call. He might as well get this over with.

"Yeah?"

"Where are you?"

"I'm still in Manhattan. I found your daughter by tracking Chloe McCarthy, but the FBI got to her first. They have Ashlee in their custody in their New York office."

"Was she arrested?"

Jamieson stares up at the building's façade. "No, I don't think so."

"Did she contact them?"

"She must have," the lawyer concludes, unable to conjure any other reasonable explanation for their appearance. "They arrived at her location moments after I did."

Tomasso curses under his breath. It's masked by shouts, muted sirens, and a muffled roar in the background.

"I will deal with them. I need you to return to Newark immediately. There's been a development."

"What happened?"

"Our office was torched. I'm here now. It's a three-alarm blaze the fire department is still trying to get under control."

"Damage?" Jamieson asks.

"It's a total loss. There will be an investigation, but the fire chief on the scene has already told me it's likely arson."

"Who would…? John Prock."

"Return to Newark and find out for sure. If you prove it was him or his people, he will get the war he's begging for."

Jamieson glances back up at the federal building. Payback for the embarrassment outside the museum will have to wait, as will retrieving Tomasso's rebellious daughter. He has no idea how her father plans on handling that, but it's his problem now. Jamieson is happy to pursue a new assignment.

"I'll get there as soon as I can."

The lawyer ends the call and is about to stow his phone when another call comes in. He answers this one more eagerly as he walks to his vehicle parked a dozen blocks away.

"This isn't a good time, Dusty. Make it fast."

"I heard about the fire up in Newark."

Jamieson sighs. "Bad news travels fast. Do you happen to have any information on who did it? There is almost no doubt it's arson."

"No. I don't have many contacts in New Jersey. We need to talk."

"Okay, talk," Jamieson orders.

"In person."

Jamieson doesn't react to the demand as his mind goes into overdrive. That's an odd request from Dusty. He's not the type to insist on personal contact. Most of his business transactions are done over the phone or via email and texting. What could he possibly want to meet about?

"That's easier said than done. I need to get over to Newark immediately."

"Then get on the road. Meet me at the Hudson River Greenway near the clay courts off 96th Street in twenty minutes," Dusty orders.

It's out of the way, but his curiosity is piqued. Jamieson looks at his watch and thinks about the traffic on the West Side Highway and Henry Hudson Parkway. The NYPD likely set up a roadblock following the museum attack to snag him trying to leave the island. It will be dismantled by the time he reaches it, but the resulting congestion will take some time to clear out.

"Make it thirty."

CHAPTER SIXTY-TWO
SSA ZACH FORTE

JACOB K. JAVITS FEDERAL BUILDING
NEW YORK, NEW YORK

Zach finishes his slices and wishes that the ladies had bought two pies. New York pizzas are anything but diminutive in size, but Zach hadn't realized how famished he was. His last meal was at the diner with Boston, but that feels like days ago.

Nadiya returns from her trip to the vending machine with a trio of Cokes to wash their meal down. New York has the best pizza on the planet. Anyone who thinks Chicago's deep dish fare is better is flat-out wrong. He'd get into a brawl over that opinion.

He's going to regret this later. Zach is sensitive to acids. Citrus causes him agony without a bottle of antacids handy. Coffee, tomatoes, alcohol, and vinegar are common triggers. Basically, all the foods he likes are fast becoming off-limits. There will come a point when he asks a doctor to put him out of his misery.

Remsen opens up a videoconference. The trio looks at each other before Nadiya punches the button on their end to fire up the technology. Matt doesn't look happy.

"I hope I'm not interrupting your meal," he says sarcastically after noticing the pizza box, Cokes, and used napkins. "We can get to the part later where you disobeyed a direct order to return to Belvoir. Right now, I need to know what the hell is going on there."

"It's been a long night."

"Apparently. Why don't you do something novel, Zach, and report exactly why it was long. I seem to be getting updated from everyone except you."

Forte takes a deep breath and rattles off the story, starting with the trip up to Scarsdale, the call from the diner, and the ordeal at the Met Cloisters. Matt listens, making faces that are either intestinal distress, hemorrhoid flare-up, or abject annoyance with Zach.

Remsen leans closer to the camera. "Do you have any idea what kind of firestorm this has started?"

"No, that's what we have you for."

"I'm glad you're finding humor in this. Trillo has been on the phone with senators, congresspeople, and the governor of New Jersey. Hell, he's probably called the FBI director and White House by now."

"Congresspeople?"

"Whatever," Matt says. "He's threatening to go public with this. The Bureau is getting calls from angry politicians demanding answers, and Brass is getting calls from the Hoover Building."

"It sounds like the U.S. government is running up its phone bill."

Matt slams his hand on his desk. "Dammit, Zach, this is serious! You need to return Ashlee Trillo to her father, and I mean right now."

"I can't. She's with Boston."

"Okay…where is Boston?"

"He's not here. I'm not sure where he is."

Matt rubs his forehead as Forte suppresses a smirk. He chose those words on purpose. Remsen considers him a glorified babysitter, not a team leader. By confessing that he doesn't know where Boston is, he essentially admits to failing his primary responsibility. At least, that's how Matt will see it.

"Zach, you and I are going to have a long chat when you get back to Watchtower. Until then, find him. Have the girl remanded to FBI custody for transport to New Jersey. Make it happen, and soon."

He doesn't leave the door open for debate when he ends the call. It was a direct order and not one that Zach could ignore without repercussions. The burner just got turned up on the pot of hot water he's already bathing in.

"Remsen looks tense. He needs a massage," Emma says.

"Yeah, one with a happy ending," Nadiya adds as Emma's phone chirps on the conference table. "Not that I'm offering."

Zach stretches his neck before standing. "Call Boston. Tell him what's going on."

"Are you going to collect him?"

"No. I'm going to the men's room to throw up."

"You might want to hear this before you go," Emma says, staring intently at her phone. "We have a development in Newark."

CHAPTER SIXTY-THREE
"BOSTON" HOLLINGER

FBI SAFEHOUSE
CHINATOWN, NEW YORK, NEW YORK

I've never been overly fond of Chinese food. First, its authenticity is dubious at best. Early restaurants adapted their cultural dishes to suit American palates by making them sweeter, boneless, and deep-fried. Broccoli, an unheard-of vegetable in China, appeared on menus. And don't get me started on fortune cookies, which are thought to be from Japan.

Still, this is Chinatown in one of the greatest immigrant cities in the world, so takeout was a no-brainer. And it's good. The place down the street might as well have a Michelin star for its lo mein. Ashlee isn't complaining either, but this is a treat for a grad student who likely has devoured her fair share of ramen noodles.

As we eat, I endure a healthy dose of mockery at my attempted use of chopsticks. The conversation meanders to any subject that isn't what happened in Salisbury. I've seen everything I need to. All I need is a motive, which I'm optimistic we'll eventually get to. Until then, I want to understand what makes this woman tick. I'm learning more than I bargained for. Despite her abusive father and nightmarish teenage years, she's a bright young woman with a fantastic sense of humor.

My cell vibrates, and I check the caller id. It's from the federal building.

"I need to take this," I tell my guest. "Hello?"

"Boston, it's Emma. You're on speaker with Nadiya."

"And Zach?"

"He's in the men's room nursing an aneurysm."

I can't suppress a smile. Zach would never approve of my being alone with Ashlee. It's a liability for him, the FBI, Watchtower…pretty much everyone. That's why begging for forgiveness is better than asking for permission.

"It's good for him. What's the word?"

"Nothing good. The boys upstairs got an angry call from Tomasso Trillo. After some ranting, he threatened to go public that the FBI has his daughter in custody."

"That's not true."

"Do you think the media cares?" Nadiya asks. "They have made dragging us through the mud a contact sport. Our reputation couldn't get worse if the Bureau was named as accomplices in the Kennedy assassination."

She has a point. I spent too much time working in Congress to ignore the politics involved. I used to be an optimist about the function of government. Then I began working in Washington. Politicians and bureaucrats are after the same thing: protecting their reputations, enhancing their power, and enriching themselves. It's a sad but near-universal truth.

"It's a PR nightmare for the Bureau, especially considering we're involved," Emma concludes. "It threatens to expose us. Remsen ordered Zach to get you under control."

"What's he going to do? Chain him to a chair and force him to watch the first three seasons of *The Real Housewives of Salt Lake City*?"

"I doubt Matt would resort to torture," Emma deadpans, "but you're still going to be forced to bring her here. It's only a matter of time. Tomasso played the one card we can't beat with anything in our hand."

"Okay. I'll discuss it with Ashlee and get back to you. Can you keep Forte out of my hair until the morning?"

"That shouldn't be a problem," Emma says. "He's pissed but hasn't marched downstairs to a Suburban to collect you, either. He ran interference with Matt to buy you time."

"Interesting."

I am going to be up late thinking about that nugget of information. Zach exists on both sides of the same coin. He's either with me one hundred percent like in Mexico or the bane of my existence. I'm looking forward to finding out why he's sitting on the fence.

"There's one more thing you should know about," Nadiya interjects. "Watchtower informed us of a structure fire underway in Newark. The details are sketchy, but the fire department already suspects arson."

"Let me guess: Brick City Development."

"Bingo."

"Any suspects?"

"They haven't started their investigation yet, but you don't need much imagination to know who's likely behind it."

"Prock will have a rock-solid alibi, which will enrage Trillo even more. What I don't get is why. John Prock is practically allergic to media coverage. He has to know that he'll be at the top of the suspect list. Why invite scrutiny by torching Trillo's company?"

"Just because he manufactures fentanyl doesn't mean he's a criminal mastermind, Boston. He's angry about losing his son and wanted to lash out at somebody."

I frown. It's still out of character. If what Brody said about his father is true, he's smarter than that. There is something at play here that I don't yet understand. When the Trillo drama is over, I'll shift my focus to the Fentanyl King of Scarsdale.

"Okay. Keep me informed."

CHAPTER SIXTY-FOUR

ASHLEE TRILLO

Shawshank ends the call and pockets his phone. He returns to his chair, picks up the rest of his carton of lo mein, and goes back to work on it without saying anything. Ashlee finds that odd. He wasn't hiding the conversation or its subject matter. He was adamant and firm, yet nothing from that conversation is blowing back on her.

"Was that your wife?" Ashlee asks, knowing that it wasn't.

"I'm not married."

"Girlfriend?"

"They're the colleagues of mine that you met at the Cloisters."

Ashlee stabs at a piece of broccoli with her fork. "They're very pretty."

"I would say 'beautiful' is a better description."

Ashlee grins. He didn't say "hot" or "smoking." Beautiful is a classy, respectful way to characterize a woman's appearance. It's not trivializing or demeaning. He meant it as a statement of fact, which she doesn't dispute.

"Have you hooked up with either of them?"

"No," he says with a violent shake of his head.

"Why not?"

"A couple of reasons. Nadiya – the blonde who doesn't like you – is my combatives instructor. She beats on people for a living and could kick my ass without breaking a sweat. Emma is a firearms instructor. She could shoot wings off a fly at thirty meters."

"Those are excuses, Shawshank, not reasons."

He grins. "They're both colleagues and good friends. Almost sisters. They have helped me…I was betrayed a couple of years ago. My fiancée…well, let's just say she wronged me in a way you read about in thriller novels. It's taken me a long time to let people back in. Relationships are messy, but I trust both of those women. I never want to be in a position where that gets jeopardized."

Ashlee presses her lips together and nods. She expected some BS reason and didn't get one. That's the most honest answer she has ever heard.

"You look a little like Matthew McConaughey."

"Thank my plastic surgeons."

Ashlee thinks that was meant to be a joke, but it sounded like an admission. "Can I ask you a personal question?"

"You mean like the last four?"

"Yes, but slightly different. Would you date me?"

Shawshank puts his fork down and wipes his mouth. Ashlee thinks he's going to either dodge the question or tell her exactly what she wants to hear.

"In a different place, time, and circumstance, yes. A lot of men would…except your baggage scares them off."

"What baggage?" Ashlee asks, surprised at the conclusion.

"You tell me," he says with a knowing look.

Shawshank may be a good man, but he's a little creepy because he knows things he shouldn't. It's like he can probe her mind. It's unnerving, but she still finds him irresistibly engaging.

"What did your colleagues want?"

"Nice change of subject. They called to tell me that your father knows you're in our custody and is demanding we return you home."

"What?"

"Jamieson must have called him right after he fled the Cloisters. Your father is threatening to go to the media and claim that we are holding you against your will. Considering the support you've mustered, it will put the FBI in a bad situation. We don't have a lot of fans right now."

"My father knows how to gain leverage. It's all he does. When that doesn't work, he calls Jamieson. That man is…."

"A psychopath. I know."

The accurate synopsis surprises Ashlee. Jamieson comes across as well-educated, dapper, and somewhat charming. He's anything but.

"You're a real man of mystery, Shawshank. So, what are you going to do?"

"I have to apologize to you, Ashlee. I lied earlier. You're here and not at the Javits Federal Building because the FBI would already have you on transport racing to Englewood Cliffs. They don't want a public scandal. Since they can't do that, they're applying pressure on me to deposit you at home."

She notices his perfectly relaxed demeanor from across the room. There is no tension or nervousness in his voice or movements. If he's stressed about his boss's ultimatum, Shawshank is a master at not showing it.

"You're not reaching for your keys, so you clearly don't want to."

"It's your choice, not mine or the bureaucrats at the FBI to decide. If you wanted to be home, you wouldn't have slipped out when nobody was looking. Twice, it seems."

"How…? I got caught on my first…how could you know that?"

"Because I'm Batman," he says, using a dusky voice that causes her to laugh. It's her first one in a long time.

"My father isn't bluffing."

"I know."

"I'm serious. My father won't stop until he gets what he wants. It's practically his mantra. You could get in a lot of trouble."

"I'm used to it. The decision isn't mine to make. It's yours."

"I don't know…."

"There's no reason to decide tonight. Sleep on it. The bedroom is yours. The lock works, so use it. I'll be out here on the couch. Tell me what you want to do in the morning."

The agent begins clearing the Chinese food cartons and wiping down the coffee table and kitchen counter. The man isn't a slob, either. He's leaving this place in better condition than he found it.

Ashlee goes to the bedroom door and stops. "You're a good man, Shawshank. I haven't had much experience with that. Good night."

She closes the door and leans against it. Maybe there are good people in this world. Shawshank may have a truckload of secrets, but he has a good heart. He's respectful and caring. Maybe she can find a man like that someday. Suddenly, she feels the rush of confidence that only optimism can bring. She doesn't need the night to think it over. Her mind is made up.

CHAPTER SIXTY-FIVE

JOHN PROCK

AMLOG CORPORATE OFFICE
HUNTS POINT, BRONX, NEW YORK

Wedged between an office supply store and a bank off Central Park Avenue in his town is a pizza place with a crust he could die for. Their Classic New York Pizza with San Marzano tomato sauce and *mozzarella di bufala* is good enough not to need additional toppings. John called ahead from the car when he was about twenty minutes away. His mouth already watering, he parks right in front of the restaurant to retrieve his pie.

The AMLOG CEO tries to be conscious of his eating, but it's been one of those weeks. Pizza is his favorite food, and it's time to indulge. He pays the bill as it is removed from the oven, boxed, and cut with a pizza wheel.

With the aroma assaulting his nose and triggering his stomach to rumble, John hurries out of the store to find his car blocked into the space. It's not a typical double-parking job. The offending driver is standing next to his gleaming black Maserati. John scans the small parking lot to confirm no strip mall patrons are inconveniently heading for their cars. As mild as these December temperatures are, nobody will be hanging around outside.

"What are you doing here?" John asks, turning his attention to the well-dressed Latino.

"Is that any way to treat your business associate? You haven't been returning my calls, *señor*. Would you rather I visit your place of business?"

"I'm sorry, Ignacio. I've been busy."

Ignacio Barerra pulls a cigarette out of its pack and taps it against a gleaming silver Zippo lighter. "I've noticed. So has our employer. The allegations against your son were unfortunate but tolerable. But then you killed him."

"I didn't kill my son!"

He lights the cigarette and takes a long drag. "Sure. And the attack on the McCarthy girl? Are you going to say that wasn't you either?"

"That's different. It can't be traced back to me."

"And the arson?" Ignacio asks, unimpressed.

John's jaw tightens. The cartels are nothing if not well-informed, so he shouldn't be surprised. Ignacio's whole purpose for living in New York is to monitor operations and report problems to his overlords in Mexico. Lothar deals with him for most of their business. Tonight is a special circumstance.

"Yes, yes, you're going to tell me you understand you're the lead suspect. Then you'll…what's the English word? Prattle? Then you'll prattle on about how you made sure your alibi is airtight. Perhaps you even lined up a patsy to take the fall. Understand that no matter what precautions you took, the authorities will know it was you."

"The state police won't make the connection."

"And the FBI?"

"They're morons," John snaps.

Ignacio chuckles before inhaling another lungful of smoke. "I thought that once. Then something happened about six months ago. A lone FBI agent crossed the border into Mexico, traveled to San Carlos Nuevo Guaymas, and killed Alejandro Salcido. You heard the report, no?"

John crosses his arms. "I read the news article online. Salcido died in a murder-suicide."

"You Americans are so funny," Ignacio says with another laugh. "You walk around telling others not to believe what they read on the Internet and then proceed to believe everything you read yourself. That level of hypocrisy is unmatched. I was in Sonora when it happened, Mr. Prock. Alejandro Salcido was murdered on his veranda by a lone FBI agent. The cartels combined forces and chased him north to the border, and he still managed to escape back into the U.S. That is no easy feat. So no, I don't believe that they are all morons, Mr. Prock."

"I'm willing to bet that one lone agent isn't here."

"Let's hope not, for your sake, because he was quite skilled. You have bigger concerns now, like whether I should tell our boss that you are no longer a viable partner."

John smirks. This isn't the first time Ignacio has threatened him. It's a part of doing business with the cartels. They are particular about how they run their operations and are ruthless against those who betray or fail them. Most of the threats are in passing. This one feels the same.

"You are many things, *Señor Barerra*: well-dressed, polished, educated…what you aren't is a liar. You have already professed our value to your superiors, so you know what you're saying isn't true. Nobody offers the combined transportation and manufacturing that we do. Nobody."

"You are a businessman. You understand assets and liabilities. I do not doubt that your company is an asset to our organization. What I'm saying is that you are becoming a liability. What your company does for us will not be beneficial if your impulses compromise the operation."

"They won't. I've seen to it."

"Hollow words from a shallow man."

The statement rattles John. In his dealings with the cartel, he's only known their mouthpiece to be professional. Even his threats have been businesslike and measured. This is different. It's personal.

"I'm good for my word."

Ignacio drops the remainder of his cigarette on the ground and crushes it under the sole of his shoe. "Then prove it. Handle your business and make these issues disappear. You have one week to clean this up, or I will make that pizza your last. Enjoy your meal, Mr. Prock."

The ultimatum and consequences of failure are clear. Ignacio has proven on multiple occasions that he's a man of his word. He speaks with authority, and no threat he issues should be considered idle. This was not like his other demands for increased production or condensed timelines. It's far more serious.

The cartel enforcer slides into his car, pulls out of the strip mall parking lot, and speeds away. John climbs into his vehicle and places the pizza on the passenger seat. He stares at it for a long moment. His grumbling stomach is now sour and turning. Suddenly, he doesn't have much of an appetite.

CHAPTER SIXTY-SIX

JAMIESON BOHMER

HUDSON RIVER GREENWAY
RIVERSIDE PARK, NEW YORK, NEW YORK

Jamieson steers his car into the parking lot and kills the engine. The New York City Parks & Recreation's 96th Street Red Clay Tennis Courts are open to the public on a first-come, first-serve basis. He's not here to smack a furry green ball over a net. From the looks of the vacant courts, nobody else is eager to be playing night tennis in mid-December air.

He walks down the grassy embankment and over a black pipe fence. The Manhattan Waterfront Greenway provides shoreline access for residents in some of Manhattan's most densely populated neighborhoods. Over the years, the city has integrated larger parks into this connected network that runs continuously around the island. The total acreage encompasses an area larger than Central Park.

Dusty is waiting for him, leaning on the fence separating the greenway from the river. As Jamieson approaches, he admires the view of Edgewater, New Jersey, situated just across the river.

"I'm short on time, Dusty. Why did you want to meet?"

The private investigator grunts as he turns and points a gun at Jamieson. The former SAS operative doesn't panic. He identifies the G48 Black chambered in 9mm Luger even in the greenway's low-light conditions. He's familiar with the weapon. It's designed for comfort with a compact grip, a built-in beaver tail, a short trigger distance, and a reversible magazine catch. It makes a good concealed-carry firearm.

"All right, Dusty. What's that about?"

"What are you and Tomasso into?" he demands.

"What the hell are you talking about?"

Dusty shakes his head. "Tell me, or I'll shoot you right here and now."

"Yeah, you're not going to do that," Jamieson says, moving closer to the railing and leaning against it. "Something's got you spooked. Let's start with what that is."

"Special Agent Andrew Dufresne. I looked into him like you asked."

"Good. What did you find?"

"Absolutely nothing. There *is* no Special Agent Dufresne. There's no record of his application to the Bureau or evidence that he's ever been to Quantico, much less graduated from it. He has no personnel record, case assignments, evaluation… anything that indicates the man exists. He's a ghost."

Jamieson rubs his chin. That's an interesting piece of information.

"It could be an alias."

"Since when do the feds give aliases? I checked out the other names you gave me. Supervisory Special Agent Zachary Forte worked in counterintelligence before landing a 'special assignment' whose details are redacted. Special Agent Emma Farris is a firearms instructor…again, on a 'special assignment.' There is no Nadiya Jesperssen in the FBI, but apparently, there is one in the CIA. So, we have a ghost, a spook, and two agents involved in something off the books. Now, I'm going to ask you again, Jamieson…what are you and Tomasso into?"

Jamieson digests that information. He was in the SAS and knows a good amount about the covert world. He met his fair share of spies from British MI6 and the American Central Intelligence Agency back in the day. The lawyer doesn't understand why they would take an interest in Ashlee's allegations against Brody Prock unless it has nothing to do with her allegations. That would explain a lot about their choice of questions at her interview. They could be looking into Brick City Development, but why?

"Nothing."

"Don't lie to me!" Dusty shouts, gripping the Glock tighter.

"Put the damn gun away, Dusty. We're too old to play these games. I have no idea why they're interested in Tomasso, but I am damn sure going to find out."

"Do it without me. My involvement with you is over. I don't conduct business like this."

"I understand," Jamieson says, slowly reaching into his pocket and pulling out an envelope filled with hundred-dollar bills. "I appreciate everything you've done for me. You're an excellent investigator. This is to cover your expenses, and I added a reward for a job well done."

Dusty grins as he holsters his weapon and reaches for the envelope. He's focused on his payday as he checks the envelope and doesn't notice Jamieson slide his right hand into his overcoat pocket. The lawyer doesn't risk withdrawing the weapon where the PI can see it. He simply points its muzzle at Dusty's abdomen and fires through his coat.

The shot hits the man in the stomach. Dusty bends forward, struggling to reach his holster. Jamieson fires twice more and props him up against the railing. The former cop stares at him, waiting for him to say something. He doesn't. One-liners are for eighties action movies. He grabs him behind the legs and shoves him over the railing.

Dusty hits the water face-first. He doesn't thrash around or try to kick for the shore. He just floats until the current catches him and drags him south. Most people don't realize that the Hudson isn't a river in this part of the state. It's a tidal estuary that stretches one hundred and fifty-three miles from Battery Park to Troy, New York. The estuary feels the ocean's tidal pulse and flows both ways. While his body may wash up near the USS Intrepid, it could also be discovered north of the George Washington Bridge. Either way, it will be found.

Jamieson looks around. Nobody is on the greenway, but someone likely heard the shots. He tosses the gun into the river, unconcerned about whether it's found. The weapon was purchased on the street, has no serial number, and there won't be recoverable prints. In short, it's completely untraceable back to him.

It's time to go. He reaches down and secures the money, tucking the envelope in his pocket as he walks. So long as Jamieson gets away clean, it can never be proven that he was ever here. It will be another tragic New York City homicide destined to join their warehouse full of cold case files.

Jamieson steps back over the black pipe railing and hurries up the embankment to the parking area. Dusty was one of the good ones. He was meticulous, efficient, and delivered results. There isn't a limitless supply of men like that. He won't be easy to replace, but it beats having him turn against them and run to the FBI. Some measures must be taken to defend the enterprise. That's what Tomasso trusts Jamieson to do.

CHAPTER SIXTY-SEVEN
ASHLEE TRILLO

Shawshank locks the door to the safe house and leads Ashlee down the stairs, out the front door, and onto the street. The smell of Chinese food assaults her senses, even at ten in the morning. She turns to see two gleaming black Chevy Suburbans parked along the sidewalk. A small brunette climbs out of the lead vehicle and waits for them.

"Do cars just arrive whenever you want them?"

He grins from ear to ear. "Well, there was this one time in Mexico…unfortunately, that's a story I can't tell you."

"You ready?" Emma says when they reach her.

Ashlee looks the woman over. Shawshank is right – beautiful is a more appropriate description. He may see her as a sister, but Emma's definitely crushing on him. It's in her eyes when she looks at him.

"I want to ride with Shawshank. Alone. Is that okay?"

Emma turns to her fellow agent and smirks. "Shawshank, eh? Yeah, okay."

The energetic woman rushes back to her own Suburban and climbs in.

"Does she think we hooked up last night?"

"She knows better. Are you sure you're ready for this?"

"Yeah, I am," Ashlee says confidently.

"All right. Come on."

The pair leads the two-vehicle convoy across Manhattan toward the Holland Tunnel. Ashlee expected her driver to pepper her with questions during this trip. This is the last chance he'll get for a while. Instead, he remains quiet. It's up to her to tell the story. He likes giving her that power.

"We were a happy family once," Ashlee says, unprompted. "My mother was a saint. I remember she used to brush my hair every night and read to me before bed – kids' books, young adult books, and even some adult books when I hit my tween years. I even convinced her to read me her Stephen King novels. *Pet Sematary*, *Misery*, *The Mist*, and…."

Ashlee looks over at the agent, who grins and shakes his head.

"*Rita Hayworth and Shawshank Redemption*. And here I thought you just watched the movie."

She smiles. "I had a great early childhood."

"What happened?" he asks, stopping at a light on the street leading to the tunnel.

"Short answer? I became a teenager who wanted the freedom that comes with it. My father was very controlling. He and my mother would fight over me all the time. When they would argue, he would say the cruelest things."

"Your mother wanted children, and Tomasso never did."

Ashlee's head shoots around to him. "You're creepy. You know that, right?"

"I've been told that once or twice."

"My mom thought I was an angel. I wasn't. My father made me rebellious."

"Teenagers know everything," Shawshank muses.

"Yeah. One night, I wanted to go to a friend's. My mother was fine with it, but my father wasn't. They argued, as usual, but my mother lost this time. He said no, and his word was gospel in that house. So, I snuck out anyway. I thought I was in the clear, but the bastard did a bed check. My mother knew where I went and jumped in the car for the short drive to my friend's house. She only made it a couple of streets."

"What happened?"

He asks the question, but Ashlee immediately gets the familiar sensation that he already knows. "She was hit by a drunk driver."

They drive in silence as Ashlee fights to control her tears. It's a painful memory and not one she's eager to relive.

"My father got the call. He collected me and took me straight to the hospital. I was devasted. She was in intensive care…there were tubes and wires…she was so pale."

Ashlee looks out the corner of her eye and notices the look on his face. It's contorted in pain. It's almost like he's feeling her grief.

"That's when it started. My father blamed me for what had happened to her. She died two days later. Internal bleeding. The doctors said they couldn't stop it. She never regained consciousness, and I never got to say goodbye."

"And because you never got to ask her for forgiveness, you could never forgive yourself."

Ashlee nods. "My father never forgave me, either. My mother was his world. He loved her with a burning passion, and I was the reason she was taken away. He became distant and, as time went on, more abusive. The mental torment was worse than the physical. I became an appendage to his life, not a part of it. I was the constant reminder of what he had lost and something that he never wanted in the first place. And then there was Jamieson."

"Did he ever hurt you?"

"Sometimes. Jamieson Bohmer is a monster who relies on fear to get what he wants. He likes control, and he's dangerous. I've been terrified of him my whole life. I've never met a man who treated me well."

"Until you did," Shawshank says as they navigate through traffic in the tunnel. "Brody. Your first date with him was great, wasn't it?"

"It was…magical. By far, the best first date ever. We laughed, shared stories…we had a real connection. When we got back to campus, Brody didn't kiss me goodnight.

I thought that was odd but passed it off as him being a gentleman. It made me want him even more. Then he ghosted me. I never knew why…until last night."

"For what it's worth, he liked you, just not in that way. He was doing what was needed to keep a certain appearance. It wasn't meant to be malicious, but for you, he was the next in a long line of men who betrayed you."

"I hated him for that," Ashlee seethes. "I wanted payback because…."

"You felt a spark. You saw a future with him."

"Unrequited love is the most dangerous thing on earth. So, I developed a plan and waited for an opportunity, just like I learned from my father and Jamieson. I got it the night of the party. You know the rest."

Shawshank just stares out the windshield. He doesn't judge or make her feel worse than she already does. She expects a dressing down or a lecture when he finally turns to her.

"Thank you for trusting me enough to tell that story."

"It was surprisingly cathartic," she says with a nervous laugh as she wipes tears from her eyes.

"Are you sure you want to do this? Go home, I mean?"

"I've lived in fear since the day my mother died. I don't want to live like…I don't like the person I've become. What I did to Brody was wrong. It's a horrible mistake that will haunt me for the rest of my life. I need to start making things right, even if the false allegation lands me in prison. I want control of my life back. That starts with confronting my father."

He doesn't argue or try to push her into a different course of action. Shawshank said that the decision was hers, and he is honoring that. She doesn't think he agrees with her approach, but he doesn't vocalize his objections as the miles pass from the windshield to the rearview mirrors. Nothing more needs to be said.

CHAPTER SIXTY-EIGHT
"BOSTON" HOLLINGER

TOMASSO TRILLO FAMILY ESTATE
ENGLEWOOD CLIFFS, NEW JERSEY

The trip through most of New Jersey has been quiet but not tense. I sense Ashlee's anxiety rise when I pull into her neighborhood, steer into the semicircular drive, and shift the Suburban into park. I'm not right in front of the double doors that lead straight into the foyer. I'm curious to see who emerges from the house, although I can offer an educated guess.

The temptation to ask her one more time if she is having second thoughts is almost overwhelming. I manage to muster the strength not to give in. This is her choice…her journey. I don't have to like it, and I don't. Not one bit.

"I'm not going to change my mind," Ashlee says from the passenger seat, seeming to notice my internal struggle. "I think it'd be too late even if I wanted to."

"It would be more complicated," I admit, "but not too late."

The Suburban is forty feet from the front door. I could fire up the engine and gun it within seconds of Ashlee telling me to drive us out of here. I turn to look at her, trying not to make it look like I'm pleading with my eyes.

"I guess this is goodbye."

So much for that. "I prefer to leave it at 'until we meet again.'"

"Okay. Before I go, is there any chance I can hear the story you won't tell me? The one about you in Mexico?"

I smile. "Sure. Graduate from law school and join the FBI."

That's not technically accurate, but she doesn't need to know that. It's a harmless white lie. Then again, most lies are harmless until they're not. She's the kind of woman who would appear on my doorstep demanding to hear the tale five minutes after graduating from Quantico.

"See ya around, Shawshank."

Ashlee climbs out, and I do the same, moving to the front of the Suburban as she begins walking up the driveway. Emma and Nadiya climb out of the trail vehicle with a sense of urgency. When I glance at the front door, I see why. Jamieson is walking straight at me. Emma and Nadiya smell trouble, even when he passes Ashlee without even a glance. The "lawyer" stops directly in front of me.

"Special Agent Dufresne."

"Mr. Bohmer."

"Thank you for returning my client's daughter. He was very concerned about her."

I make a show of looking over his shoulder at the door. "So concerned that Tomasso is rushing out of the house to embrace his daughter in the driveway?"

"That isn't his way," Jamieson says, glancing behind him.

"Clearly. I want to speak to Tomasso."

"Unfortunately, that isn't possible. I'm happy to relay to him any message you have."

There's no point in arguing. Jamieson has slipped into lawyer mode. Without a court order, I have as much of a chance of talking to Tomasso as being crowned King of England.

"Very well. If so much as a single hair on his daughter's head is harmed, there will be consequences."

"Consequences?" Jamieson asks, feigning surprise. "As in, legal ones?"

"Regular, old-school, Old Testament of the Bible consequences."

"That sounds like a threat, Agent Dufresne."

"Nah. Nothing like that. It is a warning. I don't know what your employer is hiding. Until very recently, I didn't care. But now that I have some idea, it'd be wise not to give me a reason to keep digging."

Jamieson presses his lips together and nods. "You have speculation, Agent Dufresne. That's a dangerous thing without context because it makes people believe things that aren't true. I also did some digging since our last encounter. Do you know what I learned?"

"Enlighten me, please."

"There is no Special Agent Andrew Dufresne in the FBI," Jamieson whispers after leaning close enough for me to smell his aftershave. "Yet here you are with at least one agent who is. I'm not sure about the hot blonde with her, but that's irrelevant. It naturally begs the question of who you really are."

"Who is anyone, really?" I ask, getting philosophical now. "We only see what others show us. It shapes our perceptions…manipulates them. You understand that better than anyone, right?"

Jamieson grins. "What an interesting story they would write about us, Mr. Mystery Agent. Two adversaries with dark secrets face off in a desperate attempt to see who can learn more about the other before the ultimate showdown."

I don't need to learn anything more about Jamieson. I need him to understand how serious I am.

"You don't want to cross sabers with me."

"Is that supposed to frighten me?"

"It's not designed to, but it would if you were a smart man. Are you a smart man, Mr. Bohmer?"

"Intelligence is useless without practical application. I understand my limitations, and I know those of my enemies even better. Hope we don't have a reason to run into each other again."

"I think you should get used to the fact that we will."

He nods. "If that's the case, then maybe they'll get the chance to write stories about us after all."

Jamieson turns and walks up the drive. I watch him go, not entirely sure I had the upper hand in that exchange. I'm consumed with that thought when Nadiya touches my arm and causes me to flinch. I didn't even hear her coming up from behind me.

"I want to make that guy feel pain like he's never imagined."

"You and I both, Nadiya. You and I both."

"Did you get anything from him this time?"

I shake my head slowly. "Not a damn thing. It's strange having a conversation with someone and not seeing their pain and angst play like a movie in my head. I almost feel normal."

"You know you live an interesting life when talking to a psychopath is normal."

"'Interesting' is one word to characterize it."

Emma joins us, keeping her eyes welded to the front door. She saw something she didn't like, and now her protective instincts are in overdrive. The woman has incredible instincts. There is plenty not to like about this.

"Will Ashlee be okay?"

I follow her eyes back to the house, wishing I had a better answer to that question.

"I hope so."

CHAPTER SIXTY-NINE
SSA ZACH FORTE

ZACH'S HOTEL ROOM
NEW YORK, NEW YORK

The knock on the door surprises Zach. He rolls off the bed and answers it to find Dr. Asami Kurota standing there. He gestures her in and checks the corridor, more out of habit than any reasonable fear of the boogieman.

"I figured you would want me to meet at another museum."

"Not this time. Where's Boston?"

"He's dropping Ashlee Trillo off at her father's house in New Jersey," Zach says, locking the door and flipping the bar lock to engage it.

"Where did he stash her last night?"

"She stayed with him at the safe house."

Asami purses her lips as her eyes search for her next question. "Why was he at a safe house and not here?"

Zach hates getting the third degree. He also hates the expression, partly because of the ambiguous nature of its origin. Asami was sent here to ask these questions, and despite his reluctance to answer, he doesn't want to kill the messenger.

"Short answer? Hotels keep records, and I didn't want one for this mission."

"Ah. It was smart, especially considering Matt ordered you to return to Virginia, and you're ignoring him. Since Boston isn't here with the three of you, it reduces the likelihood of Watchtower sending a team to collect you."

"Yeah, or that. You don't miss much, Asami, do you? Can I get you something?"

"Coffee. Lots of coffee. I've been driving all night." Asami drops her purse on the small table in the corner and crashes into the upholstered chair. "And I have a six-hour drive back to Virginia after we're done here."

"You aren't staying in the city?"

"Let's just say that you aren't the only ones ignoring orders. My visit isn't exactly sanctioned." Asami sits up in her chair and leans forward. "There's another reason I wanted to meet in your hotel."

"I'm flattered, Asami, but I'm not that into you."

"Thank God you aren't," she says with a weak smile. "Boston picks up memories based on trauma, but his skills are improving. Anything that causes strong discomfort could trigger a memory, and hauling you off to a place you don't want to be might lead him to pick up this one the next time he sees you."

"And you don't want him to know that you're here. Why?"

Asami sighs heavily, retrieves her pocketbook from the table, and reaches into it. "Because of this."

She pulls out a rectangular clamshell case and stares at it for a long moment. It's strange behavior for Asami. She is not a sentimental person, nor does she place value on physical objects. She hands the case to Zach.

"Did you go jewelry shopping?"

"Open it."

He complies and finds the case empty except for a single syringe. He pulls it out and turns it over, trying to read its contents. "Does this have a name in plain English?"

"You can call it 'Sweet Dreams' or 'Memory Eraser' or something equally campy if you'd like. The name is irrelevant. What it does is the important part."

"Is this what I think it is?" She nods. "How long have you had it?"

"Almost two months," Asami whispers.

Forte gently places the syringe back in the case and closes it. Brass has wanted an "off" switch developed for Boston since before his adventures in Mexico. He realizes the value of seeing memories and wants total control. If Boston goes rogue or decides to go against his masters, their administrator needs the option of destroying the weapon.

"You didn't tell Brass or Matt about this?"

Asami looks around the room nervously before answering. "They aren't chemists. Nor do they work in the pharmaceutical industry. They have no idea how long drug development takes. I hung onto it once the lab completed the batch and swore them to secrecy."

"How does this stuff work?"

"Have you ever heard of Chantix?"

"The stop smoking aid."

"Exactly. Chantix works on two levels. First, it partially activates nicotinic acetylcholine receptors. That's how new ex-smokers get mild nicotine-like effects that ease withdrawal symptoms. The drug's main benefit is stopping actual nicotine molecules from attaching to those receptors. This serum works the second way."

"I don't understand."

Asami shifts her weight in her chair and sits a little straighter. She's shifting into doctor mode. Her body language changes to something more professional when she engages in a diagnosis or offers a medical explanation.

"I've been studying Boston's CT scans for over a year. He has a unique set of neurological pathways in his brain. They interact with his brain chemistry, and that's how he engages in remote viewing."

"That's his wi-fi antenna."

"I thought I was already explaining this in layman's terms…but, yes. I think this drug will inhibit the connection between the chemicals in his brain and these new pathways."

Zach grimaces. "So, it could turn off his ability to see memories, or it could turn him into a vegetable."

"That's a possible side effect."

"Seriously?"

Asami shrugs. "There's no way to know if it works, Zach. Boston is patient zero and the only known subject. His gift can't be replicated and thus can't be tested. If it does work, I don't know for how long. I can't know if the dosage increases or decreases that duration. Will his kidneys fail, cause blood clots, form—?"

"I get the point. Why are you giving this to me?"

Asami leans back in her chair and folds her hands on her abdomen. "Because I think Boston is at a pivotal crossroads. He will embrace this power and use it to its full potential or let it destroy him. I have no idea which direction he will go."

"Why do you say that?"

She sighs and relaxes back into the chair. "Pour me that cup of coffee, and I'll tell you."

CHAPTER SEVENTY

JOHN PROCK

ETERNAL GARDENS CEMETERY
SCARSDALE, NEW YORK

Everything changes with the passage of time. History bears witness to shifts in what's proper and cool, along with people's wants and desires. Even death changes. The ritual of interring a dead body in the ground may largely be unaltered, but the rise of the industrial funeral complex has dramatically changed the perception of death. Graveyards gave way to cemeteries. Many cemeteries were renamed "memorial gardens."

John wonders if that is supposed to make people feel better. It's certainly not making him feel any better. His son is still dead, and the place he is being laid to rest is filled with granite or marble makers engraved with names and dates. It doesn't matter what the place is called.

Vegetables grow in gardens. There are no tomato plants, carrots, or radishes here. There are only large oak and elm trees whose leaves shade the area during the summer months and a smattering of evergreens and small bushes. It's peaceful and serene but doesn't assuage his pain.

Brody's service is short. The reverend speaking at his graveside didn't personally know John's son. They weren't a religious family. And he was too young to be revered for his accomplishments, so the man's remarks were filled with hollow platitudes about how life is precious and can end too soon. That works for John. He would rather people not know the truth.

John's friends, neighbors, and AMLOG co-workers are the only people in attendance. None of Brody's friends bothered to pay their final respects. Not even Lucas. That secret of their relationship likely died with his son. Lucas will never talk, considering he couldn't be bothered to attend his lover's funeral. The apathy is disgusting. He's a despicable human being.

The service ends, and the guests say their goodbyes before heading to their cars. It's not frigid for mid-December in New York, at least compared to what it could be. Still, it's cold enough that outdoor activities other than skiing or sledding are kept short, and nobody wants to hang around a cemetery longer than necessary.

John puts his hand on his son's casket. Brody was his greatest success at birth and became his greatest failure in death. He doesn't know when he failed his son, only that he did. The rape accusations brought secrets into the sunlight. It would have been better for everyone had they stayed in the shadows. That is Ashlee Trillo's fault. And Chloe McCarthy's.

One man stays behind, and it isn't Lothar. The well-dressed man comes up and extends his hand, which John takes.

"Thank you for coming, Hugh. It's good to see you."

"And you, although I wish the circumstances were different. I'm sorry for your loss, John. I truly am. The senator also sends her sincere condolences."

Hugh Barton is a long-time acquaintance who happens to be the chief of staff for the junior senator from New York, Rachael Holloway. He convinced John to contribute significant financial resources to her first senate run. He agreed and has since grown into a strong supporter. Senator Holloway rewarded that with friendship, mainly because John is the only major campaign contributor who asks for nothing in return. Then again, true friends show up at funerals.

"That's nice of her. I hoped that she would be here to convey them in person. Instead, she sent you."

Hugh clearly expected the comment. "I volunteered. Don't think that she didn't want to be here. You have always been one of our ardent supporters. We appreciate that as much as your considerable financial generosity. Unfortunately—"

"The senator couldn't be photographed at the graveside of an accused rapist. She'd be gift-wrapping a scandal for her political enemies."

Hugh looks around and then at the casket suspended over the hole in the ground. "To put it bluntly, yes."

"He didn't rape her, Hugh."

"Politics is perception, John. I don't doubt Brody's innocence. Unfortunately, the world doesn't operate that way. You know that. Please don't hold it against Senator Holloway. She's very upset about this."

"I won't hold it against her. Since you're here, I'm hoping to ask a favor from you."

"I'll do what I can."

"A pair of FBI agents showed up at my house following Brody's death."

"Right before you went on camera in your front yard and shamed the media. That was epic, by the way. What about them?"

"Can the senator find out who they are? I know she has contacts in the FBI."

"I'm sure they're lackeys from the local field office. I'll make some inquiries, and if I don't come up with anything, I'll escalate to the senator. I have to ask – why do you want to know?"

"I just do. Lothar didn't catch either of their names. I appreciate you looking into it for me, Hugh. Thank you."

"It's the least we can do. I'm truly sorry, John."

Hugh pats him on the shoulder before walking back in the direction of his car. Prock returns to staring at his son's casket. What a waste. Of life. Of energy. Of time. He takes a long look around the memorial garden. It will be the last time he likely ever comes here. Visiting would equally be a waste.

CHAPTER SEVENTY-ONE
ASHLEE TRILLO

TOMASSO TRILLO FAMILY ESTATE
ENGLEWOOD CLIFFS, NEW JERSEY

Ashlee enters the foyer and stops. She looks around at the white marble, ornate sconces, and beautiful crystal chandelier. Somehow, this entryway looks and feels different. It's not as confining as she once thought it was. The feeling is…liberating.

She turns and enters her father's study without knocking. He glares at her from his desk before standing and walking around it. He stands ten feet away with his hands in his pockets. She wasn't expecting a hug and a tearful reunion, and she didn't get one.

Tomasso grins. "Welcome home. Go to your room. I will deal with you later."

"No."

"Excuse me?"

Ashlee looks her father in the eyes. "I said no. I'm not going to my room. I'm not taking commands from you like I'm a dog."

Tomasso presses his lips together and inhales. "You don't have a choice. You will obey me if you expect to live under this roof."

"Perfect, because I don't expect to live under your roof. Why do you think I left in the first place? The only reason I'm here is that you threatened the FBI. You wanted me back. I didn't want to return."

"You insolent little bitch."

"Maybe. But what kind of scumbag human being sends his henchman to kidnap his daughter and stab her best friend?"

"That was…unfortunate."

"Tell that to Chloe."

Tomasso menacingly storms over to Ashlee, but she doesn't retreat. He thrusts his index finger into her face. "You are a problem child. My only regret is that I wasn't harder on you."

"Learn to live with those regrets. The good news is that I'll no longer be your problem once I walk out that door."

"You always will be. You are a disgrace that I am ashamed to call my flesh and blood. I lost Viviana because of you and your selfish behavior!"

Ashlee laughs, her eyes moistening at the mention of her mother. "You know, I've listened to you blame me for my mother's death for years."

"You killed her!"

"A drunk driver killed her! Do you want to know the dirty little secret? Mom didn't need to look for me the night of the accident. She knew I was at my friend's house because I told her that's where I was going. She watched me climb out my window and waved from it as I walked away."

Tomasso's eyes shift back and forth like he's at a tennis match. Somewhere in the deep recesses of his mind is a memory that leads to the truth. It's been altered and badly suppressed, but it's there. Ashlee may not have heard the argument between her mother and father that night, but she's willing to bet that her mom told him that she granted permission. That's why he was so angry. It's also why he sent Ashlee's mother to collect her instead of going himself.

"You're lying."

"You know that I'm not. I have no reason to lie. The only reason Mom went out that night is that you wanted me locked in my room. You *forced* her to go. I didn't kill my mother – you did."

The sting on her cheek registers before she can react to the movement of her father's arm. It's a blazing-fast slap he has sadly practiced on her for years. It's what happens next that she can change. Instead of crying or shying away, she defiantly turns her head and smiles.

"Hit me again."

"What?" an incredulous Tomasso asks.

"Hit me again. Slap me a dozen more times. I'm done being scared…of you, of the world…."

"You won't survive without me."

"Yeah, that's a possibility. I won't deny it," Ashlee says before leaning forward. "But I would rather die than live like this."

Ashlee turns, and Tomasso grabs her arm. She yanks it away.

"We aren't finished!"

"Yes, we are. You've done a masterful job convincing me that I should be despised. That I have no worth or owe you for what happened to my mother. I don't. You just sought to control me, much like you did her. Only I let you. That ends right now."

"You will not leave this house."

"I am leaving, and you're going to let me. Otherwise, I'll expose every secret you have." Tomasso again recoils in shock. "You're surprised? You don't think I know about your shady deals and which politicians you have in your pocket?"

"You've been talking to the FBI."

"I have, but not about that. But I will if I'm forced to. I'm leaving, Father, and you're going to let me. That's the 'or else.'"

Jamieson is standing outside the study when Ashlee exits. He glowers at her as she stops beside him, refusing to make eye contact.

"I know you were listening. That threat also applies to you, in case there's any doubt."

Ashlee ascends the stairs and stops at the top. She looks down at the psychopath, willing to face his withering glare for the first time.

"By the way, Jamieson. You didn't manage to kill Chloe. She's tougher than you thought."

Content that she got under his skin, she retreats into the bedroom to pack a bag. The world is a scary place, and Ashlee doesn't know what she'll do next. But the possibilities are endless, and the promise of a fresh start and a new tomorrow has given her an energy she hasn't had since childhood. Ashlee feels free for the first time in her life. The smile about what the future may bring is the first genuine one she's had since the day her mother died.

CHAPTER SEVENTY-TWO

JAMIESON BOHMER

Jamieson twists the knob and enters the bedroom without knocking. His sudden appearance startles Ashlee, who stops packing her bag to look at him with apprehension. She slowly turns back and drops a couple of sweaters in it.

"What do you want? Did my father send you here to talk me out of this or tie me to a chair?"

"We're way beyond that now, don't you think?" Jamieson closes the door. "I've known you most of your life. I watched you grow up. I saw you graduate from high school and then college."

"Are you getting sentimental on me?"

"Do I strike you as the sentimental type?" Jamieson asks.

"No, you're the type who likes to inflict pain. So, cut the crap trip down memory lane."

"I have no interest in rehashing the past. That first part isn't entirely true."

"You stabbed Chloe. You didn't have to. She's smaller than you, so you could have tossed her aside to chase me. Instead, you stabbed her. You wanted to hurt her because you liked it."

"Yes, I stabbed your roommate. I didn't like it. I didn't dislike it, either. I did it because it had to be done."

"There are those words again," Ashlee whispers. "'It had to be done.' You're like a parrot. Do you always do things other people tell you to?"

Jamieson shrugs. "Most things I do for myself. Other people wanting it to happen is just a bonus. Take us, for example. I want to beat you to a bloody pulp. Your father would cheer that."

Ashlee freezes. She then slowly zips up her bag and slings it over her shoulder. "I'm sure he would. I'm leaving, Jamieson. Step aside."

"I'm not going to do that. I credit you for being so bold as to think you can waltz out of here. I'm afraid the reality of your situation is very different."

Jamieson grabs at her bag. She yanks it away and stands her ground. He stops for a moment. Whatever happened to her in the days she was gone profoundly impacted her confidence.

"Put the bag down. Let's talk."

"I have nothing to say to you."

He pulls out the knife he retrieved from the block in the kitchen and shows it to her. He watches her eyes track down to it before returning to him.

"I'm prepared to use this, but I'd rather talk," Jamieson says, setting it on the bed. "Put the bag down…please. See? I'm asking nicely."

Ashlee pulls the strap off her shoulder and drops the bag to the floor.

"That's better. I like seeing this side of you. It's fiery and passionate. It may be misplaced, but it's long overdue."

"Don't get too used to it. You're never going to see me again."

"I know you want to believe that. I'm betting you've spent the last couple of days convincing yourself that you could change things. It's honorable. It's also futile. Some things don't change, Miss Trillo, like gravity. It's immutable and always present. So is your father. He will never be out of your life."

"What are you going to do to stop me?"

"Look hard at that knife and know I will do what must be done. It's your choice. Decide."

That was the final push he needed. Ashlee grabs the knife and swings it at Jamieson. He was expecting the move. In fact, he was counting on it. He catches her arm and squeezes his hand against the knife's grip. He kicks her leg out and knocks her off-balance. Her momentum takes her backward, and he uses it to push her onto the bed. Jamieson straddles her abdomen, pinning her. It's déjà vu, except this time, she's trying to stab him with the knife he brought.

Content that she's immobilized, Jamieson applies pressure to the fist holding the knife. He forces the blade closer to her face. She eyes it as it gets closer to her cheek.

"What…no! What are you doing?"

"What I always do, Miss Trillo. What must be done."

The blade gets closer to her face. Then dips below it.

"No! Stop!"

"There is no stopping this…no going back. You said it yourself: You'd rather die than live like this. I'm helping you fulfill that promise."

Jamieson covers her mouth against the scream he knows is coming. Her eyes are like dinner plates. Beautiful. Troubled. And now full of the realization that there is no escape from this life except through death.

"Shh…It will all be over soon."

The knife plunges into her carotid artery. Blood begins to spray everywhere. Jamieson pushes it even deeper, keeping his hand over her mouth until he's certain she can't scream. He removes the knife and lets go of Ashlee's hand, letting it get covered by the arterial spray. He jumps off her and stands back. Excessive blood loss is fatal. She can struggle all she wants, but the outcome has already been determined. She turns her head to look at Jamieson, and he returns the stare until the life in her eyes flickers out.

CHAPTER SEVENTY-THREE
SSA ZACH FORTE

BASE GYM & FITNESS CENTER
FORT BELVOIR, VIRGINIA

Most civilians from various government agencies assigned to work on this post keep crazy hours. That's why the base gym is open late at Fort Belvoir. Exercise is a great stress reliever. The post commander made a lot of friends when he ordered it to close late and open early so his guests could get their workouts in.

A handful of people are on treadmills and in the weight room, but he only needs to follow the sound of heavy thumping. Zach has never felt affection toward inanimate objects. He doesn't get sentimental at the loss of a wrecked vehicle or personal belonging. This changes things. The way Boston is bashing the heavy bag in the corner makes him feel bad for the leather. He's also nervous for whoever owns the face he's imagining.

"I want to be alone, Zach," Boston says between strikes.

"And I want to be on a yacht in the Mediterranean with a stocked bar and the top ten finalists in the Miss Universe Pageant all fighting to oil me up. We both have to live with disappointment."

Boston hits the bag hard three more times. Zach knows it's his face that he's imagining now.

"I'm not in the mood for your bullshit tonight. What do you want?"

Zach launches into the monologue he authored in his head. He explains how he was at the top of his Quantico class and helped eliminate some of the country's most dangerous threats. Those successes ended during Operation Beaver Cage when one misjudgment almost cost him everything.

"Is there a point to this?" Boston interrupts about two-thirds of the way through.

"We were both given second chances. For you, it's a new lease on life doing something that matters. For me, it's helping you."

"Helping me? Is that what you call it? You give me crap every day. Sometimes I think you resent me."

"Because I want what you have, okay?" Zach snaps. "You want the truth? Here it is: I'm jealous of you, Boston. You have a unique opportunity to make a difference in this shitty world that I never will."

Zach scoffs and sits on the metal bench along the wall. Boston watches him but remains silent.

"You asked what I want. Simple. Redemption."

"For what?"

"Let's start with current events. Telling you about Ashlee was one of the hardest things I've ever done. It crushed me to have to do it. Emma told me she saw a side of you that she never had before. I think you saw Ashlee as a kindred spirit, and you connected."

"Nothing happened between us," Boston moans, expecting the accusation.

"I know. You treat the women you care about with a respect most men couldn't dream of reaching. Emma and Nadiya are two of the most beautiful women a guy could ever hope to meet, and you cherish them like younger siblings. I meant you connected with Ashlee in a spiritual and emotional sense, not a physical one."

Boston goes back to work on the heavy bag until the punches get weaker and weaker. Spent, he grabs and holds it for support.

"Is this where you tell me I'm too emotionally invested?"

"No. Contrary to popular opinion, I prefer you that way."

"Why?"

"Because you have a superhuman trait. You can *see* the memories of other people. Most of them are dark and painful. Ashlee's certainly were, and yet you still saw the best in her. That's important because I never want you to lose your humanity."

"You sound like Asami."

Zach lets out a gruff chuckle. "I'd prefer to play the role of your father, not your mother."

He tried to get Boston to smile, and it failed. "They killed her, Zach. I don't care what the local and state police are calling it. She didn't commit suicide. They murdered her in cold blood."

"I know."

"What's the Bureau saying?" Boston asks, his forehead still buried against the heavy bag.

"The opposite of what I am. It's convenient for the Bureau to call it suicide. Without Brody or Ashlee alive to see it through, this case goes away. They will sweep it under the rug like it never happened and move on to the next opportunity to burnish their careers."

"And Watchtower?"

"Matt has wanted us off this for a while. What do you think?"

That's not what Boston wanted to hear. He pounds the bag so hard that Forte can feel the building shaking. He stops suddenly, wheels, and strides up to Zach, out of breath and clearly furious.

"Are you okay with that?" Boston demands.

"No, but I can't do anything about it."

"And I can?" Boston asks, cocking his head.

Zach keeps his head low and only shifts his eyes to stare at the agitated man in front of him. "I don't know. *Can* you?"

Boston sits on the bench and pulls the gloves off his hands. It feels like a metaphor. He probably isn't seeing the symbolism behind that simple action. He should.

"I can't do this, Zach. I've tried. I can't do it."

"Yeah," the senior agent says, leaning back against the wall. "Asami came to the same conclusion."

"You talked to her?"

"I'm always talking to her, and before you freak out, no, she doesn't tell me everything you say. I get highlights. Attitudes. Mental outlook and stability. She said it was coming to this. I thought we had more time."

"To do what?"

Zach pulls a case out of his pocket and gives it a wag. "Offer you a choice."

He opens the rectangular case and sets it on the bench between them. It has only one content: a syringe with two milliliters of a clear fluid.

"Is that…?" Boston asks before scoffing. "She lied."

"She had to. You have no idea what hell will rain down on her and me when Remsen and Brass find out you know about this."

Boston picks up the syringe and tries to read the writing. Zach hopes he has better luck. It has over a half-dozen more syllables than the longest word he's ever seen outside of supercalifragilisticexpialidocious.

"This will stop me from seeing memories?"

Zach shrugs. "Theoretically. Nobody knows for how long. It could be hours, it could be months, it could be permanent. It could be fatal. It's tough to do clinical testing when the only person who can attest to the result is the patient himself. Or so I was told."

"Why are you giving me this?"

"You didn't ask for this. Watchtower sees you as a weapon, and every weapon needs a safety to prevent it from doing unwanted damage. That's where the syringe comes from. If you can no longer see memories, you have no value to Brass. That's your out, but it also highlights the real problem. I don't think you hate seeing memories. I think you resent not being able to do anything about what you see."

"Does Asami agree?"

Zach looks at the well-abused heavy bag and grins. "Wholeheartedly. For what it's worth, Emma and Nadiya do, too. Boston, you're a different man than you were a year ago. You dropped an MS-13 gangbanger standing over a hostage from twenty feet away without thinking twice. No agent I know could do that. And nobody walks into cartel country, dispatches a sex trafficker in his own house, and lives to tell about it. The knight riding in to rescue you in her puke-green Charger notwithstanding."

"Lime-green," Boston says, cracking a smile as he often does when Sol's heroics come up in conversation.

"Whatever."

"You think I should take that, Zach?"

Every fiber in Zach's being wants to scream at Boston. There's no way that he wants him to take an experimental drug and negate his abilities. It'd be like asking the X-Men to give up their powers. It'd be selfish and counterproductive, but he can't say that. Boston would likely grab the syringe and inject himself in front of Zach out of spite.

"I'm doing for you what you did for Ashlee: letting you make your own choice."

"It didn't work out well for her," Boston admits in a near whisper.

"No, it didn't. It might not for you, either. But Emma and Nadiya said that Ashlee was at peace, maybe for the first time in her adult life. I didn't know her like you did, so you tell me: Would she say it was worth it in the end? Without her here to answer that, you may be the only one who can."

Zach pats him on the shoulder as he leaves. He takes a long look at the treadmills, wondering when he last was on one. It doesn't matter. He isn't going to start tonight. There are bigger concerns weighing him down, like if Boston stabs himself with that syringe and what can be said to placate Remsen and Brass if he does.

CHAPTER SEVENTY-FOUR
"BOSTON" HOLLINGER

EMMA'S AND NADIYA'S QUARTERS
FORT BELVOIR, VIRGINIA

I knock on the door, and it opens within seconds. My original thought was that I'd be waking them up. It's just after two in the morning, and most of the post is asleep. I learned that after walking in the rain for the past three hours.

"You look like a drowned rat," Emma says, her eyes taking stock of the dumpster fire on her front stoop.

"And you look like a vision."

Emma blushes and lets me in. She's dressed in cute pajamas, her hair is almost perfect, and she has never needed makeup to accent her beautiful face. Nadiya is on the couch, nursing a glass of Irish whiskey. She is equally stunning in shorts that show off her long legs.

"I could have been any random stranger knocking on your door. You guys never checked to see who it was."

"Boston, use your head. If someone decided to break in here intent on assaulting us, would they have a better chance dodging Emma's bullets or my fists?"

"Fair point," I say as Emma tosses me a dishtowel to dry my face.

"We knew you would be stopping by eventually. You're soaked. If you're gonna sit, use the chair."

I do as instructed. "When were you going to call it quits waiting for me?"

"In a few hours when our alarms go off," Emma says as Nadiya pours me a glass of whiskey. "How are your hands?"

"You talked to Zach."

"Duh," Nadiya says.

"Then he told you about Asami's…concoction."

"We couldn't pronounce its name, either. Did you take it?"

"It's in my pocket," I say, tapping the case through my jacket.

"Are you going to?"

It's a complicated question. I likely would have if I had been given this offer a month ago or even a week ago. My ability to intrude into the minds of unsuspecting targets is why I was brought to Watchtower. It's what has exposed me to all kinds of horrors, none of which are mine. My own life has enough drama and tragedy. Why would I continue to subject myself to others' painful memories?

That was then. Something Zach said at the gym struck a nerve. He noted that Watchtower was the problem, not my gift. I haven't looked at it that way since I've always considered them related. But they aren't. He's spot-on about my wanting to make a difference and seems to understand that Watchtower hinders that end. What if they weren't?

"Emma, you're FBI. What will happen to John Prock and Tomasso Trillo now that their kids are gone?"

She lowers her eyes, recognizing the question for what it is: leading. "Nothing."

"They'll escape justice?"

"Most likely."

"You already knew that, Boston," Nadiya interjects, tucking her legs under her. "You didn't come knocking to confirm your suspicions. What's on your mind?"

"Dispensing justice." The women nod, but it's more of an appreciation of the honesty than tacit agreement. "You don't approve?"

"This isn't Hollywood, Boston. Zach was half-right about Mexico. You survived because of your training, but you were also *really* lucky. Luck runs out. Life isn't scripted, as you learned at Hogan's Alley."

I could have done without that reminder. "I know."

"Do you?" Emma asks. "Because this is the real world. Cemeteries are filled with dead men who tried being heroes."

"Did I ever tell you why I joined the Army?" I ask, settling deeper into the chair.

"For college? You look like the ROTC type."

I'm almost offended. "Hardly."

I explain why I signed a blank check to Uncle Sam and joined his Army. He almost cashed it. Too many of my friends died in Syria. I've spent countless days wondering what their sacrifice was for since that attack.

I didn't join the military for missions like our one in Syria. I had a sense of duty and believed nothing was more important and honorable than serving my countrymen and defending the Constitution. I still believe that, to a degree. It just needs to be on my terms, as selfish as that sounds.

"So what?" Nadiya asks. "You served your country."

"What good did it do? Was I defending the Constitution of the United States in some Syrian desert? What good was risking my life and getting blown up there? I didn't make a difference. I was nothing more than a casualty in a conflict most Americans will never remember."

"Boston…"

"Brody was a good kid. Ashlee was an incredible young woman. They're both dead, and the men responsible will never atone for that…unless I make them."

Neither woman is surprised by that statement. They have no reaction at all. Nadiya takes a sip of her drink, and Emma gives me a sliver of a smile. They expected this.

"Okay, but is this a logical or emotional decision?" Nadiya asks.

"Does it matter?"

"Yes," Emma says. "If you start down this path, there's no turning back. This isn't a game you can restart at the last save. There are no do-overs. If this is what you want, we have your back. But it needs to be for the right reasons."

Now, it's my turn to lower my eyes. It's not what I wanted to hear, but that's what I came here for. I know I'm not thinking clearly. My anger over Ashlee's death and Brock's fate is messing with my head. I trust these two women more than anyone, and I need them to spell it out for me. I knew they would do just that.

Emma grabs the whiskey bottle and refills our glasses. She holds up her glass to signify a toast. "To Brody and Ashlee. May they finally rest in peace."

"Now, tell us about Brody Prock and Ashlee Trillo," Nadiya commands after we clink glasses.

The demand catches me off-guard. "Why?"

"Because you knew them better than anyone. You saw their memories and understood their lives. They live on through you, so it might as well also be through us."

CHAPTER SEVENTY-FIVE

JOHN PROCK

ESTATE OF JOHN PROCK
SCARSDALE, NEW YORK

The air isn't cold enough for John to fire up the gas-powered standing space heaters on his covered screen patio. He likes the chill on his face and is wearing a warm enough jacket to defend against hypothermia. He's left the lights off, but the resulting darkness isn't pitch-black.

John watches the bright orange tip of his cigar as he takes a long drag on his Cohiba and pulls the smoke into his lungs. Most men puff cigars. He likes to inhale them, at least most of the time. He exhales and reaches for his tumbler of blended whiskey. Most of his stress has melted away. This is helping usher the rest of it out of his body.

There is a clamoring in the house after a door closes. John hears footsteps on the hardwood floor and then another door opening. He isn't alarmed. Lothar will find him out here eventually. Three minutes later, his operations manager opens the door to the screened patio and steps into the room.

"Here you are."

"Yup. Here I am. Drink?" John asks, grabbing the bottle and giving it a wag.

"Sure."

"Cigar?"

"No, I'll pass."

John pours a drink into an extra glass he brought with him. He knew his longtime friend and ally would swing by eventually. He hands it to Lothar, who takes a sip after easing himself onto the cushioned wicker chair.

"You heard the news, I assume?"

Lothar smirks. "It was hard to miss."

"I would love to have killed that bitch, but there's a satisfaction in knowing she took herself out."

John expects Lothar to agree. Instead, the long-time right-hand man only scowls and gestures at him. "Is that what this is? A victory lap?"

"It's a victory cigar."

"You shouldn't have lit it yet. This nightmare isn't over," Lothar says, leaning back in his chair. "I heard from Ignacio. He's displeased."

"When is *Señor Barerra* ever pleased about anything?" John moans.

"This is serious, John. Ashlee may be dead, but the media spotlight is brighter than ever. He's afraid she'll turn into a martyr."

"Yeah. Only my son is also dead, or did he forget? The media can't persecute him over these accusations unless they want to walk on his grave."

"That's true…unless they turn their attention to you."

"Why would they do that?"

Lothar sighs. "I have a source in New York – a PI named Dusty. He was working for the Trillo family. He called me on the way to a meeting with their lawyer and said that the police were questioning the coroner's final report on your son."

"He committed suicide, Lothar. He put the gun in his mouth and blew the top of his head off. I was standing right in front of him when he did it."

Lothar looks down. "And you were never there. Except detectives are skeptical about how he got his hands on your gun. They are questioning your statement, and the NYPD may keep digging without that answer. That's making the cartel nervous."

John feels the stress beginning to return. It's always something. He thought he was free of the scrutiny the rape allegations had brought. Now, he's beginning to understand that what happened at Salisbury may always haunt him. At a minimum, it gives the cartel leverage over him that he can ill-afford them to have.

"It doesn't matter. Just have your source keep an eye on the situation. I'll pay him whatever fee he wants."

"Okay, I'll let him know when I reach him. He isn't picking up his phone. There's one more order of business."

Lothar pulls a tri-folded piece of paper from his coat pocket and holds it up. He hands it to John, who sets his drink down and tries to read it in the low light.

"What's this?"

"A plane ticket. I need you to get on that flight and disappear for a while."

"Why?"

"You need a vacation and time to grieve the loss of your only son. More importantly, it will get you away from the spotlight for a while. I will handle things while you're gone, and your AMLOG execs can mind the company."

"Hamilton, Bermuda. Why there?"

"I have my reasons. I'll let you know what they are when you say yes."

"Okay, I'll go."

Lothar gives John the details of the travel arrangements and what to expect when he arrives. The man is nothing if not efficient. Schemes and plans start swirling around John's head. Christmas is coming early.

"All right. There's just one catch. I need you to book another seat on the flight for this to work."

Lothar smiles. "I'll book one right away."

CHAPTER SEVENTY-SIX

JAMIESON BOHMER

TOMASSO TRILLO FAMILY ESTATE
ENGLEWOOD CLIFFS, NEW JERSEY

Jamieson enters the study without knocking and closes the door. He moves to the bar secreted in a floor globe and pours a drink before easing himself into a seat across the desk from Tomasso. The developer doesn't look up from his laptop, instead content to peck away at whatever email or document he's drafting.

If the grumpy Italian is upset at the loss of his daughter, he isn't showing it. It would make sense if Ashlee were Jamieson's daughter. Emotions have never been his thing. His boss is his polar opposite. He's animated and loud, and expressing himself is ingrained in his DNA. Not today. While he isn't overjoyed, he doesn't have the deep sense of grief he would expect most fathers to have.

"Do the police believe it was a suicide?" he finally asks when he pauses typing.

"The detectives are suspicious, but I believe our story is holding. There's no physical evidence to say otherwise."

"They asked me difficult questions."

Jamieson hopes he was more emotional than he is now. "That was to be expected. I was questioned, as well."

Tomasso looks at his lawyer for the first time. "It had to be done."

"I believe you."

"Do you? It doesn't sound like it."

If Tomasso is looking for a cheerleader to issue a pep talk, Jamieson is among the least qualified men in the world. Ashlee was difficult. She was rebellious and ungrateful. But if she had been granted the freedom she craved, he doubts she would have gone to the police. There was never any real intent of destroying her father, but he gave the order anyway, despite the possible consequences.

"I believe it was risky."

"Not doing anything was equally risky. Ashlee was growing beyond my control."

"I understand," Jamieson says, still not agreeing with the action.

"It's over now," the developer concludes, closing his laptop. "As long as the police declare her death a suicide, the media will report the story and move on to something juicier. We can get back to doing what we do best."

Jamieson shakes his head. "That is the optimistic outcome, but I don't think it will be that simple."

"What do you mean? Are you worried about the FBI? They have nothing."

Jamieson lowers his eyes. He weighs whether to tell his boss what the late private investigator relayed before his untimely passing. The world isn't black and white. Most of life is spent in the gray area between those two extremes. He decides to tell a shade of the truth.

"I don't trust them. Do you remember Special Agent Dufresne?"

"Not really."

"He was here for your daughter's interview. There is something off about him. He's a maverick, and mavericks are dangerous."

Tomasso leans back in his chair and folds his hands on his chest. "You don't think he would try something against us, do you?"

"It would be a mistake to rule it out."

"Shall I have more security posted to the estate?"

"No. You're a grieving father who shouldn't be bothered with trivial details. I will take care of any extra measures."

"Very well. Speaking of security, the guard who allowed my daughter to escape…."

"Chaz Sabia. What about him?"

"Has he been removed from duty?" It was the announcement of an expectation more than a question.

"Not yet. I will take care of it."

"See that you do. It's been a long day," Tomasso says, rising from his chair, prompting Jamieson to do the same. "I'm going to watch some television in my bedroom and retire early."

"Have a good night."

Tomasso leaves Jamieson in the study. He looks around and spots one of the three cameras he knows are in here. A plan begins formulating in his mind. Agent Dufresne is coming. He's sure of it. It may not be today or tomorrow, but he will be coming. The threat he issued in the driveway was not an idle one. When that day comes, Jamieson needs to be ready.

CHAPTER SEVENTY-SEVEN
SSA ZACH FORTE

TEMPORARY LODGING FACILITY
FORT BELVOIR, VIRGINIA

Some things are predictable in life. The sun is going to come up in the east. Politicians are going to lie. Celebrity marriages are going to end in divorce. And Boston isn't going to take no for an answer when he sets his mind to something. That's why Zach is sitting at the bottom of these stairs in mid-December.

The Watchtower staff were all procured base housing. Emma and Nadiya share a small house where most of the junior enlisted soldiers are billeted. That explains the trails of drool Zach spotted in the street. He has billeting that's typically reserved for senior officers and warrant officers. Boston had yet to step foot on Fort Belvoir until recently, so he doesn't have housing assigned.

Every military base has temporary lodging for transient personnel or those awaiting a housing assignment. They're essentially government hotels, with small rooms good for sleeping and little else. Boston's billet is on the second floor, with an outdoor exit like in old motels. He thinks that will make it easy to sneak out. He's wrong.

"Is there a problem with your accommodation?" Zach says, hearing the footsteps stop at the top of the stairs.

He turns to see Boston hanging his head. "Were you going to wait here for me all night?"

"I knew I wouldn't need to," Zach says, standing and brushing himself off. "At least you don't have to deal with a chain link fence and woods in rural Virginia this time. I assume you've made your decision?"

Boston smiles and lets out a short laugh as he descends the stairs. He's dressed in black and has an assault pack on his back. He last made a break for freedom at their remote training center. The run he told the guards he was going on led him straight to the training area fence line, which he adeptly defeated before making his way to the main road and hitchhiking into Washington, D.C.

Boston takes Forte's seat on the stairs. He opens his assault pack and retrieves the syringe's case. Zach opens it and checks to see if it was used. It wasn't. He looks hard at Boston and nods before stuffing it in his pocket.

"Should we keep this for a rainy day?"

"That depends. Do you think we'll ever trust each other?"

Zach rubs his chin. "It depends on what we're talking about. I don't trust you to follow orders. I do trust you to do the right thing."

"Is that what you think I'm doing?"

"I can't be sure exactly what you're doing, other than I know you're not going on a date dressed like that. Who's the target? Prock or Trillo?"

"Does it matter? They're both bad men."

"No argument from me."

"All right. Is this the part where you appeal to my morality or ask me to place my faith in the American justice system?"

Forte wishes he could. The fact is, he lost faith in that long ago. It's not the system. What America devised is about the best any society could hope for. The problem is the people in the system.

Undoubtedly, cases could be built against Tomasso Trillo and John Prock. With Boston's guidance, skilled investigators wouldn't need to fruitlessly dig for leads. They would be archaeologists who know the precise location of the ruins to excavate. The problem is that, with those two men's political connections and money, no investigation will ever be launched. That's how the world works and why so many people are tired of it.

"No. It's where I give you this."

Zach picks up a small duffel tucked behind a concrete pillar and hands it over. Boston unzips it and finds SIG Sauer P226 with a threaded barrel and a suppressor. It's loaded without a round chambered, and there are five spare magazines. Boston rezips the bag.

"It's untraceable. Leave your Watchtower piece here."

He shakes his head. "I'm never going to be able to figure you out, Zach."

"Good. I'd hate to think I could ever be predictable."

"Is there a quid pro quo?"

There should be. Zach knows this could cost him his career. Watchtower is the last stop. With his colorful history, he'd never be accepted back into the Bureau. Handing Boston that weapon is an act he's not sure Matt would ever forgive. Brass sure as hell wouldn't. Either of them could send Zach packing at a moment's notice.

"Yeah. Don't get caught, and come back alive."

Boston nods. "You're going to catch hell for this. You know that."

"I've made a spectacular career of that."

"Then why do it again?"

Forte presses his lips together and doesn't answer. It's not a matter of being super-secretive. The truth is, he's not sure if he even knows why. His earlier admission of jealousy is the best he can muster. Even if he had a better explanation, Zach doesn't think it could be explained in a way that Boston would accept, given their history.

"Good hunting, Boston."

CHAPTER SEVENTY-EIGHT
"BOSTON" HOLLINGER

TEMPORARY LODGING FACILITY PARKING AREA
FORT BELVOIR, VIRGINIA

I can't help but check over my shoulder to see if Zach is coming to tackle me. He's an enigma sometimes. There's no way I would have expected him to let me walk away. Part of me expected Emma and Nadiya to pull up in a Suburban and throw a black bag over my head to spirit me down to the training center.

That might be why I'm spooked when an older model BMW tears around the corner of the parking lot and screams to a stop next to me. The window comes down, and Nadiya's head pokes out.

"Heading our way, Sailor?"

"I was in the Army. Never confuse the two. What are you doing here?"

"Offering you a ride, dumbass," Emma says from the passenger seat.

I check over my shoulder. Zach still isn't charging at me for the sack behind the line of scrimmage.

"You guys shouldn't be involved in what's about to happen."

"We're only getting involved because of it. Get in. It's cold out."

I open the rear door, drop the duffel on the seat, and slide it across to make room. If it's a trap the two women are about to spring, it's a good one.

"Are you kidnapping me, or did Forte send you to babysit?"

"Neither. We told Zach we were going, and he didn't argue. And before you try to read our memories to see if that's the truth, know that it is."

I don't bother with the memory. "I'm capable of handling this myself."

"Probably. But we're a team, and someone should be there to have your back. Sol isn't here with her lime-green car to save your ass this time."

That's a strong memory of my own. After killing Salcido, his men pinned me down at the San Carlos Nuevo Guaymas marina. Since my attempt to steal a boat proved futile, I was preparing for a last stand when the cavalry came. Sol showed up in her Charger and whisked me out of there in a hail of gunfire. I owe my life to her.

"Besides, you won't get off Belvoir without us. The MPs at the gate will be looking for a Suburban driven by an angry man trying to leave the post. Matt would have seen to that."

Nadiya pulls out of the lot and steers toward the northernmost gate. After ten minutes, she's on Route 266, heading for Interstate 95. They'll be in northern New Jersey four and a half hours from now.

"Whose car is this?" I ask, tiring of the silence.

"It belongs to some enlisted Army guy I met in our housing area."

I shake my head. "He loaned you his car?"

"I can be very persuasive," Nadiya says, flipping her hair playfully.

"No doubt. Someone will have to explain how any enlisted guy under the rank of sergeant major can afford a BMW. I barely had enough take-home pay for beer."

"Can I ask you a question, Boston?" Emma asks from the passenger seat. "Why do this?"

"Do we have to talk about this now?"

"Nope. We can sing *100 Bottles of Beer on the Wall* for the next few hours instead."

That conjures up a painful childhood memory. Part of me wants to settle in and listen to the two gorgeous women sing. Unfortunately, even if they had angelic voices, they would sing painfully off-key to annoy me, and something tells me that their vocals aren't as good as their shooting and combatives skills.

"Because of Ashlee and Brock," I mutter.

"Who says that's what they would want?"

"I do. I hope you two aren't going to spend the next four hours looking for ways to talk me out of this."

"We aren't," Nadiya says. "We just want an acknowledgment from you that revenge solves nothing."

"And if this goes wrong, it could cost everyone in this country."

Emma's comment catches my attention.

"How so?"

She turns to face me. "You have already helped so many people. Imagine how many more your abilities will benefit. If you fail or get caught tonight, that's gone forever."

I know in my heart she's right. Forte hand-selected the mission in Arizona to drive that point home. He wanted me to see the memories of those trafficked children and experience their pain, thinking it would motivate me to help people. That's exactly what it did. When I traveled to Mexico to kill Salcido, it was about something different than retribution.

"It's not revenge. It's justice."

"Are you trying to convince yourself or us?" Nadiya asks, staring at me in the rearview mirror.

I avert her gaze by staring out the window. "My gift comes with liabilities, most of which you know. It has some benefits, too. I see absolute truths, but more than that, I see the world differently."

"How so?"

"We built our society on laws and developed processes for those accused of breaking them. But the legal system is flawed because we are flawed. The guilty are rarely punished for the crimes they commit. It's nothing more than an illusion meant for deterrence, not justice."

Emma nods. "You can't right all the wrongs in the world, Boston. You're not Superman."

I can't help but chuckle. "It's funny. In our last session, Asami told me I was a superhero."

"And you chose now to listen to her? That's a new development," Nadiya concludes.

She makes a fair point. I have turned not listening to Asami into a science.

"I didn't agree with her, but I know I'm not Superman. I'm Batman. And this caped crusader may not be able to deliver justice for everyone, but he can for Ashlee Trillo and Brody Prock."

"He's lost it," Nadiya says to Emma.

"Clearly."

"Boston, Batman benefits from something that you don't have."

"A utility belt? The Batmobile?"

"Plot armor. The writers at DC Comics won't kill him off. Don't assume your story will benefit from the same sense of invincibility."

"Noted."

I return to staring out the window. Invincibility is not my problem. There may be no coming back from this, in more ways than one.

CHAPTER SEVENTY-NINE

JOHN PROCK

Newark Liberty International Airport is located just off the New Jersey Turnpike and sees the arrivals and departures of over forty-five million passengers annually. It is one of the three major New York metropolitan area airports consistently rated one of the worst in the country. John Prock understands why. He hates this airport.

Despite the reconstruction of Terminal A, consolidated rental car facility, and update to the AirTrain transportation system, its on-time performance is dreadful. It has disgustingly long security wait times and can't even do the little things right, like having useful signage, clean bathrooms, or functioning escalators.

The United States is where air travel was born. It's also where it was made miserable. This airport exemplifies inefficiency, crap design, endless waits, and an overarching feeling of chaos. It's enough to make him wish Lothar had booked him to fly out of LaGuardia. It's a sad state of affairs when that's a better option.

John checks his watch after scanning the departures area. He's here now, and she isn't. Maybe she got cold feet and decided not to come. He's about to pull out his cell to find out when he glimpses her waltzing through the door lugging a large carry-on. She looks around and spots John, and walks toward him with the excitement of someone heading into their dentist's office.

"Thank you for agreeing to come."

Emily forces a smile. "I haven't decided. I'm not sure I'm getting on that plane with you."

"What do you mean?"

"I mean, why did you invite me on this trip?"

It's not an unexpected question. John figured it would be asked once they arrived in Bermuda, not standing amongst the hustle and bustle of the international terminal departures area. It changes the calculus of the answer.

"Business."

"I'm your VP of corporate accounts. I know as well as you that we don't have any clients in Bermuda. We also don't have any hubs, and you've never once discussed expanding to the island. So, I'll ask you again and be honest. Why did you invite me?"

John lowers his eyes. "You're right. This isn't about work. The truth is, after everything that happened with Brody…I need to get away for a while."

He thought the reason sounded good. One look at Emily's body language lets him know he missed the mark.

"You're a big boy, John. You can do that on your own. I understand that you need to grieve for your son. What I don't get is why you invited me with a BS excuse about it being business."

"Does it matter?"

"It does to me. I don't think it's a secret that I've had a crush on you for a long time. But you're also my boss, and I love my job. Personal and business relationships rarely mix."

"There's no rule against it at AMLOG."

"I have a rule against it," Emily snaps. "I've been burned before."

"I'm not going to burn you."

"Not intentionally, you won't. Here's the thing – I'm not going down a path that will get my heart broken. I'm not some tramp that will breeze off to an island to be wined, dined, laid, and dumped three days later."

"Good. I'm not treating you that way because I don't think of you that way."

The response was automatic. It may have been too quick. The last thing John wants to do is sound uncaring and robotic.

"Are you sure, John? Because you've never shown any interest in me. Now you're suddenly taking me on a trip days after your son died. That doesn't sound like something a grieving man would do unless he wants a plaything to help him forget his troubles."

He nods. "I understand. I didn't intend to make you feel this uncomfortable. You shouldn't feel obligated or pressured. I only…Brody's death…well…it's forced me to look at things differently. AMLOG has been the most important thing in my life for so long. I placed it above my marriage and my son.

"Now they're both gone, and it's all I have left. Only, it's not enough. I'm coming to realize that there is more to life than work. I want someone…I have some holes to fill in my life I never realized were there. I want…and I want to see if one can be filled by a woman who has stood by me through everything."

"I'm not sleeping with you."

John isn't sure what her declaration is designed to do. Is it to dissuade him from inviting her? An attempt to trigger him to get to the root of his motives? Or a simple way to set ground rules for this trip? Not that any of that matters.

John smiles and nods. "Then that takes all the pressure off, doesn't it?"

She returns his grin. "Okay. We had better check in. Our flight leaves soon."

CHAPTER EIGHTY

JAMIESON BOHMER

TOMASSO TRILLO FAMILY ESTATE
ENGLEWOOD CLIFFS, NEW JERSEY

There isn't much to guard at Tomasso's estate. Calling it an estate may even be a misnomer. It's a house, and while not small, it isn't palatial. There are no priceless works of art or vast riches inside. Like most wealthy men, Tomasso has a safe with some spending cash. That's about it. Tomasso considers himself the most valuable asset within its four walls.

The men who watch over the house in shifts are well-compensated for precious little real work or responsibility. Mostly, they walk the grounds, watch sports on television, and help themselves to the meals prepared in the gourmet kitchen. Their presence is more of a deterrent than an active security measure. They are meant to be seen to dissuade any of Tomasso's enemies from doing something stupid.

That's what makes Chaz's failure so egregious. Tomasso issues few orders and expects the ones he does to be followed to the letter. If he tells a guard that his daughter is not to leave the house, their primary responsibility is to ensure she doesn't.

The man smoking a cigarette on the back patio doesn't have two brain cells to rub together. Jamieson knows he had designs on joining the military. Not to bag on U.S. Marines, but even the jarheads didn't think he was smart enough to join their ranks. If he had tried out for the SAS, he wouldn't have lasted fifteen minutes before washing out.

Jamieson puts his coat on and walks out the back door. He isn't quiet about it, yet the security guard is still caught off-guard at the sudden intrusion. Chaz straightens and holds his cigarette at his side.

"I know you're smoking, Mr. Sabia. There's no point in hiding it."

The big man stares at the butt pinched between his fingers. "I, uh…I just stepped outside for a quick one."

"It's your second, not counting the pair you sucked down a half hour ago. You take a lot of smoke breaks, don't you?"

"No."

Jamieson smiles. He expected some witty retort, like "what are you, the surgeon general?" He should have known better. The man with a neck as thick as a sequoia only grasps the English language at a primary school level.

"All evidence to the contrary," Jamieson says, nodding at the can filled with cigarette butts in the corner.

"Huh?"

"Never mind. Do you think you're good at your job?"

"The best."

"I see. How does someone who's the best let a young girl slip out of the house unnoticed?"

Jamieson can practically see the gears spinning in the big man's head. "It must have happened on the early shift."

"Oh, of course. I'm sure that's a possibility. So, you didn't confirm Ashlee was in her bedroom when you assumed duty?"

"The door was closed," Chaz states, thinking that fact will absolve him.

"It always is. Did you check? Yes or no?"

"No."

Jamieson turns and looks out toward the river. He can't see it from here – the property is not on the waterfront, and a highway runs alongside it. But he can feel it…smell it. Right now, he wants to drown the oaf behind him in its gray waters.

This is no challenge. He longs for another round with Special Agent Andrew Dufresne. His true identity is a mystery, and that piques Jamieson's interest. But he's also intelligent, confident, and skilled – in other words, a worthy adversary.

"So, it could have happened on your shift."

"It didn't," Chaz says after a pause.

"It did. I have a video of Ashlee leaving. You know how our cameras work. They have timestamps in the corner that show the exact date and time. Do you want to know where you were? Right where you are now. Maybe a little to the left."

Chaz looks to his left, confused. Somewhere, a village is missing its idiot.

"Did you help her escape?"

His head snaps back. "No."

"I don't believe you."

"Are you calling me a liar?"

Chaz may have the IQ of a potato, but he has a sense of honor. He takes an angry step toward Jamieson. That is a mistake.

The lawyer reaches with his right hand and grasps the big man's throat above his larynx. He squeezes hard, applying pressure through the muscle and constricting the carotid arteries. He then pushes him against the house, using the force of his body to push his hand into Chaz's windpipe.

It's an easy move to defeat. All the guard has to do is raise his beefy arms and crash them down to break the hold. Instead, he panics. Every time he starts to raise them, Jamieson squeezes harder. Size can be a force multiplier but never a substitute for skill.

"Did you help Ashlee leave the house? Yes or no? If you lie to me, I will kill you."

He shakes his head. Fear has an interesting effect on the psyche. It interrupts brain processes that regulate emotions and evaluate tactics before acting. This negatively impacts decision-making, leaving the fearful susceptible to intense emotions and impulses. In short, it inhibits the ability to lie effectively.

"Last chance. Did you help her?"

"No," he manages to say in a raspy voice.

The former SAS operator narrows his eyes before letting him go. Chaz takes a couple of deep breaths. When he looks up, he's staring down the barrel of the gun Jamieson borrowed from Tomasso's desk.

"You haven't convinced me."

"I swear, I didn't help her," he pleads, almost on the verge of tears.

"You're done working here, Chaz. Pack your gear, leave, and never come back. I'll give you five minutes to get off this property. At five minutes and one second, I will put this bullet in your chest. Your time starts now."

He doesn't waste time arguing and staggers into the house to collect his things. Jamieson pockets the weapon, making a mental note to return it. Fear is a wonderful tool, not that he has experienced it himself. That gives him a huge advantage, especially for what he knows is coming his way.

CHAPTER EIGHTY-ONE
SSA ZACH FORTE

WATCHTOWER OPERATIONS CENTER
FORT BELVOIR, VIRGINIA

Real-world military or government operations centers rarely look like they are depicted in the movies. They are pedestrian, prefer function over form, and are bland places to be except in a crisis. This one is different.

Zach has always wondered if Matt hired a Hollywood set designer to conceive this room. It's not huge, but what it lacks in size, it makes up in style. It's a combination of CTU from the show *24*, NORAD from *War Games*, and the bridge of a starship. Workstations are made of stainless steel that reflects the blue LED accent lighting everywhere, and monitors and large displays around the room display information in ultra-high definition.

The staff here works eight-hour shifts, but the room has enough seating to accommodate two shifts simultaneously. Off to the rear of the main floor are offices, work rooms, and conference areas that can accommodate additional staff in a crisis. It's a snazzy place to work for the Millennials and Zoomers who comprise most of the Watchtower staff.

The room is organized by function, and much like mission control in Houston during the Apollo program, they have headsets that allow them to communicate with other areas without shouting. Unlike those pieces of 1960s technology, these are wireless with noise-canceling ear covers with blue LED lights embedded in them. There is no doubt in Zach's mind what Matt's favorite color is.

The staff in the room monitors media, social media, satellite, and drone feeds, sorts through real-time intelligence, criminal activity reports, and counterintelligence operations. Very little happens in America and outside its borders that Watchtower isn't among the first to know about. All that information gets sorted, evaluated, filtered, and then reported to the floor commander, who converts it into hourly threat briefings.

Every branch of the government is represented here. Intelligence services make up the bulk of the personnel, but there are also members of the DoD, Homeland Security, ATF, ICE, Customs and Border Patrol, and even the IRS. Zach stays away from that guy, just in case.

He weaves through the workstations, not attracting much attention as he does. He isn't a fixture in this room like his boss is, but he knows almost everyone here. Nobody will find it odd that he walks up to Wesley's station in the front corner of the room.

"Mr. Crusher."

Wesley spins in his chair to face Zach and peels off his headset. "Are you ever going to get tired of that lame joke?"

"Not in your lifetime," Zach says with a smile.

Wesley Crusher was a fictional character portrayed by actor Wil Wheaton in *Star Trek: The Next Generation*. He also appeared in the *Star Trek: Nemesis* film and *Star Trek: Picard*. Despite his best intentions, Wesley Crusher is one of the Star Trek franchise's most despised characters among the fanbase. Disdain for the character is almost universal, and Jean-Luc Picard's "Shut up, Wesley" line is one of the series' most recognizable quips. That's why this Wesley hates the nickname so fiercely.

"What do you want, Forte?"

"Your help."

"You have a funny way of asking for it with that Crusher BS. I don't work for you."

"No, you don't. And you're under no obligation to assist. Just understand that Boston will likely find himself in a heap of trouble if you don't."

He shakes his head. "That's not my concern, either."

"Except the dream machine has done favors for you. They'll be the last if he ends up in police custody…or worse."

"How did you know about that?" Wesley asks, causing Zach to smirk. "Okay, fine, dumb question. Why didn't you put an end to it?"

Zach thinks about that for a moment. He doesn't have a good reason for letting Boston trade the use of his abilities for favors, despite it violating every written and unwritten rule that Watchtower has. It might be because he would have done the same if the roles were reversed.

"It was important to Boston to help you."

"He told you that?" Wesley asks.

"He didn't have to."

Zach has no idea if that's true, but it sounded damn good. Asami would be better positioned to answer that, assuming he even told her, which he likely didn't. It doesn't matter.

"What do you need me to do?"

"Start by keeping the New Jersey police busy."

"What do you want me to do, rob a bank?" Wesley asks before getting a disapproving grin from Zach. He sighs. "Local or state?"

"Both. Englewood Cliffs. While you're at it, I need you to find out everything you can about Tomasso Trillo's house. Alarms, home assistants, video surveillance systems…you name it."

"Gee, anything else, Zach? Boston didn't do me *that* many favors."

Zach pulls up an ergonomic rolling chair from the empty workstation adjacent to Wesley and eases into it.

"Yeah, I'll need you to convince your colleagues to not try to find Boston when the order is given."

Wesley stares blankly at Zach. "You're asking them to disobey...what makes you think they'll listen to me?"

"Call it a gut feeling."

Wesley may be a junior operative in the Watchtower hierarchy, but he knows how favors work. He asked Boston for a couple and did him a few in return. If he's willing to horse-trade with the dream machine, Zach is betting he's made deals with most people in this room. Once a hustler, always a hustler.

"You're going to get me fired," Wesley whines.

"Then we can stand together on the unemployment line. I need you to get to work. The clock's ticking."

Crusher isn't just an analyst – he's a man who knows how to get things done. He has skills but would never be considered elite at any of them. He improvises, utilizes resources, adopts strategies, and leverages situations to get results. That makes him worth his weight in gold to Watchtower. He isn't going anywhere.

"Where can I find you if I need anything?"

"Right here. I have nothing better to do tonight."

"I had better get busy updating my resume while I'm at it."

"Make it so, Mr. Crusher," Zach orders, using an awful impression of Captain Picard.

CHAPTER EIGHTY-TWO
"BOSTON" HOLLINGER

TOMASSO TRILLO FAMILY ESTATE
ENGLEWOOD CLIFFS, NEW JERSEY

I wish this were easier. If Tomasso Trillo's mansion were on the riverfront, I could scale the cliff like Army Rangers at Pointe du Hoc in Normandy during D-Day. Or, I could slip through farm fields like Jack Reacher in one of Lee Child's novels if it were rural. Instead, I'm in a suburban New Jersey manor surrounded by other suburban houses. There are too many cameras, eyes, dog walkers, and cars to make this work without being seen.

Making matters worse, the sole avenue of approach to Tomasso's house is through his backyard. To get there, I must navigate the streets dressed like the love child of a ninja and Arnold Schwarzenegger's *Commando*. Then I need to skulk through someone's yard without alerting a dog, motion camera system, or old man who yells at kids all day to keep off his grass. Give me a steep cliff along the French coast any day.

Somehow, I've managed to pull it off. I work my way into the tree line that separates Tomasso's property from his eastern neighbor. Pulling the binoculars to my eyes, I scan the house, switching to night vision and then to thermal. It's quiet.

"You read me, Boston?" Emma asks through my wireless earpiece.

"Miss me already?"

"Not as much as I will in an hour. You'll make a beautiful corpse."

"Thanks for the vote of confidence," I whisper, continuing my scan.

"We heard from Watchtower."

"Let me guess, Matt told you not to let me do anything stupid and to return to Belvoir."

"No. It was Wesley who called."

That gets my attention. "What did Mr. Crusher have to say?"

"He did a workup on the Trillo house. The alarm system is off, and the back door is unlocked."

I lower the binos as I try to understand why my favorite Watchtower analyst took it upon himself to do that. Unfortunately, I have more pressing concerns, like whether I'm stumbling into a trap.

"That makes no sense. It's like rolling out a red carpet when the house should be buttoned up tighter than Area 51. What about security?"

"Tomasso employs three guards from a company called Hudson Sentinel. They work eight-hour shifts. You have to assume the night guy is on now."

"I don't think so. I haven't seen anyone."

"They're rent-a-cops, Boston, not the guards of the Tomb of the Unknown Soldier. He's probably inside watching porn or reruns of *I Love Lucy*."

"Hopefully not at the same time," I mumble. "Keep me informed. I'm moving to get a closer look."

"Be careful."

Chance favors the bold. Of course, I'm pretty sure that's what I told myself in Mexico, and I barely escaped with my life. I cross the backyard and move along the house's back wall. I step up on the patio and notice a can of discarded cigarette butts. I'm willing to bet it belongs to the guards.

I stop when I reach the back door. There are no signs of external surveillance around the house, but that doesn't mean there isn't any. Money buys a lot of things, including cameras that are invisible to guests and potential thieves.

My hand moves to the knob, and I give it a slight turn. It moves easily. I slowly ease the door open, creep into the house, and then close the door behind me. The house is still. There are no televisions on or other ambient noises that indicate anyone is awake.

The kitchen is nice, at least, what I can see of it in the darkness. It connects to the foyer, with its grand staircase, via a short hall. The soft rubber soles of my shoes mute the sounds of my footfalls. I noted that when I heard my steps bouncing around my first time here.

"Boston, we did a drive-by," Nadiya whispers. "The study light is on. The rest of the house is dark."

I don't respond. My voice will sound like a bass speaker in here. I move around the staircase, checking the upstairs for activity. Like Nadiya reported, it's quiet. I take a deep breath and glide to the study, swinging open the door and expecting to see Tomasso. I figured the quick movement would catch him by surprise. Instead, I'm the one who's surprised.

Jamieson is sitting at a desk with a gun pointed in my direction. There is no emotion on his face as he simply stares at me.

"Nice of you to join me, Agent Dufresne, or whoever you are."

CHAPTER EIGHTY-THREE

JOHN PROCK

Horseshoe Bay Beach is consistently rated one of the top beaches in the world and is absolutely one of the most photographed ones. It appeals to everyone from small children to senior citizens and is widely regarded as a premiere cruise ship destination appropriate for the entire family. Natural limestone cliffs border the expansive horseshoe-shaped beach and large reefs popular with snorkelers.

John and Emily have spent a sizable chunk of the day in rented lounge chairs under an umbrella. She looks magnificent in a bikini, so it wasn't a harrowing experience. She jumps at the invite to head to the beach bar for a snack and some drinks.

The December weather here is hardly scorching at seventy degrees, but the rain that was falling when they arrived has moved on. Bermudan tourism is lowest this time of year, but that doesn't mean the beach is desolate. The Rum Bum is doing some healthy business.

John is tipsier than he wants to be, and Emily is even worse as they down rum-based drinks to the sound of live Reggae music. He didn't expect to be at the beach all day. It just has worked out that way. He turns his attention to a family of three sitting at the far corner of the bar. Tourists, clearly. He's seen the parents with the college-age girl at the hotel. They have made a day of it as well.

"Are you with me, John?" Emily says, grabbing his hand.

He forces a smile. "I have a question for you. What would you do to defend your kids?"

"I don't have any children. You know that."

John lowers his eyes to the table. "If you did?"

Emily is two drinks past the limit where a person can still think logically. It's an emotional question now. That's the answer he wants.

"Anything I had to."

"Would you kill for them?"

"Yes, absolutely," she says without hesitation.

The girl gets up from her table after her parents pay the bill. She and her parents head in opposite directions. Family time must be over. She wants to be alone. He can sympathize with that.

"So would I, but I didn't. I failed my son. I failed him as a father. I failed him in every way possible."

"John, you couldn't have known he would commit suicide."

He clenches his jaw and looks out at the beach as he fights back the tears forming in the corner of his eyes.

"If I had been there more for him, maybe…I'm sorry. I need to take a walk and clear my head."

"Sure. We can walk on the beach along the water."

John closes his eyes briefly. "I'm sorry, Emily. I think I'd like to be alone for a while. It's nothing about you…or us. I need to…I need to ask my son for forgiveness."

"I understand," Emily says softly with a sympathetic look.

"Why don't you return to the hotel and order us some room service. I'll be there in an hour and a half or so."

"Okay."

"Here. Take my phone. I don't want the distraction."

"Won't you need it?"

"The only person I want to talk to while I'm here is you, and I get to do that in person."

John watches Emily head down the sand to the sidewalk leading to the parking lot. There are still plenty of taxis there, and any one of them would be eager to earn the fare back to Hamilton. She'll be okay.

He checks the time on his phone. It's 6:30 pm. It's nautical twilight, where both the horizon and the brighter stars are visible and make it possible to navigate while at sea. The weather is clear today, and the eastern horizon is faintly visible. He makes his way out of the beach bar and onto the wide crescent of sand and an uncertain destiny.

CHAPTER EIGHTY-FOUR

JAMIESON BOHMER

TOMASSO TRILLO FAMILY ESTATE
ENGLEWOOD CLIFFS, NEW JERSEY

The man holds his weapon steady. Suppressors add weight to the end of the barrel, making the gun unbalanced and unstable. His isn't. That makes him trained…practiced. That's something worthy of note. Shooting is a perishable skill that atrophies with time. Jamieson hasn't even been to a range in eight months. A gunfight with this man would be laughingly one-sided.

Jamieson places Tomasso's gun on the desk. It's a risky move but one worth taking under the circumstances.

"There. Lower your weapon. I'm unarmed."

"What makes you think I care whether you are or aren't?"

Jamieson nods. "That's a fair point. You don't care. You also didn't come here to kill me. You came for Tomasso."

"You'll have to do better than that if you expect to be breathing five seconds from now, Jamieson."

"You're right. Did you wonder why I dismissed our security guard and left the back door unlocked with the alarm off?"

"No. I knew exactly why you did. Which is the other reason I'm not putting this weapon down."

Jamieson smiles. "That's smart, but not smart enough. Here's what's going to happen. If your trigger finger even twitches, I'll press this button."

He holds up a small black fob cradled between his curled index finger and thumb. The agent stares at the device and then back at Jamieson. Again, there is no panic in his eyes.

"This panic button sets off the alarm. Police will respond within three minutes and eleven seconds. I know what you're thinking – that's more than enough time for you to take care of your business. You'd be correct, except it also activates every camera on the premises. As you already know, this room is wired for audio. Cameras cover it from three angles. That's three different perspectives the police will have of an FBI agent shooting an unarmed man in cold blood. And, I assure you, the resolution is very good."

Agent Dufresne scans the bookcases above Jamieson's head.

"It's actually over there," he says, pointing up and to his right. "Well, one of them is. Murder wouldn't even be your biggest problem, Special Agent Dufresne. No, when the police investigate, they'll learn that you aren't in the FBI at all. That's going to be very uncomfortable for you. More so for agents Forte and Farris. They *are* in the FBI. The delectable Agent Jespersen works for the CIA, so it will be interesting to learn why she's operating on American soil."

The agent smiles as he lowers his gun and walks over to place it down on the corner of the desk. "I'm thoroughly impressed, Jamieson. You thought this through."

The lawyer takes his finger off the button. That was a surprising move. He expected whoever this man really is to panic. Now he's intrigued as Agent Dufresne helps himself to a seat. He's relaxed. Not sweating. At ease. He either has a lot of experience or is very well-trained.

"You know, you were right when I dropped Ashlee off. They may write novels about us. Two ghosts meeting each other in a library…yes, I know this is technically a study, but 'library' sounds better," the agent says, gesturing around the room. "It's the kind of story writers dream of. Especially when you consider your background."

"To keep the metaphor going, I'm an open book. Go ahead – tell me what you've learned after reading it."

"An open book? Maybe for the past twenty years when you attended Cornell Law, passed the New York and New Jersey bar exams, and began practicing for the Trillo family and his business interests. No wife, no kids…just your work and the house you own in Montclair. A good life, at least on the surface. What's most interesting is what happened before that."

Jamieson gestures for him to continue.

"After you became a parachutist and served in the airborne regiment, you passed the grueling UKSF selection process. That's impressive. The British SAS is no joke."

"Who dares wins," Jamieson says, quoting their motto.

"Then came the Iraq deployments. Your last one was conducting counterterrorist operations in Baghdad with Task Force Black. You were a decorated operative who excelled at short-notice precision raids. You were efficient. Valuable. Then something happened. The missions suddenly stopped. You were medically discharged, and your records were scrubbed and sealed. It was like you never existed."

"Bravo," Jamieson says with a trio of theatrical claps. "That information couldn't have been easy to find. It's my turn to be impressed."

"I wish I could take the credit. What was missing in all that was why you were discharged. It's nothing physical, so it had to be mental or emotional. The easy excuse for your behavior would be PTSD. Plenty of Iraq War veterans suffer from the horrors of post-traumatic stress. I think it's something else. I think your unit kicked you out when they learned you're a psychopath."

Jamieson beams. "They did, but that's not the whole story."

"Tell me."

"Uh, uh," he says, wagging a finger. "You first. Quid pro quo. There isn't an FBI agent in America who could have obtained my personnel record. So, tell me, Agent Dufresne, who are you, and who do you really work for?"

CHAPTER EIGHTY-FIVE
"BOSTON" HOLLINGER

TOMASSO TRILLO FAMILY ESTATE
ENGLEWOOD CLIFFS, NEW JERSEY

Okay. So, none of this is going as I planned. I knew something was amiss when Emma relayed that the rear door was unlocked and the alarm deactivated. I never expected to be having a cordial conversation with a man into whom I'm determined to put a bullet. He thinks he has the upper hand, and to a degree, he does. That doesn't mean I'm going to answer his questions.

"I'm Batman," I say in a husky voice as I lean forward.

"I believe you. Part of it, anyway. I saw you at the interview. You don't dress well enough to be Bruce Wayne. But I do think you're a vigilante. It's the only explanation as to why you're here now. The only question left is who you work for."

"Who says I work for anyone?"

"You did when you didn't take credit for obtaining my SAS file."

"Batman had Alfred. That doesn't mean he worked for Chief Gordon."

I have no idea if Jamieson will buy that. Probably not. It took resources and high-level contacts to gain his dossier from the Brits; a lone wolf wouldn't have either.

"Touché. So, this is some sort of personal vendetta against Tomasso? Did he wrong you in a previous life…or this one?"

"My turn," I say, changing the subject. "What happened in Iraq?"

"Who says something did?"

I cock my head in disapproval.

"I killed civilians. Seven of them. The father and eldest son were confirmed militants. It was still a war crime, although things like that happened there more than anyone admits. I figured that the family knew what the men were up to, and that made them enemies. So, I eliminated them."

"Why weren't you prosecuted?"

"Political reasons, I suppose. Nobody wanted the embarrassment – not the government and certainly not the SAS. I would have returned to duty, except my superiors learned that the killings didn't bother me. I didn't feel remorse, but I didn't enjoy it, either. I felt nothing. Like taking out the trash, it was just something that had to be done."

"That's when they ordered a psych profile and uncovered the truth. How did you manage to get into the SAS in the first place?"

"The physical part was tough. I feel that pain just like everyone else. The mental evaluation was the challenge. I've had to fake having emotions for most of my life. It's not easy. I learned to mimic the people around me. When they felt sad, I had to pretend to be. It's the same with anger, joy, fear…you get the point. My fellow applicants to the SAS had a range of emotions to emulate, so that's what I did."

"That explains why you're a good lawyer. They tend to be an unfeeling bunch."

Jamieson grins. "The law is about facts. The practice of it is best when the litigators are unmoved by emotions. I have a natural advantage over my peers."

I nod. "Your turn."

Jamieson leans forward in his chair. He plants his elbows on the desk and clasps his hands in front of his face. He stares at me with determined eyes.

"How does one become a vigilante embedded in the FBI?"

"One has to die," I say with conviction.

He studies me for a long moment before leaning back. "I actually believe you."

"What happened to you? What trauma did you experience that forced you to turn off your emotional capability?"

Jamieson inhales sharply as he looks out the window. It's coal-dark outside, and the interior lighting of the study makes it impossible to see anything out there. He's not interested in the front yard. He doesn't want to answer the question. Normally, I would get memories flashing through my vision explaining why. Not with this guy.

"I think you're wrong, Batman. This story about ghosts meeting in a study won't be entertaining if we sit here and reminisce all night."

"That's true," I say, rising from my chair. "We should get on with it."

"On with what?"

I mock my surprise. "You said it yourself, Jamieson. Things were going to end bloody between us. The story needs an ending. Let's get on with it…unless you're scared."

"You know better."

Jamieson stands and slides around the desk. He moves easily and self-assuredly. I need to remind myself that he isn't a lawyer but a trained and unfeeling killer. The SAS isn't for the weak-minded or physically inept. We're about to see how much I learned from Nadiya while at Watchtower.

"There's one more thing I need to know. Why did you kill Ashlee?"

"Who says I did?"

"Because Tomasso may have despised his daughter, but I don't believe he could kill her himself. He loved his wife, and his wife wouldn't have wanted that. Why live with the pain when you can farm it out to a man who can't feel guilt over it?"

Jamieson smirks. "You answered your own question. I killed her because he ordered me to."

CHAPTER EIGHTY-SIX

JOHN PROCH

HORSESHOE BAY COVE
SOUTHAMPTON, BERMUDA

John had a realization when he and Emily first arrived at this beach: The famous pink sand was not really all that *pink*. It could have been a failure to live up to expectations. He thought from the photos he'd seen that it looked like something in a can of pink lemonade mix. It wasn't even close. That's what he gets for believing what he sees on the Internet.

The beach he's walking across is regular sand speckled with pink dots from the pulverized shells of tiny marine creatures inhabiting offshore coral reefs. It didn't ruin the experience of the day.

A rock formation separates the beach from Horseshoe Bay Cove on the southeast side and only a few hundred yards from the Rum Bum. It's not supremely high at just over thirty meters, but it isn't the easiest of climbs, especially with this little illumination. The sand is glowing from the waxing gibbous moon overhead, and that helps his vision as he reaches the top.

The rocks near the bottom are more jagged, but the boulders on top are much smoother. John watches his footing as he makes his way along the top of the outcropping that juts into the bay. It's the perfect spot.

He saw people up here all day. It's a picturesque place. At night, both these rocks and the beach below are empty. Or nearly empty. He sees a lone figure near the edge, surveying the horizon. He walks toward the edge slowly with his head down and looks up to see her warily staring at him.

"Oh, I'm sorry, didn't know anybody was up here. I've been waiting all day for some alone time up here."

The girl who was sitting with the tourist family at the bar looks nervous, with her arms welded across her abdomen.

"Me, too," she meekly says.

"Well, you were here first. I can go if you want to be by yourself. My girlfriend didn't want me to climb up here to begin with. She thinks I'm accident-prone."

"Uh, no, it's okay. You're here with your girlfriend?"

John smiles as he takes a few steps closer to the young woman. "It's our first trip together as a couple. We were on the beach all day and then went to get dinner. She wanted to come back to the beach when it was empty for a romantic stroll. She wasn't about to follow me up here, though."

"Where is she?" the girl asks, looking back toward the beach.

John scans the entire length of sand behind them. "I'm not sure. She couldn't have gone too far. What brings you up here?"

"I just wanted some time to myself."

"Okay. I really should go. I'm ruining that."

She smiles and offers a slight shrug. "It's okay. It is a public beach."

It doesn't feel like one right now. This iconic beach hosts countless events, from volleyball tournaments to music festivals. It is a hive of activity, day and night. But that's during the summer months. In the short days of December, a whisper before Christmas, it's not a happening place.

"It is. But it's also a big one I'm happy to find another part of if you want to be left alone. I know how it feels to enjoy the peace and quiet of solitude."

"No, it's okay. Really. It's nice having a conversation with someone other than my parents. How long have you been with your girlfriend?"

"Not long," John answers honestly. "We're still in the honeymoon phase. She hasn't learned all my bad habits yet."

"You have bad habits?"

John offers the young woman a broad smile. "All men do."

He doesn't have any real data to back up that claim. John does have plenty of firsthand experience, starting with his high school girlfriend. In that case, the bad habit was infidelity. He's had others ranging from excessive drinking to drugs to abuse. He's sure there are also plenty of minor irritants, from missing birthdays and anniversaries to blatant indifference to the relationship. Women are very high maintenance.

"I suppose you're right," she says, returning her attention to the darkening horizon.

"Is that why you're up here? Boyfriend trouble?"

"Not exactly. I made some mistakes. Then I lost someone close to me."

"I'm so sorry. I should at least introduce myself. My name is Jonathan Marks."

John reaches out with his hand. She stares at it momentarily before shaking it, revealing a white bandage covering her abdomen.

"Chloe McCarthy. It's nice to meet you, Jonathan."

CHAPTER EIGHTY-SEVEN
SSA ZACH FORTE

WATCHTOWER OPERATIONS CENTER
FORT BELVOIR, VIRGINIA

No news is good news. That's what Zach hopes is the story of the night. Neither Nadiya nor Emma has checked in, meaning Boston accepted their transportation offer and is with them. That makes him feel a little better. Even with their support, a thousand things can go wrong with this. If anything does, he needs to be the first to know.

"Forte! My office…now!"

Zach closes his eyes and tries to keep his temper in check. He doesn't like being summoned. Every head in the operations center turns to him. That behavior in the corporate world would likely land a manager in human resources for an unpleasant conversation. Here, it's commonplace.

"Looks like someone just got called into the principal's office," Wesley warns in a child's voice.

"It wouldn't be the first time he handed me a detention slip."

"I'll keep an eye on our boy," Wesley whispers.

"Do it quietly."

Zach weaves his way through the workstations and off the operations center floor. Matt maintains a work area here but spends most of his time at Watchtower in his office. It's modern, in a Cold War kind of way. It feels like an ambassador's office was moved to a bomb shelter with LED mood lighting installed. It's an architecture and décor style that Matt should package to designers as Modern-Retro Chic.

"Boston isn't in his quarters," Matt declares, standing behind his desk as he stares at his computer screen.

"I know."

"Where is he?"

"Off-post."

Matt lifts his eyes. "No kidding. Where off-post?"

Zach rubs his chin theatrically. "I'm not entirely sure."

"You aren't…? It's your *job* to know his whereabouts at all times."

"Do I look like a human GPS tracker to you?"

Matt stands a little straighter. "No, you look like a washed-up FBI counterintelligence agent who's blowing his second chance at a career."

Everything always comes back to Beaver Cage. Grimman used that leverage to get Zach to tail Boston and try to frame him as a traitor. Remsen is using it to force the senior agent into doing his bidding. Zach has had enough. He was a superstar counterintelligence agent until that debacle derailed his career, and he is tired of it being used against him.

"Why? Because I'm not deferential to my Watchtower overlords? You told me to run my team as I see fit because you didn't want the responsibility. Boston is a member of that team."

"Boston is an asset. He's not in the FBI. He doesn't even legally exist! I rely on you to keep him with the program, including being his *babysitter* when necessary."

"Okay. Your child is on the loose, so I'll leave it to his parents to find him."

"We're not done here. Zach. You're not dismissed!"

"I'm sorry, I missed the memo that explains I joined the Marines. I don't wait to be dismissed, so I'm leaving unless you think you can stop me."

Zach figures that's the end of the conversation until he's shoved from behind. He slams into the door jamb and bounces back into the office. That took guts that he figured Matt didn't have.

There is no hesitation. Zach uses the momentum from the shove to twist and swing with his left. His fist plants into Remsen's face with a satisfying thud. It wasn't a haymaker. His left is nowhere near as powerful as his right. He proves that when he follows with a right cross that spins Matt.

Even that punch wasn't enough to put the director down. Matt regains his balance and lunges at him, forcing Zach into the wall and sending framed pictures crashing to the floor. The director lands several kidney punches before shoving his subordinate deeper into the office.

Zach lands a quick jab as Matt's roundhouse kick strikes his thigh. The two men lock arms and grapple, each looking for leverage to get the other on the ground. Monitors are knocked from the desk as the men dance around the office.

They both have the same thought: End this. Their grip on each other is broken, and Matt lands a right on Zach's chin as he pops his boss in the solar plexus. Both men crumple to the ground. Matt moans as he leans against his desk, trying to force air back into his lungs. Forte rubs his ribs and chin as he leans his head against the wall.

"Oh, we're getting too old for this shit, Zach," Remsen gasps.

"Yeah, we are. I think you knocked some of my teeth loose."

The two men start laughing. It begins with chuckles and escalates into belly laughs that actually begin to hurt.

"I'm still pissed at you," Matt says as the laughter dies.

"And I still don't care."

"I don't expect you to understand my orders, Zach, but—"

"Good. Because I don't," the senior agent says, not allowing him to finish wherever that sentence was heading.

"How long have we been friends?"

"Long enough to know when to stop a fight before someone lands in the infirmary."

"Yeah. Watchtower is important to me. It's the chance I always wanted."

"To do what?" Zach asks with a sneer.

"The right thing."

"Jeez, Matt. Then why don't you stop being such a wuss and start? You have the ultimate weapon and refuse to unlock his potential."

Remsen shakes his head. "That's not what Watchtower is."

"Then what is it? Hmm? A clearinghouse for information? The government has a dozen of those, and none are effective. Success comes down to people, and you have a walking, talking polygraph machine capable of doing what every other agency can't."

"I *will not* stand by and let Boston become a vigilante. That's not how the system works. It's not what Brass wants. The consequences could be severe."

Zach stands and brushes himself off. "It's how every system works in the background, and you know it. Ever wonder what the consequences will be if you don't let Boston use his talents? You created this monster, Dr. Frankenstein. You thought you could control him when you unleashed him on the world. Guess what. You can't. What happens next is up to you. I suggest you figure it out before Boston starts making those decisions for you."

CHAPTER EIGHTY-EIGHT

JAMIESON BOHMER

The admission of what happened to Ashlee isn't sitting well with the fake agent. Emotion can be a powerful motivator but also a net negative. Rage and anger cloud judgment and inhibit rational thoughts and actions. That's what he's counting on. Whatever skills this mystery man has, he wants them impaired. By the look on his face, Jamieson accomplished that.

Both men crouch into a low squat in the middle of the study, their feet slightly more than shoulder-width apart. It creates balance and a foundation to execute a number of possible moves. Their arms are out, ready to strike or defend. This is where the games begin.

Devotees of one martial art or another are easy to defeat. Fighting in a dojo is much different than hand-to-hand combat in the real world. To defeat his opponent, Jamieson needs to recognize his preferred fighting style and choose from his arsenal of techniques to counter and defeat it.

The SAS didn't train him in a particular martial art. Instruction primarily consisted of a comprehensive system of a dozen disciplines, including judo, kickboxing, Brazilian and Japanese jiu-jitsu, karate, and aikido. Jamieson employs a holistic fighting style by amalgamating the most useful techniques and adding his own.

The former SAS operative moves in first to test the waters. He slaps at the agent's arm with his left and tries a reverse punch that is deflected. The distraction sets him up for a quick right that is easily parried. Stymied, he shoves the agent back with both hands. Very interesting.

Most fighters like to keep their distance from an opponent. Pugilists in a boxing ring like to use reach as an advantage. This man is comfortable fighting close in. Worse, he hasn't noticed any discernible fighting style. Still, he's bound to have a flaw, and Jamieson is certain he'll find it. He hasn't been in a proper scrap in years and welcomes the challenge.

The two men reset their stances and exchange sly grins as they focus on each other. Jamieson moves in, leading with another two-handed push transitioning into a blazing quick right elbow that is blocked, along with a left uppercut the agent knocks away with his right arm. That sets him up for a left kick that Jamieson partially lands and knocks the agent off-balance backward. He was ready for the kick. Most men aren't. They like fighting with their fists, not their feet.

Jamieson gestures the agent closer with his fingers.

"How cliché. I'm disappointed in you, Jamieson."

This time, the agent moves first. He grabs at the lawyer's left arm with both hands. Jamieson breaks the attempt by slamming down with his right. The move opens him up, and the agent aims a right at his midsection, which Jamieson is lucky to block. Flat-footed, Dufresne narrowly escapes a sweep kick that would have knocked him off his feet.

Keen on harnessing his momentum, Jamieson twists into a spin kick that the man ducks under. It's a bad move. Off balance and low to the ground, the agent has no place to go. He leans back and tries an off-balance roundhouse kick that Jamieson catches, knocking him to the ground. He raises his heel and thrusts it toward the parquet floor, but the agent rolls away from the stomp and springs to his feet.

Unfazed by the near miss, he feigns a kick to get Jamieson to lower his guard and attempts a flurry of left and right strikes. The lawyer blocks them and avoids the right elbow heading for his jaw. The men hand-check each other, alternating between blocks and strikes until the agent catches his arm, slides under it, and swings an elbow that connects with Jamieson's temple.

Stunned, Jamieson kicks down to disable the man's knee, but he slides out of the way. The lawyer goes for a left-side strike and catches a knee to the abdomen for his trouble. On his back foot, the agent attacks with punches that he ducks under or blocks. Jamieson counterattacks with rights and lefts before trying a kick that is caught under the knee. Balancing on one leg, he reaches for the agent's throat and squeezes.

The upward pressure on his leg threatens to knock him off balance, so he raises his leg, pushes up off the floor, and twists his torso, lifting the agent and slamming him on the ground. Eager to end this, Jamieson rushes forward and catches a blow on the knee, causing his leg to buckle. He rolls onto his back and kicks out, knocking the agent backward.

Jamieson isn't feeling so cocky. This man has power and aggression, but he effectively controls it. His movements are instinctual but also a sign of excellent and consistent training.

"Maybe I should have shot you when you walked in."

"What's the matter, Jamieson? Do you need a nap?"

It's time for a change in tactics. Since they are both proficient at fighting close-in, it's time to try attacking from a distance. The mystery man has the same thought.

He throws a series of punches that Jamieson is barely able to block. The agent has quick hands and swings a haymaker with his right. The lawyer ducks under it and catches him in the body before missing with a haymaker of his own. He blocks a front kick and tries a roundhouse kick that glances off Dufresne's shoulder. He sees the quick right but is powerless to stop it.

The punch hits his cheek and turns him slightly. That opens Jamieson up to two rapid side kicks to the chest, one that lands on the back of his legs, and a final one to his face. None of the blows were hard, but they didn't need to be. The agent takes care of that with a hard right that knocks him down.

Jamieson climbs to his feet. This isn't his kind of fight. He looks at hand-to-hand combat as a sprint, not a marathon. Strike fast and end it faster. Unfortunately, this has turned into a marathon, which plays to the strength of the younger man with more stamina.

The time for fun and games is over. Jamieson reaches behind his back and slides the Sheffield Fairbairn-Sykes out of its sheath. He holds the commando dagger out in front of him. He may have met his match when it comes to fists and kicks, but nobody beats him in a knife fight.

CHAPTER EIGHTY-NINE
"BOSTON" HOLLINGER

TOMASSO TRILLO FAMILY ESTATE
ENGLEWOOD CLIFFS, NEW JERSEY

Jamieson holds the dagger out in a taunt. I don't recognize the model but would bet that it's something the SAS uses. It's a double-edged combat dagger mainly designed for thrusting. Nadiya always said knowing the weapon was the key to understanding how to defeat the man wielding it. Or the woman in her case. It rarely worked that way in our training sessions. If I had a nickel for every time she stabbed me with a rubber knife, I'd be living full-time at the Four Seasons in Bora Bora.

I'm tempted to draw my own knife. There are a couple of problems with that course of action. First, I will have committed my dominant hand to offense. A knife hand can block, but that takes the primary weapon out of action.

The second problem is a bigger one. A fundamental outcome of any knife fight is that you are going to get cut and bleed. I can't afford to have my blood sprayed all over this room. There is already enough of my DNA in here and on his fists, so I can't give investigators a reason to look closer. He is holding a stabbing weapon, so his aim is to turn me into Swiss cheese, not cut me to pieces. I'm better off focusing on defense while letting him think he has the upper hand.

We resume our stances. Jamieson is getting tired. His eyes are sharp, but his muscles aren't as relaxed. He aims to end this fast. I'm considering a taunt of my own when he comes at me with a left jab that I block, keeping my attention focused on the knife in his right hand. He thrusts it, and I use my elbow to deflect its trajectory toward my chest. I switch my focus back to another left aimed at my body. I turn sideways and slide backward, waiting for the knife thrust with the opposite hand. I catch his arm, twist hard at the torso and use Jamieson's momentum to flip him over my shoulder.

He rolls out of the fall, well-versed in the practice of judo. Returning to his feet, he twists and thrusts in case I'm charging. I don't, and he hits nothing but air.

The best counter against a thrusting weapon is to get close. It reduces the power generated behind a thrust, limits the options for attacking, and reduces the distance a blocking movement needs to travel. The downside is that you have to be quick.

I collapse the distance between us and throw an elbow that he blocks. My arm instinctively moves to the left to block the short thrust heading for my abdomen. I counter with a right to his body that he turns and absorbs. Then he gets handsy. Jamieson turns and spins me so that my back is against his chest. He spins the dagger in his hand as he shifts his hold and tries to plunge it into my neck.

It's a good thought but is executed too slowly. Predicting the move, I grab Jamieson's wrist and bend forward to use his downward momentum to throw him over my shoulder. He lands hard but recovers and holds his knife out.

Fatigue makes you slower, but it also gets in your head. As energy depletes and muscles tire, you begin thinking more about your actions than focusing on your assailant's weaknesses. My arms are already in motion before he thrusts the knife in front of me. I course-correct mid-swing, using the knife edges I form with my hands to strike his hand and wrist from opposite directions. The shock to his nervous system breaks his grip on the weapon.

Jamieson's eyes turn to track the dagger skittering across the floor. It's another mistake. My hard right hits his chin, and I follow it with a kick to the abdomen and a knife-hand strike to his collarbone.

Desperate and fearful of losing control of the engagement, he scrambles for the dagger resting near the visitors' chairs. I have different ideas. I grab Tomasso's gun from the desk's corner and hold it to Jamieson's temple. He rests his ass on his heels while hanging his head. He drops the knife, and I kick it to the other side of the study in case he wants to continue this dance.

In putting all of Nadiya's training to use, I'm breaking one of Emma's axioms. Her golden rule is to never trust a weapon you haven't fired yourself. Unfortunately, in this case, there isn't a better option. This is no time for a test fire. I only need one shot to send Jamieson off to meet his maker.

"That's a bit of a cheat, don't ya think?" Jamieson says, panting slightly.

"Says the man who pulled a dagger."

The lawyer grins. "Okay. I'll hand it to you, Mystery Man. You're a lot better than I thought you'd be."

"Clearly."

Jamieson nods. "All right. I guess we know how our story ends. The last lines have been written for my character. Go ahead. Close the book."

I glance over at the door and listen. I don't hear anything, and to my relief, Tomasso isn't standing in the doorway with a shotgun. The soundproofing in this study must be ridiculous.

"Almost," I say, boring into Jamieson with my eyes. "We're not quite done yet."

"What do you want to know now? Another sad story about my childhood? Or maybe you'd like to know how I figured out that you aren't in the FBI?"

"Nah, nothing like that. I haven't said, 'the end.'"

The psychopath grins slightly before I fire a round into his forehead.

CHAPTER NINETY

JOHN PROCK

HORSESHOE BAY COVE
SOUTHAMPTON, BERMUDA

Chloe and the man she knows as Jonathan Marks stare out at the dark, open waters of the Atlantic. She has let herself relax despite not seeing any sign of his girlfriend on the beach below. She isn't even looking for her anymore.

"The person you lost…was he or she family?"

"No," Chloe says with a shake of her head. "She was my roommate at law school. She committed suicide."

"That's horrible!"

"Yeah…"

John lowers his eyes. He wants to look remorseful but doesn't want her to see the recognition or the gleam in his eyes he gets when he thinks of Ashlee Trillo's untimely demise. He's not supposed to know any of that for this fiction. Not until he's ready to reveal it.

"I…I don't know what to say."

"It's okay. I've been at a loss for words for a while now," Chloe admits.

"I probably shouldn't tell you this," John says, kicking a stone over the edge and onto the rocks below. "I wasn't completely honest about why I'm in Bermuda. I am here with my girlfriend, but I also needed to get away for a while. I lost my son recently."

"Oh, my God!" Chloe says with genuine concern. "I'm so sorry to hear that."

"Thanks. There's no pain like losing a child. I hope that's something you'll never have to experience. Parents are supposed to die before their kids. That's how the world is supposed to work."

"I feel terrible. Here I am whining about losing a roommate I barely knew, and you lost your son."

"It's okay. Pain is pain, and people shouldn't compare it with others. It's not a contest of who is hurting worse."

Chloe looks at him and forces a smile before nodding. "How did your son die?"

John hangs his head. "It was also a suicide. The worst thing is that we were angry with each other when it happened. Never leave things unsaid. Life is too short. Brody's certainly was."

"Your son's name was Brody?" she asks, rewelding her arms across her torso.

He turns to her, and the corner of his mouth curls up. "Brody Prock."

Even in the fading twilight, he can see her face go pale. Chloe is a smart young woman. She realizes that nothing about this conversation is what it seems. She also must know that their meeting here isn't a coincidence.

"Brody Prock is your son?"

"He *was* my son. I probably also should have mentioned that my name is John Prock, not Jonathan Marks. I was his father."

Chloe shifts her weight and takes a step to the side. "Okay, I should really be going."

The fight or flight instinct may be one of the most understood human reactions. In times of peril, they're really the only two available choices. That makes them predictable. Chloe isn't a ninja. She doesn't train in martial arts or self-defense, so fighting on this outcropping is unlikely. That means she needs to flee, and John casually steps in front of her, blocking the only way off the rocks. At least, the only safe way off them.

"Ashlee Trillo lied about what happened at the party that night. That means you lied to defend her. Actions have consequences, Miss McCarthy."

"I need to…the men at my apartment. Did you send them?"

John grins. "Keep going."

Chloe takes a half step backward. "The goon that stabbed me and chased Ashlee at the Cloisters."

"That was someone else, but he would have saved me the headache if he had finished you off."

"You're crazy!"

"That word is so overused. I defend my interests. You see, social media has created a degree of societal arrogance. Everyone is safe behind a keyboard. Actions have no repercussions, and things can be said without consequence. When you apply those lessons to the real world, you learn they aren't true. There *are* consequences. Sometimes deadly ones."

"So, you're here to teach me a lesson?"

"No," John says, shaking his head. "I conduct business transactions. I close deals."

"I don't know…what does that mean?"

"It means I finish things. For example, my son was talking to the FBI. I brought the gun to Brody, hoping he would kill himself. Now I'm the man who killed you because he did."

Shock registers on her face. It will be the last voluntary act she has in this world. John thrusts his hands out and plants them violently on her chest. With her arms wrapped around herself, she cannot stop him. He shoves her, and the momentum carries her over the edge.

As she plummets to the rocks below, Chloe doesn't even have time to scream. John hears a pop when she lands, and he peers over the edge at his handiwork. She hits the boulders at the base of the outcropping, splitting her head open like a watermelon. There is no surviving that wound.

The beach is desolate but not completely devoid of activity. John knows he shouldn't stay here and admire the fruits of his labor. Every second that elapses is one closer to someone climbing the rocks and discovering what he did. Still, he needs this moment of satisfaction.

"I guess you'll never have to learn what it's like to lose a child after all," John mumbles. "The same can't be said for your parents."

CHAPTER NINETY-ONE
"BOSTON" HOLLINGER

TOMASSO TRILLO FAMILY ESTATE
ENGLEWOOD CLIFFS, NEW JERSEY

After checking in with Emma to let her know I'm okay, I survey the room. This study is a beautiful space. The bar in the corner near the double doors is a unique piece I saw online once. It's an ornate floor globe where the top half lifts to reveal an interior space for alcohol and tumblers. I reach into my pocket and make some preparations. When I close the lid to the bar, I hear the footfalls coming down the stairs.

Only a deep sleeper could slumber through the ruckus Jamieson and I made. I left the study's light on and the door slightly ajar for when sleeping beauty awoke. I wasn't sure how long that would be, but Tomasso Trillo is finally coming downstairs to investigate the fracas.

"Jamieson? Are you down here?" Tomasso Trillo calls out from the foyer.

I hear him shuffling toward the study as I move around the desk facing the windows. There is no telltale clicking on the marble, like when I first came here. He must be wearing slippers or is barefoot.

The door opens slowly. "Jamieson, why aren't you answering…me?"

"Because he can't."

A man's reaction to seeing a dead body on the floor says a lot. Most people would recoil in horror and retreat immediately. Others would freeze up, seized by fear for their own safety. Tomasso does neither of those things. He frowns and glares at me.

"Agent Dufresne, right?"

"Sure. We can go with that."

I move around the far side of the desk and gesture with my gun over to the chair. Tomasso complies without protest, stepping over Jamieson's body but unable to completely avoid the blood pooling on the floor. He tracks it over to the desk.

"Before you get any ideas, your gun is in my pocket. You can try using that letter opener as a weapon, but I don't think it'll work out well for you."

He nods. "What do you want?"

"For you to take a seat."

He slowly complies. "Murder is illegal in this country, Agent Dufresne, even for a federal agent."

"That's true, Tomasso. Then again, I'm a lousy agent. For the record, many things in this world are illegal: bribery, extortion, assault, wire fraud, money laundering, tax evasion…. Listen to me. I sound like I'm reciting an indictment. I didn't even get to *murder*. Let's just say that neither of us cares much for the laws of civil society."

"You think you'll get away with this?"

I smile. "You're a man used to getting his way, aren't you?"

"More or less."

"How does being on the other side of the equation feel?"

"Uncomfortable. How about you? You're FBI...law enforcement. How does it feel to be judge, jury, and executioner?" Tomasso asks, nodding at the body sprawled face-down on the floor.

"You're making assumptions based on the information you believe is true, like me being an FBI agent. You saw me here for the interview, so I must be FBI, only the truth is more...complicated."

For the first time, a flash of fear crosses Tomasso's face. A memory starts to play in my vision, and I fight to ignore it. Now isn't the time. It'd be easier if this "gift" came with an on-off switch.

"Our beliefs are based on perceptions. For example, I thought Ashlee lied about the rape because she sought attention. But I was wrong. She was tired of men mistreating her and wanted revenge against a boy she liked because she thought he was like the rest of them. It's a lesson she learned from dear old dad."

Tomasso shakes his head. "It's nothing she would have learned from me. Ashlee was a troubled woman."

"She was damaged because *you* made her that way."

"I loved my daughter!"

"So, you beat her. You allowed Jamieson to abuse her. But that wasn't the worst of it. You tormented her emotionally because you despised her. She was a feisty child who became a strong-willed and rebellious woman...just like your wife."

I brace myself for the flood of memories and am not disappointed.

"I am not your property!" a woman screams in the kitchen before hurling a dish at my head. "You do not dictate who I spend my time with!"

"It's always something with work! You have a family now!" she shouts in the bedroom. I can feel his anger and frustration.

"What do you want from me, Viviana?"

"To be a husband. To be a man. To be here!"

The next memory is the only room in the house that I recognize. This study hasn't changed much over the years.

"You are not getting a job. That's the end of this discussion."

"Why not? Afraid I'll dedicate more time to it than you do to yours?"

My jaw begins to ache as it tightens. "My job pays for this house. No wife of mine will work. Your place is here raising our daughter."

"You realize what century this is, don't you, Tomasso?"

"You know nothing," Tomasso says, prompting me to ignore what's playing before my eyes and return to the present.

"I wish I could say that was true…that I was guessing. Unfortunately, Tomasso, I know everything. Viviana was your world. Her death was a tragedy. It also had nothing to do with your daughter."

"I know that!"

"No, you don't. If Ashlee hadn't sneaked out, your wife never would have left that night. You blame her and have ever since you took the call in this room from the hospital. After Viviana died, you stood over there and told Ashlee it was her fault."

"I did…how? How do you know…did she tell you that?"

I shake my head. "I told you. I know everything. From that moment on, she wasn't your daughter. She was the specter of your departed wife. Ashlee looks like Viviana and acts like her. She was a living reminder of what you lost, and you couldn't stand it."

Tomasso looks like he wants to protest, but he remains silent. He's likely wondering how I could possibly know any of that. I know that's what I would be asking if the roles were reversed.

"You look like you could use a drink."

I walk over to the bar and check the selection. The bottles of alcohol here would cost me nine months' salary. I select the Lagavulin 1976 Islay single malt scotch whisky. In a different life, I knew a senator who loved this brand. He, too, was a pretentious asshole.

"You're a scumbag, Tomasso, but you have excellent taste. How much did this bottle cost?"

"Seven thousand."

I shake my head and pour with both hands to avoid spilling even a single drop. "Worth every penny, I'm sure."

"I didn't kill my daughter if that's what you think."

"I know. Jamieson did, on your orders. He was a psychopath, literally, but a loyal one."

I hand him the glass and take a long sip from my own as I sit in the chair opposite the desk. After watching me for a moment, he does the same. It's an appropriate measure to not slurp down the drink offered by a man holding a gun on you. He learned something from *The Princess Bride*, not that it did Vizzini much good. I wonder if Tomasso identifies with him since they're both Sicilian.

"It was mercy."

"It was *murder*. I get that Jamieson didn't care, but you're her father. The level of indifference you have toward your flesh and blood is what the ancient Greeks used to write tragedies about."

"I did nothing wrong. You are mistaken."

"Sure." It's all I bother saying. What's done is done.

"What happens now?"

I shrug. "We enjoy our drinks and continue talking man to man."

"If you're going to shoot me, just get it over with."

"As much as I'd love to put a bullet through your forehead, I'm not going to shoot you, Tomasso."

I'm too far away to notice if Tomasso's pupils are constricting, and his complexion makes it difficult to detect whether his skin is graying or pale. Without touching him, I won't be able to tell if his skin is cold and clammy. The one thing that I do notice is his breathing. It's growing slower and shallower.

He stares at the drink and then back at me. I might not notice the effects, but he is feeling them.

"Yeah, I should probably tell you that I slipped a fatal dose of fentanyl into the scotch. Sorry."

"You said…you…wouldn't kill me."

"No. I said I wouldn't shoot you. Here's a fun fact: Fifty-seven percent of people who fatally overdose on fentanyl also test positive for cocaine, methamphetamine, or heroin. I'm no expert, but I'm pretty sure this stuff is pure. Two milligrams is more than enough to do the job. I added about five to your glass before you walked in."

Tomasso's shallow breathing becomes labored. His limbs have gone numb. Otherwise, I would have expected him to attempt to fight back. He's powerless to stop what's happening. A man who fancies himself as able to control everything and everybody is losing the ability to breathe. He leans back in his chair and glares at me.

"You deserve much worse than this, Tomasso. Your daughter deserved far better than having her neck opened. Unlike you, she was a good person, and I pray that she finally found the peace in death that she didn't have in life. As for you…I hope you burn in hell."

Those are the last words Tomasso hears before his breathing ceases, and he collapses onto the desk. There is no need to check his pulse. He won't have one. I wipe down my weapon and press it in his hand. Satisfied, I place it on the desk and rub my gloves on his skin to transfer some gunpowder residue. Any decent crime scene investigator will see right through that, but I don't expect them to be needed.

After transferring his prints to the bag, I drop the remaining powder next to the decanter. Content that I haven't left any physical evidence behind, I walk out the back door of the estate. Watchtower can alter the security logs. The video system is already off. There is no forced entry, and nothing is missing. It's a murder-suicide from a troubled and grieving father and probably the easiest case the New Jersey State Police will investigate tomorrow, assuming they don't look too closely.

CHAPTER NINETY-TWO
SSA ZACH FORTE

The colonial-revival-style home in Jadwin Loop Village has a spacious porch, three bedrooms, two and a half baths, and a two-car garage. It also came fully furnished, including the seventy-five-inch television that's hanging on the wall. This is the nicest place Forte has ever lived in.

The doorbell rings, but he doesn't bother getting up. He knows who's at the door and left it unlocked on purpose.

"Come in, Boston."

He enters the house as Zach clicks off the television. Boston looks around before glancing at Forte and noticing the bruising and cut over his right eye.

"I thought I had a tough night. You look like hell."

"I slipped in the shower."

It was meant to be a joke, but Boston slips into his thousand-yard stare like he's searching for the memory. It's his tell. Zach has worked with him long enough now to recognize it.

"I didn't think Matt would have had combatives training."

"Me neither. Or I'm getting old and rusty."

"Spend a couple of days with Nadiya. You'll be able to kick his ass in no time. So, why am I here at Chateau Forte?"

Zach retreats to the kitchen and opens the refrigerator. "Because I can't be sure that someone from Watchtower isn't sitting in your billet waiting for you."

"That bad, eh?"

Forte returns with two beers that he pops the tops off with a bottle opener, and he shrugs before plopping down on the sofa. Boston gingerly takes a seat in the recliner. He rubs his ribs gently before sinking deeper into the cushioned back.

"Should I ask?"

Boston glances up at him. "No."

Zach thinks about pressing him for details and decides against it. If Boston squared up against Jamieson, Nadiya no doubt learned every detail on the drive back to Virginia and will be strutting around like a proud mother hen when they start work in the morning. She forced him to take his training seriously. By all accounts, it paid off tonight.

"You ever get the feeling that we aren't all playing on the same side, Zach?"

"You mean, do I wonder if Watchtower contributes to the problem it was created to solve? Yeah, from time to time."

Boston takes a long swig of the beer. "Aren't you gonna ask what happened?"

"Do I need to? I doubt you'd be standing here if it had gone wrong."

"Why didn't you stop me? I want the real reason, not some BS you pull out of thin air. Three months ago, you would have chained me to my bed. Three weeks ago, you would have blocked my path and shouted until I gave up. What changed? I want to know."

"People in hell want ice water. I did what I did. I don't owe you an explanation. Deal with it."

"Fine. Fair warning. There's more to be done."

"John Prock?"

Boston nods. "Yeah. How did you know who I was going after tonight? Did Emma and Nadiya report to you?"

"You know better than that. Because of your relationship with Ashlee, Trillo and Jamieson were the obvious first targets. You won't be doing anything about John Prock anytime soon."

"Watch me."

Forte grins. "Watchtower is keeping tabs on him for me as a personal favor. He's in Bermuda."

Boston shifts positions, grimaces, and leans back into the recliner again. "What's he doing there?"

"Business."

"Yeah, okay, what's he really doing there?"

"Shagging one of his executives, according to the analysts."

Watchtower is a unique entity. It has information accumulated from every part of the federal bureaucracy. That includes the TSA and Customs and Border Patrol systems. They have all the travel information for John Prock and his attractive vice-president of account management. Just because they booked separate rooms doesn't mean they'll be using them.

"Hell of a way to mourn the loss of your son. He's deep in the fentanyl trade, Zach. We need to build a case."

"The FBI can do that," Forte says, depositing his empty beer bottle on the coffee table next to two of its friends. "Watchtower is officially removed from inquiring about anything relating to Trillo or Prock, per Brass's order. That will be strictly enforced once he learns about whatever you did tonight."

"I'm not sure what you're talking about. Tomasso Trillo died of a fentanyl overdose tonight. It was a murder-suicide."

Zach nods. He doesn't need to ask where the drugs came from. The mechanics of how he staged this aren't what's worrying him.

"Please tell me you see the moral ambiguity in all this, Boston."

"I do. I also see justice being served when I know the courts wouldn't have."

This is more than a criticism of "innocent until proven guilty" or the sometimes maddening premise that allowing a hundred criminals to go free is better than imprisoning an innocent person. It's about a system corrupted by power, politics, and money. There wouldn't be justice because powerful people would bind the gears or stop the engine from starting at all. Tomasso bought his protection. Prock has done the same thing.

Boston warily eyes Zach from the recliner. The senior agent knows that his charge expects more of an argument than he's getting. Zach believes in the law. He believes in the mission of the FBI. What Hollinger did tonight flies in the face of both. The problem is that Zach doesn't see an alternative other than letting a scumbag walk free.

"Since I can't return to my lodging, am I crashing here?"

"Oh, hell no. I don't trust the lock on my door and am not about to give you an opportunity to strangle me in my sleep."

Boston grins. "Fair. So, what's the plan?"

"For you to go dark for a while."

Boston narrows his eyes and cocks his head. Forte cocks his thumb over his shoulder at the two black canvas duffel bags against the wall near the front door. Boston struggles to turn his head to see what Zach is pointing at.

"Those arrived for you from the training center. I'll get you a ride off the base. You need to lie low in D.C."

"Who do you have supervising me?"

It's an appropriate question. Boston has had a babysitter since he emerged from the medically induced coma after the shooting. His lack of freedom is why he bolted from the training center in the first place. Even his outings over the past few months have been chaperoned to a degree. That ends now.

"Nobody. You're on your own. Carry this," Forte says, reaching into his sweatshirt pocket and tossing over a burner phone. "Keep it on. I'll call you when I need you."

"Are you trying to tell me something?"

"Yeah, to take a vacation while I sort some things out. Maybe even heal up a bit. You deserve the downtime more than anybody I know. Spend it wisely. It may be the last you get for a while."

CHAPTER NINETY-THREE

JOHN PROCK

Every major hotel property on the planet has some sort of video surveillance on the grounds. It's necessary to ensure the safety and security of their guests, deter criminal activity, and have a record of events on the premises. After checking in, John's first order of business was determining the cameras' locations. He took mental notes of them since Emily wouldn't understand the need to document those security measures.

Obviously, John ruled out a return through the main lobby area. It's covered from every conceivable angle. The Pink Sands Resort isn't one big building. It has a main structure where most restaurants and amenities are located, along with two separate detached wings. The ground between them and the main building has cameras, but they don't cover everything.

John eases through a gate and quietly walks toward his accommodation. The lighting creates enough shadows for him to stay invisible to the other guests roaming the grounds. Most of his fellow guests are enjoying the band playing at the main restaurant as small children play around the moongate.

The eye-catching round limestone openings are found along garden walls around Bermuda. Local legend holds that happiness will endure for newlyweds who step hand-in-hand through a moongate. He's seen couples kissing and posing under these intriguing stone passageways numerous times since he's been here. Emily hasn't asked him to do that…yet.

John reaches the entrance to his building and catches a break. He didn't want to swipe his keycard to gain entry because there would be a record. He was prepared to wait until a guest exited and is fortunate that he won't need to. A young couple leaves and makes a right, not even seeing him standing ten feet away. He hustles and catches the door before it closes.

"Your timing is perfect," Emily says, opening the door after John takes the stairs to the room and knocks. "Room service was just delivered."

"Great!"

"How was your walk? Did you find the peace you were looking for?"

John forces a smile. "It's a start."

He can't pry his eyes off Emily. She's dressed only in a hotel robe with wet hair fresh from the shower. She looks amazing.

"I'm sorry," she says, noticing his gaze. "I used your shower. I hope that's okay."

"Of course."

He takes her hand and is about to say something when he hears his cell phone ring. Life is about timing. The call comes in at the worst possible moment but is right at the prescribed time. Fortunately, he made it back to the room to answer it.

"I should get that," John says, releasing her hand and walking to the desk. "Yeah?"

"Calling as instructed," Lothar says. "I assume all is well."

"It is. Anything I need to know about back home?"

"It's quiet. I'll keep you appraised if that changes. Should I expect news coming out of Bermuda?"

"Eventually. Thanks for minding the shop. You know what to do next?"

"Wait five or six minutes and then hang up."

"Good man," John says, setting the phone down without ending the call.

Alibis are a tricky thing. The feds will likely learn he was in Bermuda when Chloe died. That will be suspicious, but no evidence links him to the murder scene. So far as anyone knows, he was in his room with a lovely blonde all night and even took a call from it. The cell tower records will attest to that.

All he will need Emily to do is back up his story if it comes to that. It's a dangerous play. There is one easy way to ensure that happens, and he takes a deep breath.

"Sorry about that. Where were we?"

"Getting ready to eat."

"No, I don't think that's it," he says, pulling her close.

She looks at his eyes and then his lips, and he kisses her. She returns it even more passionately. He feels a tug at his shorts as she unfastens his belt. Emily smiles coyly as she unfastens the snap and reaches down to grab him.

"I thought you said you wouldn't sleep with me."

"I lied."

John unties the belt on her robe, opening it. Emily has an amazing body. She steps back and lets the cloth slip off her shoulders. He helps her remove his shirt and pants, and they collapse into the bed for what he hopes is a very long night.

CHAPTER NINETY-FOUR

SSA ZACH FORTE

WATCHTOWER OPERATIONS CENTER
FORT BELVOIR, VIRGINIA

The experiment with Boston is a minuscule part of the Watchtower operation. He is one cog in the machine, and this room reminds Zach of how small a role his team plays, at least so far. Nobody pays him much attention as he skirts along the side wall to the smoked-windowed conference room.

Zach expected an ass-chewing when he was summoned here. He didn't expect it to be from David Brass. The man charged with standing up and overseeing this secret squirrel society sets the tone of the conversation with some pointed questions meant to put Forte on the defensive. They were deftly answered, and now he's losing his patience.

"Special Agent Forte, Matt brought you here to manage Hollinger. It's a decision that I only reluctantly supported. But it's evident that you're failing spectacularly in that mission."

"Sir, we were handed this assignment, and Boston did exactly what was asked of him. He uncovered the truth about Ashlee Trillo's rape allegations. In the process, he also found a few things – corruption, fraud, bribery, and a possible drug smuggling operation. I would think that's the kind of intelligence that Watchtower would want."

"It is, and it should have stopped there. Then he ran off and killed Tomasso Trillo!"

Zach purses his lips. "I'm not sure what you're referring to. Trillo's death is being labeled a murder-suicide."

"Don't bullshit me, Forte! I've spent three decades in the CIA. You don't think I know what a staged scene looks like? Boston *killed* him."

"That's not what the New Jersey State Police say," Zach says, his voice remaining calm and even.

"Well, golly gee, it must not have happened that way. Where's Hollinger now?"

There it is. Zach couldn't tell Boston why he sent him away and hoped the dream machine wouldn't pluck it out of his memories when they were having beers in the living room. Brass looks at Hollinger like a tool pulled out of the box and returned when it's of no more use. Matt felt the same way until recently. He wants to control him, and Forte needs to buy some time until he uncovers how.

"I gave him some time off."

"Why?"

"Because that was Dr. Kurota's advice. The deaths of Ashlee Trillo and Brody Prock hit him hard. There were tough memories to deal with during this investigation that took a psychological toll. He needs some time to clear his head and decompress."

Brass leans back in his chair. Forte doesn't know where he works exactly. He knows it's for the Department of Agriculture and is probably somewhere in Virginia, but where is anybody's guess. The CIA knows how to keep secrets unless foreign governments are involved. Then they leak like a sieve.

"This experiment is failing. Matt, restrict Hollinger to the facility until I determine our next course of action."

"I'm not going to do that," Matt says coolly. "Boston is an agent, not a prisoner."

Brass's eyes narrow. "Really? The agents I work with follow orders. They follow procedures."

"Sir, Boston is a valued member of the Watchtower team," Matt argues.

"And he's also a massive liability. We need to—"

"Not a single person here has their movements restricted," Forte says, jumping into the fray. "If we do that again, he could disappear and never be found."

Brass learned by accident about Boston's escape from the training facility. To say he was displeased is an understatement. He knows that the ability to see and interpret memories is a powerful but dangerous weapon that could also be unleashed on a friend as well as a foe. That's why Brass is nervous and why Forte brought it up.

"Very well. I need to clean up this mess in New Jersey, Matt. More is at stake here than exposing a shady developer and drug operation. This country needs Watchtower. I will not let anyone jeopardize that. Do you understand?"

"I do."

"Good. I'm making Hollinger your responsibility. I'll hold you personally responsible if he steps out of line even once. Understood?"

"Yes, sir."

Brass takes a hard look at both men before rising from his chair. There are no more words. Nothing more needs to be said. Brass has a job to do. So do Matt and Zach.

"Well, that was fun," Zach says after the big boss leaves. "I'm beginning to think you're scared of Brass. I expected a more full-throated defense of your prize agent."

Matt rubs his temples. "Brass wasn't interested in anything you or I had to say. Watchtower is his life. He spent his career lobbying for this and staked his future on Watchtower's success. I have, too. You were right when you said that Hollinger is a misused asset, but he's also a maverick who could take the whole thing down."

"Both are points you could have made five minutes ago."

"It wasn't the time or place."

"There will never be a good time."

Matt frowns. "Where's Boston?"

"It's in Massachusetts."

There's a time for levity and a time for seriousness. Zach has never had a tuned radar that he could rely on to distinguish which is which. From the look on Matt's face, he was wrong again.

"Forte, my job is on the line here. Is there anything about what happened in the past twenty minutes that leads you to believe I'm in the mood for your games?"

"He went to D.C.," Zach says, getting the point crystal clear.

"Supervised?"

"No."

"Of course not," Matt says with a sigh. "Well, my ass is in a sling, so I might as well put yours in one. Find Boston and bring him back here before he does something stupid."

"What makes you think he will?"

"He has already demonstrated that capacity countless times, and I don't want this to be the last."

CHAPTER NINETY-FIVE
"BOSTON" HOLLINGER

1790 BISTRO
GEORGETOWN, WASHINGTON, D.C.

The 1790 Bistro didn't get its name from the year it opened like many in the city believe. It's actually a relatively new restaurant, although old enough to allow the myth to proliferate. The bistro was named after the year of the city's founding and has become one of the most popular hotspots in the district.

This isn't my kind of joint. I prefer burgers and beer to the strange delicacies that this Michelin-star restaurant offers. I received some important intelligence thanks to some friends at Watchtower. Forte would have a stroke if he knew they told me, but that's his problem. I have a different one to solve.

I focus on the man at the bar and close my eyes. The problem with crowds is that it's difficult to sort through memories. I don't know whose I'm receiving. Strong emotions from someone else in the room make finding the ones I'm after much more difficult. But I'm determined to get into this guy's life somehow.

The memory is foggier than usual because it isn't a strong emotion. A woman is screaming and cursing at me. I can't distinguish her words, but the tone and volume mean she's upset.

"I told you, Liz, I have to work," I hear myself say.

She stares at me through teary eyes. "And I need you here, Kyle! Your son needs you! It's Friday night, and you should be with your family."

"You know how important my work is."

"More important than our marriage? Our sick son?"

I don't feel anger…it's more like…impatience. Kyle doesn't want to be here.

"My salary is how we pay the bills, which means I work when they need me. I'm sorry. I have to go."

"Fine. Go. I'll be here, alone…as usual."

I can feel my blood boil as I watch the pair interact at the bar. She doesn't know. There's no way she would be out with him if she did. Taking a sip from my tumbler, I start the mental gymnastics of what to do next. That's when an opportunity presents itself.

The 1790 Bistro doesn't accept walk-in patrons. If you don't have a reservation, you aren't going to get seated. That doesn't mean you immediately will if you do have one. This place is notorious for running late, up to an hour after your appointed time. Not many restaurants can get away with that, but the 1790 is one of them.

Clearly growing impatient, Kyle whispers something and goes to the hostess stand to check on the reservation. His date is left to sip her drink and fend off the half-dozen men eyeing her from across the spacious bar. She'll be fine.

I weave through the patrons and into the busy foyer. People are standing in clusters, and a crowd has formed around the harried hostesses. Kyle folds his arms and scowls as the two women converse with a group that just arrived. I come up alongside him and shake my head when I feel him glance at me.

"I hate the wait here," Kyle says, checking his watch for dramatic effect.

I offer him a sympathetic grimace. "Yeah, they need to step it up. Your wife will be even more suspicious if you don't get home to her."

"Excuse me?"

"Your wife. Liz? I mean, your date is lovely, but even her beauty wouldn't make you forget that you're married with a sick child at home."

"I don't know what you're talking about," Kyle says, thrusting his chin out.

"Yes, you do," I state flatly.

"How do you know…? I don't know who the hell you think you are," he says, bringing his arm up to give me a shove.

He couldn't have telegraphed the move any better with a neon sign. I catch his arm as it moves toward my chest, spin him around, and put it in a wrist lock behind his back. I look around. Nobody has noticed that the man is restrained despite my standing in a busy foyer. Nadiya would be impressed.

"This is a public place, Kyle. You really don't want to assault me here. Us getting tossed out is the best-case scenario. That would be embarrassing, but what happens if you get arrested for assault while on a *date*? How do you explain that to Liz?"

I release him, and he flexes his hand, looking around to see if anyone has noticed. "What do you want?"

"For you to end your evening and go home to your wife and child."

"Or else?"

I pull out my phone. "I make a call, and your first conversation tomorrow morning is with a divorce attorney."

"Who are you?" he asks, his face contorted in utter confusion.

"A concerned citizen." I should make that my personal catchphrase. I haven't used it much since my time in Phoenix, but I feel a revival coming.

"I can't leave her here," Kyle says, looking apprehensively back toward the door leading to the bar area.

"You will, or I'll start dialing. It's your choice, Kyle. I'll be watching."

It's a bluff, but he doesn't know that. He might think I'm a private investigator hired by his wife, but then the threat wouldn't make much sense. Whatever he thinks, he knows that he doesn't have any good options.

I give him a friendly slap on the shoulder and retreat to the bar. My original seat is taken, so I choose a spot even closer to his date. Fortunately, she is turned away from me, which works in my favor.

Kyle must have composed himself and weighed his options for a few minutes. He finally returns, desperately trying not to bump into the patrons and spill their drinks. When he reaches his date and sees me, he scowls and turns to her.

"I'm sorry, something has come up, and I need to cut our evening short."

"Oh…is everything okay?" his date asks, a hint of concern on her face.

"I'm not sure. Can you take a rideshare home? I really have to go."

"Seriously?"

The concern in her voice morphed into something closer to annoyance and disbelief. Kyle glances at me as I watch from behind her. I pull my phone out and give it a wag just for the hell of it.

"Yes. I'm sorry. I have to go. Good night," he says before spinning and high-tailing it out of the bar.

"Unbelievable," she moans, digging through her purse after watching him go. It's now or never.

"He's married," I say, causing Tara Winters' head to jerk around. "I heard him on the phone with his wife in the foyer when he checked your reservation. She was getting suspicious."

I manage to finish the sentence before getting lost in my thoughts. Tara still looks amazing. With olive skin, gorgeous eyes, and an athletic figure, countless men would sign up to get PTSD just to be in the same room with her. And that's before they realize she's strong, intelligent, and funny.

"No…he can't…are you…wait, have we met?"

"Not really. I think I remember seeing you once up in Chevy Chase," I say, wondering how well I can pull off that lie.

"The coffee shop! You were there when the woman spilled coffee on me."

"That's right. I can't believe you remember that. You were wearing a lab coat."

"I'm a doctor….and, apparently, a bad judge of character when it comes to the men in my life."

I try not to take that comment personally. I'm supposed to be dead.

"I wouldn't judge that based on one scumbag. I'm Tyler. Tyler Durden."

She shakes my hand. There's no hint of recognition of the name. I didn't think there would be. *Fight Club* isn't a movie I figured she'd be interested in. Considering the character is the protagonist's imaginary alter ego, I thought it was perfect for this.

"You're sweet, Tyler. It's nice to meet you. I'm Tara Winters. If you didn't notice, I'm new to the dating scene."

I offer a smile. "With respect, you're a beautiful woman. I very much doubt that."

Tara checks her dress subconsciously. "It's true. I've been out of the game for a while."

"I'm sorry. Divorced?"

It seemed like that would be the logical conclusion to draw. Pretending not to know much about her is harder than I thought it would be.

"No. A man that I…it's complicated, but he died tragically. I haven't really been myself since."

The memory comes rushing into my vision.

I'm seated as a squad of soldiers in dress uniform march off. A lone man remains behind to stand watch at the position of attention over a casket. It's a dreary day. That's the perfect metaphor for the profound sadness I feel. I rise from my chair and walk over to the casket, clutching a folded American flag against my chest. I run a finger along the edge of the lacquered wood, not believing this is happening.

"I feel like I'm the one who's been in a dream," Tara's voice says as I speak. "I expect to wake up and see things as they were before."

"Sweetheart, this is as real as it gets," Louisiana says.

He was never the warm, fuzzy type. The words do nothing to help my anguish. I stare down at the casket – my casket.

"I don't expect you to understand."

"Boston's not the first fallen soldier I've seen buried. He's just the most recent."

"Yeah, well, he's the first one I've had to bury!" I snap, hurt, angry, and emotional.

I cut the memory short. It might seem fascinating to relive my own funeral through someone's eyes, but the anguish is unbearable. Tara's pain was profound…and real. We didn't know each other for that long and only shared one kiss in the time we did. It's amazing how much of an attachment we formed with each other. I knew I missed her. I never realized how much she missed me in return.

"I'm sorry to hear that. It sounds like true love."

Tara's eyes stare into mine. The last time we looked at each other like that was right before I confronted Gina and woke up in a CIA medical facility with Forte staring over me. Life can change in an instant. Mine certainly did.

"I'm sorry," she says, briefly breaking eye contact. "I don't mean to stare. You just feel so familiar…if I may ask, what happened to your face? It looks like you were in a fight."

"I force a smile. "Very observant. I was mugged two days ago."

"And he did that to you?"

"He got it worse, believe me."

She fidgets. "You must be able to handle yourself."

"I was in the military."

Tara's eyes bore into me. "Let me guess. Military intelligence?"

I feel a jolt of electricity in my spine. There is no way she could know. But does she suspect? I knew this would be a dangerous game. Now, I realize just how dangerous.

"In my experience, there's no such thing. Field artillery. I was a gun bunny."

"Where were you stationed?"

I don't have an answer that would deflect her from the truth. Fortunately, I don't need one when the hostess walks over and taps her on the shoulder.

"Excuse me, ma'am? Your table is ready."

"Oh, I…" Tara looks at me. "I know this is a little forward, Tyler, but do you have dinner plans this evening?"

I'm thrown by the question and need to think fast. "Uh…no, I only came here for a drink."

"Would you like to join me? It'd be a shame to let the reservation go to waste."

All men and women in the armed forces are familiar with Murphy's Laws. One of my favorites states, "No plan ever survives first contact intact." I only wanted to see her again, not join her for dinner. My overlords at Watchtower would have an aneurysm if they knew I was even in the same room as my former love interest, much less seated across a table from her.

I assumed Tara would leave the restaurant after Kyle's hasty exit. Why would she stay? I never thought she'd recognize me from a brief coffee shop encounter over six months ago. An invitation to join her for the evening is a pleasant yet unexpected surprise.

I smile. "I would love to."

We fall in behind the hostess, who expertly weaves between tables to a candlelit two-top near the window. Kyle may be a scumbag, but he has good taste. This is the best table in the house, and he had to have reserved it for Tara.

The pre-dinner ritual is performed. Napkins are placed in laps, water glasses are filled, and gourmet bread with honey butter is delivered. We order wine, and I'm about to say something when Tara leans in at me hard.

"Are you married? Tell me you aren't, and please don't lie to me."

I smile and shake my head. "I wouldn't do that, Tara. No, I'm not married. I was engaged once, but she wasn't the woman I thought she was. I work a lot and haven't had much in the way of romances since."

I press my lips together at the understatement. Gina was anything but the woman I thought I was marrying – a point that my fiancée drove home when she shot me in the head and left me for dead.

"Well, we have at least one thing in common," Tara says, beaming.

"I'm guessing that we have far more than one," I say, clinking my crystal wine glass against hers and readying myself for an evening I never thought I would get the opportunity to have.

A NOTE FROM THE AUTHOR

I didn't intend to discuss culturally sensitive topics when I started this series. It's just turning out that way. I thought it would have a more international flair, and that is likely coming in Boston's journey. But here we are.

I don't usually include these notes at the end of my novels. You just spent your time digesting a hundred thousand words, but this needs to be written. Researching this novel was as heartbreaking as the last. Human trafficking is modern slavery, but rape is one of the most horrible violations imaginable. That one human being can do that to another is sickening.

It made this novel extremely difficult to write. The story is not meant to devalue women who make sexual assault claims. Most reports, as cited in this text and taken from real research, are honest. I don't profess that all women should be universally believed, but they all should absolutely be heard. Victims should be encouraged to come forward, and every report filed should be taken seriously. Full stop. Too many women are not bothering to report the crime, as current statistics indicate. That is as much a tragedy as the assault itself.

If you are a victim of a sexual crime, my heart goes out to you. I tried my best to accurately capture the trauma, as seen through Nadiya's eyes. I'm certain I didn't do it justice. I can only hope that you find peace…and that the man responsible sees his testicles rot and fall off.

But this story, like many of mine, started as a "what if?" What if a man was accused of rape, but he was gay? That doesn't necessarily mean he didn't do it. But it is an interesting concept that deserves to be the basis of a story, especially given Brody's father's beliefs. What if he didn't and couldn't come forward or mount a defense out of fear? What then?

That leads to the discussion about homosexuality. My goal is not to pass judgment on Brody or Lucas, nor will I do it with their unaccepting families. Everyone is entitled to their beliefs, even if I don't agree with them. I have an accepting nature and don't personally judge people based on the color of their skin or who they love. That's me. Some of you will disagree with Brody's life choices. Some of you will disagree with his father's viewpoint. My intent as an author is not to sway you one way or the other.

I did my best to highlight some of the stresses members of the LGBT community face. That should never be minimized. I'm aware that this discussion in this novel only scratches the surface, and I purposely explored it from Boston's perspective as a straight man. If I in any way stereotyped or misrepresented the gay community, I apologize. It is certainly not my intent.

I would end it on that note, but there is some unfinished business I need to handle first. Some of you will find John Prock's seeming escape from justice a letdown. The truth is, an antagonist as despicable as he deserves a demise that isn't rushed. Therefore,

I promise he will return in the next novel. There is more to his story to explore, and Boston must get imaginative to take him down.

My stories involve fictional characters. While they are not recreations of people I know personally, I'd be lying if I said they were not often inspired by them. I will often use names or variations of names for some, and I borrow personality traits for others. Sometimes, it's both.

That's a good thing in some novels, especially the Tierra Campos Series. Victoria Larsen is a mix of two strong women I hold in the highest esteem. Other times, you get someone like John Prock. I'm just going to leave that written there.

ACKNOWLEDGMENTS

I write because I love sharing stories. Knowing my readers are willing to invest their time in these adventures is what makes the process fulfilling. I've won awards, and there is a financial upside, but hearing that people enjoy the work makes me the proudest. Every review that states someone was up until three in the morning because they couldn't put the book down keeps me smiling for days. Thank you for spending your precious time with my novels.

To my family – Nancy, Kristina, Ken, and Gibson – and my extended family –Jen, Jill, Simon, Sandra, Logan, and Tyler – thank you for all your love and encouragement. I also have a great group of friends who have inspired characters in my other series. Jenn, Steve, Amy, Billy, Aimee, Geraldine, Meg, Bill, Chris…I will always value and cherish your friendship.

JD&J did it again. The covers for the Watchtower Thrillers are challenging. I find the cover art concepts for my other series much easier to develop. Regardless, they come through for me every time. This latest cover didn't even need revisions.

Here is the part where I have to say something nice about my editor. It's painful. Authors and editors have a love-hate relationship, but fortunately, I have a great one. Thank you to Michael Waitz at Sticks and Stones Editing for helping correct my constant mistakes and inconsistencies. I think I'm getting better. He would likely disagree. It's okay. He's wrong. As the author, I get to say that, but remember, I write fiction.

I include her at the end of the acknowledgments to ensure my wife reads this entire section. Let this not be interpreted as a list in order of importance. I don't want to sleep on the couch. Michele, you continue to be my most ardent supporter, and I am thrilled that you are by my side in this journey, wherever it takes us. If you are a Netflix executive reading this, she really hopes the journey takes us to a red carpet premiere and the Emmys. Just putting it out there because she already has the dress.

ABOUT THE AUTHOR

Mikael Carlson is the award-winning author of *The iCandidate* and the Michael Bennit Series of political dramas. He also wrote the Tierra Campos Series and the dystopian America, Inc. Saga. The Watchtower Thrillers is his fourth series, and *The Eyes of Victims* is his fourteenth novel.

A retired veteran of the Rhode Island Army National Guard and United States Army, he deployed twice to support military operations during the Global War on Terror. Mikael has served in the field artillery, infantry, and in support of special operations units during his active-duty career at Fort Bragg and in the Army National Guard.

A proud U.S. Army paratrooper, he conducted over fifty airborne operations following the completion of jump school at Fort Benning in 1998. Since then, he has trained with the militaries of countless foreign nations.

Academically, Mikael earned a Master of Arts in American History and graduated with a B.S. in International Business from Marist College in 1996.

He was raised in New Milford, Connecticut, and lives nearby Danbury.